DEVIL'S FOOD CAKE MURDER

JOANNE FLUKE

THORNDIKE
CHIVERS

This Large Print edition is published by Thorndike Press, Waterville, Maine USA and by AudioGo Ltd, Bath, England.
Copyright © 2011 by H. L. Swensen, Inc.
A Hannah Swensen Mystery with Recipes.
The moral right of the author has been asserted.
Thorndike Press, a part of Gale, Cengage Learning.

LIBRARY OF CONGRESS CATALOGING-IN-PUBLICATION DATA

Fluke, Joanne, 1943–
    Devil's food cake murder / by Joanne Fluke.
        p. cm. — (A Hannah Swensen mystery with recipes)
    (Thorndike Press large print mystery)
    ISBN-13: 978-1-4104-3425-8 (hardcover)
    ISBN-10: 1-4104-3425-7 (hardcover)
    1. Swensen, Hannah (Fictitious character)—Fiction. 2. Bakers—Fiction.
3. Murder—Investigation—Fiction. 4. Minnesota—Fiction. 5. Large type
books. I. Title.
PS3556.L685D48 2011
813'.54—dc22   2010051772

BRITISH LIBRARY CATALOGUING-IN-PUBLICATION DATA AVAILABLE
Published in the U.S. in 2011 by arrangement with Kensington Books,
an imprint of Kensington Publishing Corp.
Published in the U.K. in 2011 by arrangement with The Kensington
Publishing Corp.
U.K. Hardcover: 978 1 445 83666 9 (Chivers Large Print)
U.K. Softcover: 978 1 445 83667 6 (Camden Large Print)

Printed and bound in Great Britain by
the MPG Books Group.
1 2 3 4 5 6 7 14 13 12 11 10

This book is for Lois and Neal Meister, perfect examples of everything that's wonderful about Minnesota.

ACKNOWLEDGMENTS

A big hug for Ruel, who's tasted every single recipe in this book. (What dedication! What loyalty!) Not only that, he's also my in-house story editor.

Hugs all around for the kids and the grandkids. I have a great family!

Thank you to: Bev & Jim Pehler, Mel & Kurt, Lyn & Bill, Lu & Sheba, Gina & Fiona, Adrienne, Jay, Bob, Laura Levine & Mark, Amanda, John B., Judy Q., Daryl Groves, Dr. Bob & Sue, Richard & Krista, R.T. Jordan, Billy, Mark B., and Angelique.

Special thanks to my incredible Editor-in-Chief and friend, John Scognamiglio, who always goes that extra mile. Life is good with John S. on my side.

Many thanks to Walter, Steve, Laurie,

Doug, David, Robin, Karen, and Maureen.

Thanks to Hiro Kimura for the delectable Devil's Food Cake on the cover. (I'd love to dive into that fudge frosting!) And thank you to Lou Malcangi for designing this gorgeous dust jacket.

Thanks also to all the other talented folks at Kensington who keep Hannah sleuthing and baking up a storm.

Thank you to my friend Trudi Nash for joining me on book tours, keeping up with my hectic schedule, taking marvelous photos, and convincing me that she actually enjoys it.

And thanks to David for holding down the fort while she's gone.

I'd like to congratulate the winners of the Mystery Guild recipe contest. Edwina Gadsby, Linda Sifuentes, and Leslie Holmes contributed recipes that are so yummy, we almost had a three-way tie. You'll find all three recipes — Edwina's Chocolate-Covered Raisin Cookies, Linda's Mocha Trifle, and Leslie's Butterscotch Bonanza Bars — in this book.

8

Thank you to Arman at House of Time Jewelry in Granada Hills, CA, for advising me on expensive jewels even though I didn't buy that impressive rose cut diamond ring I described in the book.

Special thanks to *Romantic Times* Book Review for choosing Hannah Swensen as the best amateur sleuth of 2009! (I had a wonderful time at the awards ceremony in Ohio.)

Thank you to Dr. Rahhal, Dr. and Mrs. Line, and Dr. Wallen for their expertise. And special thanks to Carol at Dr. Line's office for the information on chocolate allergies.

Thanks to John at Placed4Success for Hannah's movie and TV spots, for keeping my IT system current, and for assisting at events.

Thanks to media expert Ken Wilson for his energy, his savvy, and for knowing the word "barista."

Hugs to the nothing-short-of-marvelous food stylist, Lois Brown, for making my recipes look scrumptious on camera and

for giving some of her favorite recipes to
Hannah.

Thanks to Jill Saxton, superb copy editor
and good friend.

Thank you to Sally Hayes for sharing
recipes for all sorts of wonderful treats.
Sally's recipes really are to die for!

Thanks to Kathy Allen for testing almost
all of these recipes in her
so-small-you-can't-fall-over kitchen.

Thanks to Danny Grimm for explaining
cuts of meat to me and telling me what
they're called in various parts of the
country. I was happy to find that brisket is
brisket all over!

Thank you to JoAnn Hecht for catering
Hannah's launch parties. You'll find one of
her delicious cookie recipes, Nutmeg
Snaps, in this book.

Thank you to Jamie Wallace for keeping my
Web site, **MurderSheBaked.com** up to
date and looking great.

And big hugs to everyone who gave me

family recipes to try. Hannah's got a whole lot of baking to do!

CHAPTER ONE

"You'll never see a hearse towing a U-Haul!"

Hannah Swensen turned toward the parlor doorway as she recognized her friend Claire's distinctive voice. She could hear her laughing in the parsonage hallway, obviously delighted by the twist on the old adage, *You can't take it with you.*

"Claire?" Hannah called out, but there was no answer. That was odd. She'd clearly heard Claire and that meant Claire and her new husband, Reverend Bob Knudson, must be back from visiting sick parishioners at Lake Eden Memorial Hospital.

"Bob? Claire?" Hannah called out again, but no one appeared in the doorway. All was perfectly silent outside the cozy sitting room where Hannah had been visiting with Reverend Bob's grandmother, Priscilla Knudson, and copying the octogenarian's recipe for Red Devil's Food Cake.

13

Hannah got up and walked to the window to see if she could spot Bob's car. The scene outside could have been lifted straight from a Christmas card. The birch tree on the other side of the driveway was filled with winter birds enjoying the suet that Grandma Knudson hung from the branches. There were red birds, and blue birds, and green birds, and black birds with iridescent feathers that seemed to be perched on every branch. They reminded Hannah of gems suspended from a white gold filigreed pendant. Lake Eden, Minnesota, could be truly beautiful in the winter . . . cold, but beautiful. If the KCOW weatherman was correct, the mercury in Grandma Knudson's outside thermometer would shiver in the bulb at the bottom of the scale, poking its head up for only a brief period and then sinking down out of sight again.

Hannah's gaze dropped to the driveway that ran along the width of the house and into the garage. There were no tire tracks in the freshly fallen snow. Had Bob and Claire parked in front of the parsonage for some reason?

Puzzled, Hannah crossed to the doorway and stepped out to peer down the hall. It was deserted. She was about to return to the parlor when Grandma Knudson emerged from the kitchen, carrying a tea tray with coffee and sample slices of what she called her best company cake.

"Are Claire and Bob back?" Hannah asked, quickly relieving Grandma Knudson of the heavy tray.

"Not yet. I asked Bob to call when they left the hospital so that I could put on a fresh pot of coffee."

Hannah retraced her steps to the sitting room and set the tray down on the coffee table in front of the couch Grandma Knudson called a "davenport." It had been reupholstered last month by a member of the Holy Redeemer congregation who had chosen the material and the color. The forest green couch that had gone so well with the green and yellow striped wallpaper had been re-covered with bright pink velveteen in a hue that reminded Hannah of the contents in a Pepto-Bismol bottle.

"Would you pour, Hannah?" Grandma Knudson asked, as Hannah settled down on the pink davenport again. "I know young ladies like you prefer coffee mugs, but there's something so civilized about sipping coffee from bone china cups."

Hannah reached for the silver coffeepot and carefully filled two cups. She set them on their matching saucers and was about to hand one to Grandma Knudson when she reconsidered. "I wonder if we might be better off having our coffee in the kitchen," she suggested, glancing down at the generous slices of chocolate layer cake with fudgy frosting that her hostess had placed on matching bone china dessert plates.

"Why is that, dear?"

"I'm worried that I might spill something on your pink davenport."

"Don't give it a second thought," Grandma Knudson told her, reaching out to retrieve her cup and saucer. "Every time I sit there, I hope I'm going to spill something. Unfortunately, Donna Lempke Scotchguarded this darned thing after she recovered it. Every single stain I've managed to make just wipes off."

"Well . . . that's good."

"No, it's not. It means I'm stuck with this pink monstrosity, and it'll probably outlive me!"

Hannah wasn't sure exactly how to respond. Half of her wanted to laugh because Grandma Knudson hated the color of her davenport so much, she was actively trying to ruin it. But the other half of her wanted to cry because Grandma Knudson thought she'd die before the couch could be reupholstered again. Since Hannah really didn't know what to say, she picked up her dessert plate and took a bite of Grandma Knudson's Red Devil's Food Cake.

"Mmmm!" Hannah gave an involuntary exclamation of pure pleasure. The sweet, fudgy melt-in-your-mouth goodness of the frosting was tempered by the deep, dark chocolate of the cake.

"Thank you, Hannah," Grandma Knudson said with a smile. "I'm glad you like my cake. And I'm very flattered that your mother is going to serve it at her book launch party. Now . . . what made you think Claire and Bob were back?"

"I was sure I heard Claire's voice in the hall. And I'm almost positive I heard her laugh."

"Jacob."

"What?"

"You didn't hear Claire. You heard Jacob."

"But it was Claire's voice. I recognized it."

"Jacob can imitate Claire. What did he say?"

"You'll never see a hearse towing a U-Haul," Hannah said, repeating the words she'd heard.

"Then it was definitely Jacob. He was with Claire and Bob in the church office when they were trying to find something to put

17

on the billboard sign for Sunday. Just wait until I tell them! They'll be so pleased he learned something new."

Hannah knew there was some information she wasn't getting. "Who is Jacob?" she asked, deciding to cut straight to the heart of the matter.

"He's Pete Nunke's mynah bird. Bob agreed to keep him while Pete recovers from back surgery."

Hannah laughed. "Well, Jacob fooled me. I really thought he was Claire. Does he imitate you, too?"

"Not me. And not Bob either, at least not yet. He says two things he learned from Pete, though."

"What are they?" Hannah took another forkful of cake. It was so delicious, she wanted to just put her head down and inhale it.

"The first one is, *Brrr, it's cold out there!* And I won't repeat the second one. It has something to do with the weather and someone digging a well, though."

A possible phrase popped into Hannah's head, but she wasn't about to utter it in the parsonage. "Has Jacob learned anything else since he's been here with you?"

"No, and it's not for lack of effort. Bob and Claire have been trying to teach him to say his name, but he doesn't seem interested."

The phone on the end table rang, and Hannah took another bite of her cake while Grandma Knudson answered it. The cake layers had a slightly reddish tint and Hannah remembered that the recipe she'd copied had called for a half-cup of cocoa powder. Cakes made with cocoa powder often took on a nice mahogany color. She reread what she'd written on the recipe card that Grandma Knudson had given her and realized that the deep, dark flavor she'd failed to identify initially must be from the strong coffee that complemented the chocolate. No wonder this cake was so good!

"That was Bob," Grandma Knudson told her, replacing the phone in its cradle. "They're on their way home, and they said they're bringing a surprise for me."

"Any idea what it could be?"

"Coffee ice cream, pickled herring, or ring bologna." Grandma Knudson gave a little giggle that sounded as if it had come from the throat of someone one-fifth her age. "I'd better turn that coffee on. I have it all ready to go."

In less time than it took Hannah to finish the rest of her cake, Grandma Knudson was back. "Maybe they aren't bringing me

19

something to eat. I was thinking that they might have picked up a tall, dark-haired stranger. I'd really love it if they brought me a tall, dark-haired stranger!"

Hannah stared at Grandma Knudson in surprise. "You're thinking of dating again?"

"Good heavens, no! It's just that it would be fun to tell Pam Baxter that she was right. She was the one who told me I'd meet a tall, dark-haired stranger."

"Of course," Hannah said, remembering that Pam was the teacher who'd dressed up in a fortune-teller costume at the last Jordan High carnival.

"Did you have your fortune told, Hannah?"

"Yes. Pam told me that I was going to come into money."

"And you do every day at The Cookie Jar," Grandma Knudson named Hannah's bakery and coffee shop on Main Street. "Pam was right in your case."

"But not in yours?"

"No. My problem seems to be that there aren't many strangers who come to Lake Eden and wind up at the parsonage. As a matter of fact, I can't remember the last stranger who came to town and ended up here. There were more strangers when we had the hotel, but now . . ."

"We're back!" a voice called out, interrupting Grandma Knudson's recollections.

Hannah opened her mouth to call out a hello to Claire and Bob, but she reconsidered. Had she heard Claire's voice, or was it Jacob who'd imitated her again?

"It's Claire," Grandma Knudson said, responding to Hannah's unspoken question. "Jacob's in his cage in the bedroom, and Claire's voice came from the other end of the house."

"Here we are," Bob announced, stepping into the parlor with Claire. They made a perfect couple. Bob's dark, wavy hair and sturdy body set off Claire's blond, sylphlike beauty. "Hi, Hannah."

"Hello, Bob. Hi, Claire." Hannah couldn't help noticing that they were holding hands. Not only that, they were both smiling, and they looked supremely happy. Of course smiling and looking supremely happy wasn't all that unusual for newlyweds. Bob and Claire had married on New Year's Eve and this was only the first week in February.

"Where's my surprise?" Grandma Knudson demanded of her grandson. "Hannah and I have been on pins and needles trying to guess what it is."

"What was your guess?" Claire asked Hannah.

21

"I didn't have the foggiest notion. Grandma Knudson did, though. She told me it was probably coffee ice cream, pickled herring, or ring bologna."

"It's not any of those," Bob said with a laugh. "Try another guess, Grandma."

"If it's not those, then it must be a tall, dark-haired stranger!"

"What?" Bob looked at her in surprise.

"Don't look so shocked. Pam Baxter told me I'd meet a tall, dark-haired stranger at the last school carnival and . . . Oh goodness gracious! There he is!"

"It looks like Pam Baxter was right," the stranger said, crossing the room to give Grandson Knudson a big hug.

CHAPTER TWO

"I never would have recognized you in a million years!" Grandma Knudson said, reaching out to give the stranger who wasn't a stranger a pat on the cheek.

The man laughed. "I'm not surprised. I've changed a lot since high school. Less hair, more body fat, and I'd like to think a bigger brain."

"Well, it's just wonderful that you stopped here to see me!" Grandma Knudson turned to Hannah. "This is Matthew Walters. He lived with Bob's father and me almost thirty years ago."

"My father and mother wanted to go to Africa as missionaries, and they asked Reverend and Mrs. Knudson if I could live with them while they were gone. My uncle and aunt went with them."

"That's right," Grandma took up the story. "Matthew's father had a younger brother, and Matthew's mother had a

23

younger sister. They met at the wedding, fell in love, and got married a year later. They had a son and Matthew's cousin Paul stayed with us, too." Grandma Knudson turned to Matthew. "How is Paul? I haven't heard from him in years."

"Paul is . . ." Matthew stopped speaking and frowned. "I'm not sure how Paul is. We haven't kept in touch."

Grandma Knudson looked surprised. "But why? You were so close when you were young."

"I know we were. Since my father and Paul's father were both ministers with churches only twenty-some miles apart, our families spent a lot of time together. But remember how Paul got into trouble while he was here by breaking into school lockers?"

"Of course I remember. But he didn't actually take anything valuable. It was Bill Garrison's last year as principal, and he told me that Paul was just trying to get attention from the girls by breaking into their lockers and taking little things. He thought it was because you two had spent a lot of time together when you first got here and now that you were dating, Paul felt left out."

"That's what everyone thought, but looking back on it now, I'm afraid it was the start of something bigger, almost like a trial run just to see if he could get away with it."

"What makes you think that?" Claire asked.

Matthew drew a deep breath, and Hannah could see that he was uncomfortable talking about his cousin. "Well . . . things escalated when our parents finished their mission and Paul's family moved to Cedar Rapids."

"What do you mean, *escalated?*" Grandma Knudson asked.

"Let's just say that Paul didn't grow up to be an outstanding citizen, if you know what I mean."

"Oh, dear! I was afraid of something like that. Paul didn't seem the least bit remorseful when I talked to him about the school lockers." Grandma Knudson gave a sigh, and then she reached out to pat Matthew's hand. "You don't have to sugarcoat it for me, Matthew. Did Paul commit a crime?"

Matthew hesitated briefly, and then he dipped his head. "Yes, he did. I don't know all the details, but we heard he was serving ten to twenty in a prison in Iowa."

"Ten to twenty is a stiff sentence," Bob remarked. "Your cousin must have done something fairly serious."

"It was a burglary gone bad. I had a

private detective look into it, and he said Paul got out in five."

"But that's only half of his sentence," Hannah pointed out.

"I know. The detective thought it was probably due to prison overcrowding and a reduction in funding. All I really know is that Paul was released and a few days later the trail went cold."

"Maybe he learned his lesson and decided to become an honest person," Claire suggested. "He could have moved to another state and started a new life."

"Maybe."

Hannah noticed that Matthew didn't sound at all convinced. It was clear that he didn't think his cousin was now on the straight and narrow. "What made you hire a private detective?" she asked.

"My Aunt Sarah was diagnosed with bone cancer. She's Paul's mother, and I thought he ought to know, that maybe he'd come home, or write a letter to her, or something. But the detective couldn't find Paul. There was no trace of him anywhere after he left prison."

"Is it possible he changed his name?" Claire asked.

"He could have done that. The detective told me it's not that difficult to assume someone else's identity. For all we know, Paul's in Mexico, or Canada, or another foreign country living incognito. Or perhaps he's . . . it could even be worse."

Hannah gave an involuntary shiver. She knew exactly what Matthew meant when he said, *it could even be worse.*

"Anyway, everything will work out in the end." Matthew smiled, but to Hannah's eyes it looked a bit forced. "I'm just glad to be here with you, Grandma Knudson. This room looks almost the same except . . . this couch is new, isn't it?" Matthew reached out to pat the piece of furniture Grandma Knudson had described as a *pink monstrosity.* "I seem to remember a green couch. It was slippery."

"Green taffeta," Grandma Knudson said, reaching out to touch the pink davenport. "This is it re-covered. And after that it was cream-colored silk. That didn't last long. Then it was forest green voile. That was the best. And now there's this . . . pink!"

Hannah laughed. She couldn't help it. Grandma Knudson spit out the word as if it were a bug that had flown in her open mouth.

"I'm so glad I ran into Bob at the hospital," Matthew said, smiling at Grandma Knudson. "I stopped to say hello to Doc

27

Knight, and he introduced us. And then I met Claire and learned that they were newlyweds. We're going to have plenty of time to catch up on old times, Grandma."

"What do you mean?" Grandma Knudson asked.

"I'll be right here for the next two weeks. I promised I'd take over Bob's pastoral duties for two weeks so that he can take Claire on a real honeymoon."

A delighted smile spread over Grandma Knudson's face. "Why, that's just wonderful! And it's so kind of you to offer to help out here. But can the seminary spare you for that long?"

"They're sparing me for longer than that. I'm on a four month sabbatical." Matthew turned to smile at them all and then he turned back to Grandma Knudson. "Now how about some of that coffee and cake? Bob's been telling me how good your Red Devil's Food Cake is."

"That's because it's Bob's favorite. It always has been, ever since he was a little boy. And I've got some Lemon Poppyseed Cake for you, Matthew."

"That sounds good, but I'd rather have the devil's food." Matthew gave a little chuckle. "I'd better not let anyone at the seminary hear me saying that, though!"

Everyone except Grandma Knudson laughed. Hannah turned to look at her elderly friend and found her staring at Matthew in shock. "What's the matter?" Hannah asked her.

"Matthew can't have chocolate. He's allergic. It'll make him break out in hives."

"Not anymore," Matthew told her. "I outgrew my chocolate allergy. I've been eating chocolate for twenty years now, and it's my favorite flavor. Corrine, my secretary at the seminary, says I eat so much chocolate because I'm making up for lost time."

Shortly after she'd helped Claire serve coffee and cake, Hannah excused herself and hurried back to her downtown cookie shop. Once she'd parked her candy apple red Suburban in her regular parking spot in back of the bakery and had plugged in the heater that kept the fluids from freezing on this cold winter day, she dashed into the kitchen and almost upended her diminutive partner, Lisa Herman Beeseman.

"Sorry," Hannah said, reaching out with both arms to steady Lisa, who'd been taking cool cookies from the baker's rack.

"That's okay. I'm just glad I didn't spill any cookies. We're running low today."

"Then I'll bake more." Hannah grabbed

her apron, tied it on, and went to the sink to wash her hands. "What's the favorite today?"

"Butterscotch Bonanza Bars. I'll go get out the butterscotch chips."

"But there aren't any butterscotch chips in Butterscotch Bonanza Bars."

"I know there aren't usually, but we need to add them to this batch. I made a mistake this morning when I mixed up the bars, and I put in two cups of butterscotch chips without thinking. Bertie Straub liked them so much, she wants to buy a whole batch for her clients at the Cut 'n Curl."

"Okay. Whatever Bertie wants, Bertie gets."

"That's what I figured. Do you want to go up front while I bake? Or would you rather do it the other way around?"

"The other way around. I'll bake and you wait tables."

"That's fine with me. Marge and Dad are probably ready for a break anyway. Did you get the recipe from Grandma Knudson?"

"Yes. I'll test it tomorrow afternoon. I had a slice up at the parsonage, and it was even better than I remembered from the last church supper."

"How's Grandma Knudson doing?"

"Really well. She's completely recovered

from the stroke, and she's as sharp as ever. She's especially excited about Claire and Bob's honeymoon. They're leaving on Sunday, right after church."

"But I thought they couldn't go until the church sent someone to fill in for Bob."

"They've got someone. While Claire and Bob were making rounds at the hospital, they ran into another Lutheran minister, Matthew Walters. It turns out he lived with Grandma Knudson and her husband for a whole year while his parents were doing missionary work. When Reverend Matthew found out that Bob and Claire had just gotten married and they were waiting for the seminary to send a substitute minister so that they could go on their honeymoon, he offered to take over for Bob so that they could leave now."

"How nice! Where are Bob and Claire going?"

"Hawaii. When I left the parsonage, Bob was making reservations for a fourteen-day cruise. They leave at noon, drive to the airport, fly to Los Angeles, and hop on a cruise ship that sails that night."

"But how about Claire's shop? Who's going to mind it while she's gone?"

"Mother."

Lisa, who'd picked up the cookie jar she'd

filled and was heading toward the swinging door that separated the kitchen from the coffee shop, turned back with a shocked expression. "You mean . . . *your* mother?"

"That's right. It's only three doors down from Granny's Attic and Carrie and Luanne can handle that. Mother's completely psyched about choosing the right outfits for Lake Eden women."

"She *does* have good fashion sense," Lisa said, but she didn't sound very confident. "Do you think that asking your mother to take over for Claire is the right choice?"

"Heavens no! It's the completely *wrong* choice. When Claire told me she'd already called and asked Mother, I just about had a cow!"

"You don't think your mother can do it?"

"*Mother?* Are you kidding? She's hyper-critical and she has no tact. I predict that *Beau Monde*'s business is going to fall off drastically unless Mother wears a muzzle."

Lisa's eyes widened, and then she shook her head slightly. "Come on, Hannah. You know you don't mean that. You're just kidding around, aren't you?"

"I'm not kidding around." Hannah began to frown. Now Lisa was winking with one eye and then the other as if she were some kind of blinking traffic signal. Had her business partner suddenly developed a facial tic? "Let's be serious, Lisa. You know Mother. Just think about what would happen if Mother was behind the counter at *Beau Monde* and Betty Jackson walked in to buy a dress."

"I'm sure your mother would do her best to find something that looked good on Betty."

"Maybe, but if Betty dared to say anything about how Claire didn't carry much of a selection in her size, Mother would be all over it like a duck on a June bug."

"But I'm sure she wouldn't . . ."

"Yes, she would," Hannah interrupted. "Mother would say that nobody made anything stylish in Betty's size and Betty would look a lot better if she lost some weight."

"Your mother wouldn't be that mean!"

"Oh, she wouldn't say it to be mean. It's just that Mother believes in saying exactly what's on her mind." Hannah stopped speaking and stared hard at Lisa, who was making all sorts of strange faces at her. "What's wrong with you, Lisa?"

"Nothing's wrong with Lisa," Delores Swensen answered, coming up behind her eldest daughter and giving her a none-too-gentle tap on the shoulder.

Hannah gasped, whirling around to face the matriarch of the Swensen clan. As usual, Delores Swensen was dressed in the height of fashion. Today she wore a cherry red wool suit with jet black buttons, and a cherry-red-and-black silk scarf draped artistically around her neck. The effect was one of sleek elegance and beauty. No one meeting her for the first time would ever guess that she was approaching her sixtieth birthday.

"Mother!" Hannah gulped, not failing to notice that her mother's lovely visage was hampered by the scowl between her perfectly shaped eyebrows. The two spots of bright color just below her cheekbones, obviously caused by anger at her daughter, didn't help, either.

"Yes, *Mother,*" Delores answered, glaring at Hannah. "Now I want you to explain exactly what you meant when you said I was hypercritical and I had no tact!"

If backpedaling were an art form, Hannah would have been hailed as the next Rembrandt. Hannah had insisted that she'd never intended to hurt her mother's feelings, and Delores had readily conceded that she wasn't as practiced as she could be in the diplomacy department. The air was clear again.

"So what shall I do?" Delores asked the daughter who'd only moments before been her nemesis.

"I don't know," Hannah replied, not willing to risk a reply that might make her into her mother's adversary again.

"I hate to back out now, not when I promised Claire, but do you think I should tell her I can't do it?"

"No. All we have to do is think of someone who can help you."

"Who?" Delores looked completely mystified. "It has to be someone who's up on fashion trends. I'm sure Carrie would agree to do it, but she really doesn't know that much about fashion. We could spare Luanne, but she doesn't pay that much attention to fashion, either. And it has to be someone who's got a good eye."

"A good eye?"

"For size and for what will complement the customer's shape. For instance, you couldn't recommend that Laura Vavra dress in something severely tailored. It's much too harsh a look for her. She's all gentle curves and swirls. And Rose McDermott has to be careful of large bright flowers. It makes her look like a buffet for a bumble-bee."

Hannah burst out laughing. She couldn't

35

help it. And after a moment, Delores joined in. When the image of Rose and the bumble-bees had faded, Hannah turned serious again. "I think maybe I was wrong. You'd be really good at recommending the right dress, Mother."

"I know. I'd be good at it, but no one would buy it, because I'd say something to spoil the sale. Don't forget, I have no tact."

"Maybe I was wrong about that, too."

"You weren't wrong. I know that's one of my failings, but when anyone asks for my honest opinion, I give it. And I don't mince words. That isn't a good trait to have if you're in retail sales."

"True," Hannah agreed. "So we need someone with fashion smarts, plenty of tact, and good salesmanship. That really doesn't sound like anyone I know."

"I can't think of anyone, either."

Mother and daughter turned as the kitchen door opened and Hannah's sister, Andrea, stepped in.

"Brrr! It's got to be way below zero with the wind chill." Andrea walked over to hang her coat on the hooks by the door. "Hi, Mother. Hi, Hannah. I came in for a quick cup of coffee."

Delores and Hannah exchanged glances. Hannah's glance said, *Andrea knows more about fashion than any other woman in Lake Eden. With the possible exception of you, of course.*

And Delores's glance said, *She's got tact and she's a super salesman. Bill always said she could sell kitty litter to a nomad.*

"What?" Andrea asked, reacting to the long glance that her sister and mother exchanged and the nods they gave to each other.

"Coffee," Hannah said, fetching it quickly and settling her younger sister on a stool at the stainless steel workstation.

"And new business," Delores declared, taking the stool directly across from Andrea.

"Cookies?" Andrea queried.

"Chocolate," Delores suggested.

"Coming right up." Hannah wasted no time in placing a half-dozen Brownies Plus cookie bars on a plate and serving her mother and sister.

"I'm so glad you're here, dear," Delores said, reaching out to pat Andrea's hand.

Andrea looked wary. "Why? What's going on?"

"The opportunity of a lifetime. How would you like to increase your wardrobe by twelve *Beau Monde* dresses in the next two weeks?"

Andrea's wariness quickly turned into

suspicion. "What do I have to do? Kill somebody?"

"Not at all." Delores gave her a wide
smile. "Just listen carefully. I've got a real
deal for you!"

CHAPTER THREE

Hannah had no doubt that Andrea would take their mother up on her offer, and Andrea proved her right. Once Hannah's sister had agreed to join their mother at *Beau Monde* and help to deal with Claire's customers, Delores got up from her stool.

"Sorry, dears," she said, heading toward the door. "I really have to run now. Carrie's expecting me to cover her lunch break, and I'm already five minutes late." By that time, she'd arrived at the door, but she made no move to turn the knob. Instead, she turned back to address Hannah. "I probably should have saved one of those cookie bars for her. You know how much she loves your cookies. Every time I bring her something you baked, it puts her in a good mood. But you know how much I love chocolate. Those cookie bars were so marvelous, I just couldn't seem to stop eating them."

Hannah knew a hint when she heard one

and this one was blatant. "I'll box some up for you and Carrie," she said obediently, getting up to do just that. "Will a half-dozen do?"

"Oh my, yes. Carrie will be thrilled that you thought of her."

"Right," Hannah said, flipping one of her bakery boxes open and lining it with a sheet of wax paper. She arranged six Brownies Plus cookie bars in the bottom, covered them with another piece of wax paper, and secured the lid.

"Thank you, dear," Delores said, accepting the box that Hannah handed to her. She opened the door, stepped out, and closed it again behind her.

"Well . . . *that* was unusual!" Andrea commented the moment their mother was gone.

"What was unusual?"

"I didn't expect to get a new wardrobe this week, especially now that the Gantz sale fell through."

"That's too bad," Hannah commiserated, knowing that Andrea always felt bad when she lost a real estate sale. "Did the buyers change their minds?"

"No. The buyers still want it, but Margaret and Fred pulled it off the market this morning."

"But why? I thought they could hardly

wait to move off the farm and live in a high rise apartment in the Cities."

"That's right, but Fred ended up hating apartment living. He told me it was light all the time outside the windows, even in the middle of the night. And he said the traffic noise was awful, even worse than the time the bobcat came down and spooked his horses."

"How about Margaret? Was she disappointed, too?"

"Not as much as Fred, but she said she was looking forward to living at ground level again. She didn't like the elevators."

"I can't blame her for that. I'm not crazy about elevators, either. I keep wondering what I'm going to do if it gets stuck between floors and I have to go to the . . ." Hannah stopped speaking as Andrea's cell phone rang.

"That's Bill," Andrea told her, glancing at the display. "I'd better get it. He never calls me unless it's important."

Hannah walked over to the counter to give Andrea some privacy while she talked to her husband. This could take a while, and she had baking to do.

"It happened last week and they just got around to notifying you *now?*" Andrea asked as Hannah plucked the acetate-covered page for Butterscotch Bonanza Bars out of the three-ring binder that they kept for current recipes. While Andrea listened to her husband's answer, Hannah went to work melting butter in the microwave and measuring brown sugar for one of her very favorite treats.

"Well, I guess Winnetka County must be on the bottom rung of their ladder," Andrea commented, and Hannah could tell that her sister was miffed. Andrea always reacted badly if she suspected that her husband, Bill, the sheriff of Winnetka County, was being slighted by big city law enforcement. "What does the Minneapolis P.D. expect you to do about it now?"

There was another long pause while Andrea listened, and Hannah took that time to stir in the brown sugar. This was a simple recipe, easy to make, and it was delicious.

"They broke into a Kenwood mansion?" Andrea sounded shocked, and Hannah turned to look at her. Her sister's face was flushed and she gave a little shake to her head. "But all those people have state-of-the-art security systems."

Bill's response caused Andrea to groan. "Well, it's not going to do them much good if they forget to set it! Where is this place?"

Andrea nodded at Bill's answer. "I know

exactly where that is. It's a corner lot with a great view of Lake of the Isles shoreline with Raspberry Island off to the right. The house is a Tudor, five-bedroom, four-bath, single family dwelling, with river rock steps leading up the bank to house level, and an eight-foot evergreen hedge all around it. You enter through a gate in the hedge."

Bill said something and Andrea sighed. "You're absolutely right. The hedge hides the lower story from the street and that's perfect for a burglar. There's a delivery door at the side, and that's probably how they got in."

Hannah was surprised that Andrea knew so much about the house. She was well aware that Andrea did her homework and personally checked out every house for sale in the area surrounding Lake Eden, but Minneapolis was quite far afield.

Bill must have asked the same question that Hannah was pondering, because Andrea gave a little laugh. "It's just a co-incidence, honey. We looked at that place when I was in real estate college. I remember how shocked I was at the asking price, especially because there are only a couple of houses in Lake Eden that would go for over five figures. This one had an asking price of two point three, and it's probably worth more now."

Hannah whistled. She couldn't help it. Two point three million dollars was a whole lot of money, probably more than she'd make in a lifetime. The same was true for most people in Lake Eden, with the possible exception of Mayor Bascomb, who had family money to invest, and Del Woodley at DelRay Manufacturing.

"Do you have a list of stolen goods?" Andrea asked her husband. And then she pulled a notebook and pen from her purse and wrote down what her husband told her.

While Andrea was writing what appeared to be a lengthy list, Hannah stirred eggs and vanilla into the sugar and butter mixture and took out another bowl for the dry ingredients. She mixed the flour with the baking powder and the salt and made sure they were well blended. She added them to the bowl with the brown sugar, butter, and eggs, and mixed everything up with a wooden spoon. Then she added chopped walnuts and gave the batter a final stir.

"Oh, that's easy," Andrea said, giving a little laugh. "It's called *rose cut* because it looks like a flower. It was a popular cut way back when. And it's almost three carats?"

Hannah divided the contents of her bowl into three batches. She added the butterscotch chips to Bertie's batch and spread the batter in the bottom of a nine-inch by thirteen-inch pan she'd lined with heavy duty foil. Since she'd tripled the recipe, Hannah mixed semi-sweet chocolate chips into the second batch and white chocolate chips into the third. Personally, she preferred these yummy cookie bars plain. The butterscotch flavor from the ingredients was absolutely delicious all by itself. But several of their customers were crazy about white chocolate chips, and she knew they'd be delighted with the combination of white chocolate and butterscotch. There were also those who wouldn't dream of ordering anything without dark chocolate, and the third batch she'd made was bound to please them.

"How many diamonds did you say were around it?" Andrea asked. And then, as Hannah watched, her sister's eyes widened. "Sixteen! It's just loaded with diamonds! Did they tell you what it's worth?"

Hannah carried the three pans she'd filled to the oven and slipped them in. She turned just in time to see her sister gulp a little air.

"That's incredible, all right!" Andrea said. "But if the diamonds add up to almost four carats, it sounds reasonable."

Andrea listened for a moment and then

she laughed. "You're right, honey. It *doesn't* sound reasonable. No ring should be worth that much money. How did they get it?"

Hannah poured herself another cup of coffee and sat down on a stool across from her sister. Some people might not be able to read upside down, but Hannah was well schooled in the art. When she was growing up, she'd helped her sisters with their reading lessons. The three sisters, Hannah, the oldest, Andrea, the next in line, and Michelle, the youngest, had gathered in Hannah's room to go over their assignments for the next day. At that time, Hannah had found that reading upside down made their homework sessions shorter and increased her sleep time.

What Hannah read was a list of jewelry. There were necklaces, brooches, tiaras, bracelets, and rings. But the item at the end of the list, the item that Andrea had been discussing with Bill, was an antique ring worth more than Hannah could fathom.

"While they were sleeping," Andrea repeated, shivering slightly. "I hate to think of what might have happened if they'd woken up."

Awakened, not woken up, Hannah's mind corrected. Andrea always had trouble with that one, but this wasn't the time to point it out to her.

"No!" Andrea sounded shocked at the next piece of information she learned from her husband. "If they hit the neighbor with their getaway car and he died, is that murder?"

That's the felony murder rule, Hannah answered the question, but not out loud. *Any unlawful homicide that occurs in the commission or attempted commission of a felony is felony murder.*

"Felony murder," Andrea echoed the answer that Hannah hadn't spoken. "What I don't get is why she had all that expensive jewelry spread out in her dressing room."

Several scenarios flashed through Hannah's mind, but what Andrea confirmed next wasn't one of them.

"A charity event at the Walker? And she couldn't decide which gown she wanted to wear so she took all of the jewelry out of the safe?" Andrea frowned slightly. "I guess I can understand that, but why didn't she lock up what she didn't wear before they left the house? Or at least lock everything up when she got home?"

Hannah reached out to feel Andrea's coffee cup. It was stone cold. She picked it up, carried it to the sink to dump it out, and refilled it with fresh hot coffee.

"She thought he put it back in the safe, and he thought she did," Andrea said with a snort. "That's a pretty lame excuse, but I know it happens. Remember when I thought you put on the coffee, and you thought I put on the coffee, and when we came downstairs in the morning there wasn't any? And since we were late, there wasn't time to make it and we had to leave for work without coffee?"

Hannah shuddered at the thought. No coffee in the morning was about the worst thing she could imagine. There was no way she could get along in the morning without coffee. If she didn't have a minimum of one cup before she stepped into the shower, she'd probably fall asleep and drown!

"You want me to keep my eye out for the missing jewelry here in Lake Eden?" Andrea said incredulously. "Bill . . . honey . . . that's ridiculous! Why would it wind up here? We don't have any pawnshops, and even if we did, they wouldn't buy expensive jewelry like that. And I can practically guarantee that the burglars aren't going to stand on the corner in front of Hal and Rose's Cafe and try to sell an antique diamond ring for thousands and thousands of dollars. People don't have that kind of money."

There was silence for a moment while Andrea listened. Then she said, "Okay, honey. I love you, too. See you tonight." She clicked off her phone and dropped it into her purse. She took a sip of coffee, and then she picked up the list she'd made. "Bill wants us to keep an eye out for this stolen jewelry. The ring you heard me talk about is the most expensive piece, but they took a lot more. They're sending him pictures, and I'll make copies for you."

Hannah felt like saying that people didn't exactly get dressed to the nines to come into her coffee shop, and she was unlikely to see any antique rings worth bundles of money, but she was interested in seeing the pictures. "Maybe you'd better make copies for Mother and Carrie too, especially since that expensive ring is an antique. They can watch out for it at antique auctions."

"Good idea." Andrea glanced at the clock on the kitchen wall. "I'd better get going. I have to pick up the girls from school."

Hannah was surprised. Her oldest niece, Tracey, was in the first grade, but Andrea and Bill's youngest, Bethany, had celebrated her second birthday less than two months ago. "The *girls?*" she asked, turning to her sister. "Isn't Bethie too young for Kiddie Korner?"

"Much too young. Janice isn't taking anybody under three and a half, and they've got to be out of diapers. But I wasn't talking about Bethie. Lucy Dunwright is hosting her cousin's bridal shower tonight, so Karen's sleeping over with Tracey. Grandma McCann's making Karen's favorite meal, and then they're going to watch *Bambi*."

"Better stock up on the Kleenex," Hannah warned, remembering how Andrea had cried when Bambi's mother was killed.

"I will. I didn't want them to watch it. They're only six, and it's a really sad movie. But Grandma McCann says it's practically a rite of passage."

A rite of passage for a six-year-old? Hannah thought that was a bit of an overstatement, but as far as she knew, no first-grader had ever been harmed by watching *Bambi*. "Why don't you do a double feature?" she suggested. "Show *Bambi* first and follow it up with *Cinderella*. All the kids love that, and it has a happy ending."

"That's perfect! Then they won't go to sleep thinking sad thoughts. Thanks, Hannah. You really should think about getting married and having kids of your own. You'd make such a good mother."

Of course Hannah sent Andrea off with cookies for the kids to munch while they watched the movies. Munchies were a necessity when it came to double features, and children were always hungry for snacks. Once her sister had left with a box of mixed treats including Molasses Crackles for Tracey, Old-Fashioned Sugar Cookies for Bethie and Grandma McCann, Triplet Chiplets for Karen, and Lovely Lemon Cookie Bars for Andrea, Hannah cleaned up the kitchen, removed the pans of Butterscotch Bonanza Bars from the oven when her timer sounded, sat down at the workstation with a fresh cup of coffee, and thought about what her sister had said.

Andrea had hit the nail on the head when it came to Hannah's dilemma. She wanted children, she'd always wanted children, but she wasn't sure she wanted to get married. And if she did decide to get married, who would it be? She had two choices for a husband. One was Mike Kingston, chief detective at the Winnetka County Sheriff's Department, and the other was Norman Rhodes, the town dentist. The way things stood right now, neither choice was perfect.

Mike wasn't good husband material, and he was the first to admit it. He had a roving eye, and Hannah knew she'd always wonder if she was his only love. And then there was Norman, who'd been the clear choice two months ago. But things had changed and she was beginning to have doubts about him.

Hannah was well aware of the fact that she could be a single mother, but that wasn't her cup of tea. She liked the concept of the nuclear family, and she believed that, if at all possible, children should have both a father and a mother. Extended family was even better. She wanted her children to know their grandparents, cousins, aunts, and uncles.

Last year she'd almost made a choice. Spending the night at Norman's house, the house they'd designed together for a contest, had been a huge deciding factor. It hadn't been romance, not that night. She'd been so exhausted by chasing down leads in Ronni Ward's murder that Norman had made a unilateral decision and informed her that he wouldn't let her drive home. He'd given her his bedroom, and in the morning, he'd cooked an amazing breakfast for her using her favorite recipe for pop-overs.

In moments of levity, Hannah admitted that the breakfast might have been the part that tipped the scales in Norman's favor. No man except the cook at the Corner Tavern had ever made breakfast for her before. And then, just as she was seriously considering accepting Norman's standing proposal, he'd dropped the bombshell.

The incendiary device had a name, and it had first appeared at one of Delores's brunches at the Lake Eden Inn. Its name was Doctor Beverly Thorndike, Norman's former fiancée, and she was a perfect size three with the high cheekbones and gorgeous face of a major starlet. Norman had lobbed the grenade into their midst by introducing her as his new partner, and Hannah's dream of a happy and secure family life as his wife had exploded like a popped soap bubble.

And now Doctor Bev, as everyone called her, was here in Lake Eden, working with Norman at the Rhodes Dental Clinic and living in an apartment at Lake Eden's upscale apartment complex, The Oaks. She'd moved here in January, and everyone in town seemed to love her . . . everyone except Hannah. Even Hannah's own niece, Tracey, thought Doctor Bev was wonderful.

As far as Hannah was concerned, the jury was still out when it came to Norman's new partner. She had to admit that Bev was extremely nice. Too nice to Hannah's way of thinking. This could be an accurate personality assessment on Hannah's part, but it could also be due to the green-eyed monster that whispered warnings in Hannah's ear about how often Norman and Bev went out to lunch or dinner together, and how their working relationship might include a lot more than sharing patients, consulting as fellow dental professionals, and filling in for each other when one of them had to be gone. And that was another point that stuck in Hannah's craw.

Norman seemed to be clueless as far as Hannah's feelings about Bev were concerned. This was, in itself, a worry since he'd always been perfectly attuned to her emotional state. He'd told Hannah that the only reason he'd asked Beverly to join in at the clinic was to free him up to pursue his painting. That made some kind of sense. Hannah had admired the paintings Norman had done before he'd become a dentist, and she'd encouraged him to paint again. If that was the sole reason he'd asked Bev to join him at the clinic, Hannah could accept it. But as far as she knew, in the five weeks that Bev had been at the clinic, Norman hadn't taken any time away from his practice or painted anything at all.

"Hannah?" Lisa pushed open the swinging door between the coffee shop and the kitchen. "Bertie just called, and she wants to know if her Butterscotch Bonanza Bars are ready yet."

"Give me a couple of minutes to cut them and they will be," Hannah answered, doing her best to shake off her depressed mood as she headed to the counter to cut Bertie's cookie bars. Chocolate was in order. It was impossible to remain depressed when you were eating chocolate. But chocolate had calories, and she was already more than triple Bev's dress size. She'd have three semi-sweet chips right out of the bag and that was it.

Four chips later, Hannah felt much better. Through a supreme effort of will, she'd managed to limit herself to only one more than she'd intended to eat, and the yummy chocolate did its medicinal magic almost immediately. She carried Bertie's order out to Lisa, and then she came back to the kitchen and turned on the laptop Bill and Andrea had given her for Christmas. Norman had a Web site for the Rhodes Dental Clinic, and some famous general, she couldn't remember who, had advised his troops to know their enemy. She'd check Norman's Web site and see what she could find out about Beverly Thorndike, D.D.S.

Norman had created a new section in January, the week before Beverly Thorndike,

D.D.S., had joined his practice. It was called *Meet Doctor Bev.*

Hannah read the section with great interest. It was filled with get-to-know-you questions, the type you'd ask on a blind date. Doctor Bev had been born in Minneapolis, gone to high school in Edina, attended college in Michigan, and received her dental degree in Seattle, where Norman had met her. Her favorite movie was *Titanic,* her music of choice was classical, and her preferred cuisine was Mexican. In her spare time she loved to go dancing, see movies, and read. She had an extensive stamp collection, she liked to play tennis, and her favorite color was beige.

Hannah gave a little laugh, right out loud. She wasn't sure whether it was due to the lift she'd gotten from the chocolate or the fact she'd read Doctor Bev's profile on Norman's Web site. The reason didn't matter. All she knew was that she felt almost lightheaded with relief. She had absolutely nothing to worry about when it came to Doctor Beverly Thorndike. There was no way Norman could possibly love a woman whose favorite color was beige!

BUTTERSCOTCH BONANZA BARS
Preheat oven to 350 degrees F.,
rack in the middle position.

1/2 cup salted butter *(1 stick, 4 ounces, 1/4 pound)*

2 cups light brown sugar*** *(pack it down in the cup when you measure it)*

2 teaspoons baking powder

1 teaspoon salt

1 teaspoon vanilla extract

2 beaten eggs *(just whip them up in a glass with a fork)*

1 and 1/2 cups flour *(scoop it up and level it off with a table knife)*

1 cup chopped nuts *(optional)*

2 cups butterscotch chips *(optional)*

*** *If all you have in the house is dark brown sugar and the roads are icy, it's below zero, and you really don't feel like driving to the store, don't despair. Measure out one cup of dark brown sugar and mix it with one cup regular white granulated sugar. Now you've got light brown sugar, just what's called for in Leslie's recipe. And remember that you can always make any type of brown sugar by mixing molasses into white granulated sugar until it's* *the right color.*

Hannah's Note: Leslie says the nuts are optional, but she likes these cookie bars better with nuts. So do I, especially with walnuts. Bertie Straub wants hers with a cup of chopped pecans and 2 cups of butterscotch chips. Mother prefers these bars with 2 cups of semi-sweet chocolate chips and no nuts, Carrie likes them with 2 cups of mini chocolate chips and a cup of chopped pecans, and Lisa prefers to make them with 1 cup of chopped walnuts, 1 cup of white chocolate chips, and 1 cup of butterscotch chips.

All this goes to show just how versatile Leslie's recipe is. Try it first as it's written with just the nuts. Then try any other versions that you think would be yummy.

Grease and flour a 9-inch by 13-inch cake pan, or spray it with nonstick baking spray, the kind with flour added. Set it aside while you mix up the batter.

Melt the butter in a small saucepan over low heat on the stovetop, or put it in the bottom of a microwave-safe, medium-sized mixing bowl and heat it for 1 minute in the microwave on HIGH.

Add the light brown sugar to the mixing

bowl with the melted butter and stir it in well.

Mix in the baking powder and the salt. Make sure they're thoroughly incorporated.

Stir in the vanilla extract.

Mix in the beaten eggs.

Add the flour by half-cup increments, stirring in each increment before adding the next.

Stir in the nuts, if you decided to use them.

Mix in the butterscotch chips if you decided to use them, or any other chips you've chosen.

Spoon the batter into the prepared cake pan and smooth out the top with a rubber spatula.

Bake the Butterscotch Bonanza Bars at 350 degrees F. for 20 to 25 minutes. *(Mine took 25 minutes.)*

When the bars are done, take them out of the oven and cool them completely in the pan on a cold stove burner or a wire rack.

When the bars are cool, use a sharp knife to cut them into brownie-sized pieces.

Yield: Approximately 40 bars, but that all depends on how large you cut the squares.

You may not believe this, but Mother suggested that I make these cookie bars with semi-sweet chocolate chips and then frost them with chocolate fudge frosting. There are times when I think she'd frost a tuna sandwich with chocolate fudge frosting and actually enjoy eating it!

CHAPTER FOUR

Hannah set her purse down on the landing and unlocked her condo door. Then she backed up one step, made sure she was perfectly balanced on the balls of her feet, and opened the door. The preparations might have seemed strange to anyone who didn't know her roommate's habits, but the cat who chose to cohabit her condo had a unique style of greeting her at the end of a day.

"Uff!" Hannah grunted, staggering back a half-step as an orange and white, twenty-three-pound ball of fur hurtled into her arms. She caught her balance, walked through the doorway and carried the cat who shared her domicile to his favorite perch on the back of the couch. "Are you glad to see me?" she asked.

"Rrrow!" he answered, regarding her with one unblinking eye. He was blind in the other and he had a torn ear, a testament to his hard life on the streets before he'd ended up at Hannah's condo door. It was one of the reasons she'd named him Moishe, after the one-eyed Israeli general who'd triumphed in several wars.

Hannah ducked out to retrieve the scarred leather purse her mother hated, and constantly attempted to replace at Christmases, birthdays, and even once on St. Patrick's Day. That offering had been a snazzy little green bag that would have held Hannah's car keys, two aspirin as long as they weren't in the bottle, and a lace handkerchief.

"Are you hungry, Moishe?" she asked, shrugging out of her parka and tossing it on the chair by the door.

"Rrrow!"

"Okay." Hannah glanced at the answering machine sitting on her desk and saw that the red light was blinking. "Just let me get my messages and then I'll fix your dinner."

"RRRRRROW!"

This time the cry was irate and Hannah stopped in mid-stride. "You're right. I can get my messages after I feed you. How about chicken? I've got some I can cut up for you."

"Rrrow."

Moishe's tone was soft and appreciative, and Hannah smiled as she went off to the

kitchen. Whoever said cats didn't understand words had obviously never met
Moishe.

The kitchen was dark and Hannah flicked
on the bank of fluorescent lights overhead.
With snow white walls and white appliances
reflecting the light, this turned her kitchen
into something approaching the brilliance
of a movie set. Perhaps she should think
about painting the walls a darker color, or
replacing the bulbs with a lower wattage,
but she really needed to see what she was
doing when she tested recipes at home.

Moishe's skinless, boneless chicken breast
was in a container on the top shelf of the
refrigerator. Hannah got out a cutting board
and chopped it into feline-sized pieces.
Then she went back to the refrigerator to
take out some crumbled bacon she'd had
left when she'd made Quiche Lorraine to
take to her mother's house for one of their
weekly mother-daughter dinners.

Hannah had just shut the door when she
noticed something odd that was perched on
top of her refrigerator. It was round and
white, and she was sure it hadn't been there
this morning when she'd opened the refrigerator to get a glass of orange juice. She
reached up to get it and began to frown as
she realized it was a pair of her clean white

63

socks rolled up in a ball. Her socks were supposed to be in her sock drawer in the bedroom. How had this sock ball gotten up on top of her refrigerator?

She thought about that as she added the crumbled bacon to Moishe's food bowl. She remembered putting the laundry away on Sunday afternoon. There had been two loads to fold and her laundry basket had been heaped high with clean clothing for the coming week. She was sure she'd put all of her rolled socks away in her bedroom dresser drawer, but perhaps one pair had fallen out of the basket on her way to the bedroom, and she'd noticed it on the floor on her way to the kitchen to get a cold drink. Although she didn't remember doing it, she could have picked up that sock ball and stowed it on top of the refrigerator while she poured herself a glass of lemonade. *Out of sight, out of mind* was a saying with a lot of merit to it. She'd forgotten all about the sock ball, and that's why she'd been so surprised to see it there. People did things like that all the time. They got distracted, set things down in odd places, and then forgot they'd done it. Her own father had once confessed that he'd found his reading glasses in the refrigerator and had no recollection of putting them there.

The mystery was solved. That must be what had happened. Hannah couldn't think of any other explanation. She set Moishe's food bowl on the floor, watched as he eagerly buried his face in its contents, and carried her socks to the bedroom to put them away in the proper place.

Exactly one hour and thirty minutes later, Hannah was sitting in a booth at the Lake Eden Inn, dining on Sally Laughlin's excellent apricot glazed Cornish game hen, butterflied and served on a bed of pork sausage, wild rice, button mushrooms, and lightly sautéed baby snow peas. Mike, her dinner companion, was eagerly devouring lamb shank with an array of perfectly cooked spring vegetables.

When they'd finished their last bite of food, Sally came up to their booth. She was wearing one of her unique chef's aprons in a winter country print that was sprinkled with snowmen, pine trees, red barns with snow on their roofs, and old-fashioned wooden sleds. There was a rectangle of red material sewn to the bib with the words **LAKE EDEN INN** embroidered in white. Sally had recently hired another chef who was working behind the glass window that separated the kitchen from the dining room, and he was wearing an apron that matched Sally's. The sous-chefs on the line were dressed in solid green aprons to match the pine trees in the print, and the colorful display turned the preparation of food into dining entertainment.

"How was the game hen?" Sally asked Hannah.

"It was so wonderful it made me glad I'm an omnivore."

Sally laughed and turned to Mike. "And you enjoyed the lamb shank?"

"Delicious." Mike pointed down at his empty plate. "That sauce was just great. I didn't want to leave anything, so I mopped it up with a couple of your rolls."

"Good for you! I think the sauce is the best part. And you're right, that plate is so clean I could almost put it back in the cupboard and use it again." Sally noticed Mike's expression and reached out to pat his shoulder. "Of course I wouldn't. I'm just teasing."

"Better be careful who you say that to. We got word that the health board hired another inspector and they're going to be coming around again. Those guys have no sense of humor."

"True. Well, I guess I'd better get back to the kitchen before . . ."

"Wait just a second," Mike stopped her. "Do you have another minute? I'd like to show you a couple of pictures."

Sally slid into the booth next to Hannah. "I take it they aren't pictures of your nieces and nephews?"

"No. It's police business." Mike opened his briefcase, which sat beside him in the booth, and pulled out a file folder. He extricated a sheaf of photos and handed them to Sally. "These are from the Minneapolis P.D. Look through them and if you spot anyone wearing any jewelry that looks like this, call me immediately."

"Stolen?" Sally asked, paging through the photos.

"Yes, and someone was killed in the process. That means I want you to be careful if you spot anything. Don't ask questions and don't let on you noticed. Just call me and we'll be out here right away."

"Got it." Sally rose to her feet, but she held on to the photos. "Do you mind if I show these to my waitresses? They're out here on the floor more than I am."

"I was hoping you'd do that while Hannah and I have dessert."

When Sally had left, Hannah turned to Mike. "Do you really think the jewelry will show up out here?"

"Not really, but anything's possible. The burglars got some cash, too. It was in a drawer in her dressing table, and it was enough to stay out here at the inn until they can make arrangements to turn the jewelry into cash. I don't really think they'd come to a small place like this, but I've got to cover the bases."

"Then you'd better show those photos to the jeweler out in the mall. He buys antique jewelry and resells it."

"I was planning to stop there after dinner if you don't mind."

"I don't mind," Hannah said. She didn't get out to the mall very much, and Andrea had mentioned a new cheese shop that had opened last week, and raved about the aged mozzarella she'd sampled.

Their waitress appeared a moment later, bearing two dessert bowls topped with whipped cream and chocolate curls. "This is Sally's latest creation," she explained, "and it's on the house."

"What is it?" Mike asked, not waiting for an answer before he spooned up a mouthful and tasted it.

"Mocha Trifle. Sally got the recipe from her friend Linda Sifuentes. She owns a bed and breakfast in Illinois. This is her original recipe."

"Yum!" Hannah said, sparing no extra words in order to save her time for eating. The strong heady taste of the coffee complemented the smooth dark chocolate perfectly. The texture was nice with soft, moist cake and crunchy pecans, and the semi-sweet chocolate curls were a wonderful foil for the sweetness of the whipped cream.

"Sally says Linda calls it *Death by Caffeine* because you can't stop eating it. And it only takes fifteen minutes to make if you buy the cake. Of course Sally doesn't. She always makes her own sponge cake." The waitress reached into her apron pocket and pulled out a printed recipe. "Here," she said, handing it to Hannah. "Sally said you'd want it."

"Sally's right." Hannah read through the recipe while the waitress poured their coffee, and then she set it on the table so that she could finish her dessert.

Mike reached for the recipe and quickly read through it. "I thought so!" he said.

"You thought what?"

"This calls for coffee liqueur and chocolate liqueur. I hope Sally's not serving it to minors."

"Of course she's not!" Hannah said, frowning at him. "Sally and Dick are very careful about things like that."

Mike looked slightly embarrassed. "I know

that. I guess it's just a case of once a cop, always a cop. Sometimes I take my work too seriously."

You said it! Hannah wanted to say, but of course she didn't. Mike already knew his faults, and he didn't need her to point them out to him. "Have you ever had an alcohol-related complaint about the Lake Eden Inn?" she asked instead.

"Never. And I'm almost positive that no one coming from here has ever been pulled over for a D.U.I." Mike tapped the recipe with his finger. "Can you make this?"

"I'm sure I can. It doesn't look complicated since you layer everything in a trifle bowl."

"Could you make it for me next Sunday?"

Hannah shrugged. "I don't see why not. Lisa and I are really busy getting ready for Valentine's Day, but it only takes fifteen minutes. What's the occasion?"

"It's a birthday party."

Hannah swallowed hard. The last time she'd made something for Mike to take to a birthday party, the birthday girl had wound up dead. But she'd created plenty of other desserts for birthday parties since then, and no one else had experienced an unexpected and unwelcome last birthday. She was just being silly, borrowing trouble, acting paranoid, or all three of the above.

"How about it, Hannah? Will you?"

"Sure, I'll do it," Hannah agreed, convincing herself that nothing would happen if she made the trifle for Mike. "Booze? Or no booze?"

"You can make it without booze?"

"Of course. All I have to do is add an equal amount of liquid that's as sweet and thick as liqueur. I could use coffee mixed with corn syrup for the coffee liqueur, and chocolate syrup for the chocolate liqueur."

"But would it taste the same?"

"No, but it would still be good. So is it liqueur? Or no liqueur?"

"Liqueur. There isn't that much in it, and there won't be any kids. I'll buy something down at the Municipal and drop it off tomorrow."

"That's fine," Hannah said, hoping that the Lake Eden Municipal Liquor Store had a decent brand of liqueur. And then she asked the question that had been at the forefront of her mind ever since Mike had asked her to make the trifle for someone's birthday. "Whose birthday is it?"

"It's Bev's. You know Doctor Bev, don't you?"

"Yes," Hannah said, leaving it at that. Of course she knew Beverly Thorndike. She'd met her the night that Norman had introduced his new partner to the Swensen family. She'd seen her a couple of times after that, but only in passing. Hannah didn't really know her personally since she hadn't been into the dental office to visit Norman since Doctor Bev had started working there. She certainly wasn't interested in becoming a friend of the woman who'd changed her relationship with Norman!

"Norman asked me to organize something since she won't be going home to her mother's place until after her birthday," Mike continued his explanation. "We thought she might be lonely having a birthday here in Lake Eden without some kind of celebration."

Hannah was glad he hadn't told her earlier, or she might have refused to make the trifle for Doctor Bev. The diabolical side of her mind told her that this could be the perfect opportunity to get rid of Norman's new partner for good. That was when the practical side jumped in and pointed out that not only was it illegal to lace a birthday trifle with poison, it would be much too obvious who'd done it. The diabolical side was just suggesting less lethal but still nasty additives when Mike smiled and leaned across the table toward her.

"I've got a great idea," he said, giving her the smile that had fluttered at least half of the female hearts in Lake Eden. "Norman put me in charge of the guest list and I haven't gotten around to inviting anyone except a couple of people from work."

Hannah held her breath, waiting for the second shoe to drop. She was almost certain she knew what was coming and she wasn't wrong.

"How about you, Hannah? Do you want to come?"

DEATH BY CAFFEINE
(MOCHA TRIFLE)

You don't have to preheat your oven at all — this dessert requires no baking.

Hannah's 1st Note: If you can't find a sponge cake at your local bakery and you don't feel like baking one, you may be able to find the little round, indented cups for strawberry shortcake in your grocery store. I did, and mine were called "Dessert Shells," and one serving was two shells. (They're NOT pie shells, but squishy like a sponge.) It took 10 little cups to make 6 cups of cubed sponge cake, and the total weight of the cake was 8 ounces.

6 cups sponge cake

1 cup strong brewed coffee, cooled to room temperature

16 ounces *(6 cups)* of dairy topping *(I used Cool Whip Real Whipped Cream)*

1/4 cup coffee liqueur *(I used Starbucks Cappuccino)*

2 Tablespoons *(1/8 cup)* chocolate liqueur *(I used Godiva)*

2 six-ounce containers of chocolate yogurt★★★

3/4 cup mini chocolate chips

3/4 cup chopped pecans

*** *I couldn't find chocolate yogurt in my store so I used two 6-ounce containers of vanilla yogurt and mixed it with 1/8 cup chocolate syrup. It worked just fine.*

Hannah's 2nd Note: If you would prefer to whip your own sweetened whipped cream, that's fine. Just make sure you end up with 6 cups. To do this, start with 3 cups of chilled whipping cream, whip it up, and when it begins to hold a peak, continue beating and slowly sprinkle in a half-cup of white, granulated sugar. Continue to beat until the sugar has dissolved. (You can tell by shutting off the mixer and rubbing a bit of whipped cream between your finger and thumb. If it's gritty, it's not dissolved yet.)

Cut the sponge cake into cubes roughly twice the size of those little cheese cubes with fancy toothpicks that they serve at parties. You don't have to be exact. Nobody's going to measure.

Place the cake cubes in a bowl and add the strong coffee. Toss the cake cubes around a little so they all get soaked with coffee.

Combine the dairy topping, yogurt, and

liqueurs in a small bowl. Set the bowl aside.

In another small bowl, toss the mini chocolate chips with the chopped pecans. Set that bowl aside.

Get out a pretty bowl that will hold 12 cups, and set it on the counter. You're ready to assemble your trifle.

Place a third of the coffee-soaked cake cubes in the bottom of the bowl.

Top the coffee-soaked cake with a third of the whipped topping mixture.

Sprinkle a third of the chip and nut mixture over that.

Repeat these layers two more times, ending with the last of the nut and mini chocolate chip mixture.

Hannah's 3rd Note: Linda tops her trifle off with a few espresso coffee beans, but Sally uses chocolate curls at the Lake Eden Inn. Even though all you have to do to make chocolate curls is run the blade of a sharp knife down the side of a thick chocolate bar, I sometimes don't have time to do it. Then I just sprinkle on a few seasonal berries or more mini chocolate chips for decoration.

This dessert must chill for at least 3 hours before serving. If you have all the ingredients, you can make it in the morning in about fifteen minutes, stick it in the refrigerator while you go about your busy day, and serve it to company for dinner that night.

Yield: This trifle serves 12 unless you invite Mike. I watched him eat three helpings at the Lake Eden Inn.

CHAPTER FIVE

"So what are you going to do?" Andrea asked.

"I couldn't think of a good excuse that fast, so I said I'd go. What else could I do?"

"You could have listened to the message I left on your answering machine at a quarter to five last night. I called to warn you that Mike invited Bill to her birthday party and Bill accepted for both of us."

Hannah groaned. She'd seen the red light blinking, but she'd fixed Moishe's dinner first. And she'd fully intended to listen to her message right after she got dressed for her dinner with Mike, but her hair had been impossible after her shower, sticking up in wiry red corkscrew curls all over her head. It had taken what seemed like forever to brush it into some semblance of normalcy. Then Mike had arrived and she'd forgotten all about the message she hadn't retrieved. And when he had brought her home, she'd gone straight to bed without even glancing at her answering machine.

"You've got to start checking your messages, Hannah, especially when your cell phone is off."

"My cell phone's off?" Hannah rummaged around in the bottom of her purse until she found it. The moment she did, she remembered why she'd silenced it. "I turned it off when I catered Mother's Regency Romance Club meeting, but I'm almost sure I turned it back on."

Andrea shrugged. "It's either off, or dead. All I know is I called you and it went straight to voicemail. You probably haven't checked your voicemail in a while, either. If you don't leave any way for people to contact you, they can't tell you what you need to know."

"That's true," Hannah admitted, pressing the button to turn on her phone and holding it down. But even though she held it for double the time it usually took, there was no burst of sound and the display remained blank. "There's something wrong with my phone. It won't turn on."

"Then you probably forgot to charge it. Where's your charger?" Andrea held out her hand for the phone. "I'll go plug it in."

"It's at home. I don't have one at work."

Andrea just shook her head. "Really, Hannah! They're not expensive, and you should have a charger in both places. I'm going to the phone store anyway, and I'll pick up a second one for you. I've got one in my office, one at home, and one in my car. It's very important to keep your phone charged."

"I know it's important for you. You use your phone for work. Mine is just for personal use."

"That's important, too. Now tell me about Mike. What did he say when he asked you."

Hannah didn't say, *Asked me what?* She knew that her sister had gone back to their original topic of conversation. "He said, *I've got an idea. Do you want to come?* But that was after I'd already promised to make a Mocha Trifle for the party."

"Why did you do that? I thought you were upset about Doctor Bev moving here."

"I am, but Mike asked me to make the trifle for a birthday party, and I said I would, but that was before I found out whose birthday it was."

"Mike's an idiot," Andrea said, giving an exasperated sigh. "The man has zero sensitivity. I really don't know why he would ask you to make a dessert for Doctor Bev's party, unless . . ." Andrea stopped in midsentence and frowned.

"Unless what?"

"Unless he has his own selfish interests at heart. He wants you to get so mad at Norman that you'll fall into his arms on the rebound. Either that, or . . ."

Andrea faltered and Hannah stepped in with a possible explanation. "Either that or Mike has the IQ of a small kitchen appliance."

"Exactly!" Andrea looked very pleased at the comparison. "Which small kitchen appliance would he be?"

"A toaster."

"Because every single woman in town thinks he's hot?"

"Exactly. And any woman who thinks she's his one and only will get burned every time he looks at another woman. And he'll do it all the time."

Andrea gave a brief nod. "Sounds like you've got Mike figured out. How about Norman? Why do you think he brought Doctor Bev here in the first place?"

"I don't know. I've been trying to figure that out."

"Do you think he's trying to make you jealous so you'll fight for him?"

Hannah thought about that for a moment and then she shook her head. "I don't think so. Norman's not that devious. He brought her to Lake Eden for some other reason, but I'm not sure what it is. Whatever it is started in Minneapolis when he went to see the new dental clinic his friends from Seattle built."

"Are you sure?"

"Almost positive. He was fine when he left Lake Eden. I know because he dropped Cuddles off to stay with Moishe and he gave me a big hug and kiss when he left. But when he got to the Cities, things changed. He left a couple of messages, but he sounded . . ." Hannah paused to think of the best word to describe Norman's voice. "Cold. He sounded cold like he was talking to a stranger. And when he came back he was cold, too. He gave me a hug and thanked me for keeping Cuddles, but . . . he was cold. I don't know any other way to describe it."

"Before he left you were his love? And when he came back you were just a friend?"

"That's exactly right. And I'm still just a friend. I know something happened to change his state of mind, but I don't know what it is."

"Maybe you should find out," Andrea suggested, getting up to leave. But she turned back at the door. "And you'd better do it before you wind up baking a wedding cake for Norman and Doctor Bev."

Hannah took Andrea's words seriously, but there were orders to fill and cookies to bake, and there wasn't much she could do about it at the moment. She was knee deep in cookie dough when Lisa pushed open the swinging door from the coffee shop and announced that Grandma Knudson had come in to see her.

"She said it was important," Lisa said. "Shall I send her back here?"

"Yes. She probably wants more cookies for Sunday. I heard they were giving a bon voyage party after church for Claire and Reverend Bob."

Lisa shook her head. "I don't think that's it. When she came in she looked worried and she said she'd walked down here from the parsonage."

"She shouldn't be walking that far in this weather! It's ten below and the streets are slippery."

"I know. That's why I called Herb to take her back home. He'll be here in five minutes, and I figured that was long enough for you to warm her up with some coffee and listen to what she has to say."

As Lisa left to fetch Grandma Knudson,

Hannah did what she did at least a dozen times a day. She thanked her lucky stars she'd found such a wonderful, caring business partner. Lisa had been young, just out of high school, when Hannah had hired her two and a half years ago. At that time, Lisa had earned scholarships to several good universities, but she'd explained to Hannah that she wanted to stay at home in Lake Eden to care for her father, Jack Herman, who'd just been diagnosed with Alzheimer's disease.

A lot had happened in the intervening years. Lisa had been so good for business that Hannah had made her a full partner. And Lisa had married Hannah's classmate, Herb Beeseman, on Valentine's Day last year. Herb's mother, Marge Beeseman, had given the happy couple her family home, and she'd moved in with Jack to give the newlyweds time to themselves.

There had been talk when Marge, a widow, had moved in with Jack, a widower. But that gossip had been quickly nipped in the bud by Hannah's mother. Now the citizens of Lake Eden were used to the arrangement, and no one said a word. Jack Herman and Marge Beeseman were a couple and that was that.

"Hi, Grandma Knudson," Hannah

greeted her when she came into the kitchen. "Come sit at the workstation and I'll get you a cup of coffee."

"Thank you, Hannah."

Hannah noticed that Grandma Knudson's voice sounded shaky and she hurried to pour the coffee. The walk from the parsonage in subzero temperatures had obviously tired her. "Did Lisa tell you? Herb's going to take you back home so you won't have to walk up the hill."

"She told me, and that's very sweet of him. Herb Beeseman's always been a good boy. Did you bake anything special today? I want to take a box of something special back with me so that Bob and Claire think I walked down here to bring back a surprise for them. If they guess the real reason I came to see you, they might not leave on their honeymoon."

Uh-oh, Hannah's mind warned. Grandma Knudson looked very serious. "Of course I can pack up something special," Hannah reassured her, glancing over at the bakers' racks. "I've got Chocolate Sugar Cookies, Mocha Nut Butterballs, Walnut Date Chews, and Blonde Brownies. And if you'd like something different from cookies or cookie bars, I baked a batch of Carrot-Oatmeal Muffins this morning."

"I like the sound of those muffins. Are they new?"

"Yes. Lisa got the recipe from Lois Theilen. She says they're the best oatmeal muffins she ever made, and the recipe won first place at the Minnesota State Fair."

"Oh, my!" Grandma Knudson was clearly impressed, but she still looked worried.

"Try one to see if you like it," Hannah offered, putting a muffin on a plate and setting it in front of Grandma Knudson.

"Gladly. I know Lois and she's a wonderful cook. If this is her favorite oatmeal muffin recipe, it's going to be delicious." Grandma Knudson took a bite and nodded. "I told you. It's delicious. And these muffins are perfect for Bob and Claire. She likes oatmeal cookies, and Bob's really fond of carrots."

"How about Matthew? Do you think he'll like them?"

Grandma Knudson began to frown. "I'm not concerned about Matthew, at least not when it comes to muffins. Matthew's the reason I came down here to talk to you."

It took three cups of coffee and every bite of the Carrot-Oatmeal Muffin before Hannah had the whole story. Grandma Knudson was concerned that Matthew might not be the boy she remembered from so long ago.

She wasn't sure why anyone would assume Matthew's identity, but there were just too many inconsistencies between the Matthew she remembered as a teenager and the man who claimed to be Matthew as an adult.

"Let me see if I've got this straight," Hannah said, glancing down at the notes she'd jotted in one of the shorthand notebooks she kept in the kitchen. "The teenage Matthew was allergic to chocolate, but the adult Matthew isn't."

"That's right. And I don't think you can outgrow a chocolate allergy. My sister Bertha was allergic to strawberries for her whole life. She broke out in hives every time she tried to eat them."

"I'll check on that chocolate allergy," Hannah promised, glancing down at her notes again. "You're also suspicious that the adult Matthew isn't who he says he is because you don't think the seminary would give him all that time off. You want me to call to make sure he actually teaches there and he really *is* on sabbatical."

"That's right. I really don't think the seminary would give him a four-month sabbatical. My husband taught there before he decided he'd rather accept a calling as a minister. After the first two years, he earned a sabbatical, but it was only for six weeks."

Hannah jotted that down, and went on. "You told me that another reason you're suspicious is because Matthew sings too well?"

"Oh my, yes! That really made me think twice. I've never met a Lutheran minister that could sing all five verses of *Abide With Me* without going off-key."

"How about Matthew the teenager?" Hannah asked. "Did he sing off-key?"

Grandma Knudson thought about that for a moment and then she sighed. "I don't know. I don't think I ever heard him sing. I sat up front in church. There was a special pew for the family of the minister. The boys could have been up there with me, but they preferred to sit in the back with their friends."

"And the fact that Matthew can sing makes you doubt that he's an ordained minister?"

"Yes. If it turns out that there really is a Matthew Walters who teaches at Concordia and is an ordained minister on a four-month sabbatical, do you think you can find out if the Matthew they know has a good singing voice?"

"I can try," Hannah said, but it was a tall order. Perhaps Andrea would be better at making the seminary call. Bill always said she could charm the birds out of the trees, and Hannah knew firsthand that her sister could get personal information from practically anyone.

"There's the davenport, too," Grandma Knudson said. "I almost forgot about that."

"The pink one in your sitting room?"

"Yes. Matthew said he remembered it when it was green, but he couldn't have remembered that. I looked in my papers last night, and when the boys stayed with us, it was red. It wasn't recovered with green fabric until after they'd left."

"Yes, but . . ."

Grandma Knudson held up her hand. "Before you say it, I know he could be remembering it wrong, but when you add it to all the other things, it makes me even more uneasy."

"I can understand that."

"Can you really?" Grandma Knudson raised her eyes to Hannah's. "You don't think I'm seeing a bear in the woods when it's only an odd-shaped tree trunk?"

"No. Now that I know what you know about the teenage Matthew, I'm uneasy, too."

"Then you'll place the phone calls to set my mind at ease?"

"Of course I will."

"Oh, good!" Grandma Knudson pulled a folded piece of paper from her pocket and handed it to Hannah. "Here's the number of Concordia Theological Seminary. That's where Matthew said he teaches. His secretary's name is Corrine. He mentioned that when we talked about his chocolate allergy, and I wrote it down afterward. The number's long distance, and I'll pay you for the call."

"You don't have to do that. I'm just as curious as you are. I'll try to call Corrine later today. If I can't reach her, I'll call again in the morning." Hannah reached out to pat Grandma Knudson's hand. "Try not to worry. I'll have answers to all of your questions by noon tomorrow."

Grandma Knudson smiled for the first time since she'd walked into the kitchen. "Thank you, Hannah. I really appreciate it. I know I could have made those calls myself, but I was afraid he'd overhear me. If that man really is Matthew, he'd be hurt that I was suspicious of him. And if he's not Matthew, he's up to something and I don't want him to guess I suspect him."

"That makes perfect sense," Hannah said, closing her steno pad and standing up. "I'm going to pack up those muffins, and then I'll check with Lisa to see if Herb's here with your ride home."

CARROT-OATMEAL MUFFINS
Preheat oven to 375,
rack in the middle position.

1 and 1/3 cups flour *(just scoop it up and level it off with a table knife)*

1 cup quick-cooking or old-fashioned dry oatmeal *(I used Quaker Quick — 1 Minute)*

1 Tablespoon baking powder

1/2 teaspoon baking soda

1 teaspoon cinnamon *(I used half cinnamon and half cardamom)*

1/2 cup brown sugar *(pack it down in the cup when you measure it)*

1/4 cup finely shredded carrots *(pack them down when you measure them)*

1/2 cup raisins *(I used golden raisins)*

1/2 cup milk

1 beaten egg *(just whip it up in a glass with a fork)*

1/3 cup melted salted butter***

1 teaspoon vanilla extract

*** *One-third cup of salted butter is approximately 1/4 of a stick. Just cut a quarter of a stick off the end and melt the big part. It might turn out to be slightly more* *than 1/3 cup, but that doesn't seem to hurt a thing in this wonderful recipe.*

Grease or spray with Pam *(or another nonstick cooking spray)* the cups of a 12-cup muffin pan. Set it aside.

In a large mixing bowl, combine the flour and oatmeal.

Sprinkle the baking powder, baking soda, and cinnamon on top. Mix them in thoroughly.

Stir in the brown sugar. Mix until everything is blended.

Shred the carrots if you haven't already done so. A fine shred is best. You want them to cook in the time it takes the muffins to bake and turn golden brown and delicious.

Add the shredded carrots and the raisins to your bowl. Mix them in thoroughly.

In a separate small bowl, combine the milk, beaten egg, melted butter, and vanilla. Give it a good stir so that everything is well combined.

Dump the contents of the small bowl into the larger bowl. Gently stir just until the dry ingredients are moistened and no dry "pockets" remain.

Fill the prepared muffin cups 3/4 full.

Bake at 375 degrees F. for 20 to 25 minutes or until a toothpick inserted in the center of a muffin comes out clean. *(Of course it's not really clean — that's just what they say in the cookbooks. It just means that when you pull the toothpick out, it doesn't have uncooked batter sticking to it.)*

Set the muffin pan on a cold burner or a wire rack for 10 minutes. This cooling process is necessary because if you try to take the muffins out of the muffin cups now, they may break in pieces, and you certainly don't want that!

When the muffins have cooled for 10 minutes, slide the blade of a knife around each muffin's edge and gently pry them out. Once the muffins are out of the cups, you can try to cool them completely on a wire rack, but I'm betting that several will disappear before they're cool.

Yield: 12 truly excellent muffins

Hannah's Note: Mother really likes these even though there's no chocolate in the recipe. Believe me, this is high praise!

CHAPTER SIX

Hannah glanced up at the clock on the kitchen wall. It was a quarter to ten the next morning, and Andrea had been on the phone for forty-five minutes. Although she'd been all ears, Hannah hadn't learned much by listening to her sister's end of the conversation. She still didn't know whether Reverend Matthew was who he claimed to be. Hannah had done some research on chocolate allergies and found that it was possible to "outgrow" them. It all had to do with avoiding chocolate for so long that your body didn't react when you tried it again. This could have happened with Reverend Matthew, just as he claimed.

The clatter of spoons stirring coffee, the low hum of conversation, and an occasional laugh drifted under the swinging door that led to the coffee shop. The Cookie Jar was busy this morning. Hannah felt a little guilty for taking almost an hour out of their busy workday, but Lisa had agreed that setting Grandma Knudson's mind at ease was the top priority.

"You too, Corrine," Andrea said. "You've been a big help and I think I have enough background now. Thanks so much for talking to me. And that's Corrine with two r's and Addams with two d's?"

Hannah perked up her ears. It sounded as if the conversation with Matthew's secretary was about to end.

"Well, thanks again. It's been a pleasure."

Hannah got up to dump out Andrea's cold coffee and replace it with hot brew from a fresh pot. When she got back to the workstation, Andrea was dropping her cell phone back into her purse. "So?" she asked, setting the fresh mug of coffee in front of her sister.

"Matthew's secretary was very helpful."

"That's because you bamboozled her."

"No, I didn't. Corrine was just talkative. She's probably bored since her boss is gone."

"But you had to pretend to be a reporter from the *St. Louis Post-Dispatch*."

"Okay, so that was a little white lie, but it was for a good cause. You told me that Grandma Knudson was really worried."

"She is. I couldn't tell from all the yes or

no answers you gave, but does she have anything to worry about?"

Andrea shook her head. "Reverend Matthew Walters is an ordained Missouri Synod Lutheran minister. He's one of the senior members of the faculty, and he left last week on a four-month sabbatical. Before he drove off, he told Corrine that he planned to stop by a little town in Minnesota, Lake Eden to be exact, to meet the minister, Reverend Robert Knudson, and renew his acquaintance with Grandma Knudson."

"So that part checks out."

"Yes, and there's more. When I asked about Reverend Matthew's duties at the seminary, she said that he has a minor in music, he's written several hymns that are under consideration for inclusion in the college hymnal, and he's the tenor soloist in the seminary choir."

"That shoots Grandma Knudson's theory about tone-deaf Lutheran ministers out of the water."

"It sure does." Andrea glanced down at the notes she'd scrawled on a paper napkin. "And I found out about the davenport."

Hannah was amazed. She'd listened to everything Andrea had said, and she knew her sister hadn't mentioned the davenport. "How did you do *that?*"

"Corrine volunteered some information that clears it all up. She said Matthew is a . . ." Andrea glanced at the napkin full of notes, ". . . protan."

"Isn't that a form of color blindness?"

"Yes. How did you know?"

Hannah shrugged. "I must have read it somewhere. What else did she say about it?"

"She said Reverend Matthew sees red as a shade of green. She didn't find out about it until her first year as his secretary, and he came to the office Christmas party wearing a bright red shirt with a green tie. She told him she thought it was nice he'd gotten into the Christmas party spirit and he didn't know what she was talking about. He saw the red shirt as a shade of green and thought the tie matched it perfectly."

"Got it!" Hannah commented, catching on immediately. "The red davenport in Grandma Knudson's sitting room looked green to him."

"Exactly."

"So . . . nothing's left. Every suspicion that Grandma Knudson had can be explained away in one way or another. She's going to be so relieved when I tell her!"

"Yes. I think we should go up there and tell her now."

Hannah noticed the plural pronoun her

sister had used. "You're going to come with me?" she asked.

"You betcha! I'm hoping that Grandma Knudson's got some of that Red Devil's Food Cake left over from yesterday, the one you told me was really scrumptious. And once we give her the good news about Reverend Matthew, she'll be so happy she'll invite us to stay for coffee and cake."

Hannah was smiling as she turned the big stand mixer to the lowest speed and added salt, baking soda, and baking powder to the sugar in the bowl. She was testing the Red Devil's Food Cake recipe as promised. The mixture of water, butter, chocolate, brown sugar, and espresso powder was cooling in a saucepan, and she'd already prepared her cake pans by greasing and flouring the insides and then adding a layer of parchment paper to the bottom. Grandma Knudson had been delighted to find out that Reverend Matthew really was the teenager who'd stayed with her. And Andrea had been *spot on,* one of the phrases their mother used in her Regency romances that meant *absolutely correct.* Grandma Knudson had asked them to stay for cake and coffee, and then she'd asked Hannah to cater the bon voyage party for Claire and

Bob right after church on Sunday.

Hannah thought about Grandma Knudson's request while she added more sugar to the bowl. A tropical cookie would be perfect since Claire and Bob were going to Hawaii. Hannah had a couple of cookies that would work, but she wanted to make something new.

She thought about it as she added cocoa powder and the last of the sugar to the mixing bowl. Then she mixed in two eggs, one at a time, and the vanilla extract. The chocolate scent was lovely, and she decided that Bob and Claire's cookies should have both chocolate and coconut, a winning combination in almost anyone's book.

The mixture in the saucepan had cooled enough so that it wouldn't cook the eggs. Hannah added half of it to her bowl, along with half of the flour. Once that was mixed in, she added the other half of the chocolate mixture and the rest of the flour. When everything was thoroughly incorporated, she turned off the mixer, removed the beaters and the bowl, and gave the cake batter a final stir by hand.

Coconut cookies with mini chocolate chips would be good. Hannah thought about how she could make them more tropical as she filled the layer cake pans she'd prepared and slipped them into the oven. She was just setting the time for twenty minutes when she had what she thought was a great idea. She'd put something tropical on top of the cookie for a decoration. Now all she had to do was think of something that was tropical and would be delicious on top of a coconut and chocolate cookie.

She'd just dismissed pieces of fruit because they'd be sticky, when her mother opened the back door.

"Do you have a minute, Hannah?" Delores asked.

"Sure do. I just put my cakes in the oven and it's time for a break. Coffee?"

"I'm all coffeed out, dear. Do you have any juice?"

"Orange, grapefruit, or peach."

"I'll have orange if you can spare it. I just dropped by to talk about my launch party."

"Right," Hannah said, beginning to panic. She hadn't planned a thing for her mother's second book launch party, and it was scheduled for a week from next Sunday.

"Kelly-Anne, my friend in England, sent me a marvelous recipe that would be perfect for the refreshments."

Hannah was glad her mother couldn't see the anxiety on her face as she went to fetch the juice. English recipes needed to be converted to American measurements and they usually turned out to be odd amounts like a third of a half-cup, or nine and two-thirds ounces. Of course she always rounded off, but she didn't feel confident doing it.

When she carried the juice back to her mother, Hannah thought she'd erased the panicked expression from her face, but the anxiety in her eyes must have given her away, because Delores laughed.

"Relax, dear" she said. "I know how you hate to convert recipes, so I asked Kelly-Anne to do it. She converted everything to American measurements, right down to the British gas mark for the oven."

Hannah breathed a sigh of relief as she sat down at the workstation across from her mother. One of her worries was gone. As long as the recipe was for the type of dessert she'd made before and didn't have English ingredients that Florence couldn't get down at the Red Owl, like treacle, she could oblige her mother by making whatever it was. "What type of recipe is it?" she asked, crossing her fingers for luck.

"It's a cookie recipe. They're called Orange Creams, but you can make them into Lemon Creams if you'd rather. I thought we could have both kinds at the party."

"Sounds good," Hannah said, giving a relieved smile. "Did you bring the recipe with you?"

"Of course I did, dear." Delores extracted it from her purse and handed it to her daughter.

Hannah read it through quickly. Kelly-Anne had even written little notes next to some of the ingredients to explain that castor sugar was really superfine sugar, and icing sugar was confectioner's sugar.

"What do you think, dear?" Delores asked when Hannah put the recipe back down on the stainless steel work surface.

"They're rolled cookies. We don't usually make them here because they're more work, but we can certainly do it. And they sound really delicious."

"Then you'll bake both kinds for my party?"

"Of course we will. I think they'll go very well with champagne, and I'll bake a test batch so you can taste them."

"Wonderful!" Delores looked pleased. "I have thirty-seven acceptances so far, and I just know more will come in next week. I think you'd better plan for a hundred. If any cookies are left over, you can serve them here at The Cookie Jar."

"I don't think there'll be many left. If

these taste as scrumptious as I think they'll be, we'd better make double."

Delores began to get up from her stool. "I'd better get back . . ."

"Just a minute, Mother," Hannah interrupted before Delores could rise to her feet. "I really need your help."

"Of course." Delores settled back down again. "What is it, dear?"

"It's about Bob and Claire's party after church on Sunday. Grandma Knudson wants me to make some kind of tropical cookie since they're sailing to Hawaii, and I'm thinking about a cookie with coconut and chocolate chips."

"Chocolate chips aren't really tropical, dear."

"I know that, but chocolate goes so well with coconut."

"That's true." Delores thought about it for a moment. "Why don't you make half of your coconut cookies with chocolate and the other half with candied papaya. You could chop it up and mix it in like you did the time you ran out of raisins and you wanted to make Oatmeal Raisin Crisps."

"Good idea, Mother! I'd forgotten all about those cookies."

"Well, they were excellent. You really ought to make them again."

"I will. Any other suggestions for the bon voyage party?"

"Yes. I think you should put a macadamia nut on top of each cookie. That's so Hawaiian. And you could serve them on your father's surfboard. The top is almost flat like a big plate."

"Dad had a *surfboard?*" Hannah was amazed. She just couldn't imagine the father she'd always thought of as nonathletic on a surfboard.

"It's just decorative, dear, one of those touristy mementos they sell in the shops at the airport. As I remember, it had palm trees and waves painted all over it. Your father hung it on the wall in the living room for a couple of years after we were first married."

"And you still have it?"

"Yes. It's up in the attic where it's been ever since your father decided to take it off the wall. You can go up there and get it if you want it."

Hannah made up her mind almost instantly. "I want it. It'll make a perfect cookie platter, and I can sanitize it by covering it with plastic wrap. How about you, Mother? Didn't you bring any souvenirs home from Hawaii?"

"Yes, but they didn't last long. They sold

macadamia nuts at the airport, and I just loved the chocolate-covered ones. That was before anyone had them here, and I brought back six boxes. And that gives me another idea. Why don't you call Florence and see if she can order some? You could use plain macadamia nuts on the papaya cookies and chocolate-covered macadamia nuts on the others."

"That's perfect! For someone who doesn't bake, you have great ideas."

"Thank you, dear. I'm glad I could be of some help." Delores rose to her feet, and this time Hannah didn't stop her. "I'll see you on Saturday, dear. If you'd like to stay for dinner, I can make Hawaiian Pot Roast or E-Z Lasagna."

Hannah's stomach roiled at the thought of eating her mother's E-Z Lasagna or Hawaiian Pot Roast. It wasn't that they were bad. It was just that they were the only two entrees Delores ever made. Every week, when she went to her mother's house for their mother-daughter dinner, she had one or the other. There was no way she could face either one again on the weekend.

"Hannah?"

Her mother was waiting for an answer and Hannah put on her most regretful expression. "I'm sorry, Mother, but I have plans for Saturday night."

"Oh. Well . . . another time then. I have work to do anyway. The outline on my next Regency romance is due in two weeks."

"Do you know the title yet?"

"I'm not sure, but it has to be alliterative. My titles are always alliterative. Do you have any ideas?"

Hannah thought about that. Her mother's first book had been titled *A Match for Melissa,* and the book she was launching next week was *A Season for Samantha.* "How about *A Boyfriend for Bettina?*"

"It's too modern, dear. They didn't use the word *boyfriend* in Regency times."

"Okay. How about . . . *A Husband for Holly?*"

Delores mulled it over for a moment, and then she smiled. "I like that. Holly can be a commoner and the man she marries at the end of the book can be a titled gentleman. Some gentlemen did marry beneath their station, you know. And that elevated their brides to their station."

"If you marry a duke, you're a duchess?"

"Exactly right."

"What happens if a titled woman marries beneath her station? Does her new husband get elevated in status?"

"No, dear. It doesn't work the other way

around. As a matter of fact, when a duke died, his duchess could no longer own their land or their homes. Her oldest son became the duke, and his wife became the new duchess. She was demoted to dowager duchess status."

"What status is that?"

"It's a steep step down, dear. A dowager duchess had to live in a small cottage called the dower house, a distance away from the duke's castle. She had to give up all her jewelry and money, because they were an asset of the estate. Everything she had belonged to the new duke. And she depended totally on her son's largess for any monies she needed to live."

"That's not fair!"

"Of course it's not, but that's the way it was then."

"Maybe she would have been better off not marrying at all," Hannah speculated.

"No, dear. Unmarried women were treated worse than pariahs. You see, all the eligible young ladies were trotted out in fine clothing for the *Season* in London."

"*Season?*"

"That's what they called it, dear. It was held right after the gentlemen finished hunting on their country estates and before Parliament was called back into session. The eligible young ladies were presented to the queen, and feted at balls and parties. It was arranged so that the unmarried men could take their pick of the debutants. A young lady was expected to receive at least one proposal of marriage."

"What happened to the young ladies who didn't receive proposals?"

"That's the sad thing, dear. If a young woman went through more than one Season, she was considered to be *on the shelf*. She was often ridiculed and given uncomplimentary names like *ape-leader*."

"That's horrible!"

"Yes it is. Things are a lot better now. Look at you, dear. You're over thirty and you're not married. That would make you a spinster in Regency England. To make matters worse, you're in trade. That was something a woman didn't do unless it was to help in a shop owned by her husband."

"So I would have been totally unsuitable?"

"Oh, my yes!" Delores glanced up at the clock on the wall. "I'm late, dear. I really have to rush."

Once her mother had left, Hannah sat down to wait for her cakes to come out of the oven. Regency England didn't sound like a very good place to live if you were an independent woman. Every time she thought the current political climate was intolerable, she'd remember what happened to women then and thank her lucky stars she hadn't been born back in Regency times.

RED DEVIL'S FOOD CAKE
Preheat oven to 350 degrees F.,
rack in the middle position.

1 cup water

3/4 cup *(1 and 1/2 sticks, 6 ounces)* salted butter

1/2 cup brown sugar

1/2 cup white *(granulated)* sugar

1-ounce square unsweetened chocolate *(I used Baker's)*

1 teaspoon instant espresso coffee powder

1 and 1/2 cups white *(granulated)* sugar

1/2 teaspoon salt

1 teaspoon baking soda

1/4 teaspoon baking powder

1/2 cup unsweetened cocoa powder

2 eggs *(room temperature — float them in a cup with hot water if you forgot to take them out of the refrigerator last night)*

2 teaspoons vanilla extract

3 cups cake flour *(I used Swansdown)****

*** *If you don't have cake flour, you can use 2 and 2/3 cups all-purpose flour. Your cake won't be as light in texture, but that's not necessarily a bad thing when it comes to chocolate cake!*

Combine the water, butter, white sugar,

and brown sugar in a small saucepan on the stovetop.

Break *(or cut)* the square of unsweetened chocolate into two parts and add them to the saucepan.

Turn the heat to MEDIUM HIGH and heat the mixture, stirring frequently, until the butter melts.

Continue to stir until the mixture is smooth and the chocolate has melted.

Pull the saucepan off the heat and add the teaspoon of instant espresso coffee powder. Stir it until the espresso powder dissolves.

Let the mixture cool while you start in on the rest of the cake.

Prepare two 9-inch round cake pans by spraying the insides with baking spray *(the kind with flour in it).* Tear off two sheets of parchment paper slightly larger than the bottom of your cake pans. Stack the parchment paper, place one cake pan on top, and trace around the bottom with a pen or pencil. Staying inside the pen or pencil mark, cut out the tracing you made. Fit the paper circles into the bottoms of your prepared pans, and then spray the parchment circles with baking spray.

Hannah's 1st Note: This cake is easy to make with an electric stand mixer, but you can also do it with a hand mixer

or even completely by hand.

Measure out one and a half cups of white sugar. Add about a third of it to the mixing bowl. *(Just eyeball it — you don't have to be exact.)*

Add the half-teaspoon of salt, the teaspoon of baking soda, and the 1/4 teaspoon of baking powder to the mixing bowl.

Turn the mixer on LOW. Let it run for thirty seconds or so and then shut it off. *(If you do this by hand, make sure everything is thoroughly mixed.)*

Add the second third of the sugar to your bowl, turn the mixer on LOW again, and mix it for another thirty seconds or so.

Measure the cocoa powder and add it to your bowl. Mix it in on LOW speed *(Take it from me, you don't want it all over your kitchen!)* for another thirty seconds or so.

Pour in the final third of sugar, turn the mixer on LOW again, and mix for a full minute.

With the mixer still running on LOW, add one egg to your bowl. Mix it in thoroughly.

Add the second egg to your bowl and mix that in thoroughly.

With the mixer still running on LOW add the 2 teaspoons of vanilla and mix it in thoroughly. Turn off the mixer.

Feel the outside of the saucepan with the

chocolate and butter mixture. If it's not so hot that it could cook the eggs, you can work with it now. If it's still too hot, let it cool a little more.

When you're ready to add the chocolate and butter mixture, turn the mixer on MEDIUM speed and SLOWLY pour half of the mixture into your bowl. Mix it in thoroughly, and then shut off the mixer.

Now measure out your cake flour by scooping it up and then leveling it off with the blade of a table knife. DON'T PACK IT DOWN IN THE CUP.

Add half of the flour to your bowl, turn the mixer on LOW, and mix it in thoroughly.

With the mixer still running on LOW, add the other half of the chocolate and butter mixture to your bowl, pouring it in SLOWLY and mixing it thoroughly. Shut off the mixer.

Add the rest of the flour to your bowl. Turn your mixer on LOW and mix until everything is well incorporated. Increase the mixer speed to MEDIUM and mix for a full minute. Then shut off the mixer.

Take the bowl from the mixer and give the batter a good stir by hand, making sure to scrape down the sides of the bowl. When you're satisfied that the cake batter is well mixed, divide it as evenly as you can between the two cake pans.

Bake at 325 degrees F. for 20 to 25 minutes or until a toothpick inserted into the center of the pan comes out clean. *(Mine took 22 minutes.)*

Hannah's 2nd Note: If you want to make this cake into mini cupcakes, fill paper-lined or greased mini-cupcake tins 3/4 full with batter. Bake them at 350 degrees F. for 15 minutes.

Remove the pans from the oven and cool them completely on a wire racks. To remove the cakes from their pans, simply run the blade of a table knife around the inside edges of the pans and tip the cakes out.

How to Frost Red Devil's Food Cake (or any cake, for that matter.)

When you're ready to frost your Red Devil's Food Cake, turn one layer upside down on a cake plate so that the flat side is up. *(If it's too tippy that way, put it back in its pan and use a sharp knife to level off the top of the layer before you invert it on the cake plate a second time.)*

Use Fudgy Frosting *(recipe below)* between the layers.

Position the second cake layer, rounded side up, on top of the frosting on the first layer.

Now frost the top and the sides of your

cake. Your masterpiece is complete!

Hannah's 3rd Note: Be generous with the frosting — it's yummy!

Yield: This cake will serve at least 12 people. It's perfect paired with vanilla or coffee ice cream.

(Mother likes this cake with chocolate ice cream, but that's Mother. She convinced Dad to walk three blocks in a snowstorm when the car wouldn't start and she ran out of chocolate ice cream!)

FUDGY FROSTING

2 cups semi-sweet *(regular)* chocolate chips *(a 12-ounce package)*
1/4 teaspoon salt *(it brings out the flavor of the chocolate)*
14-ounce can of sweetened condensed milk
1 ounce *(2 Tablespoons)* salted butter
1 teaspoon vanilla extract

Hannah's Note: If you use a double boiler for this frosting, it's foolproof. You can also make it in a heavy saucepan over low to medium heat on the stovetop, but you'll have to stir it constantly with a wooden spoon or a heat-resistant spatula to keep it from scorching.

Fill the bottom part of the double boiler with water. Make sure the water doesn't touch the underside of the top.

Put the chocolate chips and the salt in the top of the double boiler, set it over the bottom, and place the double boiler on the stovetop at medium heat. Stir occasionally until the chocolate chips are melted.

Stir in the can of sweetened condensed milk and cook approximately 2 minutes, stirring constantly, until the frosting is shiny and of spreading consistency.

Shut off the heat, remove the top part of the double boiler to a cold burner, and quickly stir in the vanilla. *(It may sputter a bit, so be careful.)* Then add the butter and stir it in until it melts.

Your frosting is ready to use.

Once you have frosted your two-layer Red Devil's Food Cake *(or your Mini Cupcakes, if you decided to make those instead,)* give the frosting pan to your favorite person to scrape. Once it cools, it's just like fudge.

CHAPTER SEVEN

"He's a very good minister," Delores whispered to Hannah at the conclusion of Reverend Matthew's sermon.

"Yes, he is. That was a good sermon," Hannah whispered back. Reverend Matthew had been in Lake Eden for less than a week, and he was doing a wonderful job of substituting for Reverend Bob. Claire had confided that her husband had deliberately stood aside and urged Reverend Matthew to take over all the church duties, including today's holy sacrament of communion. It had been a test, and Reverend Matthew had passed with flying colors. So far this week, Reverend Matthew had officiated at three weddings, two christenings, and one funeral. He'd also led the men's Bible study group, gone to Lake Eden Memorial Hospital to visit and give communion to sick parishioners, written the next church bulletin, and counseled two couples on their upcoming marriages.

"He has such a fine singing voice!" Delores continued. "He's handsome too, and an older man might be good for you, Hannah."

Hannah gave her mother a cease and desist look and Delores returned the volley with a shrug. Then both of them smiled in perfect harmony. They'd played this scene many times before. Hannah's role was to object to any suggestion Delores had when it came to men. Her mother's role was to continue to suggest that her eldest daughter should consider every unattached male of Hannah's age or older as a potential husband.

The hymn was almost over. When the final note in the second to the last stanza had been reached, or nearly reached since it ended on a high note, Delores and Hannah slid from the pew and tiptoed out. It was time for Hannah to arrange the cookies on the surfboard platter, and Delores had agreed to help.

Lisa and Herb were already in the church basement with Marge. They'd put on the coffee, covered the surfboard with plastic wrap, placed it on the refreshment table, and set out napkins, cream and sugar, and lemon for those who preferred tea.

"Are you going to do half one kind and half the other?" Herb asked Hannah as he carried a box of cookies to the table. "Or are you going to mix them up?"

"I'll mix them up. They'll look prettier that way."

"I can do that," Marge offered, starting to place the cookies on the surfboard that doubled as a platter.

"I'll help," Delores said, hurrying over to do just that. "Are you going to the party tonight, Marge?"

"No. Sunday night is our board game night and Jack really enjoys it. Parcheesi is his favorite, but he loves Uncle Wiggly too. He used to play it with the kids."

Delores gave a little sigh. "I know he used to be a marvelous Contract Bridge player. He doesn't play anymore?"

"No, it's too frustrating. He forgets the conventions and he feels bad about forgetting. Board games are better and we all have a good time."

"Especially me," Lisa said, coming up with the basket of herbal teabags. "Since I was the youngest, I always had to go to bed before the game was over. And then later, when I was old enough, the other kids didn't want to play."

"What do you think of the substitute

minister?" Herb asked Delores.

"He's very good. And he also looks very handsome in black."

Marge laughed. "Do I detect a hint of interest in your voice?" she teased.

"Oh, he's too young for me."

Hannah held her breath, waiting for her mother's next comment and hoping it wouldn't come. She sent Delores a look that said, *Don't you dare!* and her mother returned it with a devilish smile.

"Actually," Delores said, "I was thinking of . . ."

Hannah had all she could do not to groan as she waited for her mother to finish the sentence. Delores was about to exact her pound of flesh.

"I was thinking of Vonnie Blair, Doc Knight's secretary. She's a lovely woman and very religious. She told me once that she'd been thinking of going into the ministry herself, but they wouldn't have taken her seriously back then."

Thank you, Mother, Hannah said silently, sending her gratitude by way of the unique mother-daughter radar that existed between the two of them. Delores acknowledged the sentiment by giving a little nod. All was well. It wasn't Get Hannah time.

There was a sound from above their

heads. Footsteps on the church floor. The service was over and Reverend Matthew had invited the whole congregation to Claire and Bob's bon voyage party.

Thirty minutes passed in less time than Hannah believed possible. Three-quarters of their cookies had disappeared, along with two forty-cup urns of coffee, and a third of their herbal tea packets. The children had drunk their fill of lemonade, little Dennis Weiler had touched five cookies before his mother had grabbed his hand, and Earl Flensburg had complimented Hannah repeatedly on the Mini Mac Cookies.

Another ten minutes and all that was left was the cleanup. Hannah and Lisa received hugs from Reverend Bob and Claire before the happy couple went off to the parsonage to collect their luggage, shook hands with Reverend Matthew who complimented them on a wonderful job, and accepted Herb, Delores, and Marge's offer to help with the cleanup. While Marge and Lisa washed the church coffee cups and spoons, and Herb folded up the church chairs and stacked them in their racks, Hannah and Delores wiped down the tables and packed up the few cookies that were left. In less than fifteen minutes they were completely through.

"See you tomorrow morning," Hannah called out to Lisa as her partner drove off with Herb and Marge.

"Earl certainly liked those Mini Mac Cookies, and Carrie ate three of the Papaya Macs," Delores commented to Hannah as they walked to their cars. "If I baked, I'd make some for Wednesday night. They're coming over for dinner."

Hannah knew when she was being tapped for cookies. "Would you like the leftover cookies, Mother?"

"I'd love them, but aren't you serving cookies at Doctor Bev's birthday party? I heard you were providing the dessert."

"Yes, but not cookies. I'm bringing something else." Hannah passed her mother the box of leftover cookies. "Just slip the box in a freezer bag and pop it in the freezer. Then take them out on Wednesday morning, let them thaw on the counter all day, and they'll still be nice and fresh."

"Thank you, dear. I do wish that I could attend the party this evening, but I'm on deadline for the outline, you know."

Hannah sighed as she parted ways with her mother and headed to her cookie truck. One half of her wished that her mother would be there to support her, but the other half was glad that Delores wouldn't be there to witness her daughter's bad behavior just in case Hannah decided to scratch Beverly Thorndike's eyes out.

Hannah backed out of her parking spot and waved goodbye to her mother. Once she'd turned onto Third, she drove almost all the way to Main, but turned into the alley before she reached the stop sign. Moments later, she was parking in her usual spot behind The Cookie Jar. It was time to do what she really didn't want to do, and make Mocha Trifles for Doctor Bev's birthday party.

It was eight o'clock in the evening, and time was passing so slowly Hannah thought she'd die. She glanced at her watch, hoping that no one would notice the sharp eye she was keeping on the time, and gave a little sigh. She was here at Doctor Bev's birthday party, it was turning out to be an ordeal for her, and she couldn't let anyone know it.

Norman had rented the banquet room of the Lake Eden Community Center for the party. The room was jammed with guests, and it was clear that Mike had done a bang-up job of inviting people. More than fifty guests were milling around, laughing and talking, and sipping drinks from the full bar that Hank Olsen, the regular bartender at the Lake Eden Municipal Bar, was manning. The nondrinkers were availing themselves of soft drinks from the row of coolers on a long table that had been set up against the far wall, and everyone seemed to be having a marvelous time. Everyone but Hannah, that is.

Someone had decorated the room with a ceiling of crepe paper streamers and metallic balloons that bobbed and swayed on strings attached to flowerpots filled with flowers. There was a six-piece band on an elevated stage, deli sandwiches brought in from the new deli out at the Tri-County Mall, and bowls of chips and dips. Hannah's trifles, all five of them, were in bowls in the walk-in cooler, ready to emerge with candles on top when it was time for dessert.

The band began to play. The party had officially begun. Hannah felt an unsettling pang as Norman took Doctor Bev into his arms. She smiled up at him as he led her gracefully across the floor and he looked down at her with obvious affection.

It was more than a little pang. Hannah felt rotten to the core. She was having great difficulty keeping the pleasant expression on her face as she watched Norman and Doctor Bev dance. It reminded her of the first romantic dance at a wedding reception when the groom took his new bride in his arms and they danced for the first time as husband and wife.

"Hannah?"

A voice started her out of her unhappy contemplation, and Hannah tore her eyes away from what appeared to all the world like a happy couple. "Mike," she greeted him, glad for the interruption.

"Come on, Hannah. Let's dance."

Mike held out his hand and Hannah took it. Dancing with Mike should keep her from dwelling on Norman and Doctor Bev. She knew from experience that it was impossible to think about anyone else when she was in Mike's arms.

Mike's sexy charisma worked like a charm the moment she began to dance, and her mind settled down into a purring idle. Hannah was so grateful to Mike for rescuing her from her unwanted spectator role that she snuggled a little closer into his arms and smiled up at him exactly the way that Doctor Bev had smiled up at Norman.

As their dance went on, Hannah was dimly aware that other couples had joined them on the area set aside as a dance floor. The song that the small band had been playing when they'd begun to dance had ended and the band had segued into another romantic tune. They'd played only a few bars before Mike stopped dancing and Hannah realized that someone else had tapped him on the shoulder to cut in.

It was Norman, and Hannah followed polite convention and stepped into his arms. Doctor Bev did the same with Mike, and the two couples separated. "Having fun?" Norman asked her.

"Fun," Hannah repeated, hoping that he would take that for assent.

"Good. I think Bev's enjoying herself, too. Most of our patients are here. Your mother even showed up. She told me she might be too busy working on her new outline, but she's here."

Hannah felt a rush of affection for her mother. Delores had come up with the perfect excuse, but she'd shown up to support Hannah. She was even on the dance floor with Doc Knight. As Hannah spotted them, Delores gave her the high sign. That meant her mother thought she was handling the situation well. It was probably a good thing Delores didn't know how close Hannah had come to losing it when Doctor Bev had stepped into Norman's arms.

Luckily, there was no shortage of partners. The men in Lake Eden liked to dance. It wasn't like some dances in other places like the Eagle, a sleazy, country-western bar and dance place in the country that everyone called a dive. There the men who didn't have dates for the evening would arrive ten minutes before the last call for drinks. They'd survey the unattached women, ask one of them to dance, buy her one drink at last call, and then attempt to arrange an after-hours date that wouldn't cost them a dime.

Hannah stayed until after the refreshments were served and the birthday gifts were opened. The trifle recipe Sally had given her was a huge success, but that was little consolation. She said goodnight and happy birthday to Doctor Bev, and pleaded an early morning at The Cookie Jar to escape after two hours of smiling so constantly that her face felt as if it might crack.

Once Hannah pushed open the door of the community center and stepped out into the subzero temperature, she gave such a big sigh of relief that her breath came out in a volley-ball-sized cloud of vapor. At least *that* was over. She could hardly wait to get home, have a steaming cup of hot chocolate laced with at least a dozen miniature marsh-mallows, pet Moishe until her blood pressure returned to normal, and go to bed.

"Hannah?"

Hannah came close to groaning as she recognized Norman's voice. She really didn't feel like talking to Norman right now. She actually considered pretending not to hear him, but it was a still and silent night, and Norman knew she didn't have a hearing problem. She told herself that she had maintained so far and she could maintain a bit longer. And then she turned around.

"Hi, Norman," she said, pasting the same smile on her face again. "Aren't you cold without a coat?"

"No. I wanted to catch you before you left, Hannah. I really appreciate you going the extra mile for Bev's party. I was going to buy a cake because I know you're busy with Valentine's Day coming up and all. But then Mike said he'd asked you if you'd bake something and you said you'd make the dessert."

"Right," Hannah responded, hoping he wasn't going to offer to pay her for the work she'd done.

"That trifle was so good, Bev said she'd like to learn how to make it. Unfortunately, she's not a very good cook. Her talents in the kitchen are pretty much on a par with your sister Andrea's."

"She's *that* bad?"

128

"Right after she moved here, she made cupcakes from a mix. They turned out like hockey pucks."

Hannah's smile turned a bit more genuine. She was so glad that there was *something* Doctor Bev couldn't do, she decided to be generous. "Maybe her oven isn't calibrated correctly."

"It was *my* oven, and I know that works just fine."

Hannah's heart sank. Doctor Bev was using Norman's oven, the one Hannah had chosen for the house they'd designed together. She reminded herself that it wasn't really *her* oven, not if she didn't marry Norman and live in their beautiful house.

"How about that trifle?" Norman asked. "Is it difficult to make?"

The time to be generous was over. Hannah gave a little shrug. "It's not difficult for *me*," she said pointedly.

"I didn't figure it was. You can bake anything. I just want to know what sort of baking's involved."

"It starts with a sponge cake," she said quite honestly, but then temptation overtook her. "Do you think Doctor Bev could bake one of those?"

"Not on a bet!"

"Well . . . I could give you my recipe for

sponge cake if you think she'd like to work on it," Hannah offered, deliberately sounding doubtful. She certainly wasn't about to tell Norman that the assembly time for the trifle was only fifteen to twenty minutes, there was no baking required, and you could buy the sponge cake along with all the other ingredients.

"Never mind. Bev burns everything she tries to bake, and it would probably depress her. She just hates it if she can't master something."

"Okay," Hannah said, wondering how long Norman would stand here in his shirt sleeves. "Aren't you cold?" she asked him again.

"No. It's just good being alone with you, Hannah. How about if I drop by The Cookie Jar tomorrow?"

"Sure. You're always welcome at The Cookie Jar."

"Morning? Or afternoon?"

"Right between the two." Hannah decided quickly. "I've got a ton of baking to do in the morning, and then I have a couple of deliveries to make in the afternoon."

"Is noon okay? I've got a patient at eleven-thirty, but it's just a quick checkup."

"Noon is fine. See you then." Hannah took a few steps toward her cookie truck, but when she turned to give a final wave, she noticed that Norman was still standing there as motionless as a statue. "Go inside before you turn into an icicle, Norman. It's below zero out here."

"Right," Norman said with a quick bob of his head. He shivered once, as if he'd just noticed how cold it was, and then he walked quickly back to the door, pulled it open, and stepped into the heated interior.

"Oh, boy!" Hannah breathed, opening her truck and sliding in on a plastic seat cover that seemed even colder than the air outside. Norman was really preoccupied if he hadn't even noticed the cold. There was something else she'd noticed, too. A worry line he'd never had before was forming between his eyebrows. Something was very wrong and she didn't have a clue what it was.

Hannah started her truck, cranked the heat up all the way, and turned up the fake fur collar on her parka while she waited for the windshield to defrost. Yes, something was definitely wrong with Norman. Could that be why he wanted to see her alone tomorrow afternoon? Did he intend to tell her what it was?

MINI MAC COOKIES
Preheat oven to 325 degrees F.,
rack in the middle position.

Hannah's 1st Note: These cookies are called "mini" for two reasons. They're made in small (mini) cupcake papers or mini muffin tins, and they have mini chocolate chips in them. "Mac" is appropriate because they're macaroons.

14-ounce can sweetened condensed milk *(NOT evaporated milk — I used Eagle Brand)*

2 teaspoons vanilla extract

2 seven-ounce packages flaked coconut *(that's approx. 5 and 1/3 cups)*

2 cups mini chocolate chips *(12-oz. package — I used Nestle)*

Hannah's 2nd Note: I always chop my coconut flakes a little finer in my food processor with the steel blade. If you don't have a food processor, you can lay it out on a cutting board and chop it with a sharp knife.

Prepare your baking sheets. You can use mini size paper baking cups *(1 and 5/8 inches diagonally, the size that will fit into a mini muffin pan)*, the mini muffin pan without baking cups, or cookie sheets. If you use the baking cups, just set them in the muffin pan. If you use the mini muffin pan without baking cups, spray it with Pam or another nonstick cooking spray and then flour it, OR use baking spray which already contains the flour. If you use cookie sheets, line them with heavy duty foil. Spray the foil with cooking spray and flour it, or simply use a baking spray that contains flour.

Open the can of sweetened condensed milk and empty the contents into a large mixing bowl. Add the vanilla extract and stir it in.

Measure out your coconut, chop it a bit finer with your food processor or a knife and stir it into the bowl. *(It's easier if you add the coconut a half-cup at a time.)*

Add your mini chocolate chips to the bowl, stirring them in as thoroughly as you can. *(The goal here is to get some chocolate chips in every single Mini Mac Cookie.)*

If you're using baking cups, drop some cookie dough inside with a teaspoon and press it down lightly with a wet fingertip. *(This dough is sticky!)* Since these cookies don't rise, you can fill the baking cup very close to the top.

If you're using mini muffin tins without

the baking cups, simply use a teaspoon to fill them up and press down slightly with a wet fingertip. They'll look best if they're a little mounded on top.

If you're using greased and floured *(or sprayed with baking spray)* cookie sheets, drop the dough by teaspoons onto the sheet and press them down slightly with a wet fingertip. Since these cookies don't spread out, you can get 16 to 20 on each cookie sheet.

Bake the cookies at 325 degrees F. for 15 to 18 minutes. *(Mine took 17 minutes.)* They're done when the coconut is toasted to a nice golden color on the tops.

Let the cookies cool on the cookie sheets, in the baking cups, or in the mini muffin pans for 2 minutes. Then remove them to a wire rack to cool completely. If you're using the baking cups, don't remove them from the paper. They're easier to serve that way, and they'll look much prettier.

Store the Mini Mac Cookies in layers of wax paper in a box or in a storage container. Make sure the cookies don't touch each other or they'll stick together and be difficult to separate. They can be frozen, but again, don't let the cookies touch each other.

Earl Flensburg and Carrie really loved

these cookies. Mother says she's going to order some from me every time they come over for dinner and serve them with chocolate ice cream.

PAPAYA MAC COOKIES

Preheat oven to 325 degrees F.,
rack in the middle position.

Hannah's 1st Note: These cookies are called "Mac" because they're macaroons.

14-ounce can sweetened condensed milk *(NOT evaporated milk — I used Eagle Brand)*

2 teaspoons vanilla extract

2 seven-ounce packages flaked coconut *(that's approx. 5 and 1/3 cups)*

2 cups chopped dried papaya *(chop it up to the size of raisins)****

*** Dried papaya isn't always available 12 months out of the year. If you can't find it, you can use any dried fruit. I've made this cookie with dried pineapple, dried apricots, and sweetened dried cranberries. I think it could very well be delicious with anything!

Hannah's 2nd Note: I always chop my coconut flakes a little finer in my food processor with the steel blade. If you don't have a food processor, you can lay it out on a cutting board and chop it with a sharp knife.

Prepare your baking sheets. You can use mini size paper baking cups *(1 and 5/8 inches diagonally, the size that will fit into a mini muffin pan)*, the mini muffin pan without baking cups, or cookie sheets. If you use the baking cups, just set them in the muffin pan. If you use the mini muffin pan without baking cups, spray it with Pam or another nonstick cooking spray and then flour it, OR use baking spray which already contains the flour. If you use cookie sheets, line them with heavy duty foil. Spray the foil with cooking spray and flour it, or simply use a baking spray that contains flour.

Open the can of sweetened condensed milk and empty the contents into a large mixing bowl. Add the vanilla extract and stir it in.

Measure out your coconut, chop it a bit finer with your food processor or a knife, and stir it into the bowl. *(It's easier if you add the coconut a half-cup at a time.)*

Add your chopped papaya to the bowl, stirring it in as thoroughly as you can. *(The goal here is to get some chopped papaya in every single cookie.)*

If you're using baking cups, drop some cookie dough inside with a teaspoon and press it down lightly with a wet fingertip.

(This dough is sticky!) Since these cookies don't rise, you can fill the baking cup very close to the top.

If you're using mini muffin tins without the baking cups, simply use a teaspoon to fill them up and press down slightly with a wet fingertip. They'll look best if they're a little mounded on top.

If you're using greased and floured **(or sprayed with baking spray)** cookie sheets, drop the dough by teaspoons onto the sheet and press them down slightly with a wet fingertip. Since these cookies don't spread out, you can get 16 to 20 on each cookie sheet.

Bake the cookies at 325 degrees F. for 15 to 18 minutes. **(Mine took 17 minutes.)** They're done when the coconut is toasted to a nice golden color on the tops.

Let the cookies cool on the cookie sheets, in the baking cups, or in the mini muffin pans for 2 minutes. Then remove them to a wire rack to cool completely. If you're using the baking cups, don't remove them from the paper. They're easier to serve that way, and they'll look much prettier.

Store the Papaya Mac Cookies in layers of wax paper in a box or in a storage container. Make sure the cookies don't touch each other or they'll stick together and be difficult to separate. They can be frozen, but again, don't let the cookies touch each other.

Claire and Bob loved these. They promised to bring back every type of tropical dried fruit they can find in Hawaii so that I can experiment with it.

CHAPTER EIGHT

When the alarm went off at four in the morning, Hannah had all she could do to squelch the urge to shut it off and pull the blankets over her head. It was Monday morning and the sun had not yet risen over the yardarm. They had fifteen batches of cookies to make for wedding receptions, two more batches for engagement parties, and one batch for a birthday celebration. And that didn't count the dozens they'd have to bake to stock the display cookie jars at their coffee shop.

Then there was Doctor Bev's birthday party and the effort she'd made to maintain her composure. And the scimitar hanging over her head, swinging lower by the tiniest increments with each second that passed. Was Norman falling in love with Doctor Bev? Perhaps she'd find out today when she saw him at noon. Maybe he was planning to break up with her. He'd said once that he was lonely living in their house all by himself, but that was before he adopted Cuddles. Cats were lots of company. Without Moishe, she might be lonely, too.

Hannah gave another heartfelt sigh. Whatever Norman was planning to tell her had to be important. She just hoped that he wasn't going to say that he couldn't date her anymore because he was going to marry his former fiancée!

She was awake now, and being awake meant that she was beginning to feel stressed. There were too many tasks to accomplish, too many problems to attempt to solve. Somehow she had to slog through it all step by step, hour by hour, and day by day. It was a fallacy that things would be better in the morning. This was morning, and things were just as bad as they'd been when she'd gone to bed five hours ago.

Today was not going to be a good day. Hannah knew that the moment she walked into her kitchen and saw that the red ready light on her coffeemaker was out. No coffee. She'd forgotten to set it last night. How could she start the morning without coffee? She should go back to bed, take a little snooze, and start her day over.

But duty called and no Swensen daughter had ever shrugged off her duty. There was the German work ethic on her mother's side and the Scandinavian work ethic on her father's side. A fifty-hour week was nothing to gripe about, and a sixty-hour week was not impossible. You worked until your job was finished, even if you were tired.

Two minutes later, the coffeemaker was activated and Hannah was opening the refrigerator to have a glass of juice. She poured some spicy tomato juice in a glass, returned the bottle to the top shelf of the refrigerator, and was about to close the door when she realized that there was a round white sock ball on top of the refrigerator again.

"Moishe?" She turned to look at her feline roommate, who was sitting on the kitchen floor by his food bowl, waiting patiently. "How did these socks get up here?"

Had ever a cat looked more innocent? For a moment, Hannah had doubts. Perhaps she'd taken her socks from the drawer, carried them to the kitchen, and absent-mindedly placed them on top of the refrigerator when she opened it to pour her juice.

"No, I didn't!" Hannah said aloud. She knew she hadn't carried her socks into the kitchen this morning, and the sock ball hadn't been there last night. Moishe must have done it, but how? He couldn't pull out her sock drawer, and she hadn't done a load of laundry since Saturday.

Hannah grabbed the sock ball and turned to look at her cat again. He still looked innocent. She tossed it in the air, and Moishe followed it with his eyes, but he made no move to intercept it. Then she bent down and rolled it across the floor so that it landed right next to him, hoping he might do something to incriminate himself, like grabbing it in his mouth, jumping up to the counter and then to the top of the refrigerator, and dropping it there.

Of course it didn't work. Moishe ignored the sock ball. He ignored her also and concentrated on an area of the wall immediately behind her head. His fur bristled slightly and his eyes widened, causing her to swivel around to see what he was reacting to, but there was absolutely nothing there.

Trying to establish a cat's guilt or innocence was a time waster. There was no way she'd solve the mystery of the sock balls this morning. Hannah tabled it for another time and filled Moishe's bowl with his favorite kitty crunchies. Once she'd given him fresh water, she poured her coffee and sipped it on her way to the bathroom to take her shower and get ready to go to work.

"Hi, Norman," Hannah greeted him as he pushed through the swinging door at The Cookie Jar and joined her in the kitchen. "I've got a great new cookie. How about trying one of Mother's Orange Creams?"

Norman stared at her for a moment, an expression of complete astonishment on his face. "Your mother bakes Orange Creams?"

"Not Mother." Hannah gave a little laugh at the concept. Delores did not bake and never had. "Mother got the recipe from an Irish woman who lives in England. You can make them in lemon or orange, and I'll give you one of each. We're going to serve both kinds at her launch party."

Norman looked at the cookies with interest as Hannah delivered them to the workstation, along with his cup of coffee. "They're pretty," he said.

"That's what Mother thinks. She said the burst of citrus flavor would have been a huge hit in Regency England, where only the wealthy had orangeries." Hannah noticed Norman's puzzled look and went on to explain. "Orangeries are interior greenhouse gardens with fruit trees and exotic flowers."

"Like Wayne Bergstrom's penthouse garden?"

"Exactly right." Hannah remembered the garden well. She'd been back several times since Jenny had moved into the penthouse with Anna, and the only change they'd made to the garden was to add several fruit trees. One had been a mandarin orange tree so Norman was doubly right. Not only did it look like an orangery, it *was* an orangery.

As Norman picked up an Orange Cream and tasted it, Hannah tried not to think about the department store mogul and how he'd died.

"Very tasty," Norman said, pulling Hannah out of her contemplative mood. "The orange flavor is really intense."

"Lots of orange zest. Try the lemon."

Norman put down the rest of his orange cookie and picked up the lemon. He took a bite, and made a little sound of enjoyment. "Very good. I think I like the lemon best, but I'd better give the orange another try in the interest of fairness."

Hannah began to smile. "Just in the interest of fairness."

"Yes." Norman popped the rest of the orange cookie in his mouth. Once it was gone, an expression of mock horror spread over his face. "Uh-oh! I didn't mean to fin-

145

ish it. I wasn't through comparing the lemon with the orange."

Hannah laughed and went to fetch two more cookies. She could hardly wait to tell Delores how much Norman liked them.

"Did they have their new pastrami burger on the menu when you went out to The Corner Tavern with Mike on Saturday?"

Hannah was surprised at the question. How had Norman known that she'd gone out to dinner with Mike on Saturday night? But Mike had probably mentioned it. The two men were friends, after all. "Yes, they did," she told him. "It was the first item on the burger page."

"How was it?"

"I didn't have it. I ordered the bacon cheeseburger melt. It's one of my favorites." Hannah was silent, wondering if she should ask if Norman had gone out to dinner with Doctor Bev. Several of her regulars at The Cookie Jar had mentioned that they'd seen them together on multiple occasions. "How about you?" she finally asked, hoping it sounded like a casual, friendly question. "Did you have it?"

"Oh, we weren't there. I took Bev out to Bertanelli's for a jumbo Hawaiian special."

"But I thought you didn't like pineapple on your pizza!" The words flew out of Han-

146

nah's mouth before she could stop them. She was shocked that someone had actually talked Norman into eating something he'd told her he didn't like.

"I'm still not that fond of it, but it's Bev's favorite pizza so I'm trying to learn to like it."

You always ordered a half and half with me, Hannah thought, but of course she didn't say it. *There was no way I could get you to even try one anchovy! You must like her better than you like me.*

"I'd rather be with you," Norman said, reaching out for her hand. And then, just when Hannah was beginning to feel good again, he continued, "but I get tired waiting for my turn to see you. It's great to have someone else who likes to spend time with me. If I want to go out to dinner and you're doing something with Mike, I ask Bev."

And Doctor Bev's just sitting there waiting for you? Hannah wanted to ask, but she didn't.

"Bev's usually available, so it works out just fine. She dates only one other man in town."

"One other man?" This time Hannah asked the first question that popped into her mind.

"Mike." Norman must have seen the

surprised look on her face, because he gave her hand a gentle squeeze. "I'm sorry, Hannah. I thought for sure he told you. Bev lives right across from him, and it's really convenient. If she's out with Mike, you're usually available to go out with me. And if you're with me, she goes out with Mike. It keeps everybody happy and it levels the playing field."

Hannah frowned slightly. The way Norman described it, Beverly Thorndike sounded like a fuzzy yellow tennis ball, bouncing between the two men. The analogy pleased her until she realized that she fell into that same category, dividing her time between the two players, Mike and Norman, unable to settle on one or the other side of the court.

But thinking like this would get her nowhere, and it certainly wouldn't answer the question that was foremost in her mind.

"What?" Norman asked, noticing that Hannah had fallen silent, an unusual state for her.

It was now or never, win or lose, do or die. Hannah took the bull by the horns, yet another cliche, and faced Norman squarely. "Why did you ask to see me alone, Norman?"

"I told you after the party last night. It's

148

because I haven't spent much time with you lately and I miss you."

"Then you didn't come here to break up with me?"

"Break up with you?" Norman looked truly confused. "Of course not! I came to ask if you'd like to go out to dinner with me tonight."

"Oh," Hannah said, completely taken off guard.

"Will you?"

"I . . . yes. Yes, I will."

"Good!" Norman got to his feet and carried his coffee cup to the sink. "I'll pick you up at seven, and we'll go out to the Inn, if that's okay with you."

"It's fine with me." Hannah made a mental note to call Sally this afternoon and tell her that she'd told Norman the trifle recipe was complicated.

Norman pushed back his stool and stood up. "I'd better run. I've got a patient in ten minutes. See you tonight, Hannah."

After Norman had left, Hannah sat on her stool at the workstation sorting through the new information she'd learned. Both Norman and Mike were dating Doctor Bev. Norman had come right out and told her that he'd rather be with her, but was that true? If she stopped dating Mike, would Norman stop dating Bev? And was that something she wanted them both to do?

"Hannah?"

Hannah looked up, startled, as Lisa stepped in through the swinging door. "Yes?"

"Grandma Knudson just called. She wants to know when you're going to deliver the cookies for her meeting this afternoon."

"Tell her I'm on my way," Hannah said, jumping to her feet and grabbing her parka. She didn't bother with her snow boots. The walks were shoveled every day at the parsonage, and she'd park in the rear, right next to the kitchen door. She picked up the box of cookies on the counter, grabbed her purse from its perch on top of the water cooler, and headed out the door at a trot.

ORANGE OR LEMON CREAMS

Do not preheat the oven yet — this dough must chill for an hour or two.

For The Cookies:

2/3 cup ultrafine bakers sugar *(I used C&N in the carton)* ★★★

1 cup *(8 ounces, 2 sticks, 1/2 pound)* salted butter, softened

1 egg yolk, lightly beaten *(just whip it up in a glass with a fork)*

2 teaspoons orange or lemon juice *(or an orange or lemon fruit liqueur)*

Zest of one lemon or orange *(I measured mine after zesting — it was a little less than 1/2 teaspoon)*★★★★

2 and 1/4 cups all-purpose flour *(scoop it up and level it off with a table knife — don't pack it down)*

★★★ *If you don't have ultrafine bakers sugar, you don't have to crank up the car and run to the store to get some. Simply put some white, granulated sugar in your food processor and zoop it up with the steel blade. Then measure it and use it in this recipe. (You have to measure AFTER processing because the granules will be smaller and you'll get a bit more sugar to*

151

the cup.) In England this sugar is called castor sugar.

**** The zest is the colored part of the rind. Try to grate only the colored part, not the white part under it. The white part is bitter.

For The Sandwich Cream Frosting:

1/3 cup salted butter, softened

4 and 1/2 cups powdered *(confectioners)* sugar *(no need to sift unless it has big lumps)* *****

4 Tablespoons *(that's 1/4 cup)* milk or light cream

1 and 1/2 teaspoons orange or lemon juice *(or fruit liqueur)*

***** In England this sugar is called icing sugar.

To make the cookies, beat the sugar and salted butter together until they're soft and fluffy. You can do this with an electric mixer, or by hand. *(It's easier with a stand mixer.)*

Beat in the egg yolk, fruit juice or liqueur, and fruit zest. Make sure it's well mixed. You want that zest to be thoroughly incorporated.

Measure the flour by scooping it up and then leveling off the measuring cup with a table knife. Don't pack it down in the cup for this recipe.

Stir or beat in the flour in half-cup incre-ments *(just eyeball it — you don't have to be exact)* stirring or beating after each ad-dition.

Round the dough up in the mixing bowl, and divide it into 2 parts. Pat the two parts into balls. Wrap the balls in plastic wrap, and refrigerate them for at least one hour. *(Overnight is fine, too.)*

When you're ready to bake, preheat the oven to 375 degrees F., rack in the middle position.

On a floured board, roll out the dough *(just like pie-crust)* to a 1/8-inch thickness. Use a round cookie cutter, or the rim of a drinking glass to cut out dough circles.

ALTERNATIVELY:

For those of you who don't like to make rolled cookies, let your dough come up to room temperature and then use a 2-teaspoon scooper to make dough balls. Place them on a standard-size cookie sheet sprayed with Pam (or another nonstick cooking spray) or on a parchment-covered cookie sheet. You should have no more than 12 dough balls on your cookie sheet.

Flatten your dough balls with the blade of a metal spatula, or the flat bottom of a drinking glass, pressing down until they're approximately 1/8-inch thick.

Bake the cookies at 375 degrees F. for 8 to 10 minutes or until they're very slightly golden.

Take the cookies out of the oven and let them cool on the cookie sheets for 5 minutes. Then transfer them to a wire rack to cool completely.

To make the frosting, beat the softened butter until fluffy. *(This is easy with an electric mixer. It takes a bit more effort by hand.)*

Measure out the powdered sugar and put it in another bowl. Scoop it up and level off the cup as you measure, but don't bother sifting unless it's got lumps.

Beat in approximately half of the powered sugar. *(You don't have to be exact.)* Mix it up thoroughly.

Slowly, beat in half of the milk. Mix thoroughly.

Mix in the fruit juice or liqueur.

Beat in the remaining powdered sugar, mixing it all up thoroughly.

Slowly, mix in the rest of the milk. **Careful! You may not use it all!** Stop adding milk when your frosting reaches spreading consistency.

If you goof, don't despair. This sandwich

cream frosting is very forgiving. If your frosting is too runny, add more powdered sugar until it's just right. If your frosting is too thick, add a little more milk until it's just right.

When your cookies are thoroughly cooled and you're ready to assemble the Lemon or Orange Creams, spread a small amount of frosting on the 'wrong' side of a cookie, **(that's the bottom part).** Put the 'wrong' side of another cookie on top of the frosting to make a cookie sandwich.

Kelly-Anne says that this cookie dough can be frozen for up to 6 weeks, and the frosting can be frozen for the same amount of time. She tends to stamp out her shapes, then store them between layers of greaseproof paper **(I'm guessing this is wax paper)** before freezing. She writes, "This way I can have one or two freshly baked cookies anytime I feel like it, without having to make a whole batch."

Yield: 2 dozen 2-inch round Lemon or Orange Sandwich Creams, or 1 dozen 3-inch round Lemon or Orange Sandwich Creams.

CHAPTER NINE

When Hannah opened the kitchen door at the parsonage, she found Grandma Knudson standing at the stove, stirring a big pot of soup. "That smells wonderful!" Hannah told her, stepping into the steamy warmth and immediately shedding her parka. "Is that homemade chicken soup?"

"Yes. And no."

"What does *that* mean?"

"The only homemade part is the chicken. It's a recipe I got years ago from my daughter-in-law, Janelle. She was a lawyer and she didn't have time to cook when she got home from work. Sit down at the table and I'll give you a bowl so you can try it."

Hannah's stomach growled as Grandma Knudson ladled some soup into a bowl and set the steaming vessel in front of her. The aroma was heavenly.

"It's hot. You'd better blow on it to cool it down."

Hannah did just that, but it was hard to wait when something smelled as delicious as Janelle's chicken soup. She forced herself to give it several cooling blows, but then hunger overcame caution.

The soup was still hot, but not so hot that she couldn't taste the complex flavors. It was absolutely perfect, and she had to have the recipe. "Sour cream?" she asked, dipping her spoon in again the moment the question had left her mouth.

"Yes. You put it in at the very end. I added yours to your bowl right after I dished it up."

"It's wonderful. Will you give me the recipe if I promise you my firstborn son?"

Grandma Knudson laughed. "They only did that in the Old Testament. You can have the recipe, no promises necessary. I'll copy it out for you right after you finish your soup."

"Thanks!" Hannah said, and she finished her soup in record time.

"More?"

"No, thanks. That really hit the spot, but I'm saving myself for dinner tonight. Norman's taking me out to the Lake Eden Inn."

"Then could you run over to the church and tell Matthew it's time for his lunch? I tried calling him on the phone, but he didn't answer."

"Are you sure he's there?"

"Oh, yes. When I went to bed last night, he said he was going to get up early and work on his sermon for Wednesday night services. He must have gotten up very early, because I walked past his room at six-thirty and he was already gone." Grandma Knudson gave a little smile. "He hasn't changed that much since he was in high school. Matthew still makes his bed every morning. And I noticed that he took a big piece of my Red Devil's food Cake to the office with him for breakfast."

His bed was made, Hannah's mind gave her a little nudge. *Grandma Knudson assumes that he made it this morning, but what if he never went to bed at all? What if he went somewhere else and he isn't back yet?*

"Do you suppose he was called out last night for a sick parishioner, or something like that?"

"No. Matthew's very thoughtful. He would have left me a note. Besides, there's no way he would have taken Jacob anywhere except the church office."

"And Jacob is gone," Hannah drew the obvious conclusion.

"Yes. Matthew's taken quite a liking to Jacob. He always reads his sermons out loud, hoping that Jacob will pick up some new bible verses."

"Has he?"

"Yes, one. If Matthew's not in the office, he could be in another part of the church. He said something about replacing a burned-out bulb in one of the hanging lamps. Or he could be trying to fix the furnace. Bob showed him how before he left."

"Don't worry. I'll find him," Hannah promised, standing up and carrying her soup bowl and spoon to the sink. "Just don't forget to copy that recipe for me. It's really great soup."

There was absolutely nothing frightening about a church in the afternoon. Hannah closed the kitchen door behind her, traversed the back porch, and stepped out onto the walkway that led from the parsonage to the side door of the church. But if there was nothing frightening, why was her heart racing a zillion beats a minute?

Hannah avoided an icy patch on the walkway and shoved her hands into the pockets of her parka. It was a bright, sunny winter day and as she neared the side door of the church, she told herself that there were plenty of plausible reasons why Reverend Matthew hadn't answered the phone in the church office. He could have been somewhere he couldn't hear it, like in the restroom, or out in front shoveling the snow that had fallen during the night, or checking something in the storage room at the rear of the church. It was also possible that Grandma had misdialed, or another half-dozen equally reasonable explanations. Just because Reverend Matthew hadn't responded was no reason to suspect that there was anything wrong.

Hannah's mind begged to differ. There *could* be something wrong. What if Reverend Matthew had fallen off a ladder while replacing a light bulb in the heavy colored-glass fixtures that hung from the vaulted ceiling of the church? Or how about the temperamental furnace? Reverend Bob was an expert at jiggling wires to fix it. What if Reverend Matthew had tried to do the same, and electrocuted himself in the process?

All this was speculation. Hannah gave a little laugh at her overactive imagination. Chronicling all the mishaps that could have befallen the substitute minister was silly. She was almost there, and she would find out what was the matter . . . if anything *was* the matter.

Hannah arrived at the side door to the church and unlocked it with the key Grandma Knudson had given her. She told herself again that nothing was wrong, that everything was perfectly normal. Reverend Matthew would greet her when she came into the church office, and they'd go back to the parsonage together.

A wave of stale air rolled out to meet her as Hannah pushed the door open and stepped in. It was scented with dying flowers and the faint odor of fuel oil from the old furnace. Even though the inside door to the small windowless entry room was open, only feeble light filtered in from the stained glass windows that graced the walls in the body of the church.

Hannah felt for the light switch, but she couldn't seem to find it. She debated the wisdom of leaving the outside door open for light and air, but then she remembered the huge heating bills that the church incurred every winter. This was the coldest February on record, and her eyes would adjust to the dim light.

It took a few moments after she'd closed the outside door, but at last she could see well enough to move forward in the crowded room. A tall dresser with wide, shallow drawers sat against the wall. It contained

161

the sparkling white linen for communion. The top of the dresser held a large, round silver tray that had been polished to a high gleam by Hannah's neighbors, Marguerite and Clara Hollenbeck. The tray was peppered with small indentations for tiny round glasses that would hold the communion wine. Another smaller silver tray with a cover sat next to the large tray, ready to receive the communion wafers.

Avoiding several boxes that jutted out into her path, Hannah moved toward the doorway and stepped into the main body of the church. That was much better! The sunlight streaming through the stained glass windows was gorgeous.

"Reverend Matthew?" she called out expectantly, but there was no answer to her call. Her eyes scanned the rows of oaken pews, but the only things moving in the body of the church were tiny dust motes dancing in the beams of colored light.

Hannah gave it a minute or two, just in case Reverend Matthew had heard her and was coming from another part of the church, but there was no sound of hurrying footsteps. When she'd waited long enough, in her estimation, she moved on down the carpeted center aisle, past the tall, arched stained-glass windows on both sides of the church, and headed to the church office.

The office was opposite the stairway that led up to the choir loft, and Hannah knew that Reverend Bob had recently refurbished it. The door was shut, and she hesitated. What if Reverend Matthew was deep in prayer, or meditation, or something like that? Would it be right to interrupt him for something as mundane as lunch? But Grandma Knudson's homemade chicken soup was certainly not mundane!

"Reverend Matthew?" Hannah called out again, and followed her query by knocking softly on the door. "Are you in there?"

There was no answer. Hannah felt her heartbeat quicken, and there was a lump in her throat. This wasn't good, not good at all. She wanted to turn tail and run, but that would be cowardly. What if Reverend Matthew was inside and he was injured in some way? Or he had been taken suddenly ill? Or . . . but she didn't want to think about *that!*

She called his name again. Twice. And then she reached out with shaking fingers and turned the doorknob. It took all of her gumption to push the door open slightly, just far enough so that she could see the edge of the desk. And then a bit wider. And then . . . .

The first thing she saw was the cake, a huge slice of Grandma Knudson's Red Devil's Food Cake on the rug in front of the desk. There was a plate there too, obviously thrown to the floor. Hannah stared at the cake for a moment. Grandma Knudson's mouthwatering fudge frosting was smeared into the fibers of the off-white rug, and she hoped it wouldn't stain. But she ceased thinking about that minor problem when she spotted what was behind the desk.

Hannah stood stock still and stared at the awful sight. Reverend Matthew was seated at the desk, and it was obvious that he'd been working on next Sunday's sermon because it was spread out on the desk in front of him. His head was resting on the pages, but he wasn't asleep. There was something on the sheets of paper and on the desktop in front of him. That something was blood. A lot of blood. More blood than Hannah ever would have guessed a human being could contain.

"Reverend Matthew?" she asked again, in a very quiet voice. She didn't expect an answer, and she didn't get one. Reverend Matthew was dead.

CHAPTER TEN

Hannah stood there staring at the gruesome sight for what seemed like endless minutes. She might have stayed there, stationary and in shock, for much longer, but a voice rang out from the top of the bookcase.

"The wages of sin is death," the voice said, causing Hannah to whirl around and stare at the top of the bookcase. What she saw came very close to making her break out in hysterical laughter.

It was Jacob, the mynah bird, in his cage on the bookcase. He peered down at her with beady eyes and gave a squawk that made her jump. "The wages of sin is death," he said again in Reverend Matthew's voice.

At that moment, the phone on the desk began to ring. Hannah reached out to answer it, but she stopped short. Only when she'd taken a tissue from the box on the reverend's desk to preserve any existing

165

fingerprints did she carefully lift the receiver.

"Hello?" she said, hoping she didn't sound too shaky.

"Hannah!" It was Grandma Knudson's voice. "Did you find Matthew?"

"Oh, yes," Hannah said, deliberately avoiding the natural urge to turn and glance at the reverend.

"Is he coming over for lunch?"

"Uh . . . no, he's not . . ." Hannah stopped, wondering how she could tell Grandma Knudson that her favorite house guest and her grandson's substitute minister was dead. Certainly not on the phone. That just wouldn't be right.

"He's *not* coming over for lunch?"

"Not right now. He's not . . ." Hannah stopped. What could she say? She didn't want to lie to Grandma Knudson, but neither did she wish to tell her friend the bad news over the phone.

"He's not what?" Grandma Knudson asked.

"He's . . . not hungry at the moment," Hannah said, grasping at the first excuse she could think of. "You should turn the soup down to simmer, Grandma Knudson. I'm going to stay here with Reverend Matthew for a while, and then I'll come back to

166

the parsonage."

"All right, Hannah." Grandma Knudson gave a little chuckle. "Matthew must have had too much cake. That was a huge piece he took for breakfast this morning. He *does* love my cake."

"I can tell that," Hannah said, glancing down at the sticky goo that had once been a delicious slice of Red Devil's Food Cake. There was no way she was going to let Grandma Knudson come here to the church office to see the horrific sight. "Just sit tight, and I'll be there in less than ten minutes," she promised. "Is that all right?"

"That's fine, dear. I have to get dressed for my Bible study group anyway. Just let yourself in when you come back to the parsonage, and help yourself to more soup."

Janelle's Quick And Easy Chicken Soup

8 cups chicken broth **OR**
2 quarts water **(that's 8 cups)** and 8 chicken
  bouillon cubes
6 and 1/2 cups <u>uncooked</u> wide egg noodles
2 cans **(10 and 3/4 ounce each)** condensed
  cream of chicken soup, undiluted
3 cups cubed cooked chicken
1 cup **(8 ounces)** sour cream
minced fresh parsley

Bring broth **OR** water and bouillon to a
boil in a pot that will hold 12 to 14 cups.

Add the noodles. Cook, stirring occasionally, until the noodles are tender. **(Read
your noodle package for the time. Mine
took about 9 minutes.)** DO NOT DRAIN
the noodles. They are now part of the soup.

Turn the heat down to medium.

Add the two cans of condensed cream of
chicken soup. Stir them in well.

Add the cubed chicken and stir it in.

Heat everything through. This should take
from 5 to 10 minutes.

When the soup is piping hot, remove it
from the heat. If you're serving it all at once
and everyone's ready to eat, stir in the sour

cream, sprinkle with fresh parsley, and ladle into soup bowls.

CHAPTER ELEVEN

"No, don't call them!" Grandma Knudson frowned at Mike. "I won't let anything spoil their honeymoon." Hannah cast Grandma Knudson an admiring look. Her elderly friend looked a bit shaken from the bad news Mike had just delivered to her, but her voice was firm.

"Are you sure?" Clara Hollenbeck asked her. The Hollenbeck sisters, Clara and Marguerite, had arrived early for the Bible study group in order to help Grandma Knudson with the refreshments.

"Reverend Bob would come home in a flash if he knew," Marguerite said. "He wouldn't want you to be alone at a time like this."

"I'm not alone." Grandma Knudson paused and Hannah wondered if they were about to get an affirmation of her faith. "I have you, Clara," she reached out to pat Clara's hand, and then she reached for

Marguerite's hand. "And you, Marguerite."

Both sisters looked proud to be counted as Grandma Knudson's friends. "But will Reverend Bob be angry at us for not telling him?" Clara posed another possibility.

"I can't see why he would be. It's not like he can hop on a plane and get here right away. He's on a ship sailing for Hawaii, and he won't even get there for another three days. Don't you think it would be a real shame for Bob and Claire to dock at such a beautiful island and have to go straight to the airport to come home?"

Clara nodded and so did Marguerite. "You're right, Grandma Knudson," Marguerite said, and Hannah noticed that the normally soft-spoken lady had picked up a bit of Grandma Knudson's firmness. "If we all pull together, we can get along just fine until the seminary sends us another minister. In the meantime, I think our brother's minister, Reverend Collins from Grey Eagle, might agree to perform some of the duties."

"Hank Collins is a nice young man," Grandma Knudson agreed. "I'm sure he'll fill in as best he can. And there's Tom Sherman from Little Falls. Bob helped him out once when he was on vacation."

Mike cleared his throat, and everyone

turned to look at him. "Excuse me, ladies," he said. "I need to ask Grandma Knudson some questions."

"Of course you do, son." Grandma Knudson turned to Clara and Marguerite. "I'm putting the two of you in charge of the Bible study meeting. When the other ladies come, take them straight to the living room, tell them that there's been an accident at the church, and get their input on who we can get to fill in until the seminary sends another minister to substitute for Bob. If you make a list of their suggestions, I'll look it over when I join you and we'll place some calls. I put on the coffee, so that should be ready, and Hannah brought a box of . . . what are they, Hannah?"

"Big Soft Chewy Molasses Cookies. They're Lois Thielen's recipe."

"I've had those. They're delicious," Clara said, and then she turned to look at Grandma Knudson. "We could bring coffee and a plate of them in here if you'd like."

Grandma Knudson nodded. "That would be nice. Thank you, Clara. You girls are always so thoughtful."

When Clara and Marguerite had left, Hannah turned to Mike. "Would you like me to leave so you can talk to Grandma Knudson alone?"

"That's okay. You don't have to leave on my account."

"Nor on my account," Grandma Knudson added. "Besides, you should tell Mike everything you and Andrea found out about Matthew." Grandma Knudson turned to Mike. "We missed you at church services on Sunday, Mike. If you'd been there, you would have had the chance to meet Matthew in person."

Mike took the gentle chiding in stride, but Hannah knew him well enough to know he was slightly embarrassed. She was willing to bet he'd be in church this coming Sunday.

"When was the last time you saw Reverend Walters?" he asked.

"About nine last night when I went to bed. I said goodnight to him, and he told me that he was going to get up early and work on his sermon in the church office."

Hannah gave a little shiver as she remembered the blood-soaked pages spread out on the desk. She wondered if Reverend Matthew had finished his sermon, and then she wondered if it really mattered at all.

"Do you know if Reverend Matthew had any enemies?" Mike asked his second question.

"I don't know of any. Except . . ." Grandma Knudson stopped and looked thoughtful. "He may have had a falling out with his cousin Paul. Or perhaps it was the other way around and his cousin Paul had a falling out with Matthew. In any event, they hadn't seen each other for years. When they were here, staying with me while their parents went off to do missionary work, Matthew and Paul were quite close. Toward the end of the year, Paul did get into a bit of trouble, but we suspected it was because Matthew had a girlfriend and Paul was jealous of the time Matthew spent with her."

"What kind of trouble?"

"Minor trouble. He broke into lockers at school and took mementos, little things that weren't valuable. The principal at the time thought it was a bid for attention, but Matthew thought it was the start of something. He said Paul committed a crime and was sent to a prison in Iowa. Matthew wasn't sure of the details because Paul's parents didn't want to talk about it, but he thought it was some kind of burglary gone bad."

"Do you know Paul's parents?"

"I did. Not well, but we exchanged Christmas cards and they always sent me a little something for my birthday. They're both dead now. Paul's mother died six years ago, and his father died last year."

Hannah interpreted the tightening of the

muscles around Mike's mouth. He was disappointed that he couldn't interview Paul's parents. "So when was the last time Reverend Matthew saw his cousin Paul?"

"I'm not sure, but it has to be when Matthew was in his twenties. I know he tried to contact Paul after his cousin got out of prison in Iowa, but the private detective he hired couldn't find him."

"Why did Reverend Matthew want to contact his cousin?"

"To tell him that Paul's mother was dying of cancer. Matthew said he owed it to Paul to tell him. He thought Paul might want to come home to see his mother, or write a letter, or do something, but he couldn't find Paul to notify him."

Mike made a couple of quick notes in his notebook. "All right. How about when Reverend Matthew was here in Lake Eden? Were there any incidents with local people? Altercations? Disagreements? Old grudges from when both boys stayed here with you?"

"Nothing I can think of. Matthew was a lovely person. He liked everyone and everyone he met liked him." Grandma Knudson stopped talking as Marguerite came into the sitting room carrying a tea tray. "Oh, thank you, Marguerite. Just set it right here and Hannah will pour, won't you, dear?"

"Of course," Hannah said, handling the delicate bone china with care as she poured coffee and passed the cookie plate.

Once they'd sipped their coffee and pronounced it good, and taken bites of their cookies and pronounced those excellent, Grandma Knudson turned to Hannah again.

"Tell Mike what you and Andrea found out when you called the seminary to check Matthew out for me," she said.

Mike's eyebrows raised. "You checked out Reverend Matthew?"

"Yes," Hannah said, and proceeded to tell him everything they'd learned about the minister who'd become the unfortunate victim of violent crime.

"Why don't you go home," Lisa said after the third time Hannah had forgotten to put sweetened dried cranberries in a batch of Boggles. "Your mind's not on baking, and I can finish up here by myself. Are you okay to drive home? Or should I call Herb to give you a ride?"

"I'm fine," Hannah told her, even though she was about as far from fine as she could get and still manage to function. She was still rattled after finding Reverend Matthew's body, but that wouldn't affect her ability to step on the accelerator, apply the brakes, or steer her cookie truck down the road to her condo complex.

Lisa noticed the play of emotions on Hannah's face and wrinkled her brows in concern. "What is it? You look really sad."

"It's silly," Hannah said. "I'm anthropomorphizing."

"Attributing human characteristics to something not capable of having them?"

"Yes. I keep thinking about Jacob."

Lisa looked lost for a moment and then she asked, "Who's Jacob?"

"Pete Nunke's mynah bird. They're keeping him at the parsonage while Pete recovers from back surgery."

"But Jacob's okay, isn't he? The killer didn't . . ."

"No, Jacob's fine," Hannah interrupted Lisa's thought to reassure her. "But Jacob was in his cage at the church office when Reverend Matthew was murdered. He must have seen the whole thing."

Lisa gave a little shiver. "That's awful, all right! They say mynah birds are very intelligent. I wonder if Jacob could identify the killer."

"Only on a bad TV detective show."

"You're right." Lisa gave a little laugh. "I guess Jacob's lucky he's a bird. After all, what is he going to say if they put him on the witness stand? Polly wants a cracker?"

Now it was Hannah's turn to shiver. And she shivered so hard, Lisa noticed.

"Now what's the matter?" Lisa asked her.

"I just remembered what happened right after I found Reverend Matthew's body."

"What's that?"

"I was just standing there staring at Reverend Matthew's body and his voice said, *The wages of sin is death*."

"*His* voice? You mean . . . Reverend Matthew's voice?"

"Yes."

"Then he wasn't dead?"

"Oh, he was dead. One look and I knew that. But his voice came from above and behind me. For a split second there, I actually thought something supernatural was going on."

"Like the restless spirit of someone who'd suffered a terrible wrong and died in the process?"

"Exactly. And then I looked up and saw Jacob in his cage and realized that he must have learned to imitate Reverend Matthew's voice. I know everyone at the parsonage was trying to teach Jacob to repeat Bible verses, and that must be one he learned from Reverend Matthew."

Lisa gave another little shiver. "Or maybe . . . just maybe . . . Jacob learned it when Reverend Matthew said it to his killer."

"Now *that's* really creepy!"

"I know. Can I use it tomorrow at story time?"

Hannah laughed. She couldn't help it. Lisa loved to embellish the story of how Hannah had found the most current murder victim, and their customers looked forward to hearing the tale. By the time Lisa performed her one-woman show, and it *was* a show, no doubt about that, Hannah probably wouldn't recognize herself.

"Can I?" Lisa prodded.

May I, not can I, the grammarian in Hannah's mind corrected, but she didn't say it out loud. That might embarrass Lisa. "It's fine with me," she said instead. "Do you want me to tell you how I found the body? Or would you rather fabricate the whole thing?"

"Tell me," Lisa said quickly, rushing to the drawer where Hannah kept her stash of shorthand notebooks, and coming back to the workstation with notebook, pen, and fresh cups of coffee for both of them. "I'm ready," she said, opening the notebook and readying her pen. "Shoot."

"Don't say shoot."

"He was shot?" Lisa looked horrified when Hannah nodded. "Oh, dear! That's just awful! I wish he'd been stabbed, or bludgeoned, or smothered, or something."

"Why?" Hannah was puzzled at Lisa's reaction.

"The shooting sports are going to take it in the chops again when people find out that Reverend Matthew was shot. The politicians are already making noise about declaring our guns illegal. If they do that to us, they ought to make knives, and hammers, and pillows illegal, too!"

"I'm sorry, Lisa," Hannah commiserated. She knew Lisa and Herb enjoyed competitive shooting.

"So am I. Herb and I love to shoot trap and skeet, and he says I'm getting pretty good at it. And we love to get all dressed up in Wild West outfits to compete at cowboy shoots. If they make our guns illegal, we'll have to . . . to . . . to go *bowling* instead!"

Hannah came very close to laughing, but she managed to contain herself. Lisa had spit out the word *bowling* the way Hannah and her sisters used to spit out watermelon seeds in the backyard to see who could reach the greatest distance. "Careful, Lisa. Alice Vogel wouldn't be happy to hear you say that. And she's one of our best customers."

"You're right." Lisa looked a little sheepish. "There's nothing wrong with bowling. A lot of people love to bowl. And Alice does a great job running the leagues down at Ali's Alley. But I like shooting a million times better than bowling. Just think about it, Hannah. You could kill a person with a bowling ball, too!"

Hannah could tell that Lisa was getting worked up again, and she gave her a comforting smile. "It's really unlikely that they'll make guns illegal in Minnesota. We need hunting to keep down the deer population, and people come from all over to hunt and fish. Those tourist dollars speak loudly. They stimulate the economy of towns all over Minnesota. And there are the farmers who live way out in the country. They have to protect their livestock from predators."

"That's right. And there's something else about the farmers, especially in the winter when they live miles from their nearest neighbor. Remember when Arnie Carson fell down and broke his ankle during that storm last year, the one that took down the phone lines?"

"I remember."

"Well, Arnie couldn't walk on it and Sadie

couldn't get him into the house by herself."

"I can understand that. Arnie's a big guy and Sadie's really tiny."

"That's why Sadie went into the kitchen, brought back Arnie's shotgun, and fired it off three times at a snowbank. It was a signal they'd worked out with their neighbors. You can hear a shotgun blast a long ways away and that's how she let them know that she needed help."

"That's very smart."

"Yes, it is. And it goes to show that guns can be used for other things, not just for weapons. I just hope you're right about Minnesota voters, Hannah. I don't want to have to give up the new shotgun Herb gave me as a wedding present."

"That's a new twist on a shotgun wedding."

"I know. Everybody makes that joke." Lisa was smiling as picked up her pen again. "Now tell me exactly what happened after Grandma Knudson sent you over to the church office to fetch Reverend Matthew for lunch."

BIG SOFT CHEWY MOLASSES COOKIES

Do NOT preheat oven yet — this cookie
dough needs to chill.

**Hannah's 1st Note: Lois does this all
by hand, but we use our stand mixer
down at The Cookie Jar. She also makes
these as rolled cookies, rolling out the
dough a quarter-inch thick on a floured
board and using a 3 and 1/2 inch round
cookie cutter to cut them out. In the
interest of saving space and time, we do
ours as refrigerator cookies.**

1 and 1/4 cups white **(granulated)** sugar

1 teaspoon salt

1 and 1/2 teaspoons baking soda

1 and 1/2 teaspoons ground ginger

1 cup light molasses **(I used 1/2 cup dark
molasses mixed with 1/2 cup light Karo
syrup)**

2 beaten eggs **(just whip them up in a glass
with a fork)**

1 cup **(2 sticks, 8 ounces, 1/2 pound)** salted
butter, melted

2 Tablespoons **(1/8 cup)** hot water **(hot
water right out of the tap is fine)**

4 cups quick-cooking oatmeal **(dry, right
out of the package — I used Quaker's**

Quick-1 Minute)

4 cups all-purpose flour *(don't sift, but don't pack it down either — scoop it out with your measuring cup and level it off with a table knife)*

1 and 1/2 cups raisins *(I used golden raisins)*

1 cup chopped nuts *(I used walnuts)* approximately 1/2 cup white *(granulated)* sugar for a topping

Put the sugar in the bottom of the bowl of your mixer and turn it on LOW speed.

Add the salt, baking soda, and ground ginger. Mix them in thoroughly.

Now add the cup of light molasses. Keep mixing until everything is thoroughly blended.

Add the beaten eggs. Mix until they're well incorporated.

Melt the butter, either on the stovetop in a small saucepan, or in a microwave-safe bowl on HIGH for 90 seconds in the microwave. *(Stir the butter around after microwaving and if it's not melted, give it another 20 seconds.)*

Add the melted butter to the your bowl and mix it in.

Add the 2 Tablespoons of hot water to your bowl and mix it in.

With your mixer still on LOW speed, add the oatmeal in one cup increments, making sure to mix after each addition.

With the mixer still on LOW speed, add the flour in one cup increments, making sure to mix after each addition.

Add the raisins and mix them in.

Finally, add the nuts and mix thoroughly.

Remove the bowl from the mixer and give it a final stir by hand. This dough will be fairly thick.

Cover the cookie dough with plastic wrap and put the mixer bowl in the refrigerator for an hour. This dough will be easier to work with if it's chilled.

There are THREE ways to bake these cookies. They all turn out about the same, so you choose the way you like best. I'll give you the way Lois uses first:

Way to Bake #1 — The Rolled Method
Divide the chilled dough in half. Put one half in the refrigerator and round the other half into a big ball.

Sprinkle your breadboard with flour. Set the dough ball in the center and flatten it with your palms.

Sprinkle the top of the flattened dough ball with flour.

With a rolling pin, roll out the cookie

dough to 1/4 inch thick. Cut the dough into 3 and a half inch circles with a round cookie cutter. *(If you don't have a cookie cutter that size, I'll bet you have something in your kitchen that you can use for a cookie cutter. I had a plastic drinking glass that measured 3 and a half inches across, and I used that.)*

Place the round cutouts on a greased cookie sheet leaving 2 to 3 inches between the cookies. A standard-size cookie sheet will hold 6 cookies of this size.

Brush the tops of the cookies with water and sprinkle them with sugar.

Bake at 375 degrees F. for 9 to 10 minutes or until slightly brown around the edges. *(Mine took the full 10 minutes.)*

Remove the cookies from the oven, leave them on the cookie sheet for a minute or so, and then remove them to a wire rack.

Cool the cookies completely and then store them in a tightly covered container or cookie jar.

If you just don't want to make rolled cookies, I've found an alternative. Here's the ball and sugar method:

Way To Bake #2 — The Dough Ball Method

This way is fun and easy, and it doesn't require a breadboard, rolling pin, or flour. You also get sugar on the tops AND bottoms!

Roll the chilled dough in 2 and a half inch balls with your fingers. *(That's approximately the size of a plum.)* Roll the dough ball in a bowl of sugar and place it on a greased *(or sprayed with Pam or another nonstick cooking spray)* cookie sheet. Flatten it to a quarter-inch thick with a wide metal spatula or your impeccably clean palm.

Repeat the process of rolling dough balls, coating them with sugar, and placing them on the cookie sheet. They should be 2 to 3 inches apart and a standard-size cookie sheet will hold 6 of these big delicious cookies.

Bake at 375 degrees F. for 9 to 10 minutes or until slightly brown around the edges. *(Mine took the full 10 minutes.)*

Remove the cookies from the oven, leave them on the cookie sheet for a minute or so, and then remove them to a wire rack.

Cool the cookies completely and then store them in a tightly covered container or cookie jar.

The third way to make the cookies is the refrigerator method. It takes a little longer, but it's very simple. Here it is:

Way to Bake Cookies #3 — The Slice Method

Divide the chilled dough into 2 parts. Return the 2nd part to the refrigerator while you work with the 1st part.

Tear off a sheet of wax paper that's approximately a foot and a half *(18 inches)* long. Flip it over so it doesn't roll right back up again for you and lay it out on your counter with the long expanse facing you.

Plunk your chilled dough down on the wax paper and use your hands to shape it into a foot-long log. *(This may remind you of playing with modeling clay in kindergarten.)*

Center the cookie dough log at the edge of the long expanse of wax paper and roll it up.

Twist the ends of the wax paper to secure the log of cookie dough inside, and place it in your refrigerator.

Leave it there overnight so it's chilled thoroughly.

In the morning, when you're ready to bake, preheat the oven to 375 degrees F., rack in the middle position.

While you're waiting for your oven to preheat, grease *(or spray with Pam or another nonstick cooking spray)* your cookie sheet.

When your oven comes up to temperature, remove the log of cookie dough from the refrigerator. Unroll it and use a sharp, thin knife to slice off 6 quarter-inch slices.

Put some white sugar in a bowl with a fairly flat bottom and, one by one, lay the cookie slices in the bowl. Flip them over to coat the other side with sugar and then place them 2 to 3 inches apart on the cookie sheet. A standard-size cookie sheet will hold 6 of these large cookies.

Bake at 375 degrees F. for 8 to 10 minutes or until slightly brown around the edges. *(Mine took the full 10 minutes.)*

Remove the cookies from the oven, leave them on the cookie sheet for a minute or two to set up, and then use a flat metal spatula to remove them to a wire rack. Cool the cookies completely and then store them in a tightly covered container or cookie jar.

It doesn't really matter which way you choose to prepare the cookie dough for baking. Whether you roll them out with a rolling pin, form them into dough balls, or slice them, the bake time will be approximately the same, the cookies will be delicious, and the yield will remain approximately the same.

Yield: 3 dozen large, Big Soft Chewy Molasses-Oatmeal Cookies.

Hannah's 2nd Note: Lois told Grandma Knudson that these were her dad's favorite cookies. We can certainly see why!

Hannah's 3rd Note: My great-grandmother, Elsa Swensen, had a trick for keeping cookies like this soft and chewy. She put some orange or lemon peel in the bottom of her cookie jar. The moisture in the citrus peel kept the cookies soft and any slight orange or lemon flavor the cookies absorbed was all to the good! When citrus fruit wasn't in season in Minnesota, she used a chunk of apple to keep the cookies moist.

CHAPTER TWELVE

"Are you okay?" Norman asked when she opened her condo door at seven that night.

"I think so." Hannah thought about his comment for a moment. "Don't I look okay?"

"You look great! You know I love to see you wear that outfit."

Hannah smiled, but she declined to do the little pirouette that was called for by his compliment. Her heart was too heavy for that. "I love this skirt and sweater set," she said. "I wore it because I needed . . ."

"What?" Norman asked when her voice trailed off.

"I guess I needed a little cheering up."

"Then that's exactly what I'll do," Norman promised. "Let me get your coat and we'll go. I know what happened this afternoon, Hannah, so we can talk over dinner and sort things out."

It wasn't exactly a miracle, but it felt like

one to Hannah as she thrust her arms into the dress coat Norman held for her, watched him toss Moishe several fish-shaped kitty treats to keep him busy while they were gone, and escorted her out the door. One thing about Norman — he always seemed to know what she needed. And this time the gorgeous-enough-to-be-a-model Doctor Bev didn't enter into the equation. Norman was here, and Hannah planned to keep him with her for a good, long while. Doctor Bev was home alone. She had to be. Mike was tied up with Reverend Matthew's murder, so Doctor Bev would just have to cool her heels.

"It's good to see you smiling," Norman said, opening the passenger door for her.

"That's because I'm with you," Hannah said, and left it at that. It was true. She always felt better when she was with Norman. There was a second factor that accounted for her improved mood, but Hannah decided not to mention that the image of Doctor Bev languishing in her apartment alone made her feel much better.

"Hannah? We're here."

A voice roused Hannah from her extremely pleasant nap. It was a nice voice, a caring voice, and for a moment she thought her father was waking her in the morning so that she could get ready for school. But it wasn't her father's voice. It was . . . Norman. And she'd fallen asleep on their first date in a whole month!

"Oh, Norman! I'm so sorry! I didn't think I was that tired, but . . . why are you parking here? It's a loading zone."

"I called Sally and cleared it. She said there won't be any deliveries tonight. I didn't want you to have to walk all the way from the parking lot."

"Thank you, Norman." Hannah gave him a big smile, even though the cold night air might have chased away the cobwebs in her mind and the almost overwhelming urge to go back to sleep. But even the short distance from the car to the front door of the inn did the trick. By the time Norman opened the door, Hannah was feeling much more alert.

Once they'd hung up their coats and switched from boots to the shoes they'd brought with them, Hannah and Norman headed straight for the dining room. As they stepped inside, Sally greeted them.

"I was wondering when you'd get here," she said. "I have a new dessert tonight and there are only a few servings left. Do you want me to save you a couple?"

Norman nodded. "That would be great.

What is it?"

"Pear Crunch Pie. It's Rhanna's recipe. You remember her, don't you Hannah? She managed the whole place for me during our first year."

"I remember. You were fit to be tied when she retired and moved to California."

"What's the best thing on the menu tonight, Sally?" Norman asked her. "Hannah needs to relax with a nice glass of wine and some really great comfort food. And actually . . . I could use the same thing. Not the wine, though. It's fizzy water for me. And whatever you have in the way of comfort food would be perfect for me, too."

"You came to the right place," Sally said, smiling broadly. "I figured a lot of folks would need something hot and hearty tonight. It's so cold out there. So I made Brisket and Veggies."

"That's what I want!" Hannah said quickly.

"Me, too," Norman echoed her choice.

"Wonderful. Just relax and leave everything to me." Sally turned to pat Hannah's shoulder. "I saved one of the private booths for you. That way nobody can come to your table to ask you questions."

Hannah was grateful. She hadn't even considered that possibility, but Sally was right. Everyone from Lake Eden would want to hear the story of how she found Reverend Matthew's body. "Thanks, Sally. That was really thoughtful."

"I'll tell Dot to seat you and pull the curtains."

Sally gestured and Dot Larson, Sally's head waitress, led them up the steps to the raised part of the dining room and seated them in the end booth.

"How's the baby, Dot?" Hannah asked, before Dot could pull the curtains.

"Growing like a weed. He's got one speed and that's full throttle. If we had a bigger house, Mom would never be able to keep up with him."

"Your mother babysits while you're at work here?" Norman asked.

"That's right. It works out really well. I have the five to ten shift during the week, and Mom comes over at four-thirty. She fixes supper for Jimmy when he gets home at five-thirty, feeds Jamie and puts him to bed, and she's back home in time to watch her favorite shows. Taking care of Jamie gives her something to do now that Dad's gone."

"I'm sorry to hear your father died," Norman said quickly.

"Oh, he's not dead!" Dot gave a merry

laugh. "He's just up in Alaska with the dogs for the season. Mom usually goes with him, but there's not much for her to do up there while he's off mushing. To tell the truth, I think she's glad she could use babysitting with Jamie as an excuse not to go this year."

When Dot bustled off to get their drinks, Hannah amused herself by peeking through the curtains at the other diners. "Howie and Kitty Levine just walked in," she reported to Norman. "And there's Pam and George Baxter. And right behind them is . . . Mother!"

"Yours, or mine?"

"Mine. She's all alone."

"Would you like to ask her to join us?"

Hannah debated for a moment. She really wanted to be alone with Norman, but she knew Delores hated to dine by herself.

"Hannah? I'll do whatever you want."

Norman was waiting for an answer. Hannah sighed deeply and dipped her head. "No, I don't really want to invite her to join us, but I suppose we should."

"Then we will. Would you like me to go over and ask her?"

"That would be good," Hannah said, crossing her fingers for luck. It was possible that Delores was meeting some friends for dinner and the rest of her party hadn't arrived yet. She'd certainly taken care with her appearance, but then she always did. Delores was definitely the most attractive woman of her age in Lake Eden, perhaps even in Winnetka County.

Tonight her mother was dressed in a designer suit. Hannah knew that it was a designer suit even though she wasn't a fashion expert like Andrea, because Delores never bought anything that *wasn't* a designer creation. Tonight's outfit was made of soft green wool in a superfine weave that reminded Hannah of luna moths with gossamer wings. It was a shade of green that was lighter than an avocado and darker than the sprout of a crocus when it poked its head above ground in the Spring. Only Delores could get away with wearing such an unforgiving material and style. The jacket was nipped in at the waist, setting any excess pounds on display for all to see. Delores, of course, had none. The skirt was pencil thin and would show any imperfections. Delores, of course, had none. In short, Delores Swensen looked ravishing. Her hair was perfect, her makeup was flawless, and her appearance was top of the line. She'd obviously taken time to get ready for tonight's dinner, and Hannah was curious to see who her dining companion or companions would be.

While Norman was gone, their drinks arrived. Dot brought sparkling water with a wedge of lime for Norman, and what she said was Sally's favorite Estate Melon wine from De Ponte Cellars in Dundee Hills, Oregon. Her eye to the crack in the curtains, Hannah sipped her wine and watched Norman talk to her mother.

Delores wasn't getting up. Hannah decided that was a good sign. Norman would be escorting her back to their private booth by now if she'd accepted their invitation to join them. But something was definitely going on, because Norman left her mother's table and headed out of the dining room.

Please don't let it be a dental emergency, Hannah's mind pleaded. *And if it is, let him call Doctor Bev to take care of it. This is the first time we've been alone in ages, and I'm not willing to cut our time short.*

Dot arrived with the bread basket before Hannah could speculate further. She lifted the napkin that covered the heated treasures inside and gave a little smile of contentment. There were three breads tonight. Nestled on the right side of the bread basket were two of Sally's cornbread and honey muffins. Three Easy Cheesy Biscuits were on the right, and that also made Hannah smile. She'd gotten the recipe from a friend and passed it on to Sally.

It was the bread in the center of the bread basket that had caused Hannah to smile in delight. Sally's Apricot Bread was delightful. Sally had given her the recipe months ago, but she hadn't gotten around to baking it yet. Perhaps tonight would be the night. She could bake a batch with Norman when they got back to her condo. A batch made two loaves and if they baked a double batch, she could give one to Norman, one to her mother, who also loved it, and keep two loaves for herself.

Hannah was just spreading soft butter on her warm apricot bread when Norman pushed back the curtain and slid into the booth. "I take it Mother's not going to join us for dinner?" she asked, her smile still in place.

"No, she's waiting for her date."

"Who's her date?"

"She didn't say. But she did ask me if you were investigating Reverend Matthew's murder."

"What did you tell her?"

"I said I thought you probably would, that I thought you felt a certain responsibility when you discovered a murder victim."

Norman leaned forward toward her. "Am I right?"

"Yes," Hannah answered, although she hadn't really decided until this very moment. "Will you help?"

"Of course. I'm already helping. I asked your mother if she'd known Reverend Matthew when he stayed with Grandma Knudson as a teenager."

"What did she say?"

"She said she knew him slightly. But she also said her date for the evening knew him much better than she did."

Hannah was silent for a moment, taking that in. It had already occurred to her that Reverend Matthew could have been killed due to an old grudge, or something that had happened in Lake Eden in the past. "That *could* be helpful, depending on what it is. I think we should all get together over coffee and dessert."

"I'm ahead of you," Norman said, looking quite satisfied with himself. "I invited them to join us for dessert. And I checked with Sally right after I talked with your mother. She said she'd save the rest of the pear pie for the four of us."

"Great! Thanks, Norman." Hannah took a bite of her apricot bread and made a little sound of contentment. And then she remembered what she had wanted to ask him. "How about later at my condo? Would you like to help me make a batch of Sally's Apricot Bread? I'll give you a loaf to take home."

Norman reached out to take her hand. "Sounds like fun," he said. "I really love to bake with you."

"And I really love to bake with you," Hannah said, putting down her half-eaten slice of bread so that she could lay her other hand over his.

BRISKET AND VEGGIES

Hannah's 1st Note: Before she would give me this recipe, Sally made me promise to tell you that although this is the easiest recipe in the world, you have to pretend you've been toiling over a hot stove all day. She says it was her mother's secret recipe, and now it's yours, too.

4 to 5 pound beef brisket *(not corned!)*
2 cans *(approx. 10 ounces apiece)* condensed golden mushroom soup
3 medium potatoes *(sweet, regular, it doesn't matter)*
5 stalks celery, leaves removed
6 small white or yellow onions
6 carrots, peeled and cut into 2-inch chunks
salt and pepper to taste
one package Lawry's brown gravy mix *(the kind that makes one cup)*

Spread a layer of soup in the bottom of a disposable roaster *(that's about 1/2 can)* and place the roaster on a cookie sheet for stability.

Salt and pepper the brisket on both sides and then plunk it, fat side up, in the middle of the roaster.

Peel the potatoes and cut each one into

six chunks. Arrange them on top of the soup and around the sides of the brisket.

Cut the celery stalks into 2-inch pieces. Arrange them on top of the soup and around the sides of the meat.

Peel the onions. Cut them in half and arrange them on top of the soup and around the sides of the brisket.

Peel the carrots. Cut them in 2-inch chunks and arrange them on top of the soup and around the sides of the meat.

Hannah's 2nd Note: If you don't want to go to all this work, just buy a couple of packages of frozen stew vegetables and dump them (you don't have to thaw them) on top of the soup and around the sides of the brisket.

Salt and pepper the veggies and then slather the remaining soup over the top of everything in the roaster. Cover the roaster with a sheet of heavy duty foil to keep the steam in.

Bake your Brisket and Veggies at 350 degrees F. for 4 to 5 hours, or until it practically falls apart.

Hannah's 3rd Note: Sally says to tell you that it's practically impossible to over-bake this dish, that it just gets better and better.

Take off the foil the last half-hour of baking.

When the time is up, remove the roaster from the oven and let it cool for another half-hour before serving.

Hannah's 4th Note: If the liquid around the brisket is too thin to use for gravy, Sally puts it in a saucepan on the stove, heats it to almost boiling, and adds a package of Lawry's brown gravy mix (the kind that makes one cup) to thicken it.

CHAPTER THIRTEEN

"Oh, good! It's Doc Knight," Hannah told Norman with a smile. She'd been peeking out of the curtain every so often between bites of Sally's wonderful Brisket and Veggies, waiting for her mother's dinner companion to appear.

"She's seen a lot of him lately," Norman commented.

"She has?"

"Mother told me that she volunteered to organize the Gray Ladies."

"Who are the Gray Ladies?"

"A group of ladies who go out to the hospital to visit the patients on off-hours. Delores makes out their schedule."

"Charity work?" Hannah was surprised, and it showed on her face. Delores wasn't known for doing charity work.

"I guess you could call it charity, but it's more like community service. The patients in the hospital get lonely, and Doc keeps strict visiting hours. This way they can see the Rainbow Ladies in-between their regular visitors."

Hannah was confused. "Wait a second. You said they were Gray Ladies."

"They were, but your mother changed the name."

"Why did she do that?"

"They used to wear gray smocks. Can you imagine your mother wearing a gray smock?"

"No, I really can't," Hannah said quickly. Her mother was fond of colorful clothing and she didn't consider gray a color.

"Mother said Delores went to Claire's shop and they ordered brightly colored jackets for all of the volunteers. They're lightweight and washable, so the Rainbow Ladies wear them over a black top and black pants. Mother just loves hers. It's turquoise and that's her favorite color. Your mother brought a color wheel to their first meeting, and everyone chose a favorite color."

Hannah glanced out through the curtains again. Her mother was deep in conversation with Doc Knight. Perhaps they were discussing the Rainbow Ladies.

Norman waited until she'd taken her last bite of brisket. "Do you have any leads yet?"

"Not yet. I haven't even started."

"Did you bring your murder book with you?"

Hannah reached down to pat the leather saddlebag-size purse that her mother and Andrea kept trying to replace. She readily agreed that it was "ratty," her mother's word for all the scratches on the leather, but everything she needed to survive was in there . . . and then some.

"Do you want to brainstorm about it now, before your Mother and Doc join us? Or would you rather just relax?"

"Brainstorm," Hannah said instantly, reaching into her purse for her shorthand notebook and a pen. "First let me describe the scene of the crime, and then you can help think of possible motives."

Describing the scene didn't take long. Hannah had already done it twice in the past six hours, once in response to an official interrogation by Mike, and once at The Cookie Jar for Lisa. Each time she described it, it got a little easier, and she wondered if she was becoming jaded. She hoped not. Violent death was nothing to take lightly!

"And the murder weapon was a gun?" Norman asked when she'd finished.

"Yes, and he fell forward on the desk."

"Did they find the murder weapon?"

"No. I asked Mike about that. But just as soon as the autopsy is . . . Doc!"

Norman gave a little laugh. "Yes, Doc. He'll probably tell us his opinion. Doc's seen a lot of gunshot wounds as county coroner, and chances are he'll be right."

"It'll give us something to go on until the ballistics lab sends their report. Mike said that would take at least three days, maybe as long as a week."

Norman was silent as Dot arrived. She cleared their plates and told them that Delores and Doc would be joining them in five minutes or so. Then she left with Norman's credit card.

"Let's talk about motives while we're waiting for them," Norman suggested. "Why would anyone want to kill a minister?"

"Maybe it had nothing to do with the fact that Reverend Matthew was a minister. Don't forget that he lived here for a year when he was a senior in high school. Maybe someone with an old grudge seized the opportunity and killed him."

"Okay. Old grudge. What *kind* of old grudge?"

"I don't know. It could be jealousy. Grandma Knudson said that when Matthew was a senior at Jordan High, he was the quarterback and he dated the head cheerleader. She also said that the principal at the time thought Reverend Matthew's cousin Paul was jealous of the time they spent together."

Norman thought about that for a moment. "But why would cousin Paul wait all these years to kill Reverend Matthew when the reverend didn't end up marrying the cheerleader? And if cousin Paul was jealous of the time Reverend Matthew spent with the cheerleader, why didn't he kill the cheerleader?"

"I don't know. Those are good points. I guess we'll have to leave Paul out of it. No one knows where he is anyway. Reverend Matthew hired a private detective to find him when Paul's mother was dying, but the detective couldn't find Paul. The trail went cold at the state prison in Iowa right after Paul was released."

"Hold the phone! Reverend Matthew's cousin Paul was in prison?"

"That's right. And he got out early due to prison overcrowding. No one knows exactly what his crime was, only that it was a burglary gone bad, but he got out in five years so it couldn't be murder."

"I agree. I think we can write off cousin Paul. Do you know if Reverend Matthew had any enemies when he was here in Lake

Eden as a teenager?"

"Grandma Knudson didn't think so, but she wouldn't necessarily know. She was busy with her husband and the church, and teenagers, especially ones whose parents are thousands of miles away, don't usually confide in relative strangers."

"Right. We need to find a list of Matthew's classmates and see if any of them are still around. They may remember something."

"Good idea!" Hannah gave him a big smile and then she jotted it down. Norman had said, *We need to find a list of Matthew's classmates.* His use of the plural pronoun meant that Norman wanted to be a part of her investigation. "Marge Beeseman has a shelf full of Jordan High yearbooks down at the library. All we have to do is find the right year."

"First thing tomorrow morning, I'll run over to the library to check. Bev can cover for me. Marge may even remember Matthew."

"It's possible. She's lived here all her life. We can ask Lisa's father, too."

Norman looked concerned. He knew Lisa's father had been diagnosed with Alzheimer's. "Do you think Jack will be able to tell us?"

"Maybe, if it's a good day. And if it isn't,

we'll come back the next day."

"This is a strange case," Norman said, his brows furrowing slightly. "It's almost as if we're investigating two murders."

"One back when Matthew was in high school, and the other in the present?" Hannah guessed.

"Exactly right. Reverend Matthew was killed in the present, but the motive for his murder could be in the past. On the other hand, the motive could be right now in the present. And you know what *that* means."

"Double the work?" Hannah guessed.

"That's right. You're really going to need me to do legwork for you this time around."

"I certainly am," Hannah said, noticing that Norman looked very pleased with himself. He really did like to help her, and there was no denying that they made a good team.

"Bev can take over for the week," Norman said, drawing out his cell phone. "I'll tell her not to overbook. And if she gets in a jam with too many patients, she can always bring in Doc Bennett to help her. That way I can be all yours for the week. Sound good?"

"Sounds great," Hannah said, wishing he hadn't added the words, *for the week.*

"Do you mind if I call her right now?"

"Not at all," Hannah said, wondering how Doctor Bev would take the news that Norman wouldn't be in at all this week. Would she be jealous that he was Hannah's for the week? Or would she console herself with Mike when he came home from work at night?

"Hello, darlings," Delores greeted them as she slid into the booth with Doc Knight. The next thing she did was to reach out to pat Hannah's hand. "I heard all about it from Lisa. What a terrible experience for you! Are you all right?"

"Yes, I'm all right . . . at least for now."

"Of course you are. You're with Norman." Delores turned to Norman. "You take care of my little girl now."

"Little girl?!" Hannah couldn't stop her incredulous question.

"Sorry, dear, but I do get so worried about you all alone. Andrea's got Bill, and Michelle's got those friends of hers living with her at college. But you've got no one."

Norman reached for her other hand, which was resting on the bench seat between them, and gave it a firm squeeze. Hannah knew what that meant. Hannah should remain silent because protesting that she wasn't lonely would do no good. Her mother would go on in the *poor lonely Hannah* vein until she'd exhausted the subject.

"Enough, Delores," Doc Knight said, entering the conversation for the first time. And then, before anybody could say anything else, Dot arrived with their coffee and dessert.

Dot began by filling their cups and spooning on sweetened whipped cream with a little brown sugar sprinkled on the top. Once she'd served coffee to everyone, Delores turned to Hannah. "I wish you could make this for my launch party, dear. Sally's Cinnamon Supreme Coffee is my very favorite."

"You'll like the Pear Crunch Pie, too," Dot promised cutting four generous pieces and transferring them to dessert plates. "Just try it. It's one of my favorites."

Hannah watched as her mother took a dainty bite of the pie. And then she continued to watch as Delores cut off a huge bite and wasted no time slipping it into her mouth. Even though she'd always cautioned her daughters that it wasn't ladylike to gobble food, Delores was the first to finish both coffee and pie.

"That was marvelous!" she said, smiling at Hannah. "I wish I could have both of them for my launch party."

213

"You're in luck, Mrs. Swensen," Dot said, reaching into her apron pocket and handing the recipes to Hannah. "Sally said you'd probably want them."

Hannah bit back a grin. She'd lost count of the number of sweet treats her mother wanted her to make for her book launch party. If Hannah served everything her mother had mentioned, everyone there would go into a sugar coma. And then Mike and Bill would have to arrest her for attempted desserticide!

For long moments the only sounds were the clinking of silverware against cut glass dessert plates. When everyone had finished coffee and dessert, Doc turned to Hannah.

"I suppose you want to know about the autopsy and not wait for Andrea to wheedle it out of me."

Hannah's mouth fell open in surprise, but Delores turned to Doc with laughter in her eyes. "Andrea wheedles?"

"Yes, if she can't get a copy from Vonnie, or take it from Bill's briefcase when he's sleeping. You raised some sneaky girls, Lori."

Lori? Hannah stared at her mother, waiting for the explosion but Delores said nothing. As a matter of fact, she smiled at Doc Knight.

"I tried to set a good example," she said.

Doc Knight threw back his head and laughed. And then he reached out to put his arm around Delores and give her a squeeze. "That's my girl."

His girl? This was too much information for Hannah, who exchanged shocked looks with Norman.

"At least for tonight," Delores replied, giving him what Hannah could only describe as a come-hither smile.

Immediately, Hannah felt better. Her mother was having fun flirting with Doc Knight. And why shouldn't she? Hannah had seen her flirt with Joe Dietz and Bud Hauge, to name only a few of the men her mother had dated in the past few months. Hannah was pretty sure they were all just friends. But if they weren't, she'd simply have to deal with it. If anyone had asked, she would have admitted that it was a bit disconcerting watching her well-over-fifty mother flirt with local men, but Hannah was glad her mother was having a good time.

"What was your estimate of the time Reverend Matthew died?" Norman asked Doc.

"Between twelve and two."

"But I was there at twelve-thirty and he was already . . ." Hannah stopped speaking

215

as the light dawned. "You mean early on Sunday morning?"

"That's exactly what I mean. When you found the body, he'd been dead at least twelve hours, maybe a little longer."

"But how could you . . ." Hannah cut off her question as she noticed her mother's expression. "Never mind. That's too much information, and we don't really need to know."

"Thank you, dear," Delores said, giving her daughter a grateful glance, and then she turned to Doc. "I have a question for you."

"Ask away," Doc said, smiling at her.

"I'd like to know if he got to eat any of that luscious cake Hannah found at the scene . . . only as a matter of curiosity, of course. And I don't want to know the details of how you could tell."

"Yes. He had a bite or two."

"Did the killer eat cake before he murdered Reverend Matthew?" Hannah sat back, waiting for the answer.

Doc gave a little laugh. "I'm a doctor, not a psychic. There's no way of telling."

"I'm glad we had pie and not cake!" Norman said, and everyone laughed.

Hannah gave him an approving glance, and then she asked Doc another question. "Do you think I could get a copy of the

216

autopsy report?"

Doc shook his head. "I can't do that, Hannah. Besides, you don't need it. Your sister already got a printout from Vonnie."

Hannah smiled. Andrea was really on the ball. She'd known that Hannah would investigate Reverend Matthew's murder, and she was already collecting official reports for her. "Before you came to join us, Norman and I were talking about possible motivations for Reverend Matthew's murder. We decided it could be something current from his return here as a substitute pastor, or something that happened in the past when he went to Jordan High as a senior."

"Or something completely unrelated to Matthew Walters at all," Doc suggested a third possibility.

"But how could that be?" Delores asked him.

"Let's say that someone broke into the church in the middle of the night, not knowing that he was there in the church office. It could have been a botched burglary, and whoever it was didn't want to leave a witness."

Hannah immediately thought of Matthew's cousin Paul. He'd been convicted due to a burglary gone bad. She looked over

217

at Norman, knowing the same thought was running through his mind, and he gave a little shake of his head to remind her they'd decided that Paul wasn't a viable suspect.

"What would someone break into a church to steal?" Delores asked.

"The collection money?" Doc suggested.

Hannah thought about that for a moment. "That makes sense. The church was packed on Sunday because we held Reverend Bob and Claire's bon voyage party right after the service. There would have been more money than usual."

"You're good at this, Doc," Delores complimented him.

"Thanks. I should be good at it after all the practice I've had."

"You've solved crimes before?" Norman asked him.

"No, but it's a lot like diagnosing a patient. You add up all the facts, eliminate the diseases that don't fit the profile, and test for the ones that do. That's what I'm trying to teach my interns. Marlene's getting good at it, but Ben still has a ways to go." Doc reached out for the coffee carafe to pour more for Delores and then offered it to Hannah and Norman before he filled his own cup. "Lori thought you'd want to know about how Matthew got the quarterback job

218

on the Lake Eden Gulls."

"Please tell me," Hannah said, flipping to a fresh page in her shorthand notebook and reaching into her purse for her pen.

SALLY'S CINNAMON SUPREME COFFEE

Hannah's 1st Note: Sally uses a drip coffeemaker to make this coffee. She has a 30-cup pot, but I've reduced the recipe to fit in a household drip coffeemaker.

4 whole cinnamon sticks
3 Tablespoons brown sugar, well packed
1 teaspoon ground cinnamon
1 cup freshly ground coffee **(Sally uses French Roast beans and grinds her own)**
10 cups water

Place the cinnamon sticks and the brown sugar into the glass **(or metal)** carafe.

If your coffeemaker uses a filter, place it in the brew basket. Then put the freshly ground coffee and the ground cinnamon inside the basket.

Pour in 10 cups of water and turn on the coffeemaker. Let the water drip through completely.

Remove the carafe with the freshly made coffee and stir it to dissolve the brown sugar. Put it back on the heated pad at the bottom of the coffeemaker. It should sit there for at least 5 minutes so the flavors will meld.

This coffee is best topped with sweetened

whipped cream. Use one cup of whipping cream, 2 Tablespoons powdered sugar, and 1/2 teaspoon vanilla extract. Whip it up and place it in a pretty bowl so that people can top their coffee with it.

Hannah's 2nd Note: If you really truly don't feel like making sweetened whipped cream, you can buy it in a tub or a canister. Although sweetened whipped cream is always better when it's homemade, this coffee is so tasty, the ready-made sweetened whipped cream will be fine.

To serve, pour the coffee into a serving carafe, or if you're making just one pot, use the carafe from the coffee-maker. Transfer the cinnamon sticks to whichever carafe you use. This coffee will just get better and better as it sits.

Pour generous cupfuls and top with sweetened whipped cream. If you like, sprinkle a bit of brown sugar over the top of the sweetened whipped cream for an extra treat.

Yield: Serves 5 because everyone will want a second cup.

CHAPTER FOURTEEN

Hannah had to hunt for the pen she'd dropped in her purse only moments before. The roomy interior of her saddlebag-type purse reminded her of a claw arcade game. You operated the steam shovel to grasp a prize from the jumble of items in the glass box. Sometimes you lucked out and managed to get what you wanted. Other times you came up with a prize you could easily live without. This time Hannah was lucky, and she drew out the pen she wanted on the very first try.

"Ready?" Doc asked her.

"Yes."

"When Matthew came to school at Jordan High, he tried out for the football team and made it as an alternate quarterback. Hugh Kohler was the regular quarterback and had been for the past two years. I saw a couple of the games. The kid was good."

"So Hugh Kohler was the quarterback

and Matthew was second string?" Norman asked.

"For the first three games. But everything changed when Coach Telleson took the whole team on a camping trip at Eden Lake. It was the weekend before the big home-coming game, and they were supposed to bond together as a team. Unfortunately, it didn't work."

"What happened?" Hannah asked him.

"The first thing Coach Tellson had them do was gather firewood. They could go in groups or individually. He said later that he did it to see which boys worked best to-gether and which boys preferred to go it alone. I asked him why, and he told me that it would help him make decisions about which boys to play in certain positions."

"Okay," Norman said, but he didn't sound convinced. "What did he say about Mat-thew?"

"He said that Matthew went off alone, and so did Hugh. Hugh's younger brother, Adam, stood there for a minute and then he went off alone, too. The same for Mat-thew's cousin, Paul."

"Paul was there?" Hannah was surprised. Grandma Knudson hadn't mentioned that he'd played football.

"Paul was on the junior varsity team. I

don't think he got in more than a few minutes of playing time, but any boy who wore a uniform was there."

"Tell them about the other boys," Delores prompted.

"Except for Matthew, Hugh, Adam, and Paul, all the other boys paired up, or went in groups of three or four."

"And that told the coach something about football?" Delores sounded as dubious as Hannah felt.

"That's what Coach Telleson said. When the boys came back, he watched the amount of wood they brought, and made certain assumptions from that. He explained what these assumptions were at the time, but I don't remember now. It probably didn't make a lot of sense to me."

"Did Matthew bring back much wood?" Hannah asked.

"He brought back more wood than anyone else, but he came back late."

"There was a time limit?" Norman asked the question before Hannah could.

"Yes. They had to be back in fifteen minutes. Coach Telleson said the groups started coming in first after they'd been out for thirteen minutes. The paired boys were next, then Paul, and then Adam. Matthew arrived at the twenty-minute mark."

224

"How about Hugh?" Hannah asked the obvious question.

"He didn't come back at all. They found him a ways away, in a stand of birch with a broken leg."

"Tell them what happened," Delores urged.

"Hugh said he'd seen Matthew go down the same path, so he'd gone a different way to an area where he thought there'd be more firewood. When he saw that there wasn't any, he went back to the path that Matthew had taken, hoping that Matthew had left some wood. A little ways down the path, he found the perfect log for the campfire. He headed straight for it and that's when he fell in a deep hole that was hidden by fallen leaves and broke his leg in two places."

Hannah was already a step ahead of Doc's story. "And Hugh blamed Matthew?"

"That's right. He thought Matthew had dug a deep hole, filled it with fallen leaves to camouflage it, and placed a perfect log just beyond it as bait. And that prompted a real rift in the team. Hugh's best receiver pointed out that the hole had been there for a while since there were decaying leaves and mud at the bottom from the rain they'd had at the beginning of the week."

"So Hugh apologized and all was well?"

"No. A couple of the boys had seen Matthew going down that path. They knew that part of Hugh's story was true. And the hole had been filled to the top with leaves. That probably wouldn't have happened naturally. Even if Matthew hadn't dug the hole itself, he might have filled it with leaves and baited it with the log."

"You said there was a rift," Hannah pointed out. "Does that mean some of the boys believed that Matthew was innocent?"

"Yes. Coach Telleson did, for one. He told me that Matthew didn't have it in him to be that mean. And some of the older members of the team agreed with him. The split was about fifty-fifty, but the accusation was almost forgotten when Matthew played brilliantly in the homecoming game and the Gulls beat the Browerville Tigers twenty-eight to three."

"What do you think?" Delores asked him. "Did Matthew do it?"

"I could be wrong, but I don't think so. I asked him point blank when he came to visit Hugh in the hospital after the game. Hugh wouldn't see him, of course. He still believed Matthew had set him up so that he could have the quarterback spot. Matthew told me that he had nothing to do with it, that he'd seen the hole and avoided it and the log hadn't been there. He insisted that someone must have come along after he'd left, filled the hole in with leaves, and baited it with the log."

"Who do you think did it?" Delores asked, leaning toward Doc.

"It could have been anyone on the team. Coach Telleson said Hugh had decided he was the greatest thing since the first rhubarb pie, and he had an exaggerated notion of his importance to the team. He seemed to think that without him, they couldn't win. There were quite a few other players who didn't like his attitude, especially when he lorded it over them. It could have been any one of them."

"Or *several* of them," Norman suggested.

"True. Maybe one of those groups of three boys started talking about what fun it would be to see Hugh fall in a hole."

"Perhaps it wasn't even malicious," Delores suggested. "They might not have thought it through at all. They just decided to set a trap for him and they never expected him to fall so hard that he would break his leg and be out for the whole season."

"For the whole year, and then some," Doc corrected her. "It was a nasty break."

"If it wasn't some of the other boys, how about his brother Adam?" Hannah made the suggestion. "Was there a lot of sibling rivalry between Hugh and Adam?"

"It was a lot more than sibling rivalry," Doc said.

"What do you mean?" Norman asked.

"While Hugh was in the hospital, I heard him fight with Adam. It got pretty vicious, verbally of course, since Hugh was in traction. I felt sorry for Adam. It was clear that Hugh had bullied his younger brother for years. Now that Adam was older, he was beginning to fight back, and I figured no good could come of it."

"Do you think Adam could have filled in that hole and set the trap for his brother?" Norman followed up.

Doc shrugged. "It's possible. If Hugh pushed him to the bitter end, Adam could have done it. On the other hand, I don't know if he had the guts to do it."

"What happened to Adam? He doesn't live around here, does he?" Hannah asked.

"Not anymore. Adam earned an academic scholarship to Yale. He went on to another Ivy League school for his master's and doctorate, and I believe he's teaching at UCLA. He's never come back here, and I don't think he ever will."

"Did Hugh go to college?" Hannah was curious.

"No. He might have if he'd gotten an athletic scholarship, but after he broke his leg, that was out of the question. It took him a year to recover, and no college coach wanted to take a chance on a quarterback with a pin in his leg."

"He must have been bitter about that," Delores ventured.

"Oh, he was. Or maybe I should say, he *is*. He's sure that broken leg ruined his life and now he's saddled with a bad back on top of it." Doc Knight paused for a sip of his water. "As soon as he recovered, Hugh went to work for the state on a road repair crew. It's heavy work and it was hard on him physically, but the pay was good and the benefits were great. He only worked on the roads in the summer. The rest of the time he worked in his uncle's hardware store in St. Cloud. Two years ago, he was working on the road crew, picking up caution markers from the back of a state truck, when he slipped and took a bad fall."

"And that's when he hurt his back?" Hannah felt sorry for him in spite of the fact that he didn't sound like a very nice person.

"That's right. They did X-rays and performed surgery, but the fix didn't work. Back surgery's still risky, especially for a six-foot, two-hundred-thirty-pound guy. I would have warned him against it, but he didn't ask me. And now he's living in the family cottage out at Eden Lake, getting state disability."

"Is he badly injured?" Norman asked, and Hannah knew exactly what was running through his mind. If Hugh blamed Matthew for the origin of all his troubles, he'd have a motive for murder. Was Hugh capable of walking into the church in the middle of the night and killing Reverend Matthew?

"I don't know. I haven't seen him since he came back here to Lake Eden. He's holed up out there like a hermit, feeling sorry for himself, no doubt. Hugh's always been good at self-pity. Not that he doesn't have his cross to bear. He does."

"Do you think he still hated Matthew enough to kill him for something he thought Matthew did all those years ago?" Hannah asked.

Doc considered that for a long moment and then he nodded. "Oh, yes. In my opinion, Hugh's not quite right in the head. But I could be wrong. Maybe you two should check him out and see for yourselves."

Pear Crunch Pie
Preheat oven to 425 degrees F.,
(that's a very hot oven,)
rack in the middle position.

The Crust:
one 9-inch deep-dish pie shell, unbaked***

The Topping:
1 cup all-purpose flour *(Scoop it up in a measuring cup and level it off with a table knife.)*

1/2 cup brown sugar *(pack it down in the measuring cup)*

1/4 teaspoon cinnamon

1/4 teaspoon nutmeg *(freshly grated is best, but only use 1/8 teaspoon)*****

1/2 cup salted butter *(1 stick, 4 ounces, 1/4 pound)* cut into small pieces

1/2 cup chopped pecans *(measure after chopping)*

*** *If you're pressed for time, you can buy a frozen one at your grocery store.*

**** *Unlike some herbs and spices, freshly grated nutmeg is stronger than dried.*

231

The Filling:

one large *(20 and 1/2 ounces)* pear halves in syrup OR juice

one small *(8 and 1/2 ounces)* pear halves in syrup OR juice

1/4 cup white *(granulated)* sugar

2 Tablespoons *(1/8 cup)* cornstarch

1/8 teaspoon nutmeg *(half that amount if you use freshly grated)*

1/8 teaspoon salt

1 and 1/2 cups pear liquid *(if you don't have enough, fill in with water)*

1 Tablespoon salted butter *(that's 1/8 of a stick)*

1 teaspoon lemon juice *(freshly squeezed is best)*

You're going to make the topping first, and that's easy. In a small bowl *(or a food processor with the steel blade)* combine the flour, brown sugar, cinnamon, and nutmeg.

If you're doing this by hand, use your fingers or 2 knives and cut the butter into the flour until it looks like cornmeal. *(If you're using a food processor, use the steel blade and process with an on-and-off motion until the resulting mixture looks like cornmeal.)*

Mix in the chopped pecans by hand and

set aside on the counter.

Drain the pear halves, but DON'T THROW AWAY THE JUICE. You'll use it later.

Dry the pear halves thoroughly on paper towels.

On a COLD BURNER, combine the sugar, cornstarch, nutmeg, and salt in a medium-size saucepan. Stir them together until they're thoroughly combined.

Mix in the pear liquid, stirring it well.

Turn the burner on MEDIUM HIGH.

Cook, stirring constantly, until the mixture loses its milky appearance and turns clear. This is a little tricky for anyone who's not used to working with cornstarch. A good rule of thumb is to heat the mixture, stirring constantly with a wooden spoon or a heat-resistant spatula until it just barely reaches the boil. Set your timer for 5 minutes and keep stirring the entire time. That guarantees you've cooked it long enough.

When 5 minutes are up, remove the saucepan from the heat and move it to a cold burner. Stir in the butter and the lemon juice, and let the filling sit there cooling while you work with the pear halves.

Arrange the pear halves, rounded side up, in the bottom of your unbaked pie shell. You don't have to worry about being too artistic, because the pears will be covered with the crunch topping.

When the pear halves are arranged to your satisfaction, place the pan with the pie shell on a drip pan. *(I use a cookie sheet with sides.)* Pour the hot pear pudding you just made over the top of the pear halves as evenly as you can.

Give the topping you made earlier a final stir with a fork. Then sprinkle it over the tops of the pear halves as evenly as you can. This will form the sweet "crunch" part of Pear Crunch Pie. Rhanna's recipe calls for a lot of crunch topping, so heap it on and press it down to form a bumpy, golden brown top crust.

Bake the Pear Crunch Pie at 425 degrees F. for 20 to 25 minutes, or until the topping turns dark golden brown and looks delicious. *(In this case looks are NOT deceiving — it's yummy!)*

Yield: Rhanna's recipe says you can get 8 pieces from this 9-inch pie, but those people must not be big dessert eaters. I always have to make two pies when I invite the family for dinner. Counting Bethany *(who's too little to eat Pear Crunch Pie yet)* there are only 7 of us!

Rhanna used to make a slew of these pies for Sally's Thanksgiving buffet. The

Pear Crunch Pies were a great addition to Sally's wonderful pumpkin pies.

CHAPTER FIFTEEN

Hannah woke up at four in the morning, fifteen minutes before her alarm clock was due to give its series of irritating beeps. She switched it off, clicked on the lamp sitting on her bed table, and swung her legs over the side of the bed. Even though the facts did not support it, she felt well rested in both mind and body, and supremely happy. In short, Hannah felt wonderful, much better than she had in months.

"It was good seeing Norman again, wasn't it Moishe?" she addressed her feline roommate, who was staring at her with wide, startled eyes. The sight of her astonished cat so amused her, she burst into laughter.

The hair on Moishe's back began to stand up as she continued to laugh. He was obviously shocked by her high-spirited alertness at this hour of the morning, and that sent her into another gale of laughter. Normally, she let out a groan of dismay when the alarm woke her. More often than not, she got her slippers on the wrong feet, and she stumbled her way down the hall to the kitchen in dire danger of falling back asleep on the way.

"Rowww!" Moishe protested and jumped off the bed. She heard him run down the hallway, and then there was a thump as he leaped up onto the top floor of the Kitty Kondo Norman had given him. It was clear that Hannah's cat wasn't sure what to make of this new happy person who was inhabiting his mistress's body, and he'd chosen to hide in the safest place he knew while he attempted to figure it out.

"Relax. It's just Norman's influence," she called out as she padded down the hallway, her slippers on the correct feet, to the kitchen to pour her first cup of coffee. The mug in hand, she peered around the kitchen doorway. Moishe was still in his Kitty Kondo. He may have thought he was hidden, but his tail was hanging out of the doorway. "It's okay. I promise not to laugh again until the sun comes up."

Three of the four loaves of apricot bread she'd baked last night with Norman were still on the rack on the counter. Hannah debated cutting a slice for her breakfast. She was saving one loaf for her mother.

Delores loved Sally's Apricot Bread. She'd take the other two loaves down to The Cookie Jar with her and see if she could make a dessert with them that Lisa could serve if they ran out of cookies.

Would they run out of cookies? Hannah thought it was a distinct possibility. Everyone loved to come in, have a cup of coffee and two cookies, and listen to Lisa tell the story of Hannah finding a murder victim. The last time Lisa had performed her "Hannah Finds The Body" story, they had run out of cookies by early afternoon and had closed by two!

There was no way Hannah wanted to serve plain slices of apricot bread. They could get that out at The Lake Eden Inn in Sally's bread basket. She had to think of another dessert, one that used cake or bread. Sally's Apricot Bread was halfway between the two.

Hannah closed her eyes and thought about it for the space of several seconds. Then her eyes popped open again, and she began to smile. She'd make bread pudding with apricot bread. She'd never heard of anyone doing it before, but there was no reason why it couldn't work. But there should be a second ingredient, something that went well with apricots. And that second ingredient should be . . . chocolate! Chocolate and apricots were a natural. Everyone loved them. Cream cheese would be a good addition, too. It would give it a little zing without adding sweetness.

It didn't take long for Hannah to write out her recipe. It would have to be tested, of course, and there was no time like the present.

Less than five minutes later, she'd made the syrup, sliced the apricot bread, and was preparing to assemble her dessert. She poured her syrup, a combination of brown sugar, butter, and apricot pancake syrup in the bottom of her baking pan. Then she spread half the slices of apricot bread with whipped cream cheese and sprinkled them with mini chocolate morsels. There was no reason to think it wouldn't work . . . was there?

She was just spreading the last slice of apricot bread with cream cheese when the phone rang. She glanced at the clock, saw that it was four-thirty in the morning and frowned. Who could be calling her this early? Thoughts of critical illness, car accidents, and broken limbs ran through her mind as she reached out to answer it.

"Hello?" she asked tentatively.

"Hannah. I figured you'd be up by now.

I'm right, aren't I?"

"You're right," Hannah said with a smile. It was Norman, and she was glad to hear from him. "What are *you* doing up this early?"

"I was doing a little research online. I woke up with an idea, and it panned out."

"How so?"

"I'll tell you when I see you. How about breakfast at the Corner Tavern?"

Hannah glanced over at the preparations she'd made. Everything would keep, but she hated to stop now before she'd even tested her new recipe. "I'd love breakfast, but I really should get down to The Cookie Jar. I'm testing a new recipe."

"Okay. You go test your recipe and I'll bring you breakfast. How about bacon and cheese scrambles?"

Hannah's stomach gave a little growl of hunger before she could even say that it was her favorite breakfast dish. "Sounds good to me!" she said instead.

"How about Lisa? Will she be in early?"

"I think so. She usually is."

"I'll get one for her, too. And a big order of hash browns to go with it. Maybe a side or two of bacon, extra crispy, too. Is anybody else likely to be there that early? I can pick up more."

Hannah thought about that for a moment. "I don't think so, but I don't know for sure."

"Okay. If anyone else comes in, call me on my cell phone."

"Will do."

"What time shall I meet you?"

"Let's see . . . I'll just finish up here, take a quick shower, and you can meet me there in . . ." Hannah stopped and looked up at her apple-shaped kitchen clock. As she did so, her eyes grazed the top of the refrigerator. Another sock ball! What in the world was going on?

"You cut out for a minute there," Norman told her. "What time shall I meet you?"

Hannah quickly calculated the time it would take her to drive to town, and how many batches of cookies there were to bake from the dough she'd mixed up last night with Lisa. She could be through assembling the bread pudding in ten minutes, done with her shower in another ten, at The Cookie Jar twenty minutes after that, another ten minutes for the oven to come up to temperature, and even allowing for traffic that shouldn't be present at this hour of the morning, car trouble she hoped would not occur, and other delays that might happen to slow down her departure or her arrival, she could be ready to eat breakfast with

Norman by six-thirty.

"Hannah?"

"It took me a while to figure it out. How about six-thirty?"

"I'll be there. It's going to be great to see you, Hannah."

Hannah was smiling as she echoed his sentiment and hung up the phone. Norman had spent hours with her last night, and he still thought that it would be great to see her this morning. What woman could ask for more than that?

"It smells incredible," Lisa said, mixing up one of her favorite recipes, Raspberry Vinegar Cookies.

"It *should* be okay. They're all good ingredients, and they go together, I think."

"So do I, especially the chocolate and the apricots. Don't worry, Hannah. It's bound to be good."

"I'm not worried that it won't be good. I'm worried that it won't be spectacular."

Lisa laughed. "Good will suit me just . . . is that somebody at the back door?"

Hannah stopped chopping nuts in the food processor and listened for a minute. Lisa was right. Someone was knocking. But it was much too early for Norman. Unless he just couldn't wait any longer to see her and he'd rushed right over here and . . .

"I'll get it," Lisa said when Hannah didn't move from her spot. She hurried to the door, pulled it open and greeted whoever was standing there. "Hey! What are *you* doing up this early?"

"Working. Is she here yet? There's one more thing I need to ask her."

Hannah almost groaned. It was Mike. She wasn't upset to see him. That wasn't it at all. But if he had further questions for her, it would put a damper on their breakfast. She told herself that thinking that was no way to greet the man who'd probably been working all night on Reverend Matthew's murder case. Then she pasted a smile on her face, and gave him a big cheery wave as he came in the door.

"Hi, Mike," she said. "What do you mean, *Is she here?* Of course I'm here. Where else would I be?"

"Taking the day off to recover from shock?"

Hannah shook her head. "No time for shock. We've got cookies to bake, orders to fill, and places to go."

Mike walked over to put his hand on her shoulder. It felt good resting there, and Hannah had the crazy feeling that she was somehow being disloyal to Norman. That

243

was absurd, but she was still uncomfortable. "You said you had a question for me?"

"You bet. Do I smell apricots?"

"You do." Hannah was torn for a moment, but her conscience prodded her into doing the right thing for the man who probably hadn't had time to stop to eat. "It's Apricot Bread Pudding. Norman's going to be here pretty soon with some bacon and cheese scrambles and hash browns from the Corner Tavern. Would you like to stay and have breakfast with us?"

"Yeah! Thanks, Hannah."

"So what's your question?" Hannah asked, deciding to get anything unpleasant out of the way before the food arrived.

"I was going to ask you if you wanted to go out to breakfast, but you asked me to stay to breakfast first."

Lisa went over to pour Mike a cup of coffee while Hannah finished mixing up a triple batch of cookie dough to bake later. Once she'd carried that into the walk-in cooler, she took her cell phone from her apron pocket and gave Norman a quick call.

"Norman?" she said when he answered, "We've got one more. Mike just got here. He's been working all night and I invited him for breakfast with us."

"Okay," Norman said, and he didn't

sound at all upset. "I'll pick up some sausage, too. And maybe an order of biscuits and honey. He's bound to be hungry if he's been working all night. Call me again if anybody else shows up."

Once she stepped out of the walk-in cooler, Hannah had time for only a few sips of coffee before the oven timer rang. She took her bread pudding out of the oven, checked to make sure that the custard had set, and slid the pan on the baker's rack to cool. She was just returning to her coffee when there was another knock at the back door. Norman had arrived. Hannah went to let him in and was shocked to see her mother standing there.

"Hello, dear. I know it's early, but I found out something you really ought to know about . . ." Delores paused, catching her eldest daughter's panicked look. Hannah stepped aside slightly, and her mother put on a quick smile. "Hello, Mike."

"Hi, Delores. Whatever you were about to tell Hannah doesn't affect my murder case, does it?"

"Good grief, no!" Delores looked shocked at the thought. "It was just a little tidbit I learned on the phone last night, but I probably shouldn't repeat it anyway."

"I'm glad you're here, Mother," Hannah

jumped in quickly before Mike could ask her mother another question. "Would you like to stay for breakfast and try a little piece of my experiment?"

"Is that your experiment?" Delores gestured toward the pan on the baker's rack.

"That's it. It's Chocolate Apricot Bread Pudding."

"Made from Sally's Apricot Bread?" Delores guessed.

"That's right."

"Then wild horses couldn't drag me away. I had one piece of that wonderful bread last night and I kept waking up during the night, wishing I had another."

"You didn't wrap a slice in a napkin and stick it in your purse?"

"Hannah!" Delores began to frown. "I only did that once, and it was because I knew I wouldn't have time for breakfast in the morning."

Hannah seated her mother at the workstation and went off to get her a cup of coffee. On the way, she got Norman on her cell phone. "Mother's here," she said, wasting no time on pleasantries.

"Gotcha," Norman said. "Let me know if anyone else comes in."

Hannah had no sooner delivered her mother's coffee than there was another

246

knock at the back door. Hannah opened it to find Andrea standing there, and her sister looked a bit like an avenging angel.

"I need to talk to you alone, Hannah," Andrea said. "Could you step outside a minute?"

"Sure. Just a second," Hannah said, stepping back in and grabbing her cell phone. "Andrea's here," she said the second Norman answered. "I'm expecting the backfield of the Jordan High Gulls next."

Once she'd dropped her cell phone back in her apron pocket, Hannah stepped outside to oblige her sister. Andrea was still looking extremely disturbed. "What is it, Andrea?"

"Hannah!" Andrea exclaimed, the moment the door closed behind them. "How *could* you?"

"How could I what?"

"How could you possibly buy that hot pink top Claire had on sale? I saw it, and it's the totally wrong color for you. You know it doesn't go with your hair!"

Hannah almost laughed out loud. Andrea looked fit to be tied. "You're right, Andrea. I know it doesn't go with my hair."

"If you know it, why did you buy it? I didn't think you were the type of person

247

who'd buy something just because it was on sale."

"I'm not that type of person."

"Then why? You're going to look so awful in that top, Hannah. I just can't bear thinking about it. Promise me you won't wear it anywhere in Lake Eden."

"I promise."

"Thank goodness!" Andrea gave a huge sigh of relief. "And you won't wear it when you're with me . . . right?"

"Right."

"Are you going to wear it at home where no one can see you?"

"No."

"On a trip somewhere that I don't know about?"

"No. Relax, Andrea. I'm not going to wear it at all."

"You're not going to . . ." Andrea stopped and a puzzled expression spread over her face. "If you're not going to wear it at all, why did you buy it in the first place?"

"To send to Edwina Gadsby for her birthday. She sent me one of the best recipes I've ever tried. Everybody loves Edwina's Chocolate-Covered Raisin Cookies."

Bright spots of color began to appear in Andrea's cheeks. She was obviously embarrassed. "Sorry. I really thought you were going to . . . well you know what I thought. I'm sorry I jumped down your throat, Hannah. I was going over Claire's billing last night to see who might like something from the new shipment we just got in, and I saw your name. And then I realized what you'd purchased, and . . . I guess I overreacted."

"Just a bit, but that's okay. It's nice to know that the fashion police are on patrol. Come on in. Mother and Mike are here, and Norman should be arriving any minute."

"Thanks," Andrea said, following as Hannah pulled open the door and stepped in. "What smells so heavenly?"

"Chocolate Apricot Bread Pudding. It's an experiment."

"Can I help you taste test it?"

"Yes. We're all going to have some."

Andrea had just finished greeting Lisa, Mike, and their mother when Norman came in. "Good thing I got extra," he said, handing the take-out boxes from the Corner Tavern to Hannah. "It smells great in here."

Lisa set out plates, silverware, and napkins while Norman began to dish out the eggs, bacon, sausage, hash browns, and biscuits. He passed the plates to Hannah, who delivered them to the hungry guests.

For long moments there was nothing said.

Everyone was too busy eating. Then Norman broke the silence. "Seconds, anyone? We've got plenty."

"Just set the boxes in the center of the table, dear," Delores suggested. "You don't have to wait on us. We can dish it up ourselves."

In a few more minutes, they'd done justice to what Hannah had thought would be way too much food. "What do you think?" she asked the group. "Shall we have Chocolate Apricot Bread Pudding for dessert?"

"Dessert for *breakfast?*" Delores asked. And then, when everyone else nodded, she gave a little shrug. "Why not?"

There was another moment of silence as Hannah passed around bowls filled with bread pudding and topped with heavy cream. Then everyone began to eat. Hannah listened to the sounds of silverware clinking against the sides of the bowls, and smiled. There were a few little moans of enjoyment and an occasional sigh of contentment, but no one took the time to speak. They were all too busy polishing off their desserts. Looking around at the happy and satisfied faces of her family and friends, Hannah knew that if she asked them to name their favorite meal, they'd all answer, "Breakfast! Especially *this* breakfast!"

250

SALLY'S APRICOT BREAD
Preheat oven to 350 degrees F.,
rack in the middle position.

3/4 cup softened butter *(1 and 1/2 sticks, 6 ounces)*

1 package *(8 ounces)* softened cream cheese *(the brick kind, not the whipped kind)*

2 cups white sugar *(granulated)*

2 beaten eggs *(just whip them up in a glass with a fork)*

1/2 teaspoon vanilla extract

1 and 1/2 cups mashed apricots ★★★

3 cups flour *(don't sift — pack it down in the cup when you measure)*

1/2 teaspoon baking powder

1/2 teaspoon baking soda

1/2 teaspoon salt

1 cup chopped pecans

★★★ *You can use fresh apricots and peel and slice your own, or you can buy them already sliced and prepared in the ready-to-eat section at your produce counter, or you can use canned apricots. (I used well-drained canned apricots, two 15-ounce cans, and pureed them in a blender.)*

Hannah's 1st Note: This is a lot easier with an electric mixer.

Beat the butter, cream cheese and sugar together until they're nice and fluffy.

Add the beaten eggs and mix well.

Add the vanilla extract and mix thoroughly.

If you're using fresh apricots, peel and slice them. If you're using jarred or canned apricots, drain them thoroughly. Mash them in a food processor with the steel blade, or puree them in a blender, or squash them with a potato masher until they're pureed. Measure out 1 and 1/2 cups of mashed apricots and add them to your mixing bowl. Mix well.

In another bowl, measure out the flour, baking powder, baking soda and salt. Mix them together.

Gradually add the flour mixture to the apricot mixture, beating at low speed until everything is incorporated.

Mix in the chopped pecans by hand.

Coat the inside of two loaf pans *(the type you'd use for bread)* with Pam or another nonstick cooking spray. Spoon in the apricot bread batter, dividing it as equally as you can between the two pans.

Bake at 350 degrees F. for approximately one hour, or until a long toothpick or skewer inserted in the center comes out clean. *(Mine took exactly 60 minutes.)*

Check your loaves at 50 minutes. If you think the tops are browning too fast, tent a piece of foil over the top and continue to bake until done.

Hannah's 2nd Note: You can also bake this apricot bread in 6 smaller loaf pans, filling them about half full. If you use the smaller pans, you'll need to bake the loaves approximately 45 minutes at 350 degrees F.

Remove your pans from the oven and cool your loaves on a wire rack. Leave them in the pans for 30 minutes.

When 30 minutes have passed, loosen the edges of your loaves by running a knife around the insides of the pans and then turn the loaves out onto the wire rack to cool completely.

This is a dense, moist bread. It should be stored in a cool, enclosed place. When my loaves are completely cool, I slip them in food-size, sealable plastic bags and keep them in the refrigerator. You can also wrap them in a clean kitchen towel and store them in a breadbox . . . if they still make breadboxes, that is.

This bread freezes beautifully if you wrap it in plastic wrap or foil and slip it into a sealable freezer bag.

Yield: This recipes makes two bread-sized

loaves or 6 small loaves.

Hannah's 3rd Note: If you want to make this apricot bread into apricot muffins, spoon the batter into greased (or cupcake papered) muffin tins, filling them 2/3 full, and bake them at 375 degrees F. for 25 minutes or until golden on top.

If you'd like to make mini apricot muffins, fill your mini muffin tins 1/2 full and bake them at 375 degrees F. for 15 to 20 minutes or until slightly golden on top.

CHOCOLATE APRICOT
BREAD PUDDING

Do not preheat the oven yet — this recipe needs to sit for a while before baking.

1/2 cup salted butter *(1 stick, 4 ounces, 1/4 pound)*

1 cup brown sugar, firmly packed

1/2 cup apricot pancake syrup***

1 cup chopped pecans

1 and 1/2 large loaves of Sally's Apricot Bread *(the recipe makes 2 large loaves)*

1/2 cup whipped cream cheese

1/2 cup miniature chocolate chips *(I used Nestle Mini Morsels)*

8 eggs, beaten

2 Tablespoons *(1/8 cup)* white *(granulated)* sugar

2 cups heavy cream *(whipping cream)*

2 teaspoons vanilla extract

1/2 cup salted butter *(1 stick, 4 ounces, 1/4 pound)*

Powdered *(confectioner's)* sugar to sprinkle on top

*** *If you can't find apricot pancake syrup in your grocery store, you can make it yourself by mixing 1/4 cup apricot jam with 1/4 cup light Karo syrup.*

Heat the 1/2 cup butter, the brown sugar, and the apricot syrup in a microwave-safe bowl on HIGH for 2 and 1/2 minutes *(I used a quart measuring cup)* or in a pan on the stove, stirring constantly, until the butter has melted. Take it off the heat or out of the microwave, and set it aside on the counter.

Spray a 9-inch by 13-inch cake pan with Pam or another non-stick cooking spray.

Pour the apricot syrup mixture into the bottom of the pan.

Sprinkle the apricot syrup mixture with the chopped pecans.

Cut the ends off a loaf of Sally's Apricot Bread. Then cut the remainder of the loaf into 14 slices.

Cut one end off the second loaf of Sally's Apricot Bread. Cut the loaf in half. Working with the half without a heel, slice it into 6 pieces.

Lay out all 20 slices of apricot bread on the counter on a piece of wax paper. Spread all of the slices with whipped cream cheese.

Arrange 10 slices of apricot bread, cream cheese side up, in the syrup at the bottom of your baking pan. I put 3 slices against the long side of the baking pan with the bottoms of the slices against the pan wall. The opposite long side also got 3 slices with the bottoms of the slices against the pan wall. One slice went on the short side of the pan with the bottom against the pan wall, and another slice went against the opposite short wall with the bottom side against the pan wall. Two slices went in the middle of the pan with the bottoms of the slices facing each other. You can crowd the slices, even squeeze them to make them fit, but do not overlap the slices.

Sprinkle the 1/2 cup of mini chocolate chips over the cream cheese on the apricot bread slices.

Now place the remaining slices of apricot bread, cream cheese side down, on top of the apricot bread with the chocolate chips. You're making cream cheese, chocolate chip, cream cheese sandwiches.

Press the sandwiches down with a flat metal spatula, or the palms of your impeccably clean hands. That will make the tops adhere to the bottoms when they bake.

Beat the eggs with the sugar. Add the cream and the vanilla, mixing thoroughly. Pour this mixture over the apricot bread sandwiches in the pan.

Cover the pan with plastic wrap or foil and let it stand out on the counter for a minimum of twenty minutes. *(If you're planning a nice dinner party, you can make this in the morning, cover and refrigerator it, and slip it into the oven when your guests arrive so that it's ready to serve for dessert.)*

Preheat your oven to 350 degrees F., rack in the center position.

Take off the plastic wrap. Melt the second stick of butter and drizzle it over the tops of the cream cheese chocolate chip sandwiches.

Bake the Chocolate Apricot Bread Pudding at 350 degrees F., uncovered, for approximately one hour **(60 minutes)** or until the top has browned. Let the pan cool on a wire rack for at least five minutes before you serve.

To serve: Sprinkle the top of the pan with powdered sugar before you carry it to the table. This will make it look more attractive. Use a metal spatula to lift out the individual sandwiches which you've transformed into yummy Chocolate Apricot Bread Pudding. One sandwich is one serving.

Hannah's Note: I like to flip my sandwiches over when I put a serving into a dessert dish. Then my guests can see all the syrupy goodness on the bottom. I also like to top this delicious bread pudding with sweetened whipped cream or

a scoop of softened vanilla ice cream.
Yield: 10 large and yummy servings.

CHAPTER SIXTEEN

"Look at these," Norman said, after Mike had left, laying four pieces of photo paper out on the metal surface of the workstation. "All the school yearbooks are online at the Jordan High Web site. I found Paul's photo and printed it out. And Matthew's senior photo is right here next to his cousin's."

"They look like twins!" Lisa said, her eyes traveling from one to the other and then back again.

"This one," Delores tapped one of the photos.

"That's Paul," Norman answered her unspoken question.

"Paul has more prominent cheekbones, but perhaps that's because he's thinner. You probably could tell which was which if you saw them together."

"Which one is the youngest?" Andrea asked.

"Paul," Norman answered her. "He's two

years younger than Matthew."

"Why do they look so much alike?" Lisa asked.

It was Hannah's turn to explain. "Matthew's father had a younger brother and Matthew's mother had a younger sister. The two younger siblings met at their wedding and got married a year later."

"I wonder if they still look alike," Andrea mused. "I think Reverend Matthew looked like an older version of his yearbook photo. I wish we knew what his cousin Paul looks like now."

"We don't have any way to find out," Hannah told her. "If the private detective Matthew hired to find Paul couldn't do it, our chances aren't very good either."

"Here's the rest of Matthew's senior class," Norman informed them, pointing to the third photo. "And here's a picture of Matthew at the senior prom. He's with his high school girlfriend, and everybody thought they'd get married right after they graduated. Her name was Alice Roste."

"Now it's Alice Roste Vogel," Delores told him. "And they *didn't* get married. According to one of my telephone sources, Matthew broke Alice's heart and she married the oldest Vogel boy on the rebound."

"And that's *our* Alice?" Hannah was surprised.

"That's right," Delores confirmed it. "That's what I was going to tell you when I came in this morning. Then I saw Mike, and I decided I'd better wait. I didn't want him bothering Alice with a lot of questions. This must be terribly hard on her. My source said Alice never really got over loving Matthew."

Andrea reached out to grab Hannah's arm. "Mother's source is right, Hannah. Remember when I told you that I was going over Claire's sales information?"

"I remember."

"Well, one of the invoices was for Alice Vogel. She bought a new dress the day after Reverend Matthew arrived in town."

"That's a big leap to a conclusion," Hannah warned her sister. "What does that sales receipt really prove? Hasn't Alice ever bought a dress from Claire before?"

"No, at least not in the past twelve months. I went through a whole year's worth of invoices, and I think the only reason Alice bought such an expensive dress was so she'd look nice for Reverend Matthew."

"That *does* make sense," Delores said. "It's natural to want to look good when you're meeting an old flame after all these years."

Hannah turned to stare at her mother. Delores had been dressing even better than usual, and that was going some! And she'd bought at least one new dress every week from Claire's most expensive collection. Come to think of it, Bertie had mentioned that Delores had come in to the Cut 'n Curl to have her hair done at least once a week, and she'd gone for the works with a facial and a manicure. Was it because Delores was dating old flames again?

"Don't look so worried, dear," Delores leaned closer to Hannah so that she could speak in an undertone. "Your father was my only old flame. The men I'm dating now are just sparks."

Hannah laughed and gave her mother's hand a squeeze. Sometimes Delores was amazingly perceptive.

"Was Alice at the bon voyage party for Reverend Bob and Claire?" Lisa asked, putting an end to Hannah's speculation about her mother's love life. "I didn't see her there."

"Neither did I," Andrea said.

"I didn't either," Delores told them.

"I honestly don't remember," Hannah said, turning to Norman. "How about you?"

"I don't think so, but there were a lot of people. Of course I was only there for a couple of minutes. Once you're through with your baking, I think we should drop by to see Alice at the bowling alley and ask her."

"She's got Mothers League this morning from ten to noon," Andrea told them. "I know because Lucy Dunwright belongs. She always drops Karen at school, comes in to have a cup of coffee with me at the real estate office, and then goes off to bowl. She says she does it to keep in shape."

"Bowling *is* good exercise," Norman commented. "I wonder if we ought to wait until after twelve. Alice might be too busy with Mothers League to talk to us earlier."

"I don't think so," Delores said quickly. "Once you get your shoes, or put on your own if you have them, there's really nothing for Alice to do. She has automatic pin setting machines and automatic scoring machines. Unless they malfunction, Alice just sits on a stool behind the snack bar counter and reads a book."

Hannah was shocked. As far as she knew, her mother didn't bowl. "How do *you* know?" she asked.

"I'm on a Seniors' League team with Bud Hauge, Joe Dietz, and Doc. We bowl every

Sunday afternoon."

Hannah managed to keep a straight face, but she couldn't help imagining her mother flirting with all three men she was dating, and playing them off, one against the other.

"Is it like bowling for dollars?" Lisa asked. "Herb and I did that once."

"In a way. Our league bowls for beer."

"For *beer*?" Hannah was surprised. "But you don't even *like* beer."

"That's true. The only time I ever liked it was once when I was dating your father. It was a really hot day, the beer was ice cold, and we were watching a softball game at the lake."

"So what do you do if your team wins the beer?" Norman asked her.

"We give it to Joe. He likes beer. Doc doesn't drink it and neither does Bud."

"What does the Mothers League play for?" Lisa asked Andrea.

"Babysitting. The lowest scoring member on the losing team has to give two hours of babysitting to the highest scoring member of the winning team. Lucy got stuck with the Janowski twins last week." Andrea lowered her voice even though no one was there except the five of them. "Lucy loves kids and she's great with them, but she said the twins were holy terrors."

■ ■ ■ ■

Norman opened the glass door to Ali's Alley for Hannah, who was armed with a bag of cookies for Alice. The din of loud female voices, bowling balls hitting the wooden surface with resounding thuds, and the good-natured catcalls between the team members rolled out to greet them.

"It's noisy in here," Hannah said. "I didn't expect the Mothers League to be so noisy."

"They make more noise than the men," Alice said, coming over to greet them just in time to hear Hannah's comment. "And you ought to hear the seniors. They're positively rowdy."

Hannah handed Alice the bag of cookies. "These are for you, Alice. Lisa made Raspberry Vinegar Cookies and she said they were your favorites."

"Lisa's right. They're a lot like shortbread, and I love shortbread." Alice turned to Norman. "You're not pulling teeth today?"

"Not today. I'm helping Hannah."

Just for a second, a puzzled expression crossed Alice's face. And then her pale complexion turned even paler. "Matthew," she said. "That's why you're here. You're investigating Matthew's murder."

"I'm afraid so," Hannah responded and then she recalled what Delores had said about never getting over your first love. "I'm sorry for your loss, Alice."

"My loss?" Alice gave a bitter laugh. "My loss happened a week after graduation when Matthew left Lake Eden for good. I really thought that he'd at least come by to say goodbye, but . . ." she stopped speaking and swallowed hard. "That's not important now. It's all in the past and better off forgotten."

Jilted. That's a motive for murder. Hannah's mind spun into high gear. *Matthew disappointed her. Maybe she even thinks he ruined her life, since she married Butch Vogel less than three months later and that didn't turn out well at all.*

Hannah mentally reviewed what she knew about Butch Vogel. He was a fast-talking, hard-drinking guy with more muscle than brain who hung out at the Eagle. If she remembered correctly, the marriage had lasted less than a year. There was a scandal involving Butch and one of the waitresses, and Alice had filed for divorce.

"Why so quiet, Hannah?" Alice asked her. "Are you trying to figure out if I killed Matthew?"

"Yes," Hannah said. Alice had the reputation for saying exactly what was on her mind, and the only way to address such candor was to be just as outspoken herself. "It's a good motive, Alice."

"You bet it is! If he'd come back to Lake Eden during that first year, I might have actually done it. But now . . . ? It's too late, Hannah. Matthew was a different person, and so am I. Do you know I bought a new dress when I couldn't really afford one just to impress him with how I'd kept my looks? I even had Bertie do a weave to cover up the gray in my hair."

"I thought you looked different," Norman said. "Your hair's beautiful, Alice. Whatever a weave is, it looks good on you."

Alice laughed. "Thanks! I wouldn't expect a man to know what it is. Matthew noticed it, though. I know he did. He called me and invited me to to dinner on Monday night. I was excited about going out with him again. I was even going to go down to Claire's on Monday morning and buy another new dress. But then . . ." she stopped and blinked several times. "Then I heard the news on KCOW radio and Jake and Kelly said that Matthew was dead."

"Thanks for driving, Norman." Hannah said as she slid into the passenger seat. "I've got to make some notes."

Norman glanced over at her as he started the car. "You're adding Alice to the suspect page?"

"Yes, but just so that I can cross her out. You don't kill your high school boyfriend when he's just asked you to go out with him again."

"I don't get it." Norman pulled away from the curb and out into the street.

"What don't you get?"

"Why you wrote down Alice's name when you already knew you were going to cross her out."

"It's simple. It gives me a record of who I interviewed and why. Alice no longer has a motive, but she did until Matthew asked her to go out for dinner. And that reminds me. Do you have your cell phone handy?"

"Of course. Who do you want to call?"

"Sally. I want to see if Matthew made a reservation for Monday night. If he did, that'll substantiate Alice's story."

"You think she's lying?"

"No, but if Alice *did* kill Reverend Matthew, it would be a great cover-up, wouldn't it?"

RASPBERRY VINEGAR COOKIES
Preheat oven to 325 degrees F., rack in the middle position.

1 cup *(2 sticks, 8 ounces, 1/2 pound)* salted butter, softened

1 cup white *(granulated)* sugar

1 teaspoon raspberry vinegar***

1 teaspoon baking soda

1 teaspoon rum extract****

1 and 1/2 cups all-purpose flour *(pack it down in the cup and level it off)*

1 cup chopped pecans *(measure after chopping)*

*** *If you can't find raspberry vinegar in your store, you can use any fruit flavored vinegar or just plain old white vinegar. The vinegar is there to react with the baking soda, so any kind will do. I would caution against Balsamic. It has a heavy flavor that might not be good in these cookies. Then again, I haven't tried it. It could be wonderful.*

**** *If you don't want to use rum extract, use any other flavor of extract you like, including vanilla.*

Combine the softened butter and the sugar. Mix them until they're light and fluffy. *(You can do this with an electric mixer if you like.)*

Add the raspberry vinegar and mix it in.

Add the baking soda and mix that in.

Add the rum extract and mix it in.

Add the cup and a half of all-purpose flour. Mix thoroughly.

Mix in the chopped pecans.

Drop by spoonfuls on a greased *(I sprayed mine with Pam)* baking sheet, 12 cookie mounds to a sheet. *(Lisa and I used a 2-teaspoon scooper down at The Cookie Jar.)*

Bake at 325 degrees F. for 18 to 20 minutes, or until slightly golden on top.

Remove from the oven and let the cookies cool on the cookie sheet for 2 minutes.

Transfer the cookies to a wire rack and let them cool completely.

Store these cookies in a cookie jar or an air-tight container so that they remain moist and soft.

Hannah's Note: These cookies remind me of Lorna Doone shortbread cookies, except they're better. If you'd like to experiment with them, try adding mini chocolate chips to a batch, or pressing a chocolate candy into the center of each cookie before you bake it.

Yield: approximately 3 and 1/2 dozen to 4

dozen sweet and buttery cookies, depending on cookie size.

CHAPTER SEVENTEEN

Eden Lake was pretty in the winter. Actually, Eden Lake was pretty at any time of the year. During the spring, the water looked fresh and clear, surrounded by trees sprouting tiny new leaves in vivid green, and wildflowers gracing the banks. There were yellow and purple irises that someone had planted years ago, and white flowers called bloodroot that would stain your hands red if you snapped off the stems to pick them. Violets in pink and yellow nestled at the edges of the wooded hollows, and there were pussy willows with furry gray flowers called catkins. When Hannah was a child, she'd hoped that if she left them in water long enough, they'd turn into little cats. If you were very lucky in the spring and you had sharp eyes, you might catch a glimpse of a rare showy lady's slipper, the Minnesota state flower, protected by law, and hidden in the damp, dark depths of the woods.

Summer was beautiful, too, bringing blooms to the area surrounding the lake. There were gypsy flowers along the sides of the gravel road that circled the shoreline, their small red blooms on the very ends of their stalks, waving at you with pretty little flags as you drove by. Gray-headed corn-flowers vied for attention with their bright yellow blooms around dark gray centers. Field thistle joined them in the sunny areas, their blooms spotting the wild grasses with pink and purple color.

Then there was the lake, itself. The sparkling water was dotted with white and yellow water lilies, and yellow lotus. Norman had shown her one quiet inlet containing a veritable garden of aquatic color that someone had planted there years ago. The surface of the lake created a waving reflection of the trees and sky, and the sunsets were simply spectacular with their vivid oranges, pinks, and reds mirrored in the gently rippling waters.

Fall brought another kind of beauty to Eden Lake. Cattails thrived on the shoreline and in the shallow areas of the lake, standing tall in the autumn breezes. Bulrushes sported brownish flowers on the ends of their stems. Field thistle was still blooming. It would continue until cold weather set in, and heath aster with its white and yellow flowers bloomed on the dry hillsides. The water took on a greenish cast from the algae that multiplied in the last hot months of summer, and long-legged cranes patrolled the banks. Canada geese flew overhead in ragged vees, and the deciduous trees around the lake wore orange, yellow, red, and mahogany-colored leaves.

Then winter came, and everything except the evergreens donned black and white. Trees lifted their bare twisted branches heavenward to catch the rays of feeble winter sun, and the lake was covered with snow. Today the surface of the lake was a sheet of glistening white, unbroken but for the hillocks of snow formed by the wind. The glare was almost blinding, and Hannah looked down at her notebook again to rest her eyes. Hugh Kohler lived in the fourth cabin past the huge oak tree with a yellow Minnesota Breeder's sign nailed to its trunk. It was a faded blue cabin, and someone had propped up the sagging front porch with cinderblocks.

"There's the tree Doc told us about," Hannah pointed to the huge oak with a faded sign on its trunk. "Hugh's cabin is the fourth one on our right. It's blue."

Norman drove carefully, and Hannah was

glad. The snow had blown across the gravel road in drifts that almost reached the hubcaps, and this was no place to get stuck! She hadn't seen any cell phone transponders since they'd left the main road and not many people wintered at the lake. If they got hung up in a snowdrift and Hugh Kohler wasn't home, they'd have to hike out to the road to get help.

"That's it," Hannah said as she spotted a faded blue cabin. "It's the one with the moose antlers over the door."

Norman took one look at the driveway and shook his head. "I don't want to risk pulling in. Unless that's a really short mailbox, the snow's a lot deeper in the driveway."

"That's okay. I'm wearing my boots. How about you?"

"I've got mine in the back seat. They're on the floor behind my seat. Can you reach them?"

Hannah reached back, retrieved the boots, and Norman pulled them on. Then she got out of the car and walked toward the house. Norman had been right. The snow was a lot deeper in the driveway, and Hannah was glad that they hadn't attempted to drive up. It took a while to wade through the knee-deep drifts, but they managed to get to the door.

Norman knocked and Hannah pasted a smile on her face. She still wasn't sure what questions to ask to determine whether Hugh was guilty or innocent, and she just hoped she could come up with something before the door opened.

A split second later, the door opened and Norman and Hannah blinked in shock as they found themselves staring down the twin barrels of a double-barreled shotgun.

"I'm really sorry about that," Hugh said, "It's just that it's pretty isolated out here, and they still haven't caught that murderer who escaped from Stillwater last week. I was listening to Jake and Kelly on the news this morning, and someone reported that they'd seen him around here."

"That's okay. No harm done," Norman told him.

"I'm kind of helpless, you know? Being in this wheelchair and all. I've got the phone, but the lines are down and my truck won't start."

"If you need a ride to town, we can take you," Hannah offered. "What's wrong with your truck?"

"The battery gave out on Sunday and I'm

the only one around for miles. I'm just lucky I made it back here with my supplies before it gave up the ghost."

"Then you have enough food?" Norman asked.

"Plenty." Hugh turned to Hannah. "It's nice of you to offer to give me a ride, but all I really need is for someone to call the garage and ask Cyril to send out one of his mechanics with a new battery."

"Are you sure?" Hannah asked.

"I'm sure. I can stand up and even walk a little with a walker. It's just that I'm not supposed to put a strain on my back."

"That must make it tough to cook for yourself," Norman commented.

"Not really. I'm all set up here. I eat a lot of sandwiches and I've got the microwave on a table I can reach from the wheelchair. Soup and a sandwich is a pretty good meal."

"Well, I brought you cookies." Hannah held out the bag of cookies she'd packed for Hugh.

"Hey! That's nice of you. What brings you all the way out here, anyway?"

"Church work," Norman said before Hannah could open her mouth. "We heard you were injured, and we wanted to make sure you had everything you needed."

"Well, you sure came at the right time!

Thanks, guys. I really appreciate it. You're not going to pray over me, or try to save me, or anything like that, are you?"

Norman shook his head. "It's not that kind of church work."

"We've got more visits to make, so we'd better go," Hannah said, getting to her feet.

"Right. And don't worry about a thing," Norman added. "We'll call Cyril and tell him what you need."

When the door closed behind them, Hannah gave a huge sigh of relief. She waited until they'd waded several feet from the house, and then she reached out to tap his arm.

"Church work?" she asked with a grin.

"It *is* church work, in a way," Norman said.

"Just how do you figure that?"

"We're trying to solve Reverend Matthew's murder, and it happened in the church office. If that's not church work, I don't know what is."

CHAPTER EIGHTEEN

"I'll help you bake," Norman offered when they got back to The Cookie Jar.

"Okay, but do you really want to bake?"

"Yes. Ever since you showed me how easy it was to make popovers, I *like* to bake. I think I could be good at it if I follow your recipes."

Hannah smiled. That was a compliment, and it deserved her acknowledgment. "How about starting with brownies?"

"That's a great place to start! Is it okay if I make your Brownies Plus? They're delicious."

"That's fine with me." Hannah flipped through her sheet-protected recipe book and turned to Brownies Plus. "I think I have some Symphony bars in the pantry. Everybody loves those in the middle layer."

Once she'd gotten Norman started with her standard-size bowl and pan, Hannah turned to the next recipe on her list. It was another bar cookie, and she couldn't think of a single customer who didn't like it.

"What are you making?" Norman asked her.

"Chocolate Euphoria Cookie Bars."

"What are they?"

"Six-layer cookie bars with chocolate cookie crumbs on the bottom, semi-sweet chocolate chips next, miniature marshmallows on top of that, white chocolate chips sprinkled on the marshmallows, chocolate cereal layered on top with some milk chocolate chips over everything."

"Wow! That's a chocolate euphoria, all right!"

"You'd better believe it. I tested the recipe last week on Andrea, and she said that after eating only two, she felt like she was walking on air."

"That's a good testimonial."

"Tracey's is even better. She said her mother was in a good mood all day, even when she brought up the subject of a puppy again."

"I think I should try one of those."

"You got it. I'll just assemble them, pop them in the oven, and we can try them when they've baked and cooled. And then I'll help you with the Brownies Plus if you need it."

Hannah grabbed the ingredients and

281

several pans, and made short work of assembling the cookie bars. She put them into the oven, set the timer for twenty-five minutes, and turned to see how Norman was coming along.

"Done," Norman said, gesturing toward his pan of brownies.

"You're fast," Hannah complimented him. "You finished at the same time I did."

"But you made four pans and I only made one."

"That doesn't matter. I've been doing this at least four times longer than . . ." Hannah stopped speaking as Marge came into the kitchen with two empty cookie jars. "You need *more* cookies?"

"Yes. Everyone loves Lisa's story. A couple of people have been here twice, and new people are coming in the door in droves."

"What's a drove, anyway?" Norman asked Hannah.

"Cowboys who went on cattle drives to take livestock to market were known as drovers," Hannah told him. "I guess that means that the droves were herds of cattle."

"Makes sense to me."

Marge filled the cookie jars from the cookies on the baker's racks and headed back out to the coffee shop. "I don't want to miss this part," she said. "It's my favorite. Lisa's really good today. Do you want me to stuff a dishtowel in the door so you can hear?"

"Yes," Norman answered, and Hannah could do nothing but agree. It wasn't that she didn't like Lisa's stories. It brought them lots of business. But she'd already found Reverend Matthew's body once, and she wasn't too keen on hearing it again.

". . . knocked once, but there was no answer," Lisa's voice carried to the kitchen. "So our Hannah knocked again. *Reverend Matthew? Are you in there?* Hannah asked, but again there was no answer. So Hannah, whose heart was beating like a caged lion, turned the knob and inched open the door."

Norman looked over at Hannah. "A *caged lion?*" he repeated.

"Don't ask me. Lisa tells these stories in her own way."

"But is that what happened?"

"Not exactly, but it's close enough."

"Then, when she opened the door a bit wider," Lisa continued, "Hannah saw the one sight in the world that turned her blood to ice."

There were gasps from Lisa's audience and a low murmur that carried all the way to the kitchen. Everyone knew what was coming next. Hannah thought she recognized Florence's voice. She must have called in one of her extra checkers and left the Lake Eden Red Owl so that she could come to hear Lisa's story. And then a very familiar voice said, "Go on, Lisa."

Hannah turned to Norman in shock. "Was that Michelle?" she asked, wondering if she'd heard wrong.

"It was Michelle," Norman answered with a nod. "She must have taken the bus down when she heard about Reverend Matthew's murder."

"I don't know about you, but I would have turned tail and run," Lisa addressed her audience directly. "How about you?"

"No way I'd go in there!" a familiar voice declared, and Hannah knew it was Bonnie Surma.

"I might have, but I would have thought long and hard about it first."

"Doug Greerson," Hannah said to Norman.

"I would have kept the door closed and called the police from my cell phone," another voice stated, a female voice that Hannah didn't recognize.

"That's Bev," Norman told her. "She must have walked up here on her lunch hour."

Hannah gave silent thanks that she hadn't decided to tell the story herself. Even though they were here, together, on a quest for the killer, she was still enjoying her day with Norman. She didn't want to be reminded of Doctor Bev and how much time Norman's former fiancée spent with him on every other day at the dental office.

"Tell us more, Lisa. I can't stand the suspense!" a male voice urged her.

"Earl Flensburg," Hannah said to Norman.

"What happened next?" Carrie's anxious voice rang out.

"There's my mother," Norman said with a smile. "I don't think they've been apart more than ten minutes since they got married."

"Our Hannah didn't stop or call for reinforcements," Lisa continued. "She didn't even hesitate. She just squared her shoulders, took a deep breath, and walked right in. She may have *felt* like turning tail and running, but she didn't. Her legs were trembling, her breath was coming in little gasps like an old-fashioned steam locomotive just pulling away from the roundhouse, and her teeth were chattering, but she forced herself to move forward toward Reverend Matthew to feel for a pulse."

"Why did she do *that?*"

"Doug Greerson again," Hannah said

softly to Norman. "He's really getting into it."

"Hannah felt she owed it to him," Lisa explained, "that if there was any thread of life remaining, she'd pick up the phone and call for the ambulance. But of course there wasn't. Reverend Matthew was stone-cold dead. And then, right then and there, is when it happened, the most unexpected sound in the world."

"The phone?" Doug guessed.

"No, not the phone. It was a voice from above. Reverend Matthew's voice."

There were more gasps, a whole roomful of them, and several startled exclamations.

"And Reverend Matthew's voice said, *The wages of sin is death*."

"Come on, Lisa," Earl broke the stunned silence. "Everybody here knows that's impossible. You said Reverend Matthew was dead, and dead men don't talk."

"It wasn't Reverend Matthew," a voice called out from the back of the office shop. "It was Jacob!"

"Pete Nunke," Hannah explained to Norman.

"Who's Jacob?" Carrie asked Pete.

"That's my mynah bird. Reverend Bob and Claire kept him for me when I was in the hospital, and Grandma said he could stay with her until I could get out of this darn wheelchair. She told me that Reverend Matthew spent a lot of time with Jacob, trying to teach him Bible verses and stuff like that."

"You heard it from Jacob's owner himself," Lisa said, taking charge of her story again. "But our Hannah didn't know that Reverend Matthew had taken Jacob to the church office with him and set his cage on the bookcase. When Jacob said, *The wages of sin is death,* in an imitation of Reverend Matthew's voice, our Hannah nearly jumped out of her skin!"

"Gracious, yes!" Bertie Straub said, and Hannah wondered if she'd canceled all of her appointments for the afternoon. Bertie had come in when they opened, Hannah had seen her, and she'd spotted Bertie again when she'd left with Norman. Now Bertie was back once again. The owner of the Cut 'n Curl must have every one of Lisa's lines memorized by now.

"As soon as Hannah realized that Jacob was the one imitating Reverend Matthew's voice, she gave a deep sigh of relief. But then there was another sound that startled her. The phone on the desk, right next to Reverend Matthew's head, began to ring."

The phone rang, and for a split second

Hannah wondered how Lisa had arranged that. Then she realized that it was The Cookie Jar phone, and she leaped up to answer it. "The Cookie Jar. This is Hannah."

"Hannah!" Grandma Knudson's voice was quavery and breathless. "Hannah!"

"Grandma Knudson, are you okay?" Hannah asked, keeping her voice as calm as possible. Grandma Knudson sounded upset beyond belief.

"Yes. Yes. I am. Oh, Hannah! The most amazing thing has happened!"

"What is it, Grandma Knudson?" Hannah wondered if the shock of Reverend Matthew's murder and the stress of the past twenty-four hours had taken its toll on Grandma Knudson's health.

"It's Matthew! You've got to come right away, Hannah! Matthew isn't dead. He's alive!"

CHOCOLATE EUPHORIA COOKIE BARS
Preheat oven to 350 degrees F.,
rack in the middle position.

1/2 cup butter *(one stick, 4 ounces, 1/4 pound)*

1 and 1/2 cups chocolate wafer crumbs *(or Oreo cookie crumbs)****

1 cup *(6 ounces)* semi-sweet chocolate chips

2 cups miniature marshmallows

1 can *(14 ounces)* sweetened condensed milk *(NOT evaporated milk!)*

1 cup *(6 ounces)* white chocolate chips *(or vanilla chips)*

2 cups Cocoa Puffs cereal *(or any other chocolate crunchy cereal)*****

1 cup *(6 ounces)* milk chocolate chips

*** *My store had Nabisco Famous Chocolate Wafers, but they weren't crumbed. I zooped them up in my food processor with the steel blade. The 9-ounce package of Nabisco Famous Chocolate Wafers made about 2 cups of crumbs.*

**** *I couldn't find Cocoa Puffs in my neighborhood grocery store, so I used chocolate Cocoa Krispies (like Rice Krispies, only chocolate).*

Spray a 9-inch by 13-inch cake pan with Pam *(or another nonstick cooking spray)* and set it aside to wait for its yummy contents.

Melt the butter in a small microwave-safe bowl on HIGH for 50 seconds.

If you bought chocolate wafers, break them down into crumbs with your food processor or put them in a large, sealable plastic bag and crush them with a rolling pin. Measure out the chocolate wafer crumbs *(or the Oreo cookie crumbs)* and add them to the bowl with the melted butter. Stir the cookie crumbs and the butter until everything is moistened. *(The resulting mixture will resemble wet, dark sand.)*

Spread the butter and cookie crumb mixture in the bottom of your cake pan and spread it out as evenly as you can. Pat it smooth with the palms of your impeccably clean hands or with the blade of a metal spatula.

Sprinkle on the semi-sweet chocolate chips. Try to distribute them as evenly as possible.

Arrange the miniature marshmallows on top of the chips as evenly as you can.

Open the can of sweetened condensed milk and pour it over the top of the marshmallows as evenly as you can.

Sprinkle the white chocolate chips on top, trying for an even distribution. Your goal is to get something of every ingredient in each cookie bar when you cut them.

Measure out the Cocoa Puffs *(or whatever chocolate cereal you used)* and spread it out on top of the white chocolate chips. Again, try for an even distribution.

Sprinkle the milk chocolate chips over the chocolate cereal as evenly as you can.

Press everything in the pan down with the flat blade of a metal spatula. *(If the cereal crunches a bit, that's okay.)*

Bake the Chocolate Euphoria Cookie Bars at 350 degrees F. for 20 to 25 minutes. *(Mine took 24 minutes.)*

Remove the cookie bars from the oven and cool them in the pan on a cold stovetop burner or on a wire rack.

When the Chocolate Euphoria Cookie Bars reach room temperature, cut them into brownie-sized pieces right in the pan. Don't take them out unless you're going to eat them immediately.

You can now refrigerate the cookie bars in their pan to set up firmly.

Hannah's 1st Note: If you don't cut the bars before you put them in the refrigerator, you may have a problem. They're very firm when they're chilled.

When you're ready to serve, use a metal spatula to remove the cookie bars from the pan. No one will be able to resist.

Yield: 23 to 35 rich, decadent cookie bars, depending on how generous you are when you cut them. *(This yield would be from 24 to 36 bars, but I know you'll eat one right away.)*

Hannah's 2nd Note: These cookie bars are a huge hit at The Cookie Jar. They especially appeal to hardcore chocoholics like Mother. Andrea warns me that they're extremely rich, so you should "save" your child by eating half of his or her Chocolate Euphoria Bar before handing it over.

Hannah's 3rd Note: Mother actually said she thought I should frost Chocolate Euphoria Cookie Bars with Fudge Frosting! She really is incorrigible.

CHAPTER NINETEEN

The first thing Hannah noticed when they pulled into the parsonage driveway was that there were no fresh tire tracks coming up the drive. Clara Hollenbeck's car had been parked at the back of the house when Hannah had left on Monday after finding Reverend Matthew's body, but the Hollenbeck sisters must have left to run some errands for Grandma Knudson. That meant Grandma Knudson was alone, and she was obviously confused if she thought that Reverend Matthew was still alive.

"I wonder if I should have put in a call to Doc Knight to meet us here," she said, turning to Norman.

"You can call him later if he's needed. Let's go in and see what's going on with Grandma Knudson first."

"Right." Hannah got out of the car and retrieved the platter of Chocolate Euphoria Cookie Bars she'd placed on Norman's back seat. Grandma Knudson would need chocolate. There was no doubt about that. She was obviously upset when she'd called Hannah at The Cookie Jar and the endorphins in the chocolate would make her feel better. There were plenty of endorphins in Chocolate Euphoria Cookie Bars with their six layers of chocolate.

Hannah motioned to Norman to follow her and climbed the back steps to the porch. They entered through the door that was never locked and walked past the table filled with several wire racks that Grandma used to cool pies and cakes in a jiffy in the cold winter weather. The kitchen door was also unlocked. Grandma Knudson opened it first thing in the morning and didn't secure it until nightfall. Hannah stepped into the warm kitchen with Norman following at her heels, and called out to Grandma Knudson.

"Hi, Grandma Knudson! It's Hannah, and Norman came with me. Are you here?"

"We're in the sitting room," Grandma Knudson answered in what Hannah thought was a surprisingly strong voice. "Help yourself to a cup of coffee and come on back."

"*We're* in the sitting room?" Norman repeated, frowning slightly.

"That's what she said. I heard it, too.

Maybe somebody from the church is here."

Norman nodded, but he didn't look convinced. "I'll get the coffee. You carry the chocolate cookie bars in."

It didn't take long for Norman to pour two cups of coffee. Since both of them drank it black, there was no need to look around for cream and sugar. Norman, a cup in each hand, followed Hannah as she led the way to Grandma Knudson's sitting room.

"We're here!" Hannah said cheerily, stepping into the room. "I brought you some chocolate . . ."

"Whoa!" Norman exclaimed, almost spilling their coffee as Hannah stopped abruptly in her tracks. "What in the world is . . . oh!"

For a long moment, no one spoke. Hannah and Norman stood there in shock, staring at the man seated on Grandma Knudson's pink davenport.

"Hello, Hannah and Norman." Grandma Knudson turned in her chair to greet them. "Meet the *real* Reverend Matthew Walters. He came to see me the second that he heard he was dead."

"You look exactly like him!" Hannah said, once explanations had been given.

"I know," the real Reverend Matthew said.

"We always looked alike. I still don't know why Paul came here pretending to be me, but I certainly intend to find out. My poor secretary was beside herself when she heard that I was dead."

"Colleen?" Hannah asked, unable to resist a little test of her own.

"Corrine," Reverend Matthew corrected her. "I was visiting some friends in Wisconsin, and I called in to see if I had any messages. I thought Corrine was going to faint when she heard my voice."

"You gave me a nasty shock, too," Grandma Knudson said, "even though you tried not to startle me."

"I know I did," Reverend Matthew said, getting up to stand behind Grandma Knudson's chair and pat her shoulder. "I'm so sorry about that. There just wasn't any easy way to tell you."

Grandma Knudson reached up to put her hand over his. "Well, I'm happy now. You have no idea how horrible I felt when I . . ."

"It's not good to dwell on it," Reverend Matthew interrupted her. "Have one of Hannah's cookie bars. The sugar will do you good."

"Not to mention the chocolate," Hannah couldn't help but add. And then she turned to Reverend Matthew. "What happens now?

Will you go down to the hospital to . . ." she stopped speaking, not wanting to upset Grandma Knudson again by mentioning that Paul's body would need to be positively identified.

"Of course I will. It's one of the reasons I asked Grandma Knudson to call someone to come and stay with her. Her friends are out getting groceries and doing some things for the church. Grandma's not sure how long that'll take, and I don't want to leave her alone. Will you stay with her?"

"Stop!" Grandma Knudson said, turning around to frown at Reverend Matthew. "It's not like I'm feeble, you know! I'm perfectly capable of staying here by myself."

"I can tell you are. You're just as feisty as you were when I was a teenager," Reverend Matthew said with a laugh. "But I don't like the thought of leaving you here by yourself. Won't you please humor me on this?"

"Well . . . since you put it that way . . . all right," Grandma Knudson conceded, and then she turned back to Hannah and Norman. "Matthew always could talk anybody into anything."

"Would you like to take a couple of these cookie bars with you for the road?" Hannah asked Reverend Matthew. Her offer had two purposes. One was exactly as she stated, to give him something to enjoy while he drove to the hospital. The other purpose was more devious. She wanted to see how he'd react to the offer of chocolate.

"Thanks, Hannah. That's really nice of you, but I'd better not. I try to be careful around chocolate. It hasn't really bothered me in years, but I talked to a doctor about it and he advised me not to overdo it. He said the allergens could build up in my system again, and I could have a bad reaction."

Interesting, Hannah thought to herself. *I'd better check that out with Doc Knight.*

Reverend Matthew bent down to place a kiss on the top of Grandma Knudson's head. "I'll be back just as soon as I can," he told her. "If you don't mind, I'll go out the front door. I parked my rental car on the street."

Hannah waited until she heard the front door close behind Reverend Matthew, and then she turned to Grandma Knudson. "Are you really all right?"

"I'm fine, thanks to these," Grandma Knudson gestured toward the platter of cookie bars. "What do you call them, Hannah?"

"Chocolate Euphoria Cookie Bars."

"Well, they live up to their name!"

Grandma Knudson reached for another. "I shouldn't, but I can't seem to stop eating them. Maybe you should call them Chocolate Addiction Bars."

"That might send the wrong message to my customers," Hannah said with a chuckle.

Grandma Knudson smiled, but she quickly sobered. "I still can't believe Paul had me fooled into thinking he was Matthew."

"From what Hannah tells me, he *didn't* have you fooled," Norman reminded her. "Hannah said you suspected that Matthew wasn't Matthew from the very beginning."

"Yes, but Hannah and Andrea called the seminary and his secretary explained away all of my suspicions."

Hannah shook her head. "Not *all* of your suspicions. You suspected that something about the adult Matthew didn't fit the memories you had of him as a teenager. You knew something was wrong, even if you couldn't identify exactly what it was, and you were absolutely right about that."

"That's true." Grandma Knudson sat up a little straighter, and Hannah knew they'd given her back her pride in her ability to judge people's character. "I was beginning to doubt myself, you know."

"Well you shouldn't have," Norman said,

"not when you were right all along. The fake Reverend Matthew fooled everyone else, but he couldn't fool you."

"The fake Reverend Matthew," Grandma Knudson repeated, and as they watched, her face turned pale.

"What is it?" Hannah asked her.

"We've got a real problem on our hands," Grandma Knudson stated, and then she stopped and took a deep breath. "Paul was never ordained as a minister. I know that for a fact. And if Matthew identifies the person who impersonated him as his cousin Paul, any holy sacraments he performed are . . ." Grandma Knudson stopped speaking and frowned. "I don't know, not for certain, but . . . oh, this is truly a disaster!"

"*What* is?" This time Norman asked the question.

"Paul wasn't a minister. He was a layman. From what Matthew believes, he wasn't even active in the church. That means that every christening, every act of holy communion, every prayer and blessing he offered, and even every marriage he performed is . . . is . . ." Grandma Knudson stopped and shook her head. "It's as if it never happened! Nothing he did will be recognized by the church!"

300

■ ■ ■ ■

"Where did you go, Hannah?" Michelle asked her when Hannah and Norman got back to The Cookie Jar.

"We went to see Grandma Knudson." Hannah paused. If she told Michelle what had happened, she'd just have to repeat herself when she told Lisa. "Will you ask Marge if she'll take over in the coffee shop for ten minutes? And then will you ask Lisa to come back here? I'll need you to come with her."

"Is there trouble with Reverend Matthew's murder investigation?" Michelle asked.

"You could say that. Please go get Lisa, Michelle. The sooner I tell you the new developments in this case, the sooner we can start figuring out what to do about it."

Michelle must have conveyed Hannah's urgency to Lisa, because they were back in the kitchen almost immediately. Hannah gave them the new facts she'd learned in as few words as possible, winding up her summary of the events at the parsonage with one final statement. "So now we're waiting to hear from Grandma Knudson. She promised to call us when the real Reverend Matthew gets back to tell us if the murder

301

victim is really Paul."

The only sound in the kitchen was the low hum of the furnace. Hannah had seen fish out of water, gasping for air, and that was precisely how Lisa and Michelle appeared. Their mouths were open, their eyes were wide, and the only thing they weren't doing was flopping around on the floor. It took several seconds for them to recover, and Michelle was the first to speak.

"You mean . . . everything just got turned upside down."

"That's it precisely. And there's the other problem, too."

"The fact that the person who said he was Reverend Matthew wasn't really a minister?"

"That's right," Norman told her. "Grandma Knudson's going to ask Reverend Matthew when he gets back from identifying the body, but she's almost positive that any holy sacraments a fake minister performs aren't recognized by the church."

"What a mess!" Lisa said, just shaking her head. "I'm just thinking about how my friend Sarah will feel. She got married last weekend by Reverend Matthew . . . or at least she *thought* it was Reverend Matthew. And now she's not really married at all!"

"You're forgetting something important,"

Hannah told them. "You're assuming that Reverend Matthew is going to tell us that the murder victim is Paul. It could be someone else entirely, maybe even another minister."

"That's true," Norman said, "but the yearbook photos I printed out last night show that Paul and Matthew looked very much alike. And today you even commented that the real Reverend Matthew looks exactly like Paul. I think it's a slam dunk."

"Slam dunk?" Hannah repeated. "Don't tell me you're watching basketball on television!"

"It's true. I am. It's all Bev's doing. She likes to watch the Minnesota Wild on my big screen. She says it's the patriotic thing to do when you make your home in Minnesota."

"And you *enjoy* watching basketball?" Hannah still couldn't believe that Norman was getting into basketball. He'd never been a big sports fan.

"It's not bad. After two or three games, you know the players and you get into it, you know?"

Hannah felt a gentle kick under the stainless steel surface of the workstation, and she glanced over to see that Michelle was shaking her head slightly. Her baby sister was right. This was not the right time to quiz Norman on why he'd agreed to let Doctor Bev watch basketball on his big screen when he'd balked at inviting her over to watch Vikings football.

"The phone at the parsonage is going to be ringing off the hook when the news hits," Lisa said with a sigh. "There were a lot of weddings last week. Sarah's not the only bride who's going to want to know if her marriage is legal."

"The relatives of the people who got buried won't be too happy, either," Hannah reminded her. "Or the parents of babies who were baptized."

"And anyone who took communion on Sunday when the fake Reverend Matthew officiated," Norman added. "Not to mention the visits to the hospital to give communion to patients."

"Is Grandma Knudson there all alone?" Michelle asked Hannah.

"No. Marguerite and Clara Hollenbeck came back. They said they'd wait to make the church bank deposit until Reverend Matthew got back from the hospital."

"When Hannah and I left, they were all eating Chocolate Euphoria Cookie Bars," Norman added.

"I'm glad you made more than one pan,"

Lisa told Hannah.

"She's right," Michelle said. "You should have heard the groan when Lisa announced that they were all gone. Are they hard to make? I could do some tonight in your oven at home. And that reminds me, I can stay with you, can't I?"

"You can *always* stay with me. You know that. I gave you a copy of my key. And the hardest thing about making the Chocolate Euphoria Cookie Bars is lining the cake pan with heavy duty foil."

"Okay. I'll do a half-dozen pans for tomorrow. Do you have any other recipes?"

"I'm sure I do. I'll just flip through the book and jot them down. They're all on my computer at home."

"When do you think I should incorporate the new information into my story?" Lisa asked Hannah.

"You'd better wait until tomorrow. We don't know any real facts quite yet."

"Okay, but I'm going to give them a little teaser, something like, *If you notice that I look a little rattled, it's because I just learned something shocking about Reverend Matthew that'll turn this murder case topsy-turvy. Hannah's waiting to have her information confirmed, and she promised me that I'll be able to tell you all about it tomorrow.*"

"That's good!" Michelle complimented her.

"Thanks. I want to get everyone to come back tomorrow. Today's only Tuesday and we already made more money this week than we did all last week."

"Murder's good for business," Hannah said. "I don't like it, but it's true."

"Intrigue and deception are also good for business," Lisa pointed out, "and that's what I'm going to talk about tomorrow. Everyone's going to want to hear how you and Andrea called the seminary and found out that every one of Grandma Knudson's suspicions could be explained away. And they'll love it even more when I tell them how she was right for all the wrong reasons. I don't think there's a single person who comes in here who doesn't love Grandma Knudson."

"You're probably right," Hannah said, reaching in her pocket for the recipe Grandma Knudson had given her as they were leaving the parsonage. "She sent this for you because she remembered that pineapple is Herb's favorite fruit. It's from her daughter-in-law Janelle."

Lisa glanced down at the recipe. "Pineapple Casserole? That's something I've never heard of before."

"Is it like a pineapple and meat hotdish?" Michelle asked her.

"No. I'm not sure *what* it is. It's got chunk pineapple, sugar, flour, salt, baking soda, and grated cheddar cheese!"

"Cheddar cheese with pineapple?" Michelle sounded dubious. "Would that be good?"

"It's delicious," Norman told them. "Grandma Knudson insisted that we have fried ham and biscuits for lunch. And she made a pineapple casserole while we sat talking to her in the kitchen. It's easy. It took her less than five minutes to make and it bakes for only a half hour or so. And the crushed cornflakes and butter on the top are really good."

"I'll try it tonight," Lisa said, sticking the recipe in the pocket of her apron. "Herb's bound to love it and I've got ham left over from Sunday dinner. It was nice of Grandma Knudson to think of us. When you go back there, please thank her for me."

"I will," Hannah said, just as the phone rang. Lisa got up to answer it, and Hannah heard her thank Grandma Knudson for the recipe.

"It's Grandma Knudson with a message for you," Lisa said to Hannah. "She says she has another clue to the identity of the killer, and she wants to know if you can come up to the parsonage right now."

"Tell her I'll be there in less than five minutes," Hannah said, jumping to her feet and grabbing her parka from the hooks by the back door.

"As long as Marge is here, I'm going with you," Michelle said, jumping up almost as quickly as Hannah. "Are you coming, Norman?"

"I'm driving," Norman said, grabbing his coat and following the two Swensen sisters out the door.

PINEAPPLE CASSEROLE
Preheat oven to 350 degrees F.,
rack in the middle position.

two 20-ounce cans of chunk pineapple *(I used Dole)*

1/3 cup white *(granulated)* sugar

3/4 cup all-purpose flour *(pack it down in the cup when you measure it)*

1/2 teaspoon salt

1/2 teaspoon baking soda

1 cup grated cheddar cheese *(pack it down in the cup when you measure it)*

1/2 cup *(1 stick, 4 ounces, 1/4 pound)* salted butter

4 Tablespoons *(that's 1/4 cup)* of the pineapple juice you reserved

1 cup crushed cornflakes *(measure AFTER crushing)*

Drain the pineapple, reserving the juice. You'll use some of it in this recipe.

Mix the sugar, flour, salt, and baking soda together in a small bowl. Make sure they're well mixed.

Spray a 2-quart casserole dish with Pam or another nonstick baking spray. Put the flour mixture in the bottom of the casserole dish.

Add the drained pineapple to the casserole

dish and mix it in.

Add the grated cheese to the casserole dish and mix that in. *(It's okay to use your impeccably clean fingers.)*

Unwrap the stick of butter. Put it in a microwave-safe measuring cup that will hold at least one cup, and melt in the microwave on HIGH for 45 seconds.

Drizzle about half of the melted butter over the mixture in your casserole dish. Mix it all up with your fingers or a spoon.

Drizzle the top with 4 Tablespoons of the pineapple juice that you reserved.

If you haven't already done so, crush the cornflakes. You can do this in a sealed plastic bag with your hands. Measure out one cup of crushed cornflakes and sprinkle them on top of your casserole.

Drizzle the remaining melted butter over the top of the crushed cornflakes.

Bake your casserole at 350 degrees F. for 35 to 40 minutes.

Yield: This casserole serves 6 to 8 unless Herb comes to dinner. Then you'd better make two casseroles.

CHAPTER TWENTY

"Now that you're here, we're off to make the bank deposit," Marguerite told them when they arrived at the parsonage. "It shouldn't take us more than fifteen minutes. We go straight into Doug Greerson's office and he does it for us personally. Is that okay with you, Hannah?"

"It's fine. We'll stay until you get back or Reverend Matthew comes in, one or the other."

"Grandma said to pour yourself a cup of coffee and come into her sitting room. She's got Jacob in there."

Of course Grandma Knudson had put on a fresh pot of coffee. There was always fresh coffee at the parsonage. Michelle poured a cup for all three of them and they walked down the hallway to the sitting room.

"There you are!" Grandma Knudson greeted them. "And Michelle, too. Did you flunk out of college?"

Michelle laughed. She knew Grandma Knudson was teasing her. Delores had bragged about her grades so much that everyone in Lake Eden knew she had a three-point-nine average. "I didn't flunk out of college, Grandma Knudson . . . at least not yet."

Grandma Knudson chuckled cheerily, and Hannah noticed that only about a quarter of the cookie bars she'd brought on the platter were left. They'd done their work well. Grandma Knudson was a lot calmer now, and there was actually some color in her cheeks.

"You said you needed to see me because you had a clue to the identity of the killer?" Hannah asked her, seating herself in a chair close to Grandma Knudson while Norman and Michelle sat down on the pink davenport. "What is it?"

"It's Jacob," Grandma Knudson gestured toward the mynah bird in his cage. "He just said something I've never heard him say before. And I can't help thinking he might have learned it the night of the murder. I'm hoping I can get him to say it again so you can all hear it."

"Come on, Jacob. Be a good bird and say it again."

They were all gathered around the bird-cage, Grandma Knudson, Hannah, Norman, and Michelle. Grandma Knudson had been trying to get Pete Nunke's bird to repeat himself for almost five minutes now, but the mynah bird just stared at them with beady yellow unblinking eyes.

"Maybe there's a reason the term *bird brain* is an insult," Hannah said, earning a laugh from the others. Jacob cocked his head, almost as if he had understood her, squawked loudly as if in protest, and said, "Brrrr, it's cold out there!" in Pete Nunke's voice.

"Is that it?" Norman asked.

"No," Grandma Knudson told him. "It's something Pete taught him."

"You'll never see a hearse pulling a U-Haul," Jacob said in Claire's voice.

"He's going through his whole repertoire," Michelle told them. "My roommate's parrot does the same thing. There's nothing she can do to get him to talk, but when he starts talking, he says everything he knows before he shuts up."

"Oh dear, I hope he doesn't say the well-digger one," Grandma Knudson said to Michelle. "If he starts, just cover your ears, dear. Pete taught him that one, too. It's not very nice."

"The wages of sin is death," Jacob said in the fake Reverend Matthew's voice, ruffling his feathers and staring at them.

Michelle shivered slightly. "That's what he said to Hannah right after she . . . well, you know."

"I've got to go. It's almost eleven-thirty," Jacob said in a woman's voice. Hannah exchanged glances with Norman. He gave a little nod, and she knew he also thought the voice belonged to Alice Vogel.

"I haven't heard that before, but it must be someone he was counseling," Grandma Knudson told them. "Matthew . . . I mean the man who was *impersonating* Matthew, scheduled counseling sessions in the mornings and he took Jacob with him. He was always back at the parsonage by noon, and that's why I was so worried when he didn't show up for yesterday's lunch."

Hannah had her doubts that Grandma Knudson was right about the fake Reverend Matthew's counselee, but she said nothing. She'd have to talk to Alice Vogel again to see precisely when she'd arrived at the church office to see the man she thought was Matthew Walters.

"It's colder than a well-dig . . ." Jacob started to say, but Grandma Knudson cut him off.

"Jacob! That's naughty!"

Jacob cocked his head and preened a bit. And then he said, in Grandma Knudson's voice, "Jacob! That's naughty!"

Hannah couldn't help it. She laughed. And so did everyone else, including Grandma Knudson.

"Whether you want weather, music, or the latest moos, tune in to KCOW for country-western or blues," Jacob sang, in a perfect imitation of their local radio station's theme song.

"That's good," Hannah said. "The fake Reverend Matthew must have listened to KCOW."

Grandma Knudson shook her head. "No, that was Claire's idea. She always left the radio on for Jacob when they went out."

"I know why you're here, and you're not going to find it!" Jacob said loudly in the fake Reverend Matthew's voice.

"That's it," Grandma Knudson said quickly. "That's what I wanted you to hear."

They all fell silent, waiting for Jacob to go on with his memorized recital, but the mynah bird was also silent. He ruffled his feathers, hopped down from his perch, and went over to the water dish attached to the wall of his cage.

"I think he's through," Grandma Knudson

315

said, watching as Jacob drank and then began to groom his feathers. "He always does that right before he takes his afternoon nap."

They watched as Jacob settled down on his perch for his nap. Grandma Knudson covered his cage with a cloth and led them all to the sofa and chairs again.

"Won't it bother him if we talk?" Norman asked.

"No. Pete told me that when he's in his little cave like this, he relaxes and goes to sleep unless a really loud noise wakes him."

"That must be true for a lot of birds, maybe all birds," Michelle commented. "I know when my roommate covers her parrot's cage, he goes to sleep."

"Pete says that's because they think it's night," Grandma Knudson said, "but I don't think you should fool them unless they really need a nap. It's just not nice."

Hannah remembered Andrea driving Tracey around and around the block with the baby blinds drawn to put her to sleep when she needed a nap. It seemed that there were lots of ways for parents and bird owners to get their young charges to take a nap, and one way was to trick them.

"Did Marguerite and Clara like the cookie bars?" Hannah asked, hoping that the oblique nudge would cause Grandma Knudson to take one. She still looked a bit shaky.

"Oh, my yes! They wanted to make them for a church group they lead, but when they found out one of the ingredients was sweetened condensed milk, they reconsidered. Store-bought sweetened condensed milk is expensive, and there are over thirty ladies in their Singles Without Partners group."

"They don't have to use boughten sweetened condensed milk," Hannah told her. "I've got a recipe that works every bit as well, and you make it at home from powdered milk and some other ingredients. Would you like it so you can give it to them?"

"Oh yes! I'd love to have it! I think there was one published in the *Farm Journal* years ago, but I clipped it out and didn't copy it into my recipe book. I looked for it not all that long ago, but I must have lost it."

"That may be the one that I have. I got it from my Grandma Ingrid, and she used to read the *Farm Journal.* I've got it down at The Cookie Jar. I'll print it out and bring it to you."

"Just e-mail it to me," Grandma Knudson said. "I'll add it to my recipe folder and that'll be fine."

"You have e-mail?" Michelle asked, looking very surprised.

"Of course I have e-mail. It's not just for young people, you know. Bob set it up for me, and it's a great way to keep in touch with friends. And I just love to surf the Internet. I learn the most incredible things. There are even a couple of Web sites for Bible passages. You can choose the Bible you want to use and type in a phrase to search for. It'll tell you how many times it was used and give you book, chapter and verse within seconds. It's just amazing."

"Will you send me a link?" Michelle asked, writing her e-mail address on a piece of paper and handing it to Grandma Knudson. "One of my roommates is doing a paper for a comparative religion class, and it sounds like a great resource."

"I'll do it tonight," Grandma Knudson promised, and then she turned to Hannah again. "You need my e-mail address to send me those recipes. Mine is Grandma K, that's all one word, at the church Web site."

Hannah glanced at Norman, who was looking at her as if to say *I told you so.* She hadn't believed him when he'd told her that almost everyone in Lake Eden had become computer literate, but now it seemed he was right. If Grandma Knudson, who was almost ninety, had mastered the intricacies of the Internet, perhaps it was time for her to become a little more skilled at it.

"Do you want the substitute version, too?" Hannah asked her. "That's the one for people who have milk allergies."

"I'd love to have that! We have several church members who have milk allergies."

"I'll send that one to you too," Hannah promised. "All you have to do is ask me for your favorite recipes, Grandma Knudson. I'll be happy to e-mail them to you."

"Hello, everyone!" a voice interrupted their quiet conversation, as Clara and Marguerite Hollenbeck came in the door.

"Oh, dear!" Marguerite said, glancing at Jacob's cage and noticing that it was draped with a cloth. "Inside voices, Clara. Jacob's asleep."

"You're speaking louder than I am, Marguerite."

"Sorry." Marguerite turned to Grandma Knudson. "We ran into what we think is a little problem at the bank."

"What's the problem?" Grandma Knudson asked her.

"We did what we always do," Clara explained. "We picked up the collection in the bank bag and took it down to Doug at Lake Eden First Mercantile."

"Doug counted it for us," Marguerite took up the story. "He always counts it, even though our tally slip with the total is in the bag and we haven't been off one single cent in twenty-two years."

"Doug's a banker," Clara said. "He has to make sure everything's accurate." And then she turned to them again. "But the tally we did on Sunday, after the service, was completely different from the total Doug gave us when we went to the bank!"

"Was Doug's tally short? Or long?" Hannah asked, quickly going to the heart of the matter.

Marguerite sighed. "Short," she said. "A lot short."

"Three hundred and twenty-five dollars short to be exact," Clara gave them the figure. "Somebody took out all the big bills and left the change and small bills."

"And nobody noticed until now?" Hannah asked, wondering how that could have happened.

"No," Clara answered her. "Nobody even thought to check the collection money. We always make church deposits on Tuesday. We go into the church office, count it three times after Sunday service when it comes in, and make out the deposit slip. It was a big collection on Sunday. I remember that instead of fives and ones, there were quite a few twenty dollar bills. That's not usually the case."

"And don't forget the gold coins," Marguerite reminded her. "There were five gold coins in the collection, but they were gone along with all the large bills."

"There's another motive for the murder," Norman commented.

"Remember what Jacob said?" Hannah asked them. "He was mimicking the fake Reverend Matthew and he said, *I know why you're here and you're not going to find it!* He could have been talking about the collection money."

"That makes sense," Marguerite said. "We always keep it in the file cabinet, filed under *C* for *collection,* but somebody moved it. That could have been the fake Reverend Matthew."

"Or maybe the fake Reverend Matthew's killer moved it after he took out what he wanted," Michelle postulated. "And if the fake Reverend Matthew moved it to hide it from his killer, he must have known his killer was coming and who he was."

Hannah nodded. She was proud of Michelle for using her head. "We're jumping to several conclusions here, but it could make sense." She turned to Clara. "How many people knew that you filed the collection money under *C?*"

"Unfortunately . . . a lot of people. They were church members. We had no reason not to trust them."

"And the church office is locked at night," Marguerite added. "The only reason it was open when the murder happened is that the reverend, whoever he is, was working."

"So it could have been a burglary gone bad," Grandma Knudson said thoughtfully. "And *that's* why Paul was in prison. He was serving time for a burglary gone bad."

"That's what the *fake* Reverend Matthew told you," Hannah reminded her. "He might have lied about that, for some reason."

The phone rang and Grandma Knudson reached out to answer it. They were all silent as she said hello and then greeted her caller. "Yes, Matthew. I'm glad you called. Where are you?"

Now that Hannah knew who the caller was, she listened even more carefully. She glanced over at Norman and saw that he was also intent on hearing the one-sided telephone conversation.

"Are you all right?" Grandma Knudson asked, and then she listened for a moment. "Yes, dear. That's what we thought. You go right ahead to the sheriff's station and tell them you made positive identification. And don't worry about me. Clara and Marguerite are here, and they said they'd stay until you got back."

So the fake Reverend Matthew was Paul. That was pretty clear from Grandma Knudson's side of the conversation. It was also clear that the real Reverend Matthew was worried about Grandma Knudson.

"Just come back here when you're through," Grandma Knudson said. "I have a nice cut of boneless chuck and I'll make something good and nourishing for your supper. It always makes a body feel better to have something good to eat."

Hannah watched as a smile spread across Grandma Knudson's face. Reverend Matthew had said something to make her happy.

"That's sweet of you to say, dear! I think of you like a grandson, too."

After Grandma Knudson hung up the phone, Hannah turned to her for confirmation. "Reverend Matthew told you that his cousin Paul was the murder victim?"

"Yes. Poor Matthew was very upset, Hannah. His voice was shaking when he called me."

"I'm sure he was," Norman said. "It must have been very difficult for him to identify his cousin."

"And even more difficult to know that someone he once trusted, his cousin Paul, had impersonated him," Marguerite said. "That's a real betrayal."

Clara nodded. "Just like Judas, except it wasn't for twenty pieces of silver. I wonder what it *was* for."

"I'm going to try to find out," Hannah promised.

"And I'm going to help her," Norman added. "I'm taking the whole week off so we can work on this together."

"Me, too," Michelle said, nodding quickly. "Don't worry, Grandma Knudson. Just leave everything to us. We're going to get to the bottom of this!"

Hannah glanced over at her sister. Michelle was doing a nice job of reassuring Grandma Knudson, but she wished her baby sister had used slightly less positive language. *Just leave everything to us* was fine. They didn't want Grandma Knudson to worry and wonder about Paul's murder. But the promise that Michelle had given her, *We'll get to the bottom of this,* was a bit too much for Hannah. Of course they'd *try* to get to the bottom of it, but there was always the chance they might fail. They'd been lucky so far in solving Lake Eden murder cases, but there was always the possibility that the solution to Paul's murder might elude them.

They visited for another couple of minutes, talking about other things. Once Hannah thought that Grandma Knudson had calmed down again, she motioned to the others, said that she had to get back to The Cookie Jar, and they left.

"If you don't mind, I'm going to jot down some notes on the drive back," she told Norman when he opened the passenger door for her.

"That's fine with me. You can read them to us when we get back to . . . just a second. I've got a call and I have to take it." Norman tossed her the keys. "Start the car so you and Michelle can keep warm."

As Hannah and Michelle watched through the car windows, Norman answered the call. He listened and then an exasperated expression crossed his face.

"I wish we could hear," Michelle said. "Norman doesn't look happy."

"No, he doesn't. It must be some sort of emergency. I hope nothing's wrong with Carrie or Earl."

Norman paced as he talked, a half-dozen steps forward, and then a half-dozen steps back. They could see his face when he moved toward them, and Hannah thought he looked annoyed with his caller.

"I don't think it has anything to do with Carrie or Earl," Michelle said. "Norman looks more irritated than worried."

"And if it was a real family emergency, he'd hurry back to the car and drive wherever he had to go," Hannah added.

Ten minutes passed before Norman came back to the car. Hannah was glad she'd turned on the heater, because he was shaking a little from the cold. "Is everything okay?" she asked him.

"No. There's a dental emergency and I have to get down to the clinic. It's going to take a while, so I'll drop you off at The Cookie Jar and catch up with you at home, if that's okay with you."

"Sure," Hannah said. "That's fine."

"If you and Michelle go anywhere, just leave a note on your door."

"Will do," Hannah promised, but she didn't feel good about it. Something was wrong. She wished she knew what it was, but Norman was being secretive again.

HOMEMADE SWEETENED CONDENSED MILK

1/3 cup boiling water
4 tablespoons butter
3/4 cup sugar
1/2 teaspoon pure vanilla extract
1 cup powdered milk **(I used Carnation Nonfat Powdered Milk, but I've also used my local grocery store brand.)**

In a blender, or using an electric mixer set on LOW, blend together the boiling water and butter.

Add the sugar and let it run for a few seconds.

Add the pure vanilla extract and let it run for several additional seconds.

Shut off the blender or mixer, pour in the powdered milk, and then blend or mix on LOW until the resulting mixture is thick.

Use immediately, or store in a covered container in the refrigerator. This homemade version of sweetened condensed milk will last for up to one week in the refrigerator.

Yield: This recipe makes the equivalent of one 14-ounce can of sweetened condensed milk that can be used in pies, cakes, cookie bars and flans.

Hannah's Note: My Grandma Ingrid made this up every Sunday morning and put it in the refrigerator to use in coffee for the whole week.

SUBSTITUTE FOR SWEETENED CONDENSED MILK
(for anyone who needs to avoid milk or dairy)

2 large eggs
1 cup brown sugar *(pack it down when you measure it)*
1 teaspoon vanilla extract
2 Tablespoons flour
1/2 teaspoon baking powder
1/4 teaspoon salt

Hannah's 1st Note: This is easy to make if you use an electric mixer. You can also make it in a blender. You must make it fresh for each recipe you bake.

Beat the eggs until they're of a uniform color and thoroughly blended.

Add the brown sugar and mix it in.

Add the vanilla extract. Mix it in.

Add the flour and beat for one minute, making sure it's thoroughly incorporated into the mixture.

Add the baking powder and the salt. Beat for another minute.

Set the resulting mixture aside on the counter until you need it in your recipe. Then add it when your recipe calls for sweetened condensed milk.

Hannah's 2nd Note: This substitute can be used in any BAKED dessert recipe, including pies, cakes, and cookie bars. DO NOT use it in frostings or candy.

Yield: One recipe makes enough to substitute for one 14-ounce can of sweetened condensed milk. *(That's the store-bought size.)*

CHAPTER TWENTY-ONE

"Hannah?" Michelle came out of Hannah's condo kitchen with a cup of hot chocolate. "Did you know there's a ball of socks on top of your refrigerator?"

"Another one," Hannah said with a sigh, glancing over at Moishe, who looked totally uninterested in their conversation.

"Moishe?" Michelle asked, noticing Hannah's glance at her cat.

"He's the only one who lives here besides me. And I really don't think I'm sleepwalking with socks in my hand. Maybe you'll be able to tell which one of us is doing it, now that you're staying here."

"But Moishe can't get your sock drawer open . . . can he?"

"Don't forget you're doubting the abilities of the stubborn feline who managed to chew his way through the back of a locked cabinet to get at his food," Hannah reminded her.

Michelle gave a little shrug. "That's true. Have you checked the back of your sock drawer?"

"That was the first thing I did."

"And?"

"No holes anywhere. The drawer is solid wood, and it's heavy. If I'm not doing it, Moishe is. But I can't figure out how he's pulling out that drawer."

"Maybe I can. I'll keep an eye on him. And on you, too. Sleepwalking's not all that unusual, you know, especially in times of high stress. Are you stressed, Hannah?"

"Who, me? What could I possibly be stressed about? Just because my cat's exhibiting unusual behavior, Mike is about to warn me not to get involved in Paul's murder case and I already am, Mother keeps adding items to the menu for her book launch party, and Norman's spending more time with Doctor Bev who's prettier, and younger, and has a perfect figure. That couldn't possibly lead to stress, could it?"

"Forget I asked. You're stressed," Michelle pronounced. "I can tell because you just got sarcastic. You *never* get sarcastic when you're not stressed."

"That's probably true," Hannah admitted.

"I saw her, you know."

Hannah knew precisely which her Michelle was referring to. "What did you think of her?"

"Everything you said with one addition. She's a fake."

"What?"

"She's a fraud," Michelle repeated. "There's something about her that doesn't ring true. Nobody's that sweet and perfect. She's like . . . a dental doll."

Hannah was confused. She'd never heard of a dental doll before. "What's a dental doll?"

"You must have see those career dolls that mothers buy for their daughters. The girl astronaut, the girl teacher, the girl lawyer, and the girl doctor. I'm sure there's got to be a girl dentist that looks just like Doctor Bev."

"You don't think she's a real dentist?"

"That's not it. I think she's a real dentist, but I also think she's playing some sort of part. She's acting, Hannah. I can spot an actress a mile off. She's playing sweet, and nice, and everybody's friend, but she's not really that way inside. I just wish I knew what she's up to."

Hannah thought about that for a long moment. Perhaps Michelle was right. When she'd seen Doctor Bev in action at the birthday party, she'd thought that there was something a bit disingenuous about her.

"Well? Do you think I'm totally wrong?" Michelle asked.

"No. I had similar feelings about her, but I thought it might be just jealousy."

"You don't have anything to be jealous about! You're a much better person than she is!"

Hannah walked over to give her a hug. The Swensen family wasn't usually that demonstrative, but Michelle deserved a hug. "What would you like for dinner?"

"Red meat. I'm taking you out to the Corner Tavern for a double burger. I worked a couple of extra hours last week and I've got the extra cash."

"But you don't have spend it on me."

"I'm not spending it on you, I'm spending it on *us*. Besides, ever since Grandma Knudson mentioned that beef stew she was going to make for Reverend Matthew, I've had a hankering for red meat!"

Of course they didn't go straight to the Corner Tavern, not after Hannah told Michelle that she'd recognized the voice of the woman Grandma Knudson thought was Paul's counselee.

"Alice Vogel?" Michelle sounded surprised. "Why was she meeting with Paul?"

"She wasn't meeting with Paul. Alice thought she was meeting with Matthew Walters. She used to date him when they were in high school, and rumor has it that she still had feelings for him."

"Interesting. And you think she was with him in the church office on Sunday night?"

"That's my guess. Doc Knight said the murder took place between midnight and two in the morning, so Alice isn't a suspect if she left before midnight. It's even possible she saw Paul's killer when she was leaving the church."

"Let's stop by the bowling alley to talk to her on our way out to the Corner Tavern," Michelle said. "I want to see her reaction when you tell her that Reverend Matthew was really his cousin Paul."

Hannah brought cookies. Hannah always brought cookies. "Ready?" she asked Michelle as they walked up to the bowling alley entrance.

"I'm ready. Which cookies did you bring?"

"Nutmeg Snaps. Alice just loves them."

"So do I. That's JoAnn Hecht's recipe, isn't it?"

"Right."

"Where did she go after she left her cater-

335

ing job with Sally?"

"She moved to California and opened her own company there. I wish she were still here. She could cater Mother's book launch party, and I could just go and have fun."

A blast of warm air, the good-natured banter of bowlers, and the smell of fresh popcorn from the popcorn machine rolled out to greet them as Hannah pushed open the door.

One look at the bowlers who crowded every lane and Hannah knew that Club League was in full swing. There wasn't a lot to do in February in Minnesota. Outdoor recreation was limited to sledding, skating, and ice fishing, and no one braved the subzero temperatures on a night that was this cold. Instead, it looked as if almost everyone Hannah knew was bowling. Club League was fun because you didn't have to actually join a league. All you had to do was belong to a club, get together with four friendly members, and take part in the tournament. If your team lost, you were out. But if your team won, you went on to play another club team. The club tournament winning team won baseball caps embroidered with their names and the date they won. That gave them bragging rights.

Several of tonight's bowlers must have

been winners in the past, because Hannah spotted Cyril Murphy wearing a green cap, and Digger Gibson sporting an orange cap.

"Alice is behind the refreshment counter," Michelle said, steering Hannah in that direction. "She waved at us when we walked in. What are you going to ask her?"

"Leading questions, the kind that are designed to get her to talk."

"Like what?"

Hannah shrugged. "I don't know, but don't worry. I'll think of something before we get there."

Gus York was standing in line, waiting for Alice to pour him a beer. Hannah noticed that Alice emptied the bottle into a large disposable paper cup before she handed it to Gus. The last time she'd bowled, which had been at least six months ago, Alice had simply given bowlers the bottle. Perhaps there'd been too many incidents with dropped or broken beer bottles.

Once they'd exchanged a few words with Gus and he'd left, Hannah turned to the person she'd come to see. "Hi, Alice," she said handing over the cookies. "These are Nutmeg Snaps. Lisa said you liked them."

"Oh, I do! They remind me of Christmas."

Hannah was surprised. "Really?"

"I think it's because of the nutmeg," Alice

explained. "I always grate some fresh nutmeg on my eggnog during the Christmas season."

"Makes sense," Hannah said, sliding onto one of the stools at the counter and motioning for Michelle to do the same. "You know my youngest sister, Michelle, don't you?"

"I sure do. Hi, Michelle. How's it going with college?"

"Really well, thanks. I've got a couple days off, so I'm home to help Hannah. She's really busy this week."

"I figured she would be." Alice turned to Hannah. "Are you going to try to catch Matthew's killer?"

"Well . . ." Hannah hedged slightly. "I generally like to leave all that to the professionals, but Grandma Knudson asked me to see what I could find out."

"That's what I thought. Well, you're about five hours ahead of Mike and Lonnie. They didn't come in to ask me questions until suppertime." Alice sighed and sat down on her own stool behind the counter. "Tell me honestly, Hannah, am I still your prime suspect?"

"Not anymore. I cleared you about an hour after Norman and I were here." Hannah was silent, waiting for Alice's response.

Alice looked surprised for a moment, and

then she smiled. "That makes me feel a lot better! How did you clear me?"

"Doc Knight set the time of death between midnight and two in the morning. And you left the church office at eleven-thirty."

As the two Swensen sisters watched, tell-tale spots of red appeared on Alice's cheeks. "How do you know that?" she asked.

"Jacob told us. Remember the mynah bird that was sitting on the bookcase in his cage?"

"Yes. But . . ." Alice stopped speaking abruptly, realizing that she'd admitted to being at the church office the night of the murder, something she hadn't intended to admit.

Hannah was silent. So was Michelle. Both of them just sat there waiting for Alice to go on.

"It's not like it looks. I mean . . . I just needed to see him again, to find out if he still . . . liked me, you know? It was just a matter of curiosity, that's all."

"And did he still like you?" Hannah asked.

"Yes. He was the old Matthew, just like in high school. And he explained why he didn't come over to see me before he left town. He said that he just couldn't bear to see me again because he knew that if he saw me, he'd do something foolish like ask me to run off with him to get married, or settle down in Lake Eden and turn down the offer he got from Concordia College. He told me he wrote me a letter saying all that, and asking me if I'd be willing to wait for him to graduate and get his first posting as a minister, and then we could be married."

"But you never got the letter," Michelle said with a sigh.

"That's right. My dad kept it from me. He didn't want me to marry Matthew and leave Lake Eden. He wanted me to stay right here and help him run the bowling alley."

"Did you believe Matthew?" Hannah asked.

"Of course! He was . . ." Alice stopped and wiped away a tear with the back of her hand. "He was kind, and sweet, and considerate, just the way he'd been all those years ago. He even said I looked wonderful, and that was when he invited me out to dinner on Monday night. Maybe nothing would have come of it. Maybe we would have gone our separate ways once he was through filling in for Reverend Bob. But I can't help wondering if . . ." Alice's voice trailed off, and tears began to roll down her cheeks.

"Here," Hannah said, pulling a couple of paper napkins from the dispenser that sat on the refreshment bar and handing them to her. "Brace yourself, Alice. I've got some news that'll change everything."

Alice looked up with tear-filled eyes. "What?"

"Matthew's alive. The minister you went to see at the church office wasn't a minister at all. He was Matthew's cousin Paul."

For a brief second Alice was silent and then she began to shake her head. "No," she said. "No, he couldn't have been Paul. I *know* he wasn't Paul. I knew Paul. They *looked* alike, sure, but they weren't anything alike really. Paul wasn't a nice person. I would have known if the man I met was Paul!"

"Matthew's here now," Michelle told her. "He drove in from Wisconsin this morning, right after he heard the news that he was murdered in Lake Eden."

"Matthew positively identified the victim as Paul this afternoon at the morgue," Hannah told her.

"But . . ." Alice swallowed hard. "I was so sure. I never doubted that it was Matthew. And now you tell me that it was Paul." Alice reached for another paper napkin and wiped her eyes again. "I just can't believe it."

"Do you want to go see the real Reverend

Matthew?" Michelle asked her. "I could fill in for you here."

Alice shook her head. "No! I've had enough for today! I just can't . . . cope with anything else. Maybe tomorrow. Or the day after. I just . . . have to get this all straight in my head."

"Of course you do," Hannah said comfortingly, sliding off her stool and motioning for Michelle to do the same. "We understand, Alice. This whole thing has been a terrible shock. I only have two more questions for you, and if you can answer them, it'll help me a lot."

"I . . . yes. I can." As they watched, Alice took a deep breath and visibly pulled herself together. "What's the first question, Hannah?"

"When you left the church on Sunday night, did you see anyone else, anyone who could have been waiting to get in, parking in the lot or on the street, or even walking?"

Alice shook her head. "There was no one around. I looked. I didn't exactly want to be seen. It's just that Matthew and I used to date and everybody thinks I'm still carrying a torch for him. No, Hannah. There was no one within a block of the church, no one but me."

"That helps, Alice. Thanks. The second

question is about Paul, so you're going to have to switch gears. Did Paul have any friends when he was here at Jordan High?"

"Only one that I can think of. Of course Matthew was his best friend. When they first got here, they palled around together. But then Matthew started dating me and Paul hooked up with Lenny Peske."

"The bartender at the Eagle?" Michelle asked her.

"Yes. They were partners in crime, if you want to call it that. Paul and Lenny did all sorts of bad things, like breaking into school lockers, and playing nasty tricks on the teachers they didn't like."

"Thanks, Alice," Hannah said quickly. She could tell that Alice was shaken and really needed to be left alone. "Call me if you need me for anything. You have my cell phone number, don't you?"

"Yes. You gave it to me this afternoon."

"Here's mine, too," Michelle took a card from her purse and handed it to Alice. "Sometimes Hannah forgets to charge hers."

"So do I," Alice said, giving Hannah a wan smile. And then she asked a question of her own. "Does Mike know that Paul was the one who was murdered?"

"He does now. The real Reverend Mat-

343

thew went into the sheriff's station to report it this afternoon."

"Then they'll probably be back tonight to ask me more questions. Maybe I'll just ask one of the bowlers to run the tournament for me and lock up when it's over. Digger's here and he's reliable. He took over for me Sunday night until I got back here at twenty to twelve. You can check with him on the time."

"Thanks," Hannah said.

"I hate to skip out again tonight, but I need some time to sort this out before the police ask me any more questions."

"Don't forget you've got an alibi," Hannah reminded her.

"Yes, but does *Mike* know that?"

"Not yet," Hannah admitted. "I'll tell him the next time I see him, but I don't think that'll be until tomorrow. Of course he doesn't know that you were at the church office, either. We just learned about it a few hours ago."

"Okay. I'm going to go home, put on my favorite old robe, and watch a movie on television with my dogs. I'm going to eat every single one of your cookies, and maybe I'll even have a couple of beers to wash them down. I'm not going to answer the door or the phone for anybody! Not even you, Hannah."

"That's fine with me. I'm not going to call you. You answered all the questions I can think of for now. Just go home and get some rest. You've been on an emotional roller coaster."

Alice thought about that for a moment. "You're right. It *has* been a roller coaster, and I always get sick on roller coasters. But I think I'm doing all right this time." She reached down to grab the bag of cookies that Hannah had brought her, and held them aloft. "This time, I didn't even lose my cookies."

Hannah laughed, and so did Michelle. It wasn't really that funny, but they were glad that Alice had recovered enough to make an attempt at humor.

"Come with me and you can talk to Digger," Alice invited. "Ask him what time I got back here Sunday night, and he'll tell you. And then I'll ask him to fill in for me again tonight."

Alice led the way to a team of bowlers in the seats behind the foul line at lane number three. Hannah noticed that Digger was there, and he was wearing a bright purple sweatshirt emblazoned with his team name, *Lucky Stiffs.*

"That's a bad pun," Michelle commented,

"especially for an undertaker."

"I know. Digger's got more humor in him than you might think." Alice stopped just short of approaching Digger and his team, and turned to Hannah. "Please don't find any more bodies, Hannah. If I get implicated in any more murders, I'm going to have to put Digger on the payroll."

NUTMEG SNAPS

Do not preheat the oven yet — this cookie dough must chill before baking.

1 cup salted butter, softened *(2 sticks, 8 ounces, 1/2 pound)*

2 and 1/2 cups dark brown sugar *(pack it down in the cup when you measure it)*★★★

2 large eggs

1 and 1/2 teaspoons baking soda

1/2 teaspoon salt

2 teaspoons ground nutmeg *(or 1 teaspoon of freshly grated nutmeg)*★★★★

3 and 1/2 cups all purpose flour *(pack it down in the cup when you measure it)*

2/3 cup dried apricots, chopped *(measure AFTER chopping)*

extra sugar *(about 1/2 cup)* for rolling dough balls before baking

★★★ *If you don't have dark brown sugar, you don't have to rush right out to buy it. As far as I can tell, there are 3 types of brown sugar. One is called "brown sugar," another is called "light brown sugar," and the third is called "dark brown sugar". Light brown sugar has the least molasses and dark brown sugar has the most. If you have regular brown sugar in the house,* just add a half-teaspoon of molasses to your mixing bowl and you'll have dark brown sugar.

**** If you're using ground nutmeg in the jar and it's old, do go out and buy a new jar. Unlike fine wine, nutmeg doesn't age well. It tends to taste like soap! If you grate your own nutmeg, that's preferable. Just use 1 teaspoon of freshly grated nutmeg instead of the 2 teaspoons of ground nutmeg that it calls for in the recipe.

Hannah's 1st Note: Although you can certainly make this recipe by hand, it's a lot easier with an electric mixer.

Place the softened *(room temperature)* butter in a mixer bowl and beat it until it's smooth.

Add the dark brown sugar and beat it until it's nice and fluffy.

Mix in the eggs. Make sure they're thoroughly incorporated.

With the mixer running on LOW speed, add the baking soda, salt, and nutmeg. Keep beating until you're sure they're evenly combined.

Add the flour in half-cup increments, beating after each addition.

Shut off the mixer, and stir in the chopped dried apricots by hand. *(They tend to stick to the beaters.)*

You can leave your cookie dough right in the mixing bowl if you wish. Just tear off a sheet of plastic wrap and press it down over the top of your dough, tucking it in on the sides so that no air gets in.

Refrigerate the cookie dough for one hour **(overnight is fine, too)** to chill it and make it easier to work with.

When you're ready to bake, preheat the oven to 350 degrees F., rack in the middle position.

Take your cookie dough out of the refrigerator and set it on the counter.

Line your cookie sheets with parchment paper, or spray them with Pam or another nonstick baking spray.

Put some white sugar, a half-cup should do, into a small bowl. You'll be rolling dough balls in the sugar before baking.

Roll the dough into 1-inch balls without making them smooth.

Roll each dough ball in the sugar, covering it completely.

Arrange the dough balls on your cookie sheets 2 inches apart. You should be able to get 12 dough balls on each cookie sheet.

Flatten each ball with the bottom of a glass, or the flat blade of a metal spatula.

Bake at 350 degrees F., for 8 to 12 minutes or until the cookies are golden brown. **(Mine** *took 11 minutes, and so did JoAnn's cookies.)*

Remove the cookies from the oven, let them cool on the baking sheets for a minute or two to firm up. Then remove them to a wire rack to cool completely.

These yummy Nutmeg Snaps can be stored in an airtight container or in a covered cookie jar up to one week. They freeze beautifully if you stack them like coins in a wrapper, roll them in foil, and place the rolls in freezer bags.

Yield: approximately 6 dozen cookies, depending on cookie size.

Hannah's 2nd Note: These cookies make great "dunkers". Bill always dunks his in his coffee when he comes into The Cookie Jar for an afternoon break. Mother does it too, but please don't mention it if you see her. I wasn't supposed to tell anyone because she says it isn't proper etiquette.

CHAPTER TWENTY-TWO

"I'm really glad I didn't have to settle for a chunk of pickled ring bologna!" Michelle said, biting into her double-double cheese mushroom burger.

Hannah waited until she'd swallowed a bite of her double-double gorgonzola burger before she replied. "What made you think you'd have to settle for pickled bologna?"

"I looked at the menu at the refreshment stand just in case Alice decided to take me up on my offer to fill in for her while she went up to the parsonage to see the real Reverend Matthew. The only things she serves are sodas, beer, chips, popcorn, and pickled bologna. She had that in one of those big glass jars behind the counter."

"No pickled pigs feet?"

"No. I guess they're too messy. A chunk of bologna's neater."

The two sisters fell silent as they ate their burgers and drank from chilled mugs of root beer. They didn't speak again until their burgers were almost gone.

"I'm thinking about ordering a burger to go for Norman," Hannah said, "but he must really be tied up. I thought he'd read my note and come straight out here."

"Maybe the dental emergency is really complicated." Michelle stopped speaking and began to frown. "Never mind. It's not."

"How do *you* know?"

"The dental emergency, if there really was one, is over. I can see through the leaves of the artificial plant sitting on top of the room divider, and Norman's here."

"Wave at him. He might not be able to see us way back here."

"I *hope* he won't. Whatever you do, don't stand up, Hannah. We need to keep a really low profile."

"What are you *talking* about?"

"Norman's at a table for two in the middle of the dining room. He must have walked in shortly after we did."

"Is he waiting for us?"

"I doubt it. He's with Doctor Bev."

At first all Hannah felt was shock, but then her spirits sank to a new low. "Then the dental emergency was just an excuse to break free from me so he could take Doctor Bev to dinner."

"Don't jump to conclusions, Hannah. If you turn around, you'll be able to see Norman through the greenery."

"I don't want to see him!"

"Oh, I think you *do*. It's pretty obvious that Norman doesn't want to be here."

"Really?"

"Really. Just turn your head and look. You'll see what I mean."

Hannah turned around. It was just as Michelle had said. There was Norman at a table for two in the middle of the dining room, and Doctor Bev was with him. She was facing away so all Hannah could see was the back of her head and her expensive haircut, but Norman was facing them and he didn't look at all happy. "He looks . . . upset," she said.

"Yes, he does. I think he looks just as upset as he did when he got the phone call about the dental emergency."

"The fake dental emergency," Hannah corrected her. "It was probably *her*."

The two sisters watched for a moment, and then Michelle said, "Look! She must have said something Norman didn't like at all. Now he looks irritated."

"He looked irritated on the phone this afternoon, too."

"They're arguing about something," Michelle said. "Look how he's clenching his hand. That breadstick he's holding is going to be nothing but crumbs in a couple of seconds. She's reaching for his other hand to try to calm him down."

Hannah narrowed her eyes. "It's not going to work. He just pulled his hand back, and he's scowling."

"Maybe it's the light, but Norman's face looks red."

"It's not the light," Hannah told her. "Norman's face *is* red. He's angry, very angry."

"Furious. Have you ever seen Norman look this mad before?"

"Never. Norman isn't the type to fly off the handle. It just isn't like him."

"Then she must have pushed him to the bitter end about something," Michelle commented.

"I wonder what she's doing now. She just picked up a napkin and she's holding it up to her face."

"Crocodile tears," Michelle informed her. "Either that, or she's actually crying. There's a girl in my drama class who can cry on command. That's really useful when you're an actress."

"Well, it's coming in handy for lady dentists, too. Norman just reached out for her hand."

Michelle gave a little sigh. "You can't blame him for that. There are some guys who just can't stand to see a woman cry. I'll bet Norman's like that."

Hannah gave a little shrug. "I'm not sure. Actually I'm not sure about a lot of things now. Norman says he loves me, but this doesn't look good. And Mike says he loves me, but that'll probably change when he finds out I'm working on his murder case. Maybe neither one of them loves me!"

Michelle motioned for their waitress and pulled out her wallet. "Maybe money can't buy you love, but it'll buy you chocolate. And that's *almost* the same thing. I'm going to order a double fudge brownie delight for both of us to go."

"To go? But we can't leave yet. We'll have to walk right past them, and I don't want to do that."

Michelle started to grin. "Afraid you'll kill her?"

"Of course not! But there may be much too much ketchup and mustard in her future."

This time a grin wasn't enough for Michelle. She started to laugh. "I wouldn't blame you. Follow me, Hannah. We can stand in the kitchen to wait for our takeout and then we'll go out the back way. We can sneak back in the front door to get our coats and boots."

Hannah considered that for a moment. "But don't you think that's the coward's way out?"

"No, it's the *cheapest* way out. The dry cleaners will charge you a fortune to get the ketchup and mustard stains out of her white cashmere sweater."

"Better?" Michelle asked, after they'd polished off their double fudge brownie delights.

"Much better. Thanks, Michelle. I was really upset when I listened to that message from Norman, saying he was still tied up with his so-called *dental emergency.*"

"I know," Michelle commiserated. "Did you remember to print out those recipes for me? I can make a couple of pans of cookie bars tonight."

"I remembered," Hannah said, walking over to her desk to pick up some papers and handing them to Michelle. "I have three bar recipes and a drop cookie recipe."

"Great! Let's bake together. That'll make both of us feel good. Where shall we start?"

"You can do Black Forest Brownies, and

I'll do Strawberry Shortbread Bar Cookies."

For ten minutes the only conversation in Hannah's kitchen consisted of questions like, "Will you please hand me the sugar?" or "Where do you keep your heavy-duty aluminum foil?"

Both ovens, upper and lower, were set for the correct temperatures, and Michelle and Hannah didn't sit down again until two pans of bar cookies were in each oven. Then Hannah put on the coffee pot and joined her sister at the kitchen table. "You know Lenny Peske, don't you?"

"Not personally, but he's one of those one-toe-over-the-line guys." When Hannah looked blank, Michelle went on. "He's a wannabe crook, but not quite."

"He skirts around the law?"

"Exactly. Lonnie's Uncle Pat knew him pretty well. They went to Jordan High together."

"Does Lonnie's uncle live around here?"

Michelle shook her head. "He's been in Chicago for years. The last time Lonnie visited him, they sat around talking for hours. It was Uncle Pat who said that Lenny's always been a one-toe-over-the-line guy. I think we should talk to him."

"Uncle Pat?"

"No, Lenny. We can always catch him at the Eagle."

Hannah was surprised. Most people in Lake Eden knew that the Eagle, a backwoods bar and dance place, was a real dive. The last time Michelle had gone out there to do undercover work on a murder case, it had almost turned into a disaster. "Do you really want to go out to the Eagle again?" she asked.

"No, but that's where Lenny works. You don't want me to go undercover again, do you?"

"Absolutely not!"

"Okay, then let's all go."

"Who do you mean by *all?*"

"You, Andrea, and me. There's strength in numbers and there's no way I want to go out there alone again. How about tomorrow night?"

"That's fine with me. I'll check with Andrea in the morning, and see if she can go. But don't mention it to Mother or she'll want to go, too. And then we'll have to look out for her."

"Do you know how mad Mother would be if she heard you say that?"

"Oh, yes. I know." Hannah turned to look at the ovens as the timer rang. "Is that yours? Or mine?"

"Yours. Your crust bakes only fifteen minutes. Then you cool it for five, put on the strawberry pie filling and the topping, and bake it for another thirty minutes. I read your recipe."

"Okay. I'll get my crust out. Tell me how long your Black Forest Brownies have to go and I'll reset the timer."

"You don't have to. I'm keeping my eye on the clock. We always bake together when I come home, so I'll run by the Red Owl tomorrow and pick up a second kitchen timer."

"While you're watching the clock, why don't you call the Eagle and find out if Lenny's working tomorrow night. It'd be a waste of time to drive all the way out there and find out he's got the night off."

Michelle reached for the phone on the wall. "Good idea. I'll do it now. My bars still have fifteen minutes to go."

Hannah's crust had cooled the required five minutes, she'd finished assembling the cookie bars, and she was slipping them back into the oven by the time Michelle hung up the phone. "What took so long?" she asked.

"Lenny was in a private meeting in the office with someone, and the door was locked. They put me on hold until he came out."

"Lenny has private meetings at the Eagle?"

"That's what one of the waitresses said. She told me her name was Silky."

"Do you think that's a real name?"

"No. Waitresses at a dive like that don't usually use their real names. They don't want the customers to know anything personal about them."

Hannah stared at her baby sister. "Should I ask you how you know that?"

"You can if you want to. One of my roommates worked in a bar for the summer, and they gave her a name tag with a fake name. Anyway, Silky said that Lenny started locking the office when he took over as manager, and he's got the only key. On the nights he doesn't work, they can't open the door."

"Really!" Hannah's mind ran through the possibilities, taking Uncle Pat's character assessment into account. "My bet is that he's using it for something borderline illegal."

"I'm sure you're right. Silky also said that up to four months ago, the waitresses were going in and out to use the phone, but now nobody except Lenny can get in."

"That makes me want to get a good look at that office when we go out there," Hannah told her.

An hour passed with the two sisters baking, talking, and generally having a good time together. They'd finished six pans of cookie bars when Hannah decided it was time for them to get some sleep.

"You'd better turn in, Michelle. You have to get up early in the morning if you want to ride to town with me."

"Sounds good." Michelle stood up and gave Hannah a hug. "Goodnight, Hannah."

"Goodnight, Michelle," Hannah hugged her back. "I'll turn in soon, and then . . ." Hannah stopped talking abruptly as the doorbell rang.

"I'll get it on my way to bed," Michelle called out as she opened the door. "It's probably Norman."

"No, it's probably Mike," Mike said, stepping in. "Didn't you look through the peephole?"

"It doesn't do any good. Hello, Mike. Good to see you. And goodnight, Mike. I'm going to bed."

"Goodnight, Michelle," Mike said as she left the room, and then he turned to Hannah. "What's the matter with your peephole?"

"It's the outside light," Hannah explained, coming over to take his coat. "I petitioned the association to move the light so my visitors' faces aren't in shadow. They approved it, but the handyman hasn't been around to do it yet."

"I'll do it on my day off," Mike promised.

"But you don't have to . . ."

"I *want* to. I want you safe, Hannah. It's after eleven at night. You should know who it is before you open the door. Besides, I'm law enforcement, and that means I'm responsible for your safety and well-being. I have a vested interest in keeping you around."

"Oh, really?" Hannah said as Mike moved closer. She tried to keep it casual, but she knew what was coming and her voice shook slightly. "What's that?"

"I'll show you."

Before Hannah could do more than draw in her breath, Mike pulled her into his arms and kissed her.

It felt good to be loved, even by the man she was almost convinced was wrong for her. He'd been dating Doctor Bev, and he hadn't even mentioned it to her. Of course he also hadn't mentioned the other women he'd dated, like Shawna Lee Quinn, her sister Vanessa, and Ronni Ward. Then again Norman, who she suspected was right for her, had been upfront about taking Bev out to dinner when Hannah had a date with Mike. Except tonight. Tonight Norman had betrayed her, and . . .

Hannah stopped thinking. Mike's kiss was too compelling to spoil with thoughts of anything but him and how very good it felt to be loved, even if it wasn't forever.

STRAWBERRY SHORTBREAD BAR COOKIES

Preheat oven to 350 degrees F.,
rack in the middle position.

Hannah's 1st Note: These are really easy and fast to make. Almost everyone loves them, including Baby Bethie, and they're not even chocolate!

3 cups all purpose flour *(pack it down in the cup when you measure it)*

3/4 cup powdered *(confectioner's)* sugar *(don't sift unless it's got big lumps)*

1 and 1/2 cups salted butter, softened *(3 sticks, 12 ounces, 1/4 pound)*

1 can *(21 ounces)* strawberry pie filling *(I used Comstock)****

*** If you can't find strawberry pie filling, you can use another berry filling, like raspberry, or blueberry. You can also use pie fillings of larger fruits like peach, apple, or whatever. If you do that, cut the fruit pieces into smaller pieces so that each bar cookie will have some. I just put my apple or peach pie filling in the food processor with the steel blade and zoop it up just short of being pureed. I'm not sure about

using lemon pie filling. I haven't tried that yet.

FIRST STEP: Mix the flour and the powdered sugar together in a medium-sized bowl.

Cut in the softened butter with a two knives or a pastry cutter until the resulting mixture resembles bread crumbs or coarse corn meal.

(You can also do this in a food processor using cold butter cut into chunks that you layer between the powdered sugar and flour mixture and process with the steel blade, using an on-and-off pulsing motion.)

Spread HALF of this mixture *(approximately 3 cups will be fine)* into a greased *(or sprayed with Pam or another nonstick cooking spray)* 9-inch by 13-inch pan. *(That's a standard size rectangular cake pan.)*

Bake at 350 degrees F. for 12 to 15 minutes, or until the edges are just beginning to turn golden brown.

Remove the pan to a wire rack or a cold burner on the stove, but DON'T TURN OFF THE OVEN!

Let the crust cool for 5 minutes.

SECOND STEP: Spread the pie filling over the top of the crust you just baked.

Sprinkle the crust with the other half of

the crust mixture you saved. Try to do this as evenly as possible. Don't worry about little gaps in the topping. It will spread out and fill in a bit as it bakes.

Gently press the top crust down with the flat blade of a metal spatula.

Bake the cookie bars at 350 degrees F. for another 30 to 35 minutes, or until the top is lightly golden.

Turn off the oven and remove the pan to a wire rack or a cold burner to cool completely.

When the bars are completely cool, cover the pan with foil and refrigerate them until you're ready to cut them. *(Chilling them makes them easier to cut.)*

When you're ready to serve them, cut the Strawberry Shortbread Bar Cookies into brownie-sized pieces, arrange them on a pretty platter, and if you like, sprinkle the top with extra powdered sugar.

CHAPTER TWENTY-THREE

"You've got goose bumps," Mike said, chuckling a bit as he reached out and shut the front door. "Sorry about that. I totally forgot the door was open."

"That's okay," Hannah said, deciding not to mention that she hadn't even noticed, and the icy air that was coming in the open door probably wasn't the cause anyway. Since it would be very easy to go straight back into Mike's arms again and continue right where they'd left off, she stepped back slightly and smiled at him. "Did you get a chance to have something for dinner?"

"No. I was going to stop by the Corner Tavern, but things got rushed at the station. Did you ask because you're going to feed me? Or was it just a matter of curiosity?"

"When have I ever failed to feed you?" Hannah answered his question with another question.

"Good! I'm starving. What did you have

in mind?"

Hannah thought fast. She had a number of quickie meals in her repertoire, and her choice depended on the ingredients she had on hand. "How about Welsh Rarebit?"

"Sounds great!" Mike said, giving her the devilish grin that always made her heart beat faster. "What is it?"

"You say it sounds good, but you don't know what it is?"

"Yeah. And that's because everything you make is good. Come on, Hannah . . . tell me what it is."

"It's like a puffy cheese sandwich with only one piece of bread. And I've got Strawberry Shortbread Bar Cookies for dessert."

"Oh, boy! I guess I knocked on the right door tonight! Can I start with dessert?"

"Of course," Hannah said, heading for the kitchen. "I'll put on a fresh pot of coffee and bring out a platter of bar cookies for you to munch on. And then I'll start the Welsh Rarebit. It only takes about fifteen minutes."

"I'm in no hurry. I'll just throw some mice for the big guy. He likes that, don't you, Moishe?"

Hannah watched as her cat turned into a shameless sycophant, rubbing up against

Mike's legs and purring so loudly she could hear him from the kitchen doorway. Moishe adored Mike. It seemed that all animals adored Mike. She'd seen him with Herb's pup, Dillon, and Mike knew exactly where to scratch his ears and which toys were his favorites. He was also really good with Norman's cat, Cuddles. Mike was the type of guy that everybody's pet loved.

Hannah had put on the coffee and she was setting the oven for the proper temperature when she happened to look at the top of the refrigerator. There was a sock ball leaning up against the ice bucket she almost never used.

"Oh, no! Not again!" she said, giving a heartfelt sigh. This was the fourth or fifth sock ball she'd found on top of the refrigerator and there was no way she'd dropped that many on her way from the laundry room to her bedroom. Either she was doing strange things in her sleep, or Moishe had somehow discovered how to open her sock drawer.

"Is there something wrong?" Mike asked, and Hannah turned to see him standing in the open kitchen doorway, a toy mouse in his hand. Moishe was right next to him, looking oh-so-ingenuous.

Hannah said nothing. She just pointed to

the top of the refrigerator where the sock ball sat.

"Rolled up socks?" Mike asked her.

"That's right. And I'm almost positive that I didn't put that sock ball there."

Mike turned to look at Moishe, who looked back up at him and started to purr. "You think *he* did?" Mike asked her.

"Yes, but I can't figure out how he does it. I keep them in a drawer in the bedroom, and it sticks. It's really hard to get open."

"Let me see," Mike said.

Hannah led the way to her bedroom and pointed to the drawer filled with similar sock balls. "Try to open it, and you'll see what I mean," she told him.

Mike grasped the handle and pulled. The drawer didn't move. He pulled again, a bit harder, and it still didn't budge. "It's really sticking," he said.

"I know. Sometimes if you jiggle and pull at the same time, it'll come open."

Mike did as she described and the drawer slid out reluctantly. "Moishe couldn't have opened this. It's a really heavy drawer," he said.

"The dresser's an antique, and they knew how to build them to last back then. Mother says it's solid mahogany, the same as my bedstead."

Mike turned to look at the bed and then he sighed deeply.

"What's wrong?" Hannah asked.

"It's your bed. It looks all soft, and comfortable, and warm, and . . . I've got to get out of here!"

Hannah laughed and grabbed his arm, pulling him toward the hallway. "I take it you haven't had much sleep lately."

"No, not much. Between that jewel robbery in the Cities, a couple of scams involving senior citizens, three stolen cars, and now the church murder case, I've been working doubles almost every day."

"Well, take a nap on the couch while I make the Welsh Rarebit," Hannah suggested. "They say that fifteen or twenty minutes of sleep can make a huge difference."

"Oh, it'll make a huge difference all right!" Mike said with a grin. "If I go to sleep, I'll *stay* asleep, and you'll have to drag me out the door in the morning."

"I'll take your word for it," Hannah said. "I'll bring the coffee and you can start eating those bars. The sugar may give you a lift."

As she arranged a tray for the coffee and put the cookie bars on a plate for Mike, Hannah thought about how she could parlay the information she'd gathered into something of value from Mike. She would tell him about Alice's visit to the parsonage on Sunday night, but she'd make sure to say that Alice had an alibi. If Mike needed to substantiate that, he could talk to Digger the way they had. That exchange should earn her a piece of information about the official investigation from Mike. And if that worked out, she might even mention . . . no, she wouldn't tell Mike about Lenny Peske and how he used to pal around with Paul, not until they'd had the chance to go out to the Eagle to question Lenny. If Mike got there first, it would take away the element of surprise, and surprise could give them the advantage. With the twists and turns this investigation was taking, they needed every advantage they could get.

"Wow!" Mike said with a sigh as he put down his fork. "That was incredible, Hannah. It had the perfect amount of hot sauce for me."

"Thanks," Hannah said, glad that she'd doubled the amount of hot sauce in the recipe for the fiery flavor-loving sheriff's detective.

Mike reached across the table to pick up the carafe to pour another cup of coffee for

Hannah. He refilled his own cup, returned the carafe to its trivet, and gave her a smile. "So how's the investigation coming?" he asked her.

"Investigation?" Hannah attempted an innocent expression. "You know I like to leave all that to the professionals."

"Right. Just like you always come to a full and complete stop at every stop sign and never ever go over the speed limit."

"How's *your* investigation going?" Hannah countered. There was no use denying that she was involved in Paul's murder case. Mike knew better.

"It's a tough case."

"Because you're suddenly investigating Paul's murder rather than Reverend Matthew's?"

"Yes, but that's only part of it. There's also the history."

"The fact that they went to school right here in Lake Eden and the murder might relate to that?"

"Exactly." Mike sat back on the couch and looked at her intently.

"What?" Hannah asked. Mike was staring at her so closely, she almost wondered if she had suddenly sprouted a second nose.

"I wish you weren't a baker."

Hannah reared back slightly. "But I

373

thought you liked what I baked!"

"I did. I *do!* I was just wishing that you were a detective and you were on my team. It'd make life a lot easier."

"How so?" Hannah asked, knowing full well that she was begging for a compliment. After what Norman had put her through tonight, she could use one!

"Because you're good at it, better than anybody else on my team. And then I wouldn't have to be careful about what I say around you."

"Why do you have to be careful?" Hannah asked, still feeling a warm glow from the compliment.

"It's police procedure. We're never supposed to discuss a case with anyone except other law enforcement personnel."

Hannah gave a little sigh, but secretly she was pleased. Perhaps he hadn't meant to do it, or perhaps he had, but Mike had opened the door to further discussion of the murder case. "Then I guess I can't tell you what I learned today," she said. "If I'm not other law enforcement personnel, you probably can't take me seriously."

"I can take you seriously. Detectives get information from many different sources."

"And sometimes you have to give information to get information, right?"

Mike's eyes narrowed. "Are you proposing some type of exchange?"

"I'm not proposing anything. I'm just saying that you might have information I'd find interesting, and I might have information that you'd find interesting."

"Sounds like an exchange to me," Mike said, clearly amused. "What have you got, Hannah?"

"You first. Mine is something I know you don't know."

"Okay . . . how about the time of death?"

"I've already got it. You'll have to come up with something better than that."

"The murder weapon?"

"You recovered it?"

"No, but we know what it is."

Hannah gave a little laugh. "So do I. It was a gun."

"Yes, but what caliber? What type? You don't know that, do you?"

"No, but is that important?"

"Not really. Not unless we find it. But just for your information, it was a twenty-two semiautomatic. We found the shell casing."

"Big whoop!" Hannah said, causing Mike to chortle. "Laugh all you want, but that's not enough. My information is worth more than that."

"Give me a little taste and I'll decide if I

should give you something better."

"Well . . . okay." Hannah thought for a moment. "You noticed the birdcage at the crime scene, didn't you?"

"Of course we did. Rick Murphy lifted the cover and recognized Pete Nunke's mynah bird."

"I covered the cage right after I found the body," Hannah told him.

"Why did you do . . ." Mike began to smile. "I get it. You didn't want the bird to see the corpse."

"Something like that, yes. But Jacob, the bird, saw the whole thing. And mynah birds talk."

Mike let out a laugh. "And the bird told you who the murderer is?"

"No, but Jacob mimics people's voices. And he was talking a blue streak at Grandma Knudson's this afternoon. He said, *It's almost eleven-thirty. I've got to get back.* And Norman and I recognized the voice."

"Really!" Mike said, sounding much more interested than he had before. "Who was it?"

"Not quite yet. You haven't told me anything of interest yet."

"Okay . . . how about this? I checked Paul's prison record. He was in for armed robbery, and he shot a security guard."

"With a twenty-two?" Hannah guessed.

"You're good, Hannah. And you're right. The gun was never recovered. Now tell me who the mynah bird fingered for being in the church office."

"Alice Vogel. She used to go out with Matthew in high school, and she met him again on the night he was killed."

"No wonder she seemed rattled when Lonnie and I talked to her this afternoon!"

"Alice is even more rattled now. Michelle and I talked to her early this evening, and we told her that Paul was masquerading as Reverend Matthew and that Paul was the one who was murdered. Poor Alice just couldn't take it in. She got Digger to fill in at the tournament for her and went straight home to try to regroup."

"I wonder if Alice guessed that the man she met wasn't Reverend Matthew," Mike speculated. "If she thought she'd been duped, that might have made her angry enough to . . ."

"Stop!" Hannah interrupted. "Alice didn't do it. She's got an alibi. We talked to Digger, and he said that Alice was back at the bowling alley by twenty to twelve Sunday night."

"Okay, but she could have gone back after she closed."

"She could have, but the time frame's wrong. Alice didn't close until after two in the morning. She had Night Owl League for the DelRay employees who get off at eleven."

Mike looked thoughtful. "Did you ask her if she saw anyone around the church?"

"Of course I did. She said absolutely nothing was moving when she walked to her car. No one walking, no cars driving by, no other cars parked in front of the parsonage, the church, or in the church lot."

"Okay. I'd better talk to her for form's sake, but it can wait until I chase down another couple of leads."

"Leads?" Hannah asked, leaning forward.

Mike leaned forward too, and cupped his hands around her face. "No," he said, giving her lips a brush with his. "That's enough for tonight. When you get more, call me and we'll do another exchange."

Mike stood up, pulled her to her feet, and gave her a hug. "So tell me what you're going to take a look at next and then I have to go. It's getting late."

Hannah thought for a moment even though thinking was difficult to do in the warm circle of Mike's arms. "I'm going to talk to some of the people Paul knew when he went to Jordan High," she said quite truthfully.

"Okay."

Hannah was surprised. "That's all right with you?"

"It's fine with me. I'm not pursuing that particular avenue, so we won't get in each other's way."

In other words, you don't think I'll find out anything important, Hannah's mind interpreted Mike's response, but of course she didn't say that.

"Now go to bed and I'll lock the door behind me," Mike said, hugging her once more and then heading for the door. "You'd better get a couple hours of sleep before it's time for you to get up again."

WELSH RAREBIT

If you don't have a toaster, DO NOT preheat the oven quite yet. If you do have a toaster, preheat the oven to 450 degrees F. *(a very hot oven),* rack in the middle position.

Hannah's 1st Note: I usually double this recipe so that it will serve 4 people, even when I make it for only 2 people. Everybody in my family wants another slice!

2 large slices good white bread *(I used egg bread from the deli — you could also use thick-sliced French toast bread)*

4 large eggs
8 ounces sharp cheddar cheese, grated
1/2 teaspoon dry mustard
Tabasco or your favorite hot pepper sauce *(I used Slap Ya Mama made by Walker & Sons)*
salt
freshly ground black pepper
1/8 teaspoon cream of tartar

Toast the bread in your toaster until it's golden brown. If you don't have a toaster, lay the bread flat on your broiler pan and toast the first side, watching carefully to make sure it doesn't burn. When it's golden brown, flip it over and toast the other side.

Remove the bread from the toaster *(or the broiler pan)* immediately. If you used the broiler, shut it off and set the oven to bake at 450 degrees F., rack in the middle position. *(Your oven will already be very close to that temperature if you used the broiler.)*

Find a baking pan that will hold both slices of bread comfortably. Spray it with Pam or another nonstick baking spray. *(I use an 8-inch square pan unless I double the recipe. Then I use a half steam table disposable foil pan placed on a cookie sheet to support the bottom.)*

Place the toast in the bottom of the baking pan.

Separate the eggs into whites and yolks. Here's how to do it for this recipe:

Crack egg #1, and pull the shell into two parts. Do a little juggling to drain off the white part into a medium-sized bowl. Dump the yolk that's left in the shell into another medium-sized bowl.

Repeat this process for egg #2 and egg #3.

Get out a little refrigerator container, the kind that will hold one egg yolk.

Crack egg #4, separate the white part into

the bowl with the other white parts, and dump the yolk into the refrigerator container so that you can add it to your scrambled eggs in the morning. Put the covered container in the refrigerator.

You now have two medium-sized bowls on the counter, one containing 3 egg yolks, the other containing 4 egg whites.

Beat the three egg yolks together until they're well mixed.

Add the grated cheddar cheese to the egg yolks, and mix everything up with a fork.

Mix in the dry mustard, stirring until it's incorporated.

Stir in the hot pepper sauce.

Add a generous sprinkle of salt and mix it in.

Sprinkle in some freshly ground pepper and stir well.

Set the bowl aside on the counter.

Add the cream of tartar to the bowl with the egg whites and stir it in. It'll help the egg whites whip up faster and stiffer.

Whip the 4 egg whites until they stand up in stiff peaks. You can use an electric mixer or do this by hand with a whisk. *(Doing it by hand takes some time and muscle — it's a lot easier with a mixer.)*

Add a large spoonful of stiff egg whites to the yolks and cheese mixture, stirring it in until it's well combined. That's called "tempering."

Add the rest of the egg whites to the cheese mixture. Fold them in gently with a rubber spatula, trying to keep as much volume and air as you can in the mixture.

Hannah's 2nd Note: To fold in the egg whites, simply place the side of the rubber spatula blade in the center of the bowl, dig it all the way down to the bottom, and then bring it toward you until it touches the side of the bowl nearest you. Keeping the rubber blade flat so that you lift as much of the mixture as possible, move the spatula up the side of the bowl, and flip the mixture you carried on the rubber blade in the center on top. Now give a bowl a little turn on the counter, and do the same thing all over again. It's like carefully stirring with the flat of your spatula. Do this until there are no big clumps of egg white left. There may be little clumps, but that's perfectly all right. (You just made a soufflé. It was easy, wasn't it?)

Gently spoon the resulting mixture over the toast in the baking pan.

Bake at 450 degrees F. for 10 minutes, or

until your Welsh Rarebit has browned and risen.

Hannah's 3rd Note: I made this once at Andrea's house for Andrea, Bill, Tracey, and me. *(That was before Bethie was born.)* **Tracey thought I was calling it Welsh Rabbit and she didn't want to eat it because she liked bunnies. I had to make her another piece just to show her that there weren't any bunnies in it.**

Yield: 2 extremely tasty servings.

Chapter Twenty-Four

It was almost one in the afternoon, and Hannah was exhausted. She'd talked to Andrea, who'd agreed to come in during her lunch break to talk about their trip to the Eagle, and she'd heard almost all of Lisa's newest story in bits and pieces as Marge and Michelle came into the kitchen from the coffee shop to refill the glass cookie jars they kept behind the counter. In Hannah's opinion, today's story was even better than the one Lisa had told yesterday, and the word was spreading fast. They'd been packed, standing room only, from ten in the morning on.

As Hannah took yet another batch of cookies from the oven and slid the baking sheets onto the baker's rack, there was a knock on the kitchen door. She finished her work in double time and hurried to the door to open it.

"Hi, Hannah!" Andrea dashed in and

hung her coat on a hook by the back door. "I don't think Mother saw me come in here. She invited me to dinner, but I told her I had something else I had to do."

"You didn't tell her we were going out to the Eagle, did you?"

"Of course not! I wouldn't be *that* dumb! Mother would want to go along, and then we'd have to watch out for . . ." Andrea stopped speaking, a reaction to Hannah's pained expression. "What's wrong?"

"Say hello to Mother," Hannah said, trying for humor that didn't work. "I guess the cat's out of the bag."

"Don't you take the species of my grand-cat in vain!" Delores said, marching over to the stainless steel workstation and taking a seat. "Now what's all this about going out to a horrible place like the Eagle?"

Hannah sighed deeply and plunged into the icy waters. "We really didn't want you to know, Mother. We thought you'd worry and there's really no reason . . ."

"Hannah!" Delores interrupted. "You're just wasting our time making excuses that aren't going to work anyway. I know you're going to the Eagle tonight with Andrea and probably Michelle. Why?"

"To see Lenny Peske. He used to hang around with Paul in high school and they got into trouble together."

"Not really serious trouble," Andrea said quickly. "It was things like breaking into school lockers and playing not-so-nice tricks on teachers they didn't like."

"I see. And you think Paul's murder may relate to some incident that happened in the past when he knew Lenny in high school?"

"It's possible," Hannah told her. "It's another avenue we can explore."

"Yes, I suppose that makes sense. Lenny's not a suspect, is he?"

Hannah shook her head. "As far as we know, he doesn't have a motive."

"All right, then. I won't worry if you go out there just to talk to Lenny while he's tending bar. But if he says something incriminating, I want you to promise to come straight home and let the police handle it."

"Okay," Hannah agreed quickly. "I promise we'll leave right away if anything like that happens."

"Well, then. I guess that's settled. How about some coffee, dear?"

"Of course, Mother. Andrea? You want coffee, don't you?"

Andrea shook her head. "No coffee. I'm still a little jittery from dealing with Bonnie Surma. I'll just have a soothing cookie and a small glass of milk."

Hannah did her best to figure out what constituted a "soothing cookie" as she poured Andrea's milk and her mother's coffee. She finally settled on filling half a plate with Old-Fashioned Sugar Cookies for their buttery sweetness and smooth melt-in-your-mouth texture, and the other half with squares of Candy Bar Bar Cookies for their endorphin-rich chocolate. "What happened with Bonnie Surma?" she asked as she delivered their drinks and sweet treats.

"She came in a little before noon," Delores said, motioning for Andrea to start in on the cookies. "She said she wanted to try on the little black dress Andrea put in the window this morning."

Hannah looked blank. "I didn't see it, but what's wrong with that?"

"For one thing, it has a darling draped look over the hips," Andrea told her. "And Bonnie has her *own* draped look over her hips."

Hannah began to smile. "I get it. The little black dress would have accentuated one of Bonnie's figure flaws."

"Exactly!" Delores exclaimed. "That's precisely what I told Bonnie, but for some reason she took offense."

"I told you, Mother. No one wants to be

reminded of their imperfections. There are other, better ways to suggest that the little black dress in the window just isn't the right look for her." Andrea turned to Hannah. "It took me over twenty minutes to convince Bonnie not to leave the shop and never darken Claire's door again. And it took me another twenty minutes to talk her into trying an incredibly gorgeous red dress that I'd just unpacked from the new shipment. Mother ironed it while Bonnie and I talked about which materials would enhance her effervescent personality and the vibrant, jewel-tone shades she was simply born to wear."

"The only reason she asked me to iron the red dress that didn't need ironing was to get me out of the room," Delores complained, but then she smiled at Andrea. "It turns out she was right. All that silly talk about personalities and color enhancements worked. Bonnie bought three dresses and all of them looked wonderful on her!"

They stopped talking as they heard the sound of applause coming from the coffee shop. It was obvious that Lisa had concluded this installment of *Hannah Finds the Body.* A few moments later, Lisa came into the kitchen. Her eyes were sparkling, her color was high, and she was smiling happily.

"I think that story was the best one today," she said, sinking down on the stool. "I even got a tip, and the people around here practically never tip!"

Hannah smiled at her partner. "That's great! How much did you get?"

"I'm not sure." Lisa reached into her apron pocket and pulled out a gold coin. "He said it's worth a dollar, but Herb thought it might be worth more."

"What is it?" Andrea asked her, staring at the coin in Lisa's hand.

"A Sacagawea gold dollar. Practically everybody in the coffee shop wanted to see it."

"Who gave it to you?" Hannah asked her.

"Lenny Peske."

The swinging door opened, and Michelle came into the kitchen. "They want you back for a curtain call, Lisa," she said. "By the way, that one was really good."

"Thanks," Lisa hurried back into the coffee shop, but Michelle stayed behind. "Jon Walker wants to see you," she told Hannah. "He took a look at that gold coin and he says he's got some information you need."

Michelle left and a moment later, she came back in with Jon Walker. He was dressed in his pharmacy greens, and he quickly accepted Hannah's invitation to join them for coffee and cookies.

"It's that gold coin, Hannah," Jon said, reaching for a Candy Bar Bar Cookie. "When Lisa showed it to me, I turned it over to look at the flip side. It's part of the first run of the coin. I could tell because the eagle didn't have the arrows that decorate the more recent runs."

"Does that make it more valuable?" Delores asked.

"Not really, but it's a coincidence that Lenny had one, because I put five original run Sacagawea dollars in the church collection plate on Sunday."

Hannah and Michelle exchanged glances. They knew that part of Sunday's collection had been stolen, perhaps by the person who had killed Paul.

"Are original run Sacagawea dollars rare?" Hannah asked him.

Jon shrugged. "I don't think they're *that* rare. I get them in at the drugstore occasionally. When I do, I put them in the church collection plate. Reverend Bob usually exchanges them for regular dollars and saves them for the kids who win prizes at Vacation Bible School in the summer."

"So how many Sacagawea dollars have you taken in this year at the drugstore?" Hannah followed up.

"I'm not sure. Maybe . . . ten or twelve."

"And how many of those would you say were original run Sacagawea dollars?"

"Maybe half."

"Then it wouldn't be *that* unusual for Lenny to have one?" Hannah asked the final question in the series.

"No. No, it wouldn't be *that* unusual, especially since some people save them when they get them and use them for tips. It's just a coincidence, that's all I'm saying. Lenny probably took it in while he was bartending out at the Eagle."

Once Jon had left and the door had swung shut behind him, Delores gave her three daughters a stern look. "I'm in," she said.

"You're in what, Mother?" Michelle asked. It was clear she was confused since she hadn't been a part of their original conversation.

"I'm in and we're using my car to go out to the Eagle. From what Jon just told us, Lenny could be a suspect. There's no way I'm going to let my three girls go out there alone!"

Hannah wrapped tape, sticky side up, around her right hand, and used it on her black sweater. It had been folded on top of the other sweaters in her drawer, but somehow it had picked up what looked like hundreds of orange and white cat hairs. She was almost finished when Michelle walked in.

"Cat hair on your sweater?" Michelle asked, watching her older sister pat the sweater with the tape.

"I'll say! It was in my drawer, and I don't know how it collected that much cat hair, but Moishe must be . . ." Hannah caught sight of her sister and stopped in midsentence. "You're wearing *that?*"

"Yes. I love to wear red, and the sequins really set off the color."

"You actually bought that?" Hannah asked her, wondering if her youngest sister was having some eye problems.

"Yes, and it was really cheap. I ran across the alley to the thrift store this afternoon, and I found it in the dollar bin."

"But it's at least three sizes too small for you!"

"Four sizes, but who's counting? This sweater, some really bright lipstick, and a pair of tight jeans will make me fit right in with the rest of the bar girls at the Eagle."

"I don't understand. You're not going undercover tonight. We're just going out there to talk to Lenny."

"You and Andrea are going out there to

talk to Lenny. Mother and I are going undercover to see what information we can learn about Lenny. We planned it all out this afternoon."

"But . . . how is that going to work when we're all going out in Mother's car?"

"We're not. There's been a change of plans. Mother's coming out here to pick us up, but you're going to drive her car and drop us off at Bud Hauge's place. Mother and I are borrowing his new truck."

Hannah couldn't help but be suspicious. "Mother put you up to this, didn't she?"

"Yes, but I didn't take much convincing. I think it'll be fun. I've never gone undercover with Mother before."

Hannah sighed. There wasn't much she could do about it at this late date. Delores was due to arrive in less than ten minutes. "All right. Go ahead. But you have to promise me one thing."

"What's that?"

"Remember the Karaoke contest Mother and Carrie entered at The Moosehead in Anoka?"

"Of course I remember. They sang *Bye Bye Love* and they were awful."

"Exactly. I want you to promise me that you won't let Mother sing."

CHAPTER TWENTY-FIVE

"Ready?" Andrea said as Hannah pulled into the parking lot at the Eagle and parked in the back row between a blue pickup truck and a black Ford with one door bashed in.

"I'm ready." Hannah got out and found her sister just standing there staring at the red neon sign that hung on the outside of the building, buzzing and blinking irregularly. The last time they'd come out here, they'd noticed that the manufacturer of the sign had left out the "A" in "eagle." The sign had read EGLE the last time Hannah had been here, but weather and age had taken their toll, and the sign had since gone through another transformation. The "L" in "eagle" had burned out and only the first "E," the "G," and the final "E" remained. It now read EGE with a strange gap between the letters.

"I wonder if they're ever going to fix that sign," Andrea mused.

"I doubt it. All the regulars know the name of this place and they don't have any reasons to advertise. It's not like it's a major tourist attraction."

Andrea laughed and her breath came out in a little white cloud. It was a cold evening, although not as cold as the night before.

"Let's go," Hannah said, picking up the bag of cookies she'd brought for Lenny and locking her mother's sedan before they headed across the snowy parking lot to the front door. "I want to get inside before Michelle and Mother get here."

"So that people won't suspect that we're together?"

"No, so that I won't have to look at Mother's outfit again."

"What's wrong with Mother's outfit?" Andrea asked.

"You'll see," Hannah said with a laugh. She'd picked up Andrea after she'd dropped Michelle and Delores at Bud Hauge's house, and Andrea had no idea what their mother was wearing.

As Hannah opened the door and held it for her sister, a cloud of warmth, a blast of country-western music, and the sound of raucous laughter greeted them. The smell was the same as it had been on their previous visit, one part spilled beer, one part too many people whose personal hygiene was questionable, and three parts something Hannah didn't want to attempt to identify.

"They're grilling again," Andrea gestured toward the area near the back door where portable charcoal grills had been set up to supply hamburgers and cheeseburgers. "Isn't that illegal?"

"I think so. Ask Bill when you get home, but don't say anything now. We don't want to get kicked out for being snitches."

"Don't worry, I won't say a word. There's two barstools together on the far end."

Andrea led the way to the stools, and they took a seat. That was a bit difficult because the woman on the stool next to Hannah was much larger than the circumference of her stool. Andrea moved her stool as far as she could to the wall, and Hannah managed somehow to squeeze in.

"What are you drinking?" Andrea asked.

"White wine, but I'm not going to drink it. I'm just going to spill a little on the floor now and then."

"But won't someone notice?"

"Take a look at the floor."

Andrea looked down and made a face. "Good point. I think I'll have the same. Lenny must be on break. The only person behind the bar is a woman."

"Hello, ladies," the waitress came over to them. "What can I get you tonight?"

"What kind of wine do you serve?" Andrea asked her.

"We've got white, red, and rosy. Name your poison."

"We'll each have a glass of white wine," Hannah said, before Andrea could ask what brand it was, or correct the woman's pronunciation.

The waitress was back almost immediately with two wine glasses filled with what Hannah hoped was white wine. She wasn't, however, about to find out, and she only pretended to sip.

"Thanks," Hannah said. "How much is that, please? We'll pay as we go tonight."

"Six-fifty apiece," the woman said, waiting until Hannah had handed her a twenty-dollar bill. "You want change?"

"Just the five, please," Hannah said, managing to keep the pleasant tone in her voice. No way was she going to tip the woman seven dollars for two glasses of wine that probably came out of a box!

Andrea took a sip of her wine and made a face. "This tastes like turpentine smells. And now that I think about it, it smells like turpentine, too."

"I'll take your word for it," Hannah said,

toying with the stem of her glass. "I hope Lenny gets back from his break soon. I want to ask him some questions and get out of here."

"I see Michelle," Andrea said, gesturing toward the tables that ringed the dance floor. "The guys must have picked up on her right away, because she's already dancing."

Hannah caught sight of her sister in the arms of a tall guy wearing a plaid shirt. He looked fairly normal, and that was good. But then she saw Delores. "Uh-oh! Look at Mother!"

"Where? I don't see her."

"She's dancing with a really big man. He's got to be six-four at least. He's wearing a red shirt, and he's got a beard."

Andrea was silent for a moment. "Okay. I see him, but . . . that's *Mother?!*"

"That's Mother."

"But . . . what is she *wearing?*"

"Just a little something she picked up at the mall," Hannah said with a grin.

Delores had outdone herself in the bad taste department. Their mother was dressed in shiny black leather pants with a fringe running down the outside of the legs. Her form-fitting top was also of shiny black leather and several large rhinestone butterflies flitted across the front. Bright red lipstick, long red nails, a fake blond wig, and black high-heeled boots completed the outfit.

"I don't believe it!" Andrea breathed, looking a bit ill. "You're wrong, Hannah. There's no way Mother got an outfit like that at the mall."

"Oh, yes she did. Michelle told me she rented it from the costume shop."

"But who would wear a costume like that? And why?"

Hannah shrugged. "Halloween?" she guessed. "Or maybe Dominatrix Day? I really don't know. The only thing I *do* know is I wish she'd worn something else."

"Me, too. I know mothers can disown children. But can children disown mothers?"

Hannah laughed. "You know you don't mean that. Mother looks as if she's having fun pretending to be someone else. We'd better help Michelle keep an eye on her."

"Right. I don't like the looks of that guy she's dancing with, but so far he's behaving. I've got Bill's number on speed dial just in case there's trouble. I just wish Lenny would . . ." Andrea stopped speaking and nudged Hannah. "Lenny's back. The office door just opened, and Lenny's coming out. He's carrying something."

Hannah turned to see Lenny heading for the other end of the bar. He was an average-looking guy who might have bordered on handsome if he'd lost twenty pounds, ditched the ragged sideburns, and gotten a good haircut. "It looks like some kind of a box. It's long and rounded on the ends, and it's covered with blue velvet."

"It's a jewelry case, the kind jewelers use for expensive necklaces," Andrea told her. "When Bill gave me pearls last Christmas, they came in a velvet box just like that."

As they watched, Lenny carried the box over to a man at the other end of the bar who opened it, glanced inside, and nodded. The man handed Lenny some folded bills which Lenny counted, and then Lenny shook his hand. The man, who was wearing a quilted parka vest, thrust the jewelry box in his inside pocket, and then he headed out the door.

"What was *that* about?" Andrea asked.

"I'm not sure, but the guy in the black cowboy shirt just handed Lenny some kind of ticket and a wad of money. And now Lenny's going back into the office again."

This time Lenny didn't stay in the office for long, and when he came out, he was carrying a blue velvet ring box.

"Here you go," he said handing it to the guy in the cowboy shirt. "You got this back just in time for her birthday."

The ticket, the money, and the phrase *you got this back* clicked together in Hannah's mind. "Do you think Lenny's running a pawnshop out of the office?" she asked Andrea.

"That's exactly what I think he's doing. And that's why he locks the office."

"I wonder what type of things he has in there. So far all we've seen is jewelry, and . . ." Hannah stopped speaking as Andrea grabbed her arm. "What is it?"

"What if it's more than a pawnshop? What if Lenny fences stolen goods, too? And what if he's got some of the jewelry from that robbery in the Cities?"

Hannah shook her head. "That doesn't track. It's much too rich for Lenny's blood. He can't afford to fence anything that expensive."

"Okay, so let's say he didn't fence it. Let's say he's just keeping it for the robbers and charging them storage while they look for a buyer. Does that track for you?"

"It's better, but I still don't think that Lenny could . . ."

"Shh!" Andrea hushed her. "Lenny's coming this way! You've got to get a look in that

402

office, Hannah. Some of the jewelry could be there, and then Bill would get credit for recovering it."

"Okay, I'll do my best," Hannah promised, and then she pasted a smile on her face.

"Ladies." Lenny slapped down two napkins and moved their wine glasses on top of them. "I see that Silky forgot to give you napkins. Can I get you another drink as an apology?"

"Only if you pour this out and fill our glasses with ginger ale," Hannah said, smiling at him. "I'm sorry I missed you at the coffee shop today. I was in the kitchen baking."

Lenny looked puzzled for a moment, and then he smiled back. "Hannah. I didn't expect to see you out here. Don't you like the high-quality white wine we serve?"

Hannah shook her head and leaned forward so no one else at the bar could hear. "It's awful. What kind is it anyway?"

"I don't know. It comes in a white box with a blue stripe, and it says *High-quality White Wine* on it." Lenny laughed at his own joke, and Hannah joined in. "What brings you way out here?" he asked her.

"This," Hannah answered, setting the bag of cookies she'd brought on the bar. "You left before I could give these to you. It's a new recipe I got from my friend, Edwina Gadsby, and I'm trying it out with my customers. They're called Chocolate-Covered Raisin Cookies."

Lenny cocked his head. "Edwina Gadsby. That name's familiar."

"It should be. Her folks owned the Lake Eden movie theater until it burned down when I started high school."

"Right! They called it The Great Gadsby, and they had matinees on Saturday for half price." Lenny looked thoughtful. "Are the chocolate-covered raisins in the recipe like the Raisinets we used to buy at the candy counter?"

"They're not only like them, they *are* them. Florence ordered Raisinets for me at the Red Owl, and that's what I used in these cookies."

"Then I'm going to like these a lot. Thanks, Hannah. I'd better put these away so my waitresses can't snag them all. I think I'll lock them up in the office."

"That reminds me," Hannah said quickly. "Do you have a phone in the office that I can use? I forgot to charge my cell phone and I need to make a private call."

"Sure. I'll unlock it."

"Great! Is it okay if I close the office door

so I can hear better? It's really noisy in here."

"Fine with me, but if you think this is noisy, you should hear it on Saturday night." Lenny motioned to her. "Come with me."

Hannah slid off her stool and brushed close to Andrea. "Distract him when he gets back," she said. "You can ask him about the gold dollar."

CHOCOLATE-COVERED RAISIN COOKIES

Preheat the oven to 350 degrees F.,
rack in the middle position.

Hannah's 1st Note: Edwina says that while her grandmother made a delicious oatmeal raisin cookie, she decided it was time to try an updated more "extreme" version. Her additions were: chewy chocolate-covered raisins, instant butterscotch pudding mix, and butterscotch chips. The result was definitely not her grandmother's oatmeal raisin cookie!

1 cup salted butter, softened *(2 sticks, 8 ounces, 1/2 pound)*

1 small package *(makes 4 half-cups)* butterscotch instant pudding mix *(NOT sugar-free)****

1/2 cup white *(granulated)* sugar

1/2 cup brown sugar *(pack it down in the cup when you measure it)*

1 egg, beaten *(just whip it up in a glass with a fork)*

1 teaspoon vanilla extract

1 teaspoon baking soda

1/4 teaspoon salt

1/2 teaspoon ground cinnamon

1 and 1/2 cups all-purpose flour *(pack it down in the cup when you measure it)*

1 and 1/2 cups quick rolled oats *(not instant — I used Quaker's Quick 1-minute)*

1 cup chocolate-covered raisins (*I used Nestle Raisinets, an 11-ounce bag. There was about 1/4 cup left, but not for very long!)*

1 cup butterscotch chips *(a 6-ounce package)*

*** *If you can't find butterscotch instant pudding mix, you can use vanilla instant pudding mix, the kind that makes 4 half-cup servings. You can also use a 3.5 ounce package (also makes 4 half-cup servings) of butterscotch-flavored Jell-O Cook & Serve, but NOT the sugar-free kind.*

Hannah's 2nd Note: You can mix these cookies up by hand, but it's a lot easier with an electric mixer.

Mix the softened butter, dry pudding mix, white sugar, and brown sugar together. Beat them until they're light and fluffy.

Add the egg and the vanilla extract. Mix them in thoroughly.

Add the baking soda, salt, and cinnamon. Mix until everything is incorporated.

407

Add the flour in half-cup increments, mixing after each addition.

Add the rolled oats in half-cup increments, mixing after each addition.

Remove the bowl from the mixer and stir in the chocolate-covered raisins and the butterscotch chips by hand.

Drop the cookie dough by rounded Tablespoonfuls onto an ungreased cookie sheet, 2 inches apart, no more than 6 cookies to a standard-sized sheet. You can also use a 2-Tablespoon size scooper if you wish.

Bake the Chocolate-Covered Raisin Cookies at 350 degrees F. for 15 to 17 minutes or until the edges are golden brown.

Hannah's 3rd Note: Edwina makes her cookies much larger than we do down at The Cookie Jar. Hers are triple the size of ours. We use a 2-teaspoon size scooper instead of the 2-Tablespoon size, and bake our cookies at 350 degrees F. for 10 to 12 minutes or until the edges are golden brown.

Regardless of size, cool the cookies for 2 minutes on the cookie sheets. Then remove them to a wire rack to complete cooling.

Yield: Makes approximately 2 and 1/2 dozen large cookies. If you bake the smaller size, this recipe will make approximately 6 dozen sensational cookies.

Lisa's Note: Herb adores these cookies. He says that no one can eat just one Chocolate-Covered Raisin Cookie.

CHAPTER TWENTY-SIX

It looked like an ordinary office with a desk and desk chair, two less comfortable chairs sitting in front of it, and a filing cabinet. There was a mirror on the wall opposite the door, perfectly placed to observe the door opening and see who was there if her back was turned. Somehow Hannah didn't think the mirror's placement was a lucky accident.

She closed the office door, dialed her own number, and got the answering machine. It was a little strange listening to her own voice on the outgoing message, and she found herself wishing she sounded a bit more businesslike. On the other hand, no one called her home phone for business, so casual was perfectly all right. If Lenny happened to pick up the phone behind the bar and listen in, he'd hear her talking and hang up. She hoped.

"Are you there, Norman?" she asked when

her recorded voice stopped speaking and the beep sounded. "It's me. If you're there, pick up the phone."

Of course Norman didn't pick up the phone. She didn't expect him to come to her condo because she hadn't heard from him all day.

"I hope you get this message because we really have to talk about something," she said, pulling out the first desk drawer. There was nothing there except pens, a ruler, and a telephone book. She paged through the telephone book as she told Norman that they needed to discuss his mother's birthday present, but there were no marks by any of the names or any cryptic notes.

"Whatever you do, don't tell her we're getting together on this," she said into the phone. And then she shut the center drawer and opened the top drawer on the right side.

The drawer was almost empty. There was absolutely nothing inside except a fake leather datebook. "I was thinking of perfume, but I don't know which scent she prefers," she said as she opened the datebook. It was filled with names and numbers, obviously the work schedule for the waitresses. Hannah closed it, put it back in the drawer, and tried the next drawer down.

"It seems to me I remember her wearing

Chanel," she said, choosing the first perfume name that came to mind, "but I don't think it was number five. I saw a bottle in the guest bathroom once, and I think it was a different number."

Rubber bands, paper chips, staples, and two kinds of tape. "I'd really hate to get her some brand she won't wear. Everybody's got favorites, you know. Maybe we're better off with a really good silk scarf."

Hannah closed the drawer. It contained nothing but office supplies. And then she opened the bottom drawer, the one that was intended to be a file cabinet.

There were no files inside. Instead, there was a leather pouch. "Or maybe we could find a nice dressy sweater, but you're going to have to take a peek in her closet for the size. I'll ask Mother, but she might not know."

Hannah drew out the pouch. It was heavier than she expected it to be. She unzipped it and almost dropped the contents, she was so surprised.

"A gun," she breathed, and then, when she realized that she still had the phone up to her mouth, she cleared her throat and said, "Again, you'll have to get the size somehow. I don't want to have to guess on something that important."

Hannah stared down at the gun and frowned slightly. It was a thirty-eight revolver, and it couldn't be the murder weapon. Mike had told her that the gun used to kill Paul was a twenty-two semiautomatic.

One-toe-over-the-line, Hannah thought as she zipped up the pouch and put it back exactly where she'd found it. Those were the words Lonnie's Uncle Pat had used to describe Lenny. The gun was probably illegal, but she wasn't here to nail him for illegal possession of a firearm. She was here to find out if he had the stolen jewels.

"The more I consider it, the more I think we should go more generic," Hannah said. "Maybe we should get her a new watch. You said she's always losing watches."

A search of the file cabinet was next, and Hannah stretched out the phone cord and spoke of various brands of timepieces as she riffled through the three-drawer cabinet. There were papers, nothing but papers. Hannah didn't bother to read any. She just shut the drawers after she inspected them and returned to the desk.

There was only one place left to look, and that was the bookcase against the wall. It contained video tapes in sleeves with numbers written on the spines. Some of the

413

numbers were the same, but they had alphabetic extensions. This could refer to three episodes of a television series, but Hannah doubted it.

"Of course we could buy another type of jewelry," she suggested as she walked over to the bookcase. She hadn't seen any list of movies in any drawer she'd searched. Hannah pulled out a tape at random, number forty-three C. There was no videotape inside the sleeve. Instead of a movie, she found a packet of tissue paper with a string of pearls inside.

"Pearls!" she gasped, but she recovered quickly. "I just remembered that your mother loves pearls. That's what we could get her for her birthday. Or maybe . . ." Hannah opened sleeve number twenty-seven, ". . . a nice cocktail ring."

By the time she was through checking the tissue and jewelry inside the videotape sleeves, Hannah had tired of talking to her own answering machine about a gift for Carrie's imaginary birthday.

"This would be easier in person, Norman," she said. "I'm going to use up my whole answering machine tape if I keep on talking, so I'll see you when I get home, okay?"

Once Hannah was back on her stool and

414

Lenny was relocking the office door, she leaned close to her sister. "Nothing," she said. "Bill could get him on other things, like running a pawnshop without a license, but he's not connected with that robbery in the Cities."

"Oh, drat! I was hoping."

"I know you were. I don't know if I should be disappointed, or relieved. I like Lenny, but . . . Uh-oh!"

Andrea turned to look where Hannah was pointing and her eyes widened as she saw the guy in the red shirt and another, equally large man, facing off on the dance floor.

"I'll get Mother, you get Michelle," Hannah said sliding off her stool and heading toward the fracas as fast as she could.

"I'm right behind you," Andrea said, racing to keep up with her older sister.

"Where'd they go?" Hannah asked as they reached the edge of the dance floor.

"I don't know. They were right there a second ago . . . wait! There's Mother!"

Andrea's eyes widened as she saw their mother with her elbows pointing forward, swinging wildly from side to side. It was such an odd sight that everyone around her got out of her way as she scurried through the crowd.

"Michelle's a few feet ahead of Mother,"

415

Hannah said, catching a glimpse of Michelle's sweater. "She's doing the same thing with her elbows and everyone around them is falling back."

"I didn't know Mother could move that fast!" Andrea said, sounding shocked.

"It's all about incentive," Hannah told her. "Move fast and intimidate the rest of the crowd or you get stuck."

"I'll have to remember that for Macy's next white sale," Andrea commented. "Come on, Hannah. Let's go meet them outside the door."

Hannah and Andrea hurried toward the door, but before they got there, they heard the sound of beer bottles breaking and the thud of fists hitting their mark. Andrea turned to look back as they exited and let out a whistle.

"What?" Hannah asked her as they exited and the door closed behind them, muffling the noise.

"It's a real brawl. I just saw the guy in the red shirt pick up two other guys and bash their heads together. And I thought that only happened in the movies!"

They found their youngest sibling and their mother next to Bud Hauge's truck. Hannah marched up to them and asked the important question. "What happened?"

"Later," Delores told her. "I have to get this truck back to Bud. Follow us there and pick us up. We'll all go to Bertanelli's to debrief."

Debrief? Hannah's mind repeated the word in the form of a question, but Hannah didn't ask out loud. Pizza would be good, and she could wait. "Just tell me if you learned anything."

"Oh, my yes!" Delores replied. "How about you?"

"I learned something," Hannah answered, and then she turned to Andrea. "Did you find out anything else?"

"Of course I did. I know how to pump people for information."

"To Bud's house and then to Bertanelli's," Delores said, activating the keyless entry on Bud's fancy truck. "I need to get my coat. This leather's not as warm as I thought it would be."

Forty-five minutes later, Hannah, Andrea, Michelle, and Delores were seated at one of the round tables at Bertanelli's Pizza. Delores had dropped off the truck at Bud Hauge's house, and they'd idled in front of their mother's house while Delores had dashed in to change clothes. The black leather costume was now in a bag in the trunk of her sedan, awaiting return to the costume shop at the Tri-County Mall.

"So now will you tell us what the fight was about?" Hannah asked, once their waitress had written down their order and left.

"You first," Delores replied, pointing at Andrea. "What did you discover, dear?"

"I found out where Lenny got the Sacagawea gold dollar. Silky, the waitress who delivered our horrible wine, took it in as a tip on Saturday night. Lenny cashed it in for her and he paid her two dollars for it."

"*Saturday* night?" Michelle repeated what Andrea had said.

Andrea nodded. "That's right. On Saturday night. I checked it out with Silky and she said the same thing."

"If she got it on Saturday, it couldn't have been a part of the church collection on Sunday."

"That's right," Hannah said. "It's just like Jon Walker said. It's a coincidence."

"Then Lenny's in the clear?" Delores asked.

Hannah shook her head. "Not quite yet. We need to find out if he has an alibi."

"He has," Michelle said. "The guy I was dancing with said he went drinking with

Lenny on Sunday night and they stayed out until three in the morning. Since Doc said Paul was killed between midnight and two, that means Lenny's cleared."

"It does," Hannah agreed. "Thanks, Michelle. How about you, Mother?"

"You first, dear," Delores said, taking a sip of her coffee. "If you don't mind, I'd like to go last."

It cost her nothing to humor her mother, and Hannah didn't really mind. "I found out that Lenny is running an illegal pawnshop from his office at the Eagle." And then she proceeded to tell the story of how she'd come to look inside the videotape sleeves while she was leaving a message on her own answering machine that Norman would never hear.

"I wonder if Bill will arrest him," Michelle said.

"I don't know," Hannah said with a shrug. "In a way, I hope he won't. It didn't look as if Lenny was charging exorbitant rates, and people would probably rather go to him than a pawnbroker." She turned to Delores. "Come on, Mother. Tell us what the fight was about."

"It was about me," Delores admitted. "Spike wanted to dance with Trixie, and Hub wouldn't give her up."

"Who's Trixie?" Andrea asked.

"Trixie's me. It's the name I used at the Eagle. I wasn't about to give my real name. Michelle thought it was perfect with my outfit."

"And Hub is the guy in the red shirt?" Hannah asked.

"It's short for Hubbard," Michelle told them. "I was dancing with his son."

"Hub Hubbard," Andrea gave a little shiver. "Bill mentioned him once. He said all the Hubbards were real troublemakers."

Michelle nodded. "Bill's right. Hub's son told me his dad just got out of county lockup."

"What was he in for?" Andrea asked her.

"I don't know, but he was there for three months. They were out at the Eagle to celebrate Hub's first night home."

"You sure know how to pick 'em, Mother!" Hannah couldn't resist saying.

"I didn't pick him. He picked Trixie. And you should be really glad he did!"

All three daughters stared at their mother in shock. "Why?" Andrea finally asked.

"Because I found out who made those prank phone calls to Bill about that fake job in Florida."

"You did?!" Andrea was clearly amazed.

"Yes, I did. Hub just volunteered the

420

information when I told him I'd been harassed by the sheriff last week."

"Mother!" Andrea was obviously shocked. "Bill doesn't harass anyone! You know that's not true!"

"Of course I do, but I was playing Trixie. And Trixie *might* have been harassed by the sheriff. Actually, you should be glad I said that, because Hub was very sympathetic and he tried to make Trixie feel better."

Hannah was almost afraid to ask, but she did. "How did he do that, Mother?"

"He asked if Trixie knew about the trick somebody played on the sheriff a few months ago, calling him about a great job in Florida."

"What did you say?"

"Trixie said she'd heard about it and she thought it was really funny. And then she added that she'd just love to meet the guy who did it."

Andrea was all ears. "And he told you?"

"He told Trixie," Delores corrected her. "Hub came right out and admitted that he was the one who thought up the dirty trick in the first place, and his son was the one who made the calls."

"Good work, Mother!" Hannah complimented her. "Or should I say, good work, *Trixie?*"

"Mother is fine, dear."

"I'd better tell Bill right away," Andrea said, reaching in her purse for her cell phone.

Delores shook her head. "Oh no, you don't. *I'll* call Bill. I was the one who had to wear that ridiculous costume and pretend I was having a good time."

Delores waited until Andrea dropped her cell phone back into her purse and then she turned to Michelle.

"And that reminds me," she said to Michelle. "I want to know exactly how and where you learned that trick about leading with swinging elbows!"

CHAPTER TWENTY-SEVEN

Morning came much too early for Hannah. They'd sat at Bertanelli's for an hour unwinding, and then she'd come home to an answering machine flashing with the message light. When she'd played the message, she'd expected to hear her own voice giving the fake message to Norman, but the message had been from Norman himself, saying that he'd been planning to come over, but something had come up and he'd try to contact her tomorrow. That was it. No *I love you,* no *I'm sorry,* no *I miss you.* Nothing of a personal nature whatsoever.

Bleary-eyed and definitely not bushy-tailed, Hannah wrapped herself in her old robe. She turned to look for her live-in feline, but Moishe wasn't moving. He was nestled in the center of the expensive down-filled pillow she'd bought to keep him from stealing hers, and his tail didn't even flicker when she called his name.

"Lazy," Hannah said to the cat who was snoring softly, but she didn't have the heart to wake him. Then she padded down the carpeted hallway, too tired to look for her slippers. She couldn't blame Moishe for staying in bed. No one should have to get up when it was still dark outside. When she reached the kitchen, she reached out to flick on the lights, but the lights were already on.

There was Michelle, sitting at her kitchen table, looking much more awake and pretty than anyone had the right to look at this hour of the morning. Hannah couldn't help it. She growled.

"What was *that?*" Michelle asked.

"Jealousy. Is there coffee?"

"Yes, but you're not getting any. Go back to bed and I'll reset the pot. Lisa doesn't want you to come in before ten this morning. She says you have to get some sleep so your mind's a steel trap."

"But . . . how will you get to The Cookie Jar?"

"I've got Mother's car, remember?"

"Oh. Yeah." Hannah vaguely remembered Delores saying that Michelle could use her car as long as she returned the costume to the shop at the mall.

"Go back to bed before you wake up," Michelle said, standing up, turning Hannah around, and giving her a gentle shove in the right direction. "Moishe's waiting for you."

Hannah went back to bed. She crawled in next to her softly snoring cat and shut her eyes. And she didn't open them again until the bright sun streaming in her bedroom window woke her at nine-fifteen.

Sleep was a wonder drug. Hannah was convinced. She even hummed a little tune as she loaded the shelves of her industrial oven with cookies. She set the timer, sat down at the workstation, and sipped her coffee gratefully. Lisa was the best partner in the world.

"Oh, good!" Lisa said, coming in through the swinging door from the coffee shop. "You made Molasses Crackles."

"Plus Almond Kisses, Lisa's Pieces, and Red Velvet Cookies. I'm making Mocha Nut Butterballs next."

"Perfect," Lisa refilled the empty display cookie jar she was holding from the cookies on the baker's rack and turned to go. "How about a couple of pans of Blonde Brownies? Do you have time to make those?"

"I've got nothing *but* time. Thanks to you, I got enough sleep and now . . ." Hannah stopped speaking as the phone rang. "I'll get it."

Lisa left and Hannah grabbed the wall phone. "The Cookie Jar. This is Hannah speaking," she answered.

"Hannah! I'm so glad you answered!"

"Grandma Knudson?" Hannah asked, recognizing her friend's voice despite the fact that it was quavering. "Is there something wrong?"

"Yes! I just don't know what to do, Hannah. I'm filled with doubt."

Hannah went on red alert. Grandma Knudson, usually an extremely competent and self-confident person, sounded very unsure of herself. "Does your doubt have to do with your faith?" she asked, hoping that wasn't the case. She really wasn't sure how to deal with anyone who was having a crisis of faith.

"Oh no, dear. My faith is as strong as ever. It's just . . . if you can, I'd like to see you, Hannah. I really need to talk to someone who'll understand."

"Understand what, Grandma Knudson?"

"I'm afraid I'm having some kind of breakdown. I'm beginning to doubt my own mind!"

The moment she stepped into the parsonage kitchen, Hannah knew something was drastically wrong. There was no coffee, and the pot was stone cold.

"Grandma Knudson?" she called out, carrying the box of cookie bars she'd hastily packed. They were Chocolate Euphoria Cookie Bars made with the substitute for sweetened condensed milk.

"I'm here. In my . . . my sitting room," Grandma Knudson replied, and to Hannah's ears, she sounded frail and confused.

"I'll be right there," Hannah said, heading down the hallway without stopping to put on a fresh pot of coffee or even unpacking the cookie bars she'd brought. If Grandma Knudson was ill, she'd call Doc Knight right away.

When Hannah entered the sitting room, she found Grandma Knudson in her favorite chair, an open Bible on her lap. "What's wrong, Grandma Knudson?" she asked.

"It's Matthew. But I don't think he *is* Matthew. That's the problem. And if I tell you, you're going to think I'm a senile old woman!"

"Never!" Hannah replied immediately, opening the bakery box and gesturing toward the bar cookies. "Have one. They're Chocolate Euphoria Cookie Bars made with the substitute for sweetened condensed milk that I sent you."

Grandma Knudson perked up a bit. "The

one with powdered milk and butter?"

"No, the one without any milk at all. Try one and tell me if it's almost as good as the real ones."

Grandma Knudson reached for a bar and took a bite. She chewed for a moment and then she nodded. "Different, but just as good. And much cheaper. I had Clara and Marguerite pick me up a couple of cans of sweetened, condensed milk, and they were almost three dollars and fifty cents apiece!"

"I didn't realize it had gotten that expensive," Hannah said, wondering if she should remind Grandma Knudson why she was here, or leave well enough alone. The little discussion about baking and ingredient prices seemed to have settled her down.

"Sit down, Hannah," Grandma Knudson said, gesturing toward the awful pink davenport. "I want to tell you why I called you. And then you can decide whether I've gone 'round the bend, or not."

Hannah's heart sank as she sat down on the uncomfortable davenport. It seemed she didn't have to remind Grandma Knudson of anything. The matriarch of the Lake Eden Holy Redeemer Lutheran Church had an agenda, and she was sticking to it.

"Remember when I thought the fake Matthew wasn't Matthew for all the wrong reasons?"

"Yes, I do," Hannah said, nodding quickly. "And you turned out to be right."

"I don't think so now. Now I think this Reverend Matthew is a fake. As a matter of fact, I'm sure of it. And I'm afraid that makes me into a confused old lady who doesn't know up from down."

Hannah wasn't about to touch that one. It *did* sound crazy. Instead of commenting, she decided to ask a question. "What makes you think this minister isn't Reverend Matthew?"

"That's just it, Hannah. I'm beginning to think the first Reverend Matthew was the real one. And I don't think this one is a minister at all. He did something that no real minister would do, and that's what convinced me."

"What did he do?" Hannah asked, beginning to get a little confused with names and pronouns herself. "The current Reverend Matthew, I mean."

"He stood on the Bible."

Now Hannah really was confused. "Is that like standing up for Jesus?"

"No. I mean *standing,* with his feet, right on top of the holy scriptures! That's something a real minister would never do, Hannah. It's disrespectful!"

"I can understand that," Hannah said quickly. "It would be like having a tea party with the communion glasses."

"My little sister did that," Grandma Knudson confided, "and everyone was horrified. But she was just a little child who didn't know any better. She saw the small cups and thought they were doll size. This is different, Hannah. A real minister, an adult who's gone through the seminary and been ordained, would never treat the Bible that way."

"Where was . . . the current Matthew when he did this?"

"In the church office no more than fifteen minutes ago. I called you right after I saw him. He said he was too busy to come to the parsonage for tea, so I decided to bring him a tray. I found him standing on a little pile of books so that he could look at the top of the tallest bookcase. There's nothing up there, Hannah. I don't know why he was doing that."

"And you think one of the books he stood on was the Bible?"

"I *know* it was. I knocked on the open door, and he stepped down right away. And then he came to meet me and took the tray. He said it was sweet of me to bring him tea and he appreciated it. And then he said he was doing research for next Sunday's sermon. And that's when I saw that the top book on the pile, the one he'd been standing on, was the Bible. I just wish I knew what he was looking for on that top shelf."

"Maybe he was doing research and he needed a book that was there for reference?"

Grandma Knudson shook her head. "Impossible. The only books on the top shelf are the old hymnals that Bob takes down for Vacation Bible School. The kids love to use real hymnals, but they're hard on them so he uses the old ones. There's nothing in there that's not in the new hymnals, and there are at least a dozen of those on the shelf below. He was looking for something, Hannah. But I can't figure out what it could be."

"Is he still in the church office?" Hannah asked.

"No, he's visiting the sick at the hospital. I didn't call you until he left. I was afraid he'd hear me."

"That's good," Hannah praised her for her caution. "As long as he's gone, I'm going to go over to the church office to have a look."

"Then you think he was searching for something?"

"I don't know what else to think, unless

431

he had a dust rag in his hand. He didn't, did he?"

Grandma Knudson smiled for the first time. "No. He's not as neat as the first Matthew, the one I think was real. This one leaves his clothes on the floor, just like Paul used to . . ." Grandma Knudson stopped and began to frown. "It can't be!"

"It *could* be," Hannah said. "Norman printed out some pictures of Matthew and Paul when they were in high school, and they looked a lot alike."

"That's true. Then you think this fake minister is Paul?"

"I don't know *what* to think, but it's a distinct possibility. I'm going over to search the church office. Do I need a key?"

"I don't know if he locked it, but take mine." Grandma Knudson reached into her apron pocket and pulled out a key on a key chain with a little bell charm attached.

"That's cute," Hannah commented.

"My husband gave it to me. I used to ring the church bell for him before Sunday services. What should I do if Paul or whoever he is comes back?"

"I'll probably hear his car drive in, but if you see him turn into the lot, call me at the church office."

"I will. Don't let him catch you, Hannah.

I have the terrible feeling that he killed Matthew."

"I have that feeling, too. Don't worry, Grandma. I'll search as fast as I can and be right back."

CHAPTER TWENTY-EIGHT

It was difficult to search when you didn't know what you were searching for. All Hannah knew was that Grandma Knudson had seen Paul, or Matthew, or whoever he was, searching for something in the church office. Hannah's hope was that he hadn't found it and she would find it first.

There was nothing in the tall bookcase. Hannah had checked behind every book on every shelf. She'd even opened them all to make sure none were hollow inside to provide a hiding place.

I know why you're here and you're not going to find it! Jacob had said in the fake Reverend Matthew's voice. But Grandma Knudson didn't think he'd been the fake Reverend Matthew, not anymore. Now she thought that he was the *real* Reverend Matthew, and the second man who came to Lake Eden claiming to be Reverend Matthew was really Matthew's cousin Paul.

Hannah buried her head in her hands for a moment. Just wait until she told Lisa about this newest development! It was almost too much to fathom. If she could prove that Paul had murdered Reverend Matthew and then come to Lake Eden, pretending to be Matthew so that he could identify Matthew's body as his, everyone in town would rush to The Cookie Jar to listen to Lisa's stories.

Hannah sighed as she searched the desk. If there'd been anything of interest, the crime scene techs would have found it, but this case had so many twists and turns, she dared not leave any stone unturned.

I know why you're here and you're not going to find it! Those were the words the first Reverend Matthew had spoken to his killer. And if their suspicions were correct, his killer was his cousin Paul. That meant Paul knew that Reverend Matthew had hidden whatever it was that Paul had come to Lake Eden to get. But how had Reverend Matthew gotten what Paul wanted in the first place? And where had he hidden it?

The whole thing was just too confusing for words. Hannah's mind was spinning in circles, and she knew she had to stop thinking about who was who, and what was where. Instead, she should be concentrating on where the whatever-it-was could be hidden. It wasn't in the church office. She'd checked everywhere. Where else would a minister hide something in his church?

"The baptismal font," Hannah said aloud. It had a cover, and no one would think to look in there. She got up from the desk chair and raced down the aisle to the front of the church. There it was, the white marble basin with the ornate gilt-painted cover that had witnessed thousands of baptisms.

Thirty minutes later, Hannah was ready to give up her search altogether. She'd checked every hiding place at the front of the church, including the pulpit and the statues. She'd gone through every pew, looking for anything that might be taped under the seats or inside the hymnal and Bible racks. She'd searched the little storage room where the communion supplies and the vestments were kept, and she'd even explored the choir loft. The only place she hadn't gone was the belfry and that was because she wasn't sure how to get there. Grandma Knudson would know. She'd mentioned that she used to ring the church bell when her husband was the minister.

The moment she thought of it, Hannah raced back to the church office and picked up the phone. She dialed the parsonage and was greatly relieved when Grandma Knudson answered. "I need to know how to get up in the belfry," she said.

"The belfry?" Grandma Knudson sounded surprised. "Why do you want to go up there?"

"Because Reverend Matthew could have hidden something up there to keep Paul from finding it. It seems unlikely, but I've checked everywhere else."

"All right. Whatever you think best, Hannah. To get to the belfry, all you have to do is go through the door in back of the choir loft. There's a circular staircase that leads up to the bell-ringer's platform."

"And that's the belfry?"

"Only part of it, dear. You'll see the rope for the bell and if you look to the right, you'll notice another staircase that looks like a ladder next to the wall. There's a trap door above that staircase and the bell tower's up there."

"Uh-oh," Hannah breathed, not liking the sound of that. She wasn't exactly afraid of heights, but she certainly wasn't comfortable with them. And although she didn't think she was claustrophobic, she asked her next question anyway. "Is the bell tower large?"

"It's good-sized, but you can only stand up in the center. The rest is filled with rafters that support the steeple. And of course the bell and the bellframe are in the middle. Since you're tall, you'll have to duck a little to walk around that."

Hannah sighed. The belfry didn't sound like a pleasant place to visit. And then she remembered the phrase her grandmother Ingrid had used to describe someone with only part of their faculties. "Are there bats in the belfry?" she asked.

"I don't know, dear. I've never been all the way up there, but I imagine there *could* be bats. You should be very quiet when you're up there and they'll probably stay asleep. Bats are nocturnal animals, you know."

"I know," Hannah said, not terribly relieved by that piece of knowledge. Nocturnal did not mean nonfunctional in daylight. She'd watched part of a program about bats on the animal channel. They'd debunked the old wives' tale that bats were blind in the daylight and could get tangled in your hair, but she was glad she had tightly curled hair all the same.

"At least there's no such thing as a vampire bat," Hannah said, trying for humor.

"Oh, yes there is. They're from Mexico, I

believe. Of course they're not like Count Dracula or any other foolishness like that, but I understand that they bite."

Lovely! Hannah's mind interjected. *Bats that bite. That's all I need!*

"Good luck, Hannah," Grandma Knudson said. And then she hung up the phone.

There's nothing to it but to do it, Hannah's mind echoed her great-grandmother Elsa's favorite sentiment, the one she'd uttered every Monday when she got out the big galvanized wash tubs and wheeled the old washing machine and wringer into the kitchen from its storage place on the back porch.

Time was ticking away, and Hannah knew she'd better get at it before Paul, or Matthew, or whoever he was got back from visiting the sick at the hospital. Her great-grandma was right. Sitting here thinking about what she had to do would not get it done.

On her way to the choir loft, Hannah passed the cloak room and stopped at the lost and found box. It was half-full of items that had been left behind in the church. There was a woolen head scarf on top, and Hannah reached down to grab it. She folded it into a triangle and tied it over her head, knotting the ends under her chin babushka-style. Old wives' tale or not, she felt much better about facing the bats.

She found the door behind the choir loft with no problem, and for a moment, she wondered why she'd never noticed it before. Then she realized it was probably because she'd never sung in the choir. Hannah opened the door and went up the narrow, winding staircase to arrive at a part of the Lake Eden Holy Redeemer Church that she'd never seen before, the platform for the bell-ringer.

Light filtered in through the vented windows on all four walls. The wooden slats were canted so that very little rain or snow could get in, but it didn't stop the cold air from whistling through. Hannah knew she wouldn't like the job as bell-ringer. This part of the wooden steeple was freezing cold in the winter, and she was sure it would be miserably hot in the summer. Grandma Knudson was a saint for ringing the bell to gather the flock for Sunday services when her husband was the minister.

The rope hung down from an aperture above, and Hannah looked up to see the church bell high above her. It was a huge bell and very old. Reverend Bob had once mentioned that the bell had been made in the eighteen hundreds, and it was cast bronze. The bell rope was made of thick hemp with a sleeve of cotton so the bell-ringer's hands wouldn't touch the fibers of the rope. She'd once heard someone mention that the sleeve was called a "sally," although she had no idea why.

Hannah stared at the rope for a moment and fought the insane urge to grab the rope and pull. Of course she didn't. If she rang the bell, Grandma Knudson would think there was something wrong, the parishioners would start calling the church office and the parsonage to find out why the bell was ringing, and if Paul, or Matthew, or whoever he was, caught wind of it, he'd rush right up here to see who was responsible and catch her searching the belfry.

She stepped around the rope and headed for the ladder-type staircase on the wall. At least it didn't have round rungs. She didn't like to climb ladders with round rungs. In place of rungs, this built-in ladder had regular steps like a stepladder. They were much narrower and shallower than ordinary steps, but she could handle that.

The steps went straight up at a ninety-degree angle from the floor, but there were handrails to grip. When Hannah came to the point where the top of her head was about to hit the trap door, she held on with

441

her left hand and pushed the trapdoor open with her right. The trapdoor was big enough to accommodate a large man, but it opened smoothly on its hinges and fell back against a wooden brace that held it open and in place.

It was a bit eerie stepping into the hushed and quiet belfry. There were no sounds at all except the occasional honk of a horn in the distance, the faraway bark of a dog, or the tinny growl of a snow blower clearing a sidewalk. There was no rustling, and Hannah was relieved. If there were bats, they were sound asleep.

The space, itself, was a geometric figure that Hannah couldn't begin to identify. It began as a square with five-foot walls, but the walls began to narrow and tilt in beyond that point to form the ascending steeple. The four large open windows, covered only with fine mesh, displayed the bell to passersby on the streets below. From her bird's eye vantage point in the belfry, Hannah's view of Lake Eden was spectacular. If she looked out each of the four windows in turn, the vista was only a few degrees short of a full circle.

"Incredible!" Hannah said, spotting her mother's car traveling down Main Street and heading out of town toward the highway. Michelle must be going out to the mall to return the costume their mother had rented.

The interior of the space was cluttered and crisscrossed with wooden rafters, metal braces, and heavy blocks of wood to support the structure. Just as Grandma Knudson had told her, the bell sat directly in the center, suspended between two heavy wooden wheels. There was a groove for the rope, and Hannah surmised that was how the bell was operated. A pull on the rope from below would turn the wheel, and gravity would cause the clapper to hit the side of the bell.

A cabinet hung below one of the windows. The door was open and tools were scattered across the floor as if they'd been carelessly tossed there. No workman would leave his tools in such a state. Someone had looked for something in the cabinet and tossed the tools aside.

The walk space around the church bell and its housing was minimal. In order to get to the walls, she'd have to bob, and duck, and weave her way around structural supports. And it seemed that someone else had done exactly that not long ago, because there were footprints in the thick dust on the floor!

Hannah followed the footprints, careful not to bump into rafters, or braces, or blocks on the way. As she neared the wall, she was forced to stoop lower and lower until she was in a crouching position. When she reached the wall, she saw that the boards had been pried off, exposing the space between the inner and outer walls. Someone had searched here. And she was convinced that someone was Paul.

"What are you doing up here?"

Hannah, startled by the loud voice, swiveled her head to see who was there. "Paul!" she gasped.

The word hung between them like a scimitar swinging lower and lower over her head. Hannah desperately wished there were some way to call the name back, but of course there wasn't. Perhaps he wouldn't notice?

"That's right. I'm Paul. You're smarter than you look, Hannah. You figured it out!" He stared at her with narrowed eyes. "Too bad someone didn't teach you to keep your nose out of other people's business."

Hannah gave an involuntary shudder. His voice had changed from that of a warm and friendly minister into one that was as cold as ice. The transformation shocked her so much, she stood there and stared at him like a possum caught in the headlights of an oncoming truck. And then, as she watched, he pulled out a gun and aimed it directly at her head.

CHAPTER TWENTY-NINE

It was a twenty-two semiautomatic. Hannah knew that because Lisa and Herb had one just like it, and Hannah had shot it at target practice. And she was almost positive that this twenty-two semiautomatic was the missing murder weapon.

"What are you looking for up here?" Paul confronted her.

"The same thing you're looking for. Grandma Knudson saw you standing on a pile of books, searching for something on the top of the bookcase in the church office. I figured you were trying to find something that the real Reverend Matthew hid."

"Give the lady an A," Paul said with a sarcastic laugh. "Let me get this straight. You were searching for something, trying to find it before I did, and hoping that you'd recognize it when you found it?"

"Exactly right." Hannah inched her way forward slightly, causing Paul to back away.

"Come one step closer and you're dead!" he threatened.

"Sorry," Hannah apologized quickly and switched gears. "You must have hated Matthew a lot."

"What makes you say that?"

"You killed him." Hannah managed to inch just a slight bit closer.

"I know I did, but I didn't hate him. It was . . . self defense. That's exactly what it was. I was saving my own skin. I had to shoot Matthew to keep him from calling the police. He said he wanted me to do the right thing, to turn in the jewels so they could be returned to their rightful owner."

"Jewels?"

"From the heist. I had to get them back. I've got a partner."

"The jewels from the house in Minneapolis," Hannah said, her mind whirling with this new information. "But how did Matthew get them?"

"We had to stash them in a safe place so I used part of the cash we got to fly to St. Louis. I was going to visit Matthew at the seminary and stash them somewhere at his place. I mean, who'd think to look for stolen jewels in a seminary?"

"That's a good point," Hannah said.

"But before I could even ask where he

lived, I saw him carrying suitcases and stuff out to his car."

"But he didn't see you," Hannah guessed. If Matthew had seen his cousin, he would have told Grandma Knudson that first afternoon.

"No, he didn't see me. He was saying goodbye to some guy and they talked about how long he was going to be away and how he was going to visit somebody in Wisconsin and then come here. The guy was going to teach Matthew's classes and live at his place while he was gone. I knew I didn't dare stash the jewels there, the other guy might have found them, so I waited until Matthew went back inside, and then I hid them in a box of books in his trunk, way down in the bottom."

"And you planned to pick them up when he got here," Hannah concluded.

"Right. I never thought he'd find them and hide them from me! That was like . . . blackmail!"

Hannah nodded, even though Paul's definitions of self-defense and blackmail left a lot to be desired. "And Matthew refused to tell you where the jewels were and said he was going to turn you over to the police?"

"Yeah. That's it. He told me I needed to pay for the crime I committed. Isn't *that* a laugh? He promised me that God would forgive me if I was truly sorry for my sins, and he would always love me like a brother. And then he did a really stupid thing. He picked up the phone and started to punch in the number. So I shot him. What else could I do? It wasn't like I *wanted* to shoot him. He just didn't give me any choice."

"I understand," Hannah said.

"You do?" Paul was obviously surprised at her comment. "Why do *you* believe me?"

"Partly because of that hole you dug in high school when the whole football team went camping." Hannah could hear the far-off ringing of a phone, probably in the church office. If it was Grandma Knudson and Hannah didn't answer, would she call the police? Hannah wasn't sure, but she knew she had to keep Paul talking and buy herself more time. "You filled that hole in with leaves so that Hugh Kohler would break his leg, and your cousin Matthew could take Hugh's place as the quarterback. That proves you liked Matthew."

Paul laughed, and it was not a nice laugh. "You got it all wrong, sister! I didn't dig the hole. I *found* the hole. And I didn't try to trap Hugh Kohler for Matthew. I did for *me*. Hugh was a bully, and he picked on everybody in junior varsity. According to

Hugh, nobody could do anything right, and the coach let him get away with taunting us and talking the rest of the senior squad into being vicious whenever we played practice games. That's why I was after Hugh. He deserved that and more! I just lucked out when he broke his leg in that hole and everybody thought Matthew did it. But we're wasting time here."

Paul leveled the gun, and Hannah knew her time had run out.

"Stop!" she said. "I know where the jewels are."

The gun wavered slightly as Paul considered that. "Tell me!" he demanded.

"Will you let me go if I tell you?" Hannah asked, knowing full well that he wouldn't.

"Sure."

"Then you'd trust me not to call the police?"

Paul gave a nasty laugh. "Not on a bet! I'll fix it so you *can't* call the police."

"How?" Hannah asked, even though she knew she was treading on dangerous ground.

"Well, let's see." Paul looked amused. "I can lock you up here until someone walks by the church and hears you screaming for help. Or maybe that's not such a good idea. I think I'd be better off stuffing a gag in your mouth so you can't scream at all. It'll be an educational experience for you. You can see how smart your friends are about finding you before you freeze to death. Of course, it all depends."

"On what?" Hannah asked, listening with one half of her mind while the other half was engaged in trying to think of some clever way she could throw him off balance and recover his gun. She was almost within striking range of tackling him. He'd shoot her, of course, but if she were lucky, it would be in a nonlethal spot. If she moved fast, Paul would only have time to fire one or two shots, and it was her only chance to gain the advantage.

"It depends on whether you really know where the jewels are," he said.

"Oh, I know." Hannah did her best to sound confident. "I found something you missed."

"What?"

Hannah shifted her weight, made up a story on the spot, and moved forward another inch closer to the gun. "I found the note Matthew left in the baptismal font. He knew someone would be back for the jewels, and he wrote down exactly where he put . . ."

She was interrupted by a massive burst of

sound that resonated and reverberated through the belfry, shaking the walls and causing several of the bats that Hannah had hoped weren't there to take flight and swoop through the small space. For a moment, she was so taken aback, she just stood there. And then she realized what it was.

It was the bell! Someone was ringing the church bell, and the noise was deafening at this close range.

Paul ducked to avoid a swooping bat, and Hannah didn't stop to think. She just hurtled forward like her favorite Vikings linebacker, leading with her elbows swinging wildly the way Michelle and her mother had done to get through the crowd at the Eagle.

As she barreled into him, a good thing happened, something she hadn't expected. The gun flew out of Paul's hand and went skittering along the floor to the edge of the hole that had been cut into the floor to accommodate the bell ropes. It teetered there for a split second, and then it fell through to the platform below. Immediately after that another good thing happened, or perhaps it was bad, depending entirely on your point of view.

Paul stumbled back and lost his balance. He flailed his arms and attempted to attain equilibrium, but it was too late. With a hoarse cry of terror, he fell through the hole to the floor below.

For one shocked moment, there was silence. And then a voice hailed Hannah from the bell-ringer platform below.

"Are you all right?" Grandma Knudson called out.

"Yes. Are you?"

"I'm fine. I've got the gun, Hannah. And I've got him covered."

"He's not . . . dead?" Hannah asked, not sure if she should be relieved or disappointed.

"No, but he's unconscious. It looks like he broke his leg. Mike and Lonnie are on their way. I called the sheriff before I climbed up here. They should be here any minute."

Hannah glanced out the belfry window. "I see them! They're just turning off the highway!" she called out, hoping her legs would stop shaking enough so that she could climb safely down the ladder. "I'll be right there, Grandma Knudson."

The first few descending steps were tough going, but Hannah managed them. She arrived at the bottom of the built-in ladder still shaken, but eager to give Grandma

Knudson a hug. "You saved my life!" she said.

"All I did was ring the bell. It was the least I could do. After all, I got us into all this trouble in the first place when I doubted dear Matthew. I'm so glad he never knew that. He was a good man."

"Yes, he was," Hannah agreed, greatly relieved that Grandma Knudson appeared to be handling this crisis so well.

"We'll have a memorial service when Bob and Claire get back. People should know what a fine man he was. He was already a fine man as a teenager." Grandma Knudson stopped and gave a little gasp. "Did I hear Paul say that Matthew hid the stolen jewels?"

"That's right."

"Oh, my! I probably know where they are."

"You do?" Hannah asked, staring at her in shock.

"I think so. It's that davenport, dear, the awful pink one in my sitting room. There's a space behind the cushions. It's the way it's designed. When Matthew stayed here, he used to hide his journal there so that Paul couldn't find it."

"His journal?"

"That's right. Back then, girls called them

454

diaries, and boys called them journals. It was a place to write down your private thoughts, and it was perfectly safe from Paul. I've always held my ladies' groups in the sitting room, and Paul had no interest in Bible study or charity work for the church."

The sirens were loud now, and Hannah heard tires screech as a police cruiser pulled into the church lot. Help was about to arrive. "You make a great detective, Grandma Knudson," she said. "You not only saved my life by ringing the bell, you recovered the murder weapon when it fell down the hole, and you think you know where the stolen jewels are hidden."

"Thank you, Hannah," Grandma Knudson said, and then they heard footsteps pounding up the spiral staircase. "I'll ask the deputies to check, but I'm almost certain I'm right about the davenport. That'd mean I'm three for three. I guess that's not bad for someone who's tuning ninety next month, is it, dear?"

CHAPTER THIRTY

"Wow! What a spread!" Mike exclaimed, accepting a cup of coffee from Hannah and eyeing the cookie and dessert buffet set up at the far wall of the Lake Eden Community Library. "How many desserts are there, anyway?"

"An even dozen, including three of Grandma Knudson's Red Devil's Food Cakes."

"Why so many?" Mike asked and then he reached out to pat her arm. "Not that I'm complaining, of course."

Hannah shrugged. "Mother kept changing her mind, so Lisa and I just baked some of everything she mentioned."

"Well, people are sure digging in. I think I'd better hurry up before everything's gone."

"No worries," Hannah told him, lifting up the tablecloth that covered the beverage table so that he could see the bakery boxes that were stacked there. "We have enough desserts to feed every man, woman, and child in Lake Eden."

"Not counting the dogs and cats?" Mike teased.

"Oh, I think there's enough for them, too. And speaking of cats . . . did I tell you Michelle discovered how Moishe was getting my sock balls?"

"No. He wasn't pulling out that heavy drawer, was he?"

Hannah shook her head. "He was pulling out the drawer above it. That's my sweater drawer, and Michelle figured it out when I had to use tape to lift the cat hairs from my sweater the other night."

"Okay, so Moishe was pulling out your sweater drawer and jumping inside. How did he get the socks?"

"He went fishing in the sock drawer below."

"You mean he was snagging them with his claws?"

"That's exactly what I mean. There was just enough room for him to bring up a sock ball, jump down from my sweater drawer, and run to the kitchen to put it on top of the refrigerator."

Mike laughed. "The Big Guy's a real character!"

"I'll say."

"So what are you going to do about it? Put your socks in a different drawer?"

"No, I'm going to let him do it. Michelle caught him in the act, and she said he was having a lot of fun doing it. I have to get out my socks every morning anyway, so I'll just get them from the top of the refrigerator instead of getting them from my sock drawer."

"Wait a second," Mike started to frown. "How about that sweater drawer? Didn't you think something was up when you saw it pulled out?"

"I never saw it pulled out. Moishe closed it after he put the socks on top of the refrigerator."

"No." Mike shook his head. "I don't believe any cat could be smart enough to cover his tracks like that."

"Well, the sock balls are still appearing on top of the refrigerator and the sweater drawer is closed when I get home from work. I don't have any other explanation."

Mike thought about that for a few seconds. "Neither do I," he finally admitted. "Moishe's smarter than most of the crooks I catch. And that reminds me . . . Paul talked more than Pete Nunke's mynah bird once we got him down to the station."

458

"He gave up his partner?" Hannah asked.

"That and more. He told us about three other heists they pulled. Are you going to punish him?"

"Paul?" Hannah looked at him askance.

"No, Moishe. He's stealing your socks, after all. That's at least a misdemeanor."

"It's not that bad. It's just a little feline no-no. To tell you the truth, I thought pushing the drawer back in was so clever, I made him a Good Kitty Cake."

"A who?"

"A Good Kitty Cake, except I probably should have called it a *Smart* Kitty Cake."

"How do you make that?"

"It's just like a three layer cake. There's ground chicken, ground turkey, and flaked salmon in big patties. You frost it with cream cheese and decorate it with kitty treats. I used the fish-shaped, salmon-flavored kind that Moishe loves."

"That sounds rich."

"It is. I can only give him a little bit at a time, but he's really enjoying it. There's too much for one cat to eat, so I'll probably give some to Norman for Cuddles."

There was a clinking sound, and they looked over to see Doc Knight tapping his champagne glass with a spoon in a bid for attention. When the room was quiet, he cleared his throat.

"It's my pleasure to introduce the best author in Lake Eden, Delores Swensen, also known as the famous Kathryn Kirkwood. How about a few words, Lori."

There it was again. Doc had called her mother *Lori*. Before Hannah had time to think about what possible meaning that could have, her mother began to speak.

"Thank you, Doc. I'm just so grateful to be here on this important day with my friends. I have some wonderful news from my publisher to share with all of you. My first Regency romance, *A Match For Melissa*, did so well that Kensington is going to publish it as an e-book. Isn't that wonderful?"

Everyone applauded, including Hannah. Electronic books were becoming very popular and not just with the techno-geek crowd. Grandma Knudson even had an electronic reader. Hannah had seen it on the table in her sitting room.

"My new book, *A Season For Samantha*, will also be released as an e-book. There's only one problem with e-books. I can't autograph them. But you can buy the paperback edition of my newest book from Marge today, and I'll be happy to autograph it for you." Delores gestured toward their librarian, Marge Beeseman, who was selling a rapidly dwindling stack of paperbacks at a table near the door.

"Nice sales pitch," Mike said under his breath, grinning at Hannah as he patted his jacket pocket. "I've got mine right here. Have you seen the dedication yet?"

Hannah shook her head. "I've been too busy serving refreshments. What does it say?"

"It says . . ." Mike pulled the book from his pocket and flipped to the dedication page, "This book is dedicated to Doc Knight for so many reasons I can't list them all."

"Really! I wonder what *that* means."

"So do I. That's why I brought it up. I asked Michelle and Andrea, but they didn't know, either. Maybe you should ask your mother."

"Maybe I will."

"We were wondering about it, too," a voice said, and Hannah turned to see a slightly chubby blonde with short hair, round, gold-framed glasses perched on the end of her nose, and a smile that was as wide as all outdoors. She was standing next to a man with reddish-brown hair that was thinning on top and the slender but powerful build of a long-distance runner.

"Hi, Doc Aldrich," Mike greeted the blonde, and then he turned to the man. "Doc Matson. Glad to see you here."

"We wanted to come since we know Delores," the blonde said.

The man nodded. "Yes. We see her almost every day at the hospital."

"Meet Hannah Swensen. She's Delores's daughter," Mike said, and then he turned to Hannah. "This is Doctor Marlene Aldrich, and Doctor Ben Matson. They're Doc Knight's new interns."

"Glad to meet you," Hannah said to both of them, and then she turned to Ben. "So you don't know what the dedication means, either?"

Ben shook his head. "Not unless it has something to do with The Rainbow Ladies."

"That's probably it," Marlene agreed. "They're doing a great job for our patients, and I know Delores works with Doc on a daily basis to make out schedules and go over patient request lists."

Hannah felt vaguely uneasy. Daily meetings about work were fine, but was there something else going on? She knew her mother and Doc had been friends for years, but could there be something new that she didn't know about?

As she poured coffee for Marlene and

462

juice for Ben, Hannah couldn't help worrying a bit. When the two interns had left, she turned to Mike. "Do you think Mother could be sick?"

Mike gave a little shrug. "I don't know. She doesn't *look* sick, but sometimes people don't. Look, Hannah. I'm really sorry I brought up that dedication in the first place if it's going to make you worry."

"That's all right. I would have read it tonight anyway. And this way I can catch a couple of minutes with Mother right after the party and ask her to explain it to me."

GOOD KITTY CAKE
Preheat oven to 350 F.,
rack in the middle position.

one pound ground chicken

one pound ground turkey

one large can *(14.75 ounces)* pink salmon *(I used Chicken of the Sea)*★★★

1 egg, beaten

1/4 cup cracker crumbs *(or matzo meal)*

three 8-ounce packages of cream cheese *(the brick kind, NOT the whipped kind in a tub)*

one package of nicely shaped or colorful kitty treats to decorate the top *(I used Whisker Lickin's Crunch Lovers tuna flavor treats).*

★★★ If you're giving this as a gift and you want this cake to look really colorful, use red salmon instead of less expensive pink salmon and pick off all the grey skin after you drain it. The lucky kitty recipient won't care, but the kitty's human caretaker might.

You will need 3 pie plates or 3 layer cake pans to make this cake. *(I used disposable pie pans.)*

Spray the 3 pans with Pam or another nonstick cooking spray.

Press the pound of ground chicken into the bottom of the first pan, spreading it out evenly.

Press the pound of ground turkey into the bottom of the second pan, spreading it out evenly.

Drain the can of salmon. Pick out the bones and remove the grey skin if you wish.

Pat the salmon dry with paper towels, and then flake it into a small bowl. *(You can also put it in the food processor and give it a few whirls with the steel blade to chop it all up.)*

Mix in the beaten egg *(or put it through the tube of your food processor if you used one).*

Mix in the cracker crumbs *(or put them through the tube of your food processor if you used one).*

Once the salmon, egg, and cracker crumbs are thoroughly mixed, press them into the last pan you prepared, and spread them out as evenly as possible.

Bake the ground meat and the salmon patty in the pans at 350 degrees F. for 25 to 30 minutes.

Use a turkey baster to suck out the grease and dispose of it. Let the meat and the salmon cool completely in the pans, cover them with plastic wrap, and refrigerate them for at least an hour.

Hannah's 1st Note: You can do this the night before you plan to assemble the cake and refrigerate the meat and fish overnight. If you do this, the cake will be firmer and easier to frost.

To assemble the Good Kitty Cake, first you must make the frosting. Unwrap the cream cheese and place it in a medium-sized, microwave-safe bowl. Heat it on HIGH for 30 seconds.

Try to stir the cream cheese. If it's still too firm on top to stir, flip the top brick of cheese so it's on the bottom and heat it on HIGH for another 30 seconds.

Try to stir again. If it's still too firm, give it another 15 seconds on HIGH. That should be enough to heat it through and soften it enough to spread on your Good Kitty Cake.

Hannah's 2nd Note: When I make this 3-layer cake, I like to put the salmon layer in the middle. I use either the ground turkey or the ground chicken layer on the bottom.

Take one disk of ground meat out of its pan and place it on a cake plate. Spread a little of the frosting on top.

Take the salmon disk out of its pan and place that on top of the ground meat.

Spread a little more frosting on top of the salmon layer.

Take the third disk of ground meat, put it on top of the second, and spread a little more frosting on top. Cover this disk completely with frosting since it'll be the top of your cake.

Spread frosting on the sides of your cake with a spatula or frosting knife.

If you have any "frosting" left over, swirl in a bit of jam and spread it on your toast in the morning. Now don't make a face. It's true that cats love cream cheese, but it's for humans, too!

Use some of the kitty treats to decorate the top of your cake. Arrange them artistically on the frosting. *(Actually, the lucky kitty recipient won't really care if they're artistic or not.)*

Keep this cake **REFRIGERATED** until you serve it to your favorite feline.

Hannah's 3rd Note: This Good Kitty Cake is very rich. It's the frosting. Dole it out to your kitty in very small pieces.

Yield: Enough for the "good kitty" and five or six feline friends.

CHAPTER THIRTY-ONE

The launch party was almost over when Norman arrived. He came straight over to Hannah and waited until she'd served the people in line.

"Can I see you alone for a minute?" he asked.

Hannah took one look at his miserable expression, and her mind went on full alert. Something was horribly wrong. She'd known it for a while, but today it was clearly devastating. Norman was in some kind of terrible trouble.

"Let's go back here," Hannah said, signaling for Lisa to take over the serving table and drawing Marge's library keys from her apron pocket. She led Norman to the little room that Marge used as an office, and unlocked the door.

There were two chairs against one wall. Hannah moved a stack of books from one chair and an untidy pile of papers from the other. "Sit down, Norman," she invited, sitting down in one chair and gesturing toward the other.

"I . . . really don't know how to tell you this, Hannah," Norman began, but he had to stop and clear his throat.

"It can't be that bad," Hannah said, forcing a smile, although she knew full well it *could* be that bad. "Just tell me."

"I have to find a new home for Cuddles." Norman swallowed hard, and Hannah noticed that his voice was shaking. "She's allergic."

"*Who's* allergic?" The question popped out of Hannah's mouth. It served to make Norman look even more miserable, and she almost wished she hadn't asked.

"Bev," he answered.

The name hung between them like a pirate flag, all crossbones and skulls, conjuring up dire warnings, mayhem, and death on the high seas. The silence seemed interminable, until Hannah finally broke it.

"Doctor Bev," she said, giving a tight little nod.

"Yes."

Hannah saw the telltale brightness in Norman's eyes, and she knew that he was close to tears. He loved Cuddles as much as she loved Moishe. "Can't you just bring

Cuddles out to my place when she comes over?"

"No, that won't work. Would you please keep her just until I can find someone else to . . . to love her and give her a good home?"

"You don't have to look for anyone else," Hannah said quickly, reaching out to take his hand. "Not when you have me. I'll keep Cuddles. Moishe adores her, and so do I. They'll be good company for each other while I'm at work."

"Oh, Hannah! That would be so perfect! You have no idea what this means to me! You're such a good person and I . . . I love you so much!"

You love me so much, but you're giving up your adored pet for Doctor Bev? Hannah's mind quickly got to the crux of the matter, but she didn't want to say anything that inflammatory. Maybe there was a reasonable explanation, but she'd never know what it was unless she asked. "I don't understand, Norman. Why do you have to give up Cuddles? Why don't you just visit Bev at her place and let Cuddles stay at home with you?"

"Because . . ." Norman stopped again, and an expression of pain crossed his face. "Because Bev's moving in with me." He stopped again to take several rapid breaths. "I didn't want to tell you, Hannah. I tried to think of some way out of it, but I . . . I have to marry Bev."

Hannah stared at him uncomprehendingly while he gazed at her, utterly miserable. They stayed like that for what seemed like hours and then Hannah spoke again.

"You *have to* marry her?"

"Yes. Bev gave me an ultimatum. If I don't marry her, she won't let me be a part of Diana's life."

Hold it! What was going on here?! Hannah's mind asked, and she couldn't even begin to answer. She felt a bit like an actress who'd been thrust on stage in front of a packed house without ever having read the script. "Who's *Diana?*" she finally asked.

Norman sighed heavily. "Bev was pregnant when she broke off our engagement, and she chose not to tell me. Diana is my daughter."

DEVIL'S FOOD CAKE MURDER
RECIPE INDEX

BAKING CONVERSION CHART

These conversions are approximate, but they'll work just fine for Hannah Swensen's recipes.

VOLUME:

U.S.	Metric
1/2 teaspoon	2 milliliters
1 teaspoon	5 milliliters
1 tablespoon	15 milliliters
1/4 cup	50 milliliters
1/3 cup	75 milliliters
1/2 cup	125 milliliters
3/4 cup	175 milliliters
1 cup	1/4 liter

WEIGHT:

U.S.	Metric
1 ounce	28 grams
1 pound	454 grams

Oven Temperature:

Degrees Fahrenheit   325 degrees F.
Degrees Centigrade   165 degrees C.
British (Regulo)   3
   Gas Mark

Degrees Fahrenheit   350 degrees F.
Degrees Centigrade   175 degrees C.
British (Regulo)   4
   Gas Mark

Degrees Fahrenheit   375 degrees F.
Degrees Centigrade   190 degrees C.
British (Regulo)   5
   Gas Mark

Note: Hannah's rectangular sheet cake pan, 9 inches by 13 inches, is approximately 23 centimeters by 32.5 centimeters.

ABOUT THE AUTHOR

Like Hannah Swensen, **Joanne Fluke** was born and raised in a small town in rural Minnesota, but now lives in sunny Southern California. She is currently working on her next Hannah Swensen mystery and readers are welcome to contact her at Gr8Clues@aol.com, or by visiting her website, murdershebaked.com.

We hope you have enjoyed this Large Print book. Other Thorndike, Wheeler, Kennebec, and Chivers Press Large Print books are available at your library or directly from the publishers.

For information about current and upcoming titles, please call or write, without obligation, to:

Publisher
Thorndike Press
295 Kennedy Memorial Drive
Waterville, ME 04901
Tel. (800) 223-1244

or visit our Web site at:

http://gale.cengage.com/thorndike

OR

Chivers Large Print
published by AudioGO Ltd
St James House, The Square
Lower Bristol Road
Bath BA2 3SB
England
Tel. +44(0) 800 136919
email: info@audiogo.co.uk
www.audiogo.co.uk

All our Large Print titles are designed for easy reading, and all our books are made to last.